Also by Elizabeth de Veer

The Ocean in Winter

Elizabeth de Veer

The Blazekeeper of Bowmore House

A legacy revealed.

A shoe lost at midnight.

A future rewritten.

A CINDERELLA RETELLING

Sea Crow Press

Copyright © 2026 by Elizabeth de Veer
The Blazekeeper of Bowmore House

Published 2026, by Sea Crow Press LLC
www.seacrowpress.com
Barnstable, MA 02630

Paperback ISBN: 9781961864528
Epub: ISBN: 9781961864535
Library of Congress Control Number: 2025946180

All rights reserved.
No part of this book may be reproduced in any form or by any electronic or mechanical means, including information storage and retrieval systems, without written permission from the author, except for the use of brief quotations in a book review.

This is a work of fiction. All characters, organizations, and events portrayed in this novel are either products of the author's imagination or are used fictitiously.

The Blazekeeper of Bowmore House

Prologue

Rhona, the Widow Barclay, stood in the ballroom of the king's castle beside her two daughters and fidgeted with her left foot. On the jostling carriage ride through town to the castle, a sharp bit of gravel had popped up from the road, slipped through the top of her left boot and landed beside a hole in her worn stockings. Now it was lodged above her heel, mercilessly cutting into tender skin. The pain was excruciating. Trying not to grimace in agony, she tapped her foot against the floor, but the boots were too small and the tapping did nothing to change the position of the pebble. Rhona realized only one action would relieve her discomfort, and that involved removing her boot and shaking loose the intruder. No, she thought, she would sooner die than reveal her ratty stockings and ugly feet in the king's castle on a night as wonderful and rare as this one. Rhona decided she would press on through the pain. She would stand, walk, curtsy and smile all night, never letting on that her boots were filled with blood.

Rhona had never much liked celebrations, and this night, she felt completely out of place. She could not shirk the awareness that her hair was the wrong style, her jewelry insufficient, and her dress old and dreary. At least she was warm; the chill of late fall and the wind off the ocean could not be felt inside for fires blazed in every fireplace. Indeed, the room was bright as daytime, lit by a million sparkling candles, their incandescent light bouncing off mirrors and glass, glittering like diamonds. People crowded and hovered everywhere she looked, more than Rhona had ever seen, all beautifully dressed and dancing, talking, laughing. At the head of the room, the king and queen sat upon their fine daises, handsome and composed, gazing over the throng. A small orchestra played, and the young people danced as though they had waited their whole lives for this moment. Rhona thought she'd never heard anything so marvelous as that music. She closed her eyes, and the notes resonated through her body, all the way down to her suffering heel.

She brushed her dress. It was satin, and she'd embellished it especially for the event, but it was still the same widow's black she wore every day. Her boots had been fashionable once, but even without the pebble, they were too tight to even consider dancing. No, she would not dance this night. Among all these people who sparkled like starlight, Rhona felt like a slug, a nobody who had snuck in through a door left unlocked.

Then, she supposed, perhaps that was right. She had only come to accompany her daughters; revelry like this was for the young. Rhona had not been young for many years; perhaps she never had been. She looked at her younger daughter, Liisi. Youth suited her like petals suited a flower; such a glowing, yellow-haired beauty. Rhona had even lent her an ivory brooch, and the diamonds around the perimeter reflected in Liisi's shining eyes.

Yes, the girl was stunning. She had to be. This night, Liisi needed to secure a husband, or at least a suitor, preferably wealthy or royal, who would pledge to her his everlasting devotion. Their little family might soon lose their home. And if this came to pass, Rhona did not know what course they would take. The very idea made Rhona shiver.

"But which is the crown prince?" Liisi was asking, standing on tiptoes to see above the dancing heads. "I cannot see him."

"I am not certain," Rhona said. "It's difficult to see faces when the royal family passes by in parades. Perhaps that is he, over there."

"No, mother," said Rhona's older daughter, Orla. "That young man is an ordinary in the military. The crown prince is on the other side of the room."

Liisi smirked and, with a quick gesture, flipped open her ornate fan. "You two should be able to see better," she said. "Thanks to your immense height."

Rhona smiled. Even Liisi's impatience and irritation seemed well-suited in the king's ballroom. The young were never content; perhaps, she thought, this was as it should be. Those who had lived long, hard lives would come to find joy in simple things, but the young must insist that the world improve. Somewhere in that ceaseless longing, a new world would be born, and it was not up to the elders to dream of it.

"Shall I hoist you on to my back, like when we were children climbing trees?" Orla asked her sister, teasing.

"I'm glad you think this is funny," Liisi said, fanning herself. "I'm quite serious, Orla. I will meet the crown prince tonight. And I plan to dance with him."

"I doubt not that you will get everything you wish for, Liisi," Orla said. "One way or another."

Rhona noticed how neatly Orla's hair had been fashioned to cover the scars upon her neck. Still, the marks on her face were always visible, and though the ones on Orla's heart were unobservable, Rhona knew that Orla carried a particular burden. Rhona knew she should be grateful her daughter had survived that terrible fire at all, and yet, Orla's injuries meant she had only a short time left in the world. This Rhona regretted more than she could say.

"Now, now, ladies," Rhona said, and she held up the tiny, bejeweled opera glasses that hung from her wrist on a small chain. "Let us not spend this lovely night arguing. Which one did you think it was, Orla?"

"The gentleman over there, but perhaps..." she looked about. "The young man on that side wears a gold sash bedecked with medals. Is that crown Prince Finnian or the brother, Prince Eiran? I cannot say."

Rhona looked again through the binoculars.

"Oh, mother, the horror," Liisi said. She closed her fan and pushed the opera glasses away from her mother's face. "Do not let people see you watching through that thing. They'll think we came here to ogle the royal family."

"There is no harm in looking," Rhona said.

"Everyone here has come to notice and be noticed," Orla said. "Your mother simply brought a tool to make it easier. And see, she is not the only one. That lady over there does the same."

Liisi glanced in the direction Orla pointed. "That woman with the awful dress shaped like an aubergine?" she exclaimed. "She sells pasties in the market."

"Work is not a bad thing, Liisi," Orla said.

Liisi sighed, exasperated. "Oh, it is though. Work is terribly crude. My future husband, whoever he may be, inherited his land and title and will never bow to another. And neither will his future wife."

"I fear that life will offer you many surprises, my daughter," Rhona said.

"I am sure it shall, dear mother," Liisi said. "And I cannot wait to learn what they are."

Rhona glanced at Liisi. Her daughter had misunderstood her meaning, but she would not correct her.

"I am beginning to think," Liisi said, "That standing here with you two shall not advance my cause. I must determine which is Prince Finnian and inscribe my name upon his dance card."

"Provided it is not already full," Orla said.

Liisi again popped open her delicate, lacy fan, and hid her face behind it. "Oh, sister," she said. "When His Highness sees me, room will be found on his card."

"Good luck, sister," Orla said, waving demurely with her gloved hand.

Liisi waved coyly and disappeared into the crowd.

"She needs luck," Rhona remarked. "I believe every young woman from the kingdom of Braemuir is here."

"Perhaps," Orla said.

Rhona watched her older daughter play with her dark hair, fingering the lower tendrils of her locks and pulling them to her face. Without thinking, Orla seemed to be trying to cover the scars on her neck.

"Don't play with your hair, dear," Rhona said. "It looks so lovely, and if it comes undone, I haven't any idea how to set it right."

Orla glanced at her mother. "You know, mother, not every young woman from Braemuir is here tonight," she said. "At least one lady is not present."

"Pardon?" Rhona said.

"Cinder," Orla said. "You should have let her come. There was no reason to make her sit at home in the dark house, while we attend a ball at the king's castle. Everyone was invited. The invitation said so."

"You would have had her join us wearing that dreadful rag?" Rhona said.

"That dress belonged to her own mother," Orla said. "And she tried to fix it. We could have helped her. That is what sisters do. She had every right to be here."

Rhona sighed. Orla did not know what Rhona knew, that an orphan's life was filled with difficulties and pain. Orphans did not have parents who championed their cause nor any dowry to secure an advantageous marriage. Indeed, without a lightning strike of luck, as she herself had had, orphans never rose in society. Only hardship lay ahead for her ward. Pity, for Rhona liked the girl's spirit. But she believed

Cinder was better off not attending the king's ball, not knowing what beauty and light were contained in the world. The girl's life would have been ruined by a grandeur she would never encounter again.

Rhona herself wished she did not know of so much loveliness. Tomorrow, she would wake up in a crumbling manor house and all this would be gone, evaporated as though it never happened. She felt it very unfair to be offered this vision now and know it was almost ended, already on its way to becoming a memory.

"Orla, dear, wouldn't you care to dance with some young gentleman?" Rhona asked. "Go and greet someone."

Orla turned toward her mother with an expression of bemused surprise. "Who would care to dance with me? With this?" She touched her face, skin rippled in streaks of pink and white.

"Marks on the face do not affect dancing," Rhona said. She was trying to make light of the subject, but she knew she had failed.

"No, but scars frighten possible dance partners," Orla said. "There are so many young women here tonight, why would any young man care to dance with me?"

"Oh, Orla," Rhona said. "Do not speak so."

Orla laughed. "I sound very sad, don't I? But I am only speaking of what I know to be true. Excuse me, Mother, I must investigate the confections."

Orla left Rhona's side, and suddenly Rhona felt like she had been depleted of a girder that was holding her upright. She shifted her posture and the pebble again bit into her heel. She grimaced and tried once more to move her foot and dislodge the grain, but to no avail. She glanced around. She recognized a few people, the pasty woman included, but she had no friends in the room. She had lived in Braemuir Kingdom in the country of Dalkeith for seven years, but had made few acquaintances. She'd come there to raise Gerik's daughter after his wife died. She might have met more people if their house had been closer to town, or if her daughters had become friends with the local girls, or if Gerik had bothered to introduce them. They might have held parties of their own at Bowmore House, after all, the manor had once been stately enough for entertaining. But none of these had come to pass, so she remained a stranger in her adopted village, and now she stood in a room full of people, utterly alone.

"Pardon me, you look a bit lost," came a man's voice. "May I be of some assistance?"

Rhona turned and saw a gentleman standing beside her, hands

clasped behind his back. Dressed in a foreigner's military suit, the man was tall and slender, hair thin and graying.

She curtsied slightly. "My daughters are off enjoying the festivities," she said. "Now their old mother wanders about, having forgotten what one does at a party."

"Ahh," he said. "I am sure I do not possess your daughters' beauty and charm, but my company might prove entertaining. My name is Gustave De Fontenay," he said, and he bowed his head. "I am a guest of his highness, King Humphry."

"Pleased to make your acquaintance," Rhona said. "I am the widow, Rhona Barclay."

De Fontenay gave her a humble smile. "My pleasure," he said, his accent thick. "How strange that one can be surrounded by people and feel so solitary."

Rhona smiled slightly. "I was just thinking this."

He offered her his hand, and she rested her gloved hand upon his. "I am sent from Gallia as an envoy from King Mattieu," De Fontenay said. "Let us find a servant who can bring us some wine."

"Why, that would be lovely," she said. "So, you are a visitor to our country?"

"I am," he said. "I appreciate this place, how rugged it is, the land and the people. The sparkling cities of Gallia are not here, but there is natural beauty: tall pines, cliffs that cut the coastline, the apples, oh, a fresh Braemuir apple right off the tree is matched by none."

"Since you are from Gallia, have you spent much time in the City of Light?" Rhona asked. "I have heard the city is impossibly beautiful."

"I have," Monsieur said. "The architecture is stunning, the cuisine delectable. But one grows weary of so much celebrating. As if every day was a ball like this."

Rhona looked at the spectacle before her. "I can only imagine."

Monsieur De Fontenay directed Rhona into a quiet gallery off the side of the ballroom, then asked a servant to bring them a bottle of the king's wine and two glasses. The pair strolled and gazed upon portraits of generations of royal family members, making quiet conversation.

"How long have you been away from home?" Rhona asked.

"Many weeks," he said. "My wife wrote me a letter recently and told me of all the berry cakes she had made. At that, I nearly wept. I did not know I would be homesick for something as simple as berry cake!" He chuckled at his own emotion.

Rhona laughed with him, but quietly thought, *ahh, there's a wife*.

"When I was a child," she said, "I had a dear friend whose mother was from Gallia." Rhona stopped then, for suddenly, without warning, the memory came alive before her.

Ailen.

Rhona could see the girl as she had been the last time they'd met: face tear-streaked, eyes wide with terror, grief and confusion. Rhona had been nineteen, Ailen sixteen. It was a strange moment, like the end of time. And after it, each girl fled the town where they'd lived their whole lives, but in opposite directions. "You must leave, now," Rhona told Ailen. "Go to the island of St. Kiana. You will be safe."

She had sent Ailen away on a goatherd's wagon and never saw her again.

Rhona composed herself and tried to return her mind to the king's ball. "What business brings you here," she asked, "and keeps you away from berry cake for so long?"

"I lead a faction of the cavalry and army," he said. "We depart come morning. I remained only to attend this ball, for I was invited by the king and queen. Unfortunately, we return home unsuccessful."

"Oh," said Rhona. "What was the nature of your mission?"

"It is a complicated political matter, regarding the succession to the throne in Gallia," he said. "Many years ago, King Mattieu took a lover. Some believe the woman bore a child and stole away to your country to raise the baby. They say the queen murdered the woman and the child as well. But some say the child survived. A few months ago, the queen died, never having produced an heir. So the king sent us here to see if we could locate his lover's child."

"Oh, my, such intrigue," she said. Then, the music stopped and the room became quiet. Rhona and De Fontenay strolled to the grand hall to see what had captivated everyone's attention. A young lady in an exquisite dress of green and gold had joined the ball. She was so lovely, she radiated like the first star in a summer sky.

Rhona caught her breath; she'd never seen a woman so beautiful.

Yet, something about her looked familiar. Was it her eyes, her mouth, or the shape of her face? She felt suddenly that she was looking at her dear Ailen. But that was not possible; Ailen was three years her junior, and this young woman was the age of her own daughters.

Across the crowded room, the girl's nervous eyes met Rhona's. In that moment, the girl reminded her of her ward, her own stepdaughter. But Cinder had stayed home from the ball for she had not been able to secure a proper gown. She could never have attained a dress like that, composed herself and traveled to the castle. There had not been enough time.

The crowd between them closed and Rhona lost her view of the young woman. Just as well; she did not like the tricks her mind was playing, projecting ghosts from the past in the halls of her mind. It must be the wine, she thought. *I would have been better off with whiskey.*

"I should go seek my daughters," she said. "But I have been honored to meet you."

"You as well, madame," he said, kissing her hand.

Rhona turned toward where people were dancing and saw the young man who she believed was Prince Finnian. He held out his hand to the beautiful young woman. The look on his face, on both their faces, were expressions of delight and adoration.

She stopped and watched them, and smiled to herself. *She must be the Duchess of Spitzbergen. How strange that for a moment, I thought she was Ailen. Stranger still to think upon Cinder...* The young woman and the crown prince put their arms around each other, and when the music began to play, the two danced. Nobody in the room could look away. The couple were the perfect dancing partners, their eyes held each other fast and their feet barely grazed the floor, moving in time.

And more than all that, she thought, *our Cinder does not know how to dance.*

The next morning, when all the candles in the king's ballroom had long been cold and the last bit of detritus swept from the ballroom floor, Rhona found herself at the castle door, holding the reins to the family's palfrey and rapping furiously on the door. She could not catch her breath after her galloping ride on horseback through the morning's dark, misty roads. She hated to come to the king's castle in this condition, exhausted from a sleepless night and dirty from her ride, her hair a mess; indeed, she hated to go anywhere by horseback, but she had no time to waste.

"Please," she said breathlessly to the servant who opened the door. "I must see Monsieur De Fontenay. It's urgent."

The servant looked at her with a puzzled expression. "But ma'am, you cannot bring a horse inside the king's castle."

Rhona grumbled. "I forgot the beast was here. Where do I put it?"

The servant blinked. "Usually, guests bring their horses to the stables and a groom takes care of it," she said. "Ride back out along this path and you'll see—"

"I do not have time to ride back out the way I came," she said, flustered. "I must see Monsieur De Fontenay now."

"Wait here," the servant said. A moment later, she appeared with a scruffy boy of about twelve years. "Pavel, watch this lady's horse while she comes inside."

Rhona handed the reins over to the boy, then the servant let Rhona in and closed the door behind her. "What name shall I tell Monsieur De Fontenay?"

"The Widow Barclay," she said.

The servant led her to the king's receiving room and gestured for her to take a seat, but she was too nervous to be still. She paced the room, clasping the thing she had brought to show Monsieur De Fontenay: a stack of vellum pages covered in handwriting, rolled up and bound with kitchen twine. Her heart raced. Her mind raced. She remembered Cinder's words that morning: *You once knew a girl named Ailen, didn't you? You were her friend. I can already see it on your face.*

After several minutes, Monsieur De Fontenay entered the room. "Pardon me, Monsieur," she said, curtseying. "I am so sorry to trouble you. Please excuse my appearance."

"Madame Rhona," he said. "I am happy to see you again so soon, but my officers are preparing to leave your country this day. I apologize, but I am quite busy."

"I understand," she said. "But you must listen to me. I have found the person whom you are seeking. She is my ward."

Chapter One

Some days earlier...

One dark morning, Cinder awoke upon the cot in the kitchen. The fire had died and now the hearth was cold. Henry, a black and white tabby as old as the hills, slept on a blanket beside the fireplace, curled like a potato bug. He didn't notice the chill, and Cinder was glad he did not. *It must have rained in the night,* she thought. Cinder pulled her woolen blanket around her and stood up. The room was dimly lit by the first faint glow of morning that showed through the window. She went to the hearth and touched the floor stones; as she suspected, damp. She peered up the chimney as though she might be able to see the cracks that let the rain through, but all she saw was darkness.

"Something in this house is always failing," she muttered to herself.

She took a flint and lit a single candle. Her father had built this house before she was born. It was meant to be a shipbuilder's glorious manor, where his family could live in glory and comfort while gazing out at the Morisar Sea, anticipating future adventures or awaiting the return of the captain himself. But after he died, the salt winds off the ocean had swiftly corroded the house, and they had no funds to restore it. How could five years have passed since he died? She missed him, his great, deep laugh, the smell of his pipe, the hours they spent together looking at maps.

There was much she missed.

Her auburn hair was dusty with fireplace soot. She pulled it back with a piece of twine, then, shivering, took the broom and swept the ashes into a tin pail. She built a pile of logs and sticks in the fireplace, then tucked in oiled rags, paper scraps and dry grass. She held the candle to it, and the rags and twigs quickly ignited into yellow flame. She perched down low to stir the sparks, then watched the blaze curl and char the grasses. Once the fire seemed strong enough to ignite the larger logs, she sat back against her cot and watched flames shift and dance, like orange and yellow sprites hopping about.

"Oh, embers, I wish you could tell me your secrets," she said quietly in the darkness. "I would have so many questions."

She felt a kinship with the fire, and not only because she spent so much time tending the ones that warmed the house, but also because she'd gained her family nickname from here: Cinder, a term defined as a remnant of fire, a chunk of burned wood or coal that did not emit flames, but was hot to touch and thoroughly ignitable. Her sister Liisi had assigned it; she'd meant it as an insult. Indeed, her father's second wife and her daughters seemed to have forgotten that Cinder had once had another name, and Cinder preferred it that way. It meant she had two identities: within this family, she was the house maven, the work horse, the animal-keeper, the kitchen gardener, the cook, and the chargirl. But in her heart, under that secret name her mother had given her, she would always be the ship captain's daughter, and someday she would sail away from this house that had become her prison.

The wall clock ticked steadily, and Cinder took it down to wind it. In the candle's glow, she carefully twisted the key in the back. Delicate golden hands pointed at Roman numerals painted in blue upon tiles of fine, white enamel. Her father had brought this clock to her mother from one of his voyages. It was one of very few items of value they had not sold since her father died. She turned the key and waited for the faint resistance that meant the clock was wound. One last click; she found it. Satisfied, she placed it back upon the wall.

There, clock, she thought. So begins another day.

Cinder lit a match in the candle's flame and brought it to light first one lantern and then another. Now the room was brightened, and growing warmer, and her spirits were lifted already. A few sips of hot tea and she'd be ready for the morning's chores. Then Cinder heard the floor creak in the doorway behind her.

"Cinder, are you there?" came a voice.

She turned. "Orla," she said. "Why have you wakened? It's so early. Even the cock has yet to crow."

"I couldn't sleep," she said. "I smelled smoke and I thought you were awake. Some company might be a comfort to me."

Orla was the elder of Cinder's two sisters, both older than she. Orla was of marriageable age and her nature was kind, her spirit intelligent. She wore her dark hair bound up at the back of her head in the hopes that it would hide the vicious scars on her neck, but there was no way to conceal the angry, red stripes seared upon her cheek. Cinder helped her over to the bench beside the fireplace then took her own blanket and wrapped it around Orla.

"Thank you," Orla said. "Strange how dark it is. Morning by the clock, but the sky still in shadows."

"It's early, Orla," Cinder said. "You should rest."

"I am awake now," Orla said. She glanced toward the windows. "Cinder, which direction will the sun come from?"

"East, through that window," said Cinder, gesturing toward the window opposite Orla. "I know what you need." Cinder reached down and gathered up ancient Henry, who responded with a grumbling mew at being lifted while still asleep. She drew up his legs and tail and placed him in Orla's lap. "There you go. Doctor Henry's arrived."

"Doctor Henry," Orla said, and she pressed her cheek into the cat's striped fur. "Of all the physicians I've ever met, Doctor Henry is by far the most effective at treating what ails me."

Cinder poked at the fire. "Are you warm enough? I could fetch another blanket—"

"You don't need to fuss over me," Orla said.

Cinder sighed. The room grew quiet, but for the crackling of the fire. The flames were starting to catch now, and it was almost time to add the peat.

"Why, I'm sitting upon something," Orla said. She reached beneath her and pulled up a small figure made of sticks. Its face was a large, smooth nut, and it had a small sack upon its back made of moss and a tiny hat made of wool. "Well, hello, small woodland gentleman," she said, smiling. "Cinder, did you make this?"

"Oh, it must have fallen out of my apron pocket," Cinder said. "It's just a silly thing I do with my hands sometimes...while waiting for bread to rise or some such thing. It's nothing at all, in fact." She could feel her face growing warm, and she hoped Orla would not notice. In fact, she had not fashioned the small gentleman; her friend Alban, an employee of the king's stables whom she sometimes met at the cliffs, had crafted him and left him for her. Cinder had brought him home to make a twig and moss throne chair for him. She'd hoped to bring the new king and his throne later that day to the base of the Fairy Tree, and leave them both for Alban to find.

Alban. She missed him. She hadn't seen her friend in so long, she sometimes worried the king had decamped him to some other location, or worse, recruited him into the cavalry. But no, if he had been sent abroad, he would not have left her this small figurine. He couldn't have been gone; he was simply busy with horses.

Orla held the figurine up to the candlelight to see better. "It's charming."

"Might I have it back, please?" Cinder asked, and she reached out her hand.

Orla handed her the figurine. "Why, sister, are you blushing?"

Cinder tucked the trinket into her apron pocket and touched her hand to her cheek. "I have been leaning over the hot fire. Of course, my face is warm."

"Ahh," Orla said. "You're probably worried that if Mother knew you had time to make little dolls, she would give you more to do."

"Which she would certainly do," Cinder said, smirking. "Some days I wonder if she purposely wishes to prevent me from walking outside."

"You do have a way of disappearing," Orla said. "Sometimes I envy how free you are."

"Free?" Cinder said. "Hardly..."

"In your heart, I mean," Orla said. "You have lives beyond the walls of this house. Where do you go, when you retreat to the cliffs? What do you do there?"

Cinder began to gather the vegetables she would use to cook a stew later in the day. She shrugged. "I don't know, exactly," she said. "I let my feet and mind wander."

"When your father died, we had only known you for two years. And you were quite the wildling. Mother was exasperated, trying to teach you to be a young lady when all you wanted to do was run along the cliffs and scrape your knees."

"I never wanted to scrape my knees," Cinder said as she sliced carrots.

"After your father died, you simply...left us."

"I was mourning," Cinder said. "It was a solace to me, being out there alone, in the quiet, under the stars, watching the ocean." She remembered it well, how expansive the world felt around her, and how she hoped the wind and rain would wash her grief away.

"For days, we did not see you," Orla said. "We knew you came in the night, for food went missing. Liisi wanted to lock the doors, not so much to punish you, but to force you to speak to us. Or, maybe a little to punish you. She is Liisi, after all."

Cinder tossed the carrots into a bowl and began to cut onions. "I would not argue with that."

"Mother said we should leave you be," Orla said.

Cinder was surprised to hear this. "Did she?"

Orla nodded. "Mother had the servants bake extra bread and leave it out with butter in the kitchen. She stood by the windows searching for you for hours."

Cinder crouched by the fire and poked at the embers. "I never knew your mother watched for me."

"We were so glad when you came back," Orla said. "But I always have the feeling that...some part of you is still out there, some part we cannot reach."

Cinder threw the onions in the bowl and wiped her hands. "You and your family have little to complain about. I always do what is expected."

"Of course," Orla said. "This house would fall down around us if you were not to care for it. And the animals would starve in their barn if they had to wait for Liisi to care for them."

Cinder laughed slightly then turned to scoop flour from a bin into a bowl. "Mark that those words were not spoken by me."

"Let us agree they weren't spoken at all," Orla said, grinning. "Mother is desperate to find Liisi a husband. Someday, Liisi shall marry, and she will need to learn to care for her own brood."

Cinder poured water from a pitcher into the flour. "Hopefully, no animals," she muttered.

"Hopefully, she finds a husband who can afford servants," Orla said. "Mother says she has funds reserved for a dowry for each of us. Once Liisi's marriage is settled, I am certain Mother will find you a husband as well."

"One moment," Cinder said. "Who says I want a husband?"

Orla looked at her and blinked. "Do you not want a home of your own, Cinder?" she asked. "What would you do if you did not marry?"

Cinder pressed her hands into the shaggy mixture. "My father was a builder and captain of ships," she said. "I know something of how to maneuver one. I know how to travel by night, and I know how to pilfer provisions. You know? I think I would make a fine pirate."

Orla laughed. "A pirate?"

"Perhaps I could sail a ship in the war," Cinder said, blowing a loose lock of hair out of her face. "I am as loyal as any countryman in this kingdom. Yes, I can sail a ship against the insurgents. Perhaps I could lead a fleet."

"First a pirate, then a navy officer, and the sun not even up yet," Orla said. "I wish I was brave like you. I always admired your courage, Cinder."

"I have not so much courage," Cinder said.

Orla nodded. "You do. I could never leave a warm house and live out in the wild."

After Cinder kneaded it for a few minutes, the dough became a neat, supple ball. She admired it for a moment, then set a wet cloth over the bowl and placed it beside the fire to rise. "Some days, I think I do not have enough courage to stay inside this house," she said. "If you were not here, Orla, truly, I would leave. I would find my way on to some ship, and travel wherever it might take me."

"I cannot imagine living here without you," she said. Then the look in Orla's face shifted. "Do you really think we shall go to war?"

"Men huddle together at the market and speak of it in hushed tones," Cinder said. "People wonder about the line of succession. The king's first son, Prince Finn, is a hesitator, they say. A bride has been picked for him, but why are they not wed? They wonder whether she has taken a lover. Or perhaps he has a lady on the side."

"Oh, Prince Finn, what a fickle heart," Orla said.

"There is history to consider," Cinder said. "A throne taken by force is more likely to be just so, taken by force again. And what of these soldiers from Gallia? What are they doing, wandering about, drinking all the ale in the public houses? King Humphry tells us only they are here to address some situation that has nothing to do with us. But what is that mission? And why does his highness do nothing to alleviate the simple peoples' pain? The children in the poor house, the widows whose husbands died in war, the elderly whose families do not help them?"

Orla nodded vaguely. "It is hard to complain about what we have not, when so many others have less."

"Someday, I would like to meet the king," Cinder said, rinsing her hands in a bowl of water. "I have questions. Suggestions, too."

"Indeed," said Orla. "Perhaps you should be king. But Cinder, you wouldn't really leave us, would you?"

Cinder sighed. "I suppose I could stay at Bowmore House my whole life, baking bread and feeding chickens. Or I could take a husband and keep my own house, baking bread for him, feeding chickens and children. Or become a nun...and in the name of God, bake bread, feed chickens."

"None of those sound terrible," Orla said.

"Yes, but Orla, why have we so few options? It's not fair. The world offered us is so frustratingly small. Doesn't it make you angry, Orla?"

Orla shrugged. "I suppose I am content with my station," she said. "What is it you're so filled with longing to do?"

"A million things, Orla, a million," she said as she dried her hands. "I want to travel the world and draw maps or build houses or make a pilgrimage to the holy lands and see the great monuments of other cultures. Or invent machines that fly into the heavens!"

"Goodness, such impossible dreams!" Orla exclaimed. "Cinder, you are as restless as your father."

Orla was probably right. "My mother used to tell me that nothing could get in the way of my destiny. But I don't feel that my destiny is a kitchen. There's another future for me, Orla, something of substance. But I don't know what it is, nor how to reach it."

"Perhaps ridiculous dreams are where destiny begins," Orla said. "My most ridiculous dream is that someday I will feel right again."

"You will, Orla," Cinder said. She came over and knelt at Orla's feet, petting Henry's soft fur.

Orla looked at Cinder with a bittersweet expression. "I don't think you're right about that," she said slowly. "No, I believe you're quite mistaken."

Cinder turned away so Orla would not see her grimace, for she knew that Orla spoke the truth. The doctor said Orla's time was limited, and Mother Rhona asked Cinder and Liisi to remain quiet on this topic. They had, but Orla still seemed to know.

Cinder glimpsed the eastern window, which suddenly blossomed in red and orange.

"Orla, look, the sun," Cinder said. She took Henry from Orla and led her by her hand across the room to the window to view the sunrise over the cliffs and ocean.

"Lovely," Orla said.

"The world turns, time carries on," Cinder said. "And the sun struts about like a proud rooster, parading its colors through the sky."

The girls spotted someone crossing through their yard. The individual's face was concealed, and the dark hood and cape blew in the wind.

"Cinder, who is that?" Orla asked.

"I don't know," she said. "They have been crossing for many years. Whether woman or man, I know not."

"How strange," Orla said. "We are so far from town or neighbors. Who would need to walk through our property to get somewhere? Where are they going at this time of day, even?"

Cinder shrugged. "They never knock nor stop for tea."

"It could be a selkie," Orla whispered. "A seal turned human and come upon land to enchant a human mate."

There were times when Cinder had the strange sensation that she was not only being watched, but watched over, protected from harm by some force she could not see. Perhaps the hooded figure was some sort of watcher.

"Could it be a king's guard?" Orla asked. "You know, if you travel by coastline, the castle is not so far."

Cinder shook her head. "A member of the royal sentinel would carry a weapon. I have never felt this person to be dangerous. You've lived here all these years, and you never noticed them before now."

"That is true," she said.

The figure disappeared around a bend, and Cinder looked again toward the sun's orb. "There, now the sun is fully above the horizon, so it must be time to make tea," Cinder said. She kissed Henry and placed him back in his bed. Outside, the rooster crowed to salute the morning.

Cinder filled a pot with water to the brim and set it over the fire to boil. At that moment, a bell in the kitchen began to ring; someone in one of the upstairs bedrooms was awake. Cinder went to the bell board to see which room it was coming from.

"Good morning, Mother Rhona," she said. "Tea will be ready soon." A moment later, the bell rang again. "Yes, Mother Rhona, I heard you the first time," she said.

"And on we all march," Orla said. "I must return to my room, lest Liisi finds me gone and makes some fuss about it."

"I shall bring tea in a short while," Cinder said.

"No rush on my account," Orla said.

Cinder watched Orla leave. She was amazed at her sister's ability to keep up her spirits through the pain, which Cinder knew was constant and excruciating. Then she turned back to her chores and pulled out teapots and a tin of tea leaves. She reached up to another window to push aside the curtains. Outside, the sun continued its grand entrance. The sky was filled with bands of egg-yolk golden yellow, radiant orange, and pink. The rooster crowed again.

"Even my stepmother's worst moods cannot deny me a magnificent sunrise." Cinder looked out at the rolling hills that led to the wood and to Sayre Cliffs, which bordered lands held by the king. Sayre Cliffs, the place where she might, this very day, chance to see Alban. Sweet Alban, even thinking of him warmed her heart. She pulled the small figure out from her apron pocket and smiled. She would visit the Fairy Tree that day. Maybe she would see Alban, or at least find some new treasure.

She smiled to herself. Yes, some things Mother Rhona could never take from her.

Chapter Two

The bell continued to ring, so Cinder rushed out of the kitchen and through the house, still dark with morning's shadows. The house, known as Bowmore, was set by the sea in a town called Kilderbrae, in the kingdom called Braemuir in the country of Dalkeith. She paused for a moment and looked down the hallway past the parlor toward a series of doors along a corridor. Each door was closed and locked. After her father died, Mother Rhona had sold all the furniture in those rooms—a grand dining hall, a music room, a library, her father's study, and others—then shut and sealed the doors, deeming them ghost-rooms. But they remained part of the house's architecture, and they reminded Cinder how the house used to be: bright and warm, and filled with life.

She sighed, and climbed the grand staircase up to her stepmother's chamber and knocked on the door. "Mother Rhona? You called?"

"Come in," demanded a sharp voice on the other side. Cinder pushed the door open. Mother Rhona sat at a desk in the middle of the room wearing, as always, her long woolen dress of widow's black, with sleeves that reached up her thin hands and a neckline that covered her throat. Her long hair, streaked dark and gray, was pulled back and twisted into a tight bun. How strange that Cinder's true mother and this woman shared the same name. Her mother had been so different from this Rhona: fair of hair and eyes, less tall and rounder, softer at the edges. Her own mother had been quick to smile and laugh, always noticing something beautiful in the world: dolphins splashing in the surf, a beautiful shell, the sound of rain upon the roof.

This Rhona, with her dark eyes and angular face and body, never saw anything in the world past her own daughters. Now she was rifling through a pile of envelopes, and Cinder wondered what could possibly be so urgent.

"Don't linger in the doorway, child, come all the way in," Mother Rhona demanded. "We must not wake the others; Orla needs sleep. She's been so restless of late; the pain keeps her awake." Rhona rubbed her arms. "There's an awful chill this morning. Cinder, see to my fire. Those boards do nothing to keep out the draft, and winter not yet upon us. I suppose we'll have to put up more planks to keep back the dreaded wind. Oh, bother, those do nothing to enhance the look of this shabby, old house."

Cinder winced at her description of the house as shabby and old. *It wasn't always like this,* she thought. *It was beautiful once.* "Yes, ma'am," Cinder said.

Formerly the bedroom of Cinder's parents, this room had once been full of light and air and the smell of the ocean. Back then, it was furnished with lovely mahogany chests and a test bed fit for a king, draped with a beautiful canopy. Tall, grand windows looked out over the Morisar Sea. That view of ocean, sky and cliffs had been Cinder's mother's favorite thing in all of Bowmore House. But Mother Rhona now slept in a small cot, which even Liisi said was barely suitable for a nun. Worse yet, Mother Rhona had had the windows boarded up to protect against the wind, which blacked out the view of the cliffs and the coast. This, Cinder believed, was an insult to the house itself.

"I just put water to boil," Cinder said. She went to the hearth to sweep up the ashes from the day before. "But the kitchen is cold too. Tea may take a while."

"Oh, yes, tea," Rhona said absently. "That can wait. But here, what is the meaning of this?" She held up a stack of envelopes. "I opened my desk drawer and found these invitations, all packed in. The envelopes have been opened, but I never saw them. Some of these events happened months ago. Why were these not handed to me when they arrived?"

"I always put the post on your desk, as you requested," said Cinder.

Rhona looked through them. "Social events. Dinner, a play, this one for a performance of music. Liisi and Orla should have attended these." She looked at Cinder, her eyes steely. "These matters are important. Especially while I am trying to find suitors for the older girls."

Cinder swept the ashes and looked into the darkness of the cold fireplace. She was weary of hearing Mother Rhona speak of this endless endeavor to find husbands for Orla and Liisi. As if nothing else mattered in the wide world.

Cinder turned and spoke sternly to Mother Rhona. "Pardon," she said. "I always set the post directly on your desk. Why would I care to keep Orla and Liisi from attending anything?"

"Do not address me as though I was your equal," Mother Rhona insisted. "I am your mother. Do not forget it."

Cinder smiled vaguely and bitterly to herself and looked away. *Fear not, I have not forgotten.*

"Yes, ma'am," she said.

Rhona crossed her arms and watched the girl make the fire. She ground her teeth. After all these years, the girl still infuriated her. She was relentlessly stubborn and independent, qualities Rhona suspected she inherited from her father. Though sometimes, Rhona wondered if the girl took after her mother. Had her mother taught her to be so at home in the wide world, roaming the hills and coast as though she owned all of it? Perhaps she looked like her mother. The girl's face was pretty, as the young often are, her body slender and strong, her eyes brownish-green and wide. Her hair, now tucked behind a kerchief, was the most luminous auburn color. But she had some quality that set her apart, confidence, perhaps, self-assurance, the belief that she belonged somewhere. Had her mother given her that? Rhona suspected she'd never know.

"Your father married me so I would educate you and break you of your wild ways," she said. "It was my mandate to tame you. I think I failed."

The girl smirked. "I don't know how you can look at me in this moment and wonder if you succeeded in taming me."

"Don't talk back," Rhona said. She drummed her long fingers on the desk, sighed, and pressed the heel of her other hand against her forehead and squeezed her eyes shut. "The bank is frightfully low. No thought of fixing the house, but I do not know how I shall pay the bill for Orla's doctor. And always there is Liisi. She is the daughter of a lord, raised only to become a fine lady. I would have prepared her better had I taught her to tend farm animals."

Cinder stifled a laugh. "I can't imagine Liisi caring for an animal," she mumbled as she built a pyramid of rags and twigs. "Unless it appeared on her plate under a sprig of parsley."

"When I was your age," Rhona said. "I was on my own in the world, building a life for myself from nothing."

"Indeed," Cinder said, sitting up. "You left your small town, traveled alone to London, met an older man of wealth and station. You proposed yourself to work for him as a reader, for his eyesight was failing. Then you charmed his nephew."

Rhona glared at her stepdaughter. "I suppose you do listen to me."

"I have heard these tales more than once," Cinder said.

Yes, her ward was very comfortable in the world. Rhona wondered how one achieved that. She'd never done so herself, an orphan raised by cold relatives. She'd been invisible to them, treated not with kindness like family, but also denied the respect they paid servants. She'd slept alone in the kitchen on a sack of hay upon the cold floor. Even now, Rhona wondered, did she believe she belonged somewhere? Certainly not at this house called Bowmore. She hated it. She longed to pack her things and leave it all behind, but as long as she had three girls in her care, they had to live somewhere. This desolate place was better than nothing.

Rhona watched Cinder blow the flickering twigs and leaves. The girl always performed her chores well. For whatever trouble she caused, Rhona thought, the girl did work hard. Life would be very different if Cinder did not assume so much responsibility. Cinder turned her face and Rhona watched her gather more sticks to feed into the burgeoning fire. Something about the girl always seemed familiar, yet Rhona was never able to pinpoint exactly what. Was it the shape of the girl's face? Her voice? The way she moved?

"I suppose you remind me of your father," Rhona said.

Cinder wiped the back of her hand against her head, smearing dark ash upon her forehead. "Perhaps," she said.

The girl had had another name once, Rhona mused, but now she could not recall it. Her father had always called her Princess, which annoyed Rhona to no end. When Rhona first met the girl, she lived like an animal, wandering the hills. Cinder's mother had been dead for five years then and her father had not known what to do with the child. He had sought a wife who could bear some structure upon the girl's life while he sailed the seven seas. They wed, and for two years, Rhona was the lady of the house, a role she enjoyed. She even made some progress tempering the girl's wild ways: Cinder loved learning, and if she was allowed to look at her father's atlas, she could be convinced to sit with the girls and work on her stitches.

When they received word that Gerik's ship had gone down in a storm, everything changed. Rhona worried they'd lost the girl forever to her impulses to run and wander. But she did return. Then they learned the terrible truth: Gerik had invested all his funds and worth in that last voyage and left his family with almost no resources beyond the house. Rhona had to figure what they needed to survive and let go of all else.

She'd released the staff, every last one of them. And Cinder had taken up many of those duties, even the hard, messy ones, tasks Orla was unable to perform, jobs Liisi would never try. She hated to admit it, but they desperately needed Cinder.

"You're a curious little someone, aren't you," she said.

Cinder frowned. "What does that mean?"

"You manage yourself quite adequately," Rhona said. "You must have learned something useful from your own mother."

Cinder stood up and brushed the ashes from her hands. "I suppose," she muttered.

"I think of her as Rhona the first," Rhona said. "Sometimes, at night, I imagine what I might say to her. Oh, Rhona the first, what am I to do with your daughter?"

Cinder set the iron fire poker down beside the hearth. "Say what you like to me," she said. "But do not speak of my mother. She has nothing to do with you."

Rhona glared at her. She prepared to say something sharp about showing respect to her elders, but then there came a knock on her door and Rhona let the comment go. "Come in," she called.

"Mother," whined Liisi, "I have been ringing the kitchen for ages, and nobody answers." Rhona's younger daughter came in wearing her satin morning coat and her soft sleeping mask around her neck. Her light hair was plaited down her back, and her lips were pink with a fresh swipe of salve.

"Do you think Cinder has finally—" Liisi noticed Cinder by the fireplace, then sighed. "Oh, here you are. Our room is cold. Orla is shivering in bed. We shouldn't have to wait so long. And where is our morning tea? Mother, you know I don't ask for myself, only for Orla's good."

Rhona looked at her daughter. If she had to choose which of these two was prettier, it would be Liisi with her fine, golden hair, her slender build, and the lovely dark blue eyes she inherited from her father. Still, Liisi would not get far if she'd had to work or get about on her wits.

"Cinder, go make a fire in the girls' room," she said. "And in the future, make sure all correspondences come *to me* directly."

"I told you, I always—"

"Oh, you found those?" Liisi said, fingering the stack of envelopes. "I hid them away in a drawer."

Rhona looked at her daughter. "Why on earth would you do that?"

"Mother, so many dull people invite us to their dull assemblies," she said, rolling her eyes. "A boring garden party, a sad dinner, a tedious country dance. If we let ourselves mingle with simple people, then what will the proper people think?"

Rhona looked at her golden daughter and sighed. She didn't care for this side of Liisi, but she supposed it had to be expected because of the way her father had spoiled her.

"The people inviting you I have known my whole life," Cinder said. "You might have at least sent your regrets so people knew they'd have to carry on without you."

"What, Cinder?" Liisi said. "If we respond to every invitation, then people will think we have not enough social engagements to occupy our time."

Cinder peered at Liisi. "And you find your schedule entirely occupied, do you?"

"Whether it is or is not of no consequence," Liisi said. "All that matters is how things appear."

Cinder pursed her lips as though she was holding back sour words. "Pardon me," she said. "I must go start the fire in Orla's room."

As she walked toward the door, Liisi whined. "And the fire in my room, also," she said. "Tell her, mother, the fire in my room also!"

"It is next door to Orla's room," Cinder muttered. "I shall do your room second, as I always do, fair, overly-occupied Liisi."

After she was gone, Rhona turned to her daughter. "How shall I find you a suitable husband if you do not attend these gatherings?"

"Oh, mother," Liisi said. She yawned. "I am too weary to discuss this matter so early in the morning. Can we not return to it after lunch?"

Rhona knew she would not be able to push her younger daughter in any direction. The girl was stubborn. And lazy and snobbish, also traits she learned from her father.

"Liisi, do not hide invitations from me," Rhona said. "My dearest hope is that you soon become the lady of another house. How will you find a suitor if you never meet anybody?"

"What does it matter if I meet someone if he is the wrong person?" Liisi turned toward her mother and batted her eyelashes. "Father used to say that one day, minstrels will write songs about my beauty. And they will sing far and wide of my fair hair and lovely eyes. It would be an error if I was too available, mother. I am rare and precious, like a jewel."

Rhona laughed slightly to herself. Her daughter certainly did not lack confidence.

Chapter Three

That afternoon, Mother Rhona engaged the older girls with lessons in manners. In these, she conducted the girls like a pair of trained animals, teaching them to say things like, "how lovely you look today, madame," and "why sir, what a wit you possess." Cinder delivered tea and biscuits, tended the fire in the drawing room, then, without a word, slipped out of the house.

Late afternoon, and the autumn sun was beginning to sink in the west. Cinder wrapped herself up in her hood and cape and braved the chill wind to head toward her beloved cliffs. She followed a path that led through orchards of twisting apple trees and stopped at one to fill a basket with sweet, crisp Braemuir apples. She made her way deeper into the grove and found the tree whose trunk bore a wide opening at the base, and a row of small stones led up to it like a footpath. The Fairy Tree. She crouched down and looked inside. Within was a tiny throne room fit for the smallest king and queen of the land, and all the furnishings had been made from found items: bark, moss, twigs, twine, seashells, pebbles. She pulled from her apron the trinket she had made: a throne chair for the fairy king, made from sticks and twine. Then, Cinder brought out the nut-faced fellow whom Orla had found that morning. She placed him carefully upon his chair, pleased at how well he fit. As a final touch, she placed a small acorn upon his head.

"My liege," she said. "May you always rule with wisdom, and may kindness be your guiding star."

She straightened the tiny stones that made up the path, then stood and surveyed her work. "If you see my friend, Alban, tell him his friend wishes him well." A wave of sadness and longing went through her. "Tell him his friend misses him. Dearly."

She curtseyed to the fairy king, then walked further down the path. A moment later, the trees parted and the trail opened up on the scene she loved more than any other: an eastward-facing perch cushioned in green on a cliff high over a jagged rock face. Layers of rock formed stripes and columns of brown and gray, and below that shone the silver ocean studded with white froth. The sky over the ocean was streaked with wispy clouds, gray and pale yellow. The wind blew so hard and frigid off the ocean, Cinder thought this must be what flying felt like. She inhaled the air, salty and so cold, it burned. She gazed at the sky, relieved to finally be in the one place where she could deeply breathe. She spun in circles, then ran and jumped in the wind, delighting in the cold sting. When she reached the edge of the cliff, the whole ocean opened up before her.

She sank down at the edge, just before the spot where the earth crumbled. She peered hard at the horizon and touched a small amulet that hung on a length of leather around her neck. It was a curious trinket, a piece of amber shaped like a water drop. A small insect with translucent wings was suspended inside, perfectly preserved. The amulet had been a gift from her own mother.

"Mother," she said. "I know you are out there. I will find you someday." The breeze came up off the ocean and wrapped her like a mother's hug.

After a while, she pulled an apple from her basket and began to crunch the sweet flesh. Suddenly, a young man plopped down beside her.

"Wonderful, someone picked me apples," he said, helping himself.

Cinder smiled. "You're here!" she exclaimed. She threw her arms around his shoulders for a quick, tight hug. "Is this truly you, Alban, or have you sent a spy who is your exact twin?"

"Let me check," he said. He thought for a moment. "No, today, I am only me. My twin must be dispatched elsewhere."

She laughed and put her palm on his face. "I hoped you would come," she said.

"I have missed you," he said. He took her hand in his, then, and kissed it.

He had never done that before. She gasped slightly and withdrew her hand. She looked at Alban; he also looked surprised, as though he himself was not sure how that had happened. Cinder tried to decide whether she should be shocked, angry or offended. But then, his kiss lingered upon her skin, warm as a beam of sunlight. She looked into his eyes and smiled slightly to signal to him that she was not bothered. He smiled back, but he seemed nervous.

Then, something changed. Without warning, she suddenly longed for him in some way that seemed beyond friendship. She could not work out what language went with the feeling, though in the back of her mind, a single word, fragile as a newborn songbird, whispered *love*. Love?

Love.

"It's been so long," she said, forcing herself to laugh. "I wondered if you'd stolen one of the king's horses and ridden off to another land."

"Hardly," he said, taking another bite. "I am so busy, the stable master wouldn't even let me past the border of Braemuir. Today I only escaped for I promised to exercise the steed."

"Steed? I heard no horse approaching," she said.

"I tied him up over there," he said, pointing back at a tree where a tall, dark brown horse stood roped to it. "Tiberius Nero. The king named him for some Roman emperor."

She picked up a piece of fruit, tossed it into the air and caught it. "Does his highness care for apples?"

Alban laughed. "Of course!"

She hopped to her feet and ran over to the horse, then offered him the apple from her flat palm. Tiberius bared his large teeth, gently took the fruit and crunched happily.

"Handsome fellow," Cinder said, as she stroked his nose. "Who gave you such a terrible name? You look like a Chestnut to me. Or maybe Honeysuckle."

Alban followed her to the horse. "Honeysuckle? The king would never stand for it," he said. "King Humphry likes to give horses names ready to charge into battle."

"Do you mean we might change the course of history if we gave the horses new names?" she asked. "If that's true, then I would name you Sweet Tea Rose. We could do with less war. Have you seen the widows at the Kilderbrae market? Those broods of children, all hungry and weary. They cause my heart pain. I wonder if the king thinks about those faces before he assembles his companies for the march."

"It's hard to say what the king considers," Alban said. "Aside from his own glory."

"Someone should make him talk to those women and children before sending out more fathers and brothers," she said. "He would think twice."

"You're not wrong," Alban said. "I will mention it to him when next I see him. The king is always interested in the ideas of others."

"Do you jest?" Cinder asked.

"I certainly do," Alban said. "And to correct the record, I have been coming here, and you are the one who has been absent. What has kept you so busy?"

Cinder sighed. The horse finished eating the apple, and the two wandered back to the edge of the cliffs. "The usual," she said. "I awaken every morning and battle a dragon, then I sail down an enchanted river to the mermaid's lair. There we play until lunch. Then I return home to read and nap, and, after the most delectable supper, the house fills with music and we all sing and dance until bedtime."

Alban laughed. "Your imagination is like a tonic to me."

"I wish my life was a thimble of that much excitement," she said. "You found the trinkets I left?"

"Yes," he said. "I left you one too. Did you get it? I was quite proud of my creation, the King of all Fey Folk."

"Indeed, his majesty's coronation was just today," she said. "You should go see. I built him a throne chair. After all, the king needs a proper seat to rule from."

"Indeed, he does," Alban said. "Well done."

She looked at Alban's light hair and dark eyes, and the strange feeling stirred again. For the second time that day, she felt her cheeks redden from the inside. She put her hands on them, and hoped he did not notice.

"I have missed you, Alban," she said. "Without your information about the castle, I have had to resort to listening to the chattering at the market. Which is not generally reliable."

"You would eavesdrop on others even if you saw me every day," he said.

"I suppose you're right. It's a good way to learn what's happening," she said. They found a blanket of green moss on a spot overlooking the cliffs and sat. "So, how have you been? Does the king treat you kindly? What of the princes, are they still as clever as mud stuck on pigs?"

"They're not so bad," he said. "They might be growing up of late."

"This is good news," she said. "What do you know about Crown Prince Finnian? At the market, they say his wedding to the Duchess of Spitzbergen may be...delayed."

"I have not heard this," he said, leaning back against a rock. "Tell me more."

"They say he prefers poetry over sword fighting," she said. "And music over jousting. I for one appreciate his priorities, but the king does not. King Humphry favors his second son over his first."

"Interesting," he said.

"Alban, you know the second prince personally," she said. "What kind of leader would he make?"

Alban shrugged. "Prince Eiran would do well," he said. "He's sensible, and learned in history. He's a strong swordsman. His judge of character might be hasty, but then, he is young. Though if it counts for anything, Prince Finn has been raised from birth to take the role."

"I hope it counts," she said. Suddenly inspired, she jumped up, grabbed a long stick from the ground and pointed it forward, sword-fighting an invisible assailant. "King Humphry did not inherit the crown, as Prince Finn someday will. He took it at the Battle of Chisolm Hill. King Humphry rose at dawn and met mad King Athelstan, his heart filled with vengeance." She stepped forward and stabbed the sword decisively into the air. "The sun rose over the horizon that day to find the earth soaked with the blood of the fallen king."

"Prince Finn is not the only one with a love for poetics," he said.

"The market minstrels love telling that story," Cinder said. She held the base of her pretend sword near her ear. "Is this how you taught me to hold it?" she asked.

"Yes, pull your hand back a little," he said. "Legs solid and steady. Then call, 'en guarde!'"

"En guarde!" she shouted, and pierced her sword forward in one swift motion.

"Excellent!" he said. "And, what of you? How fare the clucking capons?"

She planted her sword on the ground and leaned against it like a cane. "Nothing changes in my house," she said, her voice wistful. "Except...my injured sister, she's not doing well. I worry."

"What says the doctor?"

She let the cane fall and came to sit next to Alban. "He mixes salves for her pain, but..." She paused. "I fear there is no cure for wounds as deep as hers."

"I am sorry," he said. "And the other young lady?"

"My other sister," she said. "Well, she is, of course, radiant, dazzling, and altogether perfect."

"Don't gaze at her over much," Alban said, his mouth full of crisp apple flesh. "Lest you turn to stone from her sheer wonderfulness. And how fares the mother?"

Cinder sat up straight. "My *step*mother, you mean," she said. "She is correct in everything even when she is thoroughly wrong. And terribly cordial and warm. Or just terrible."

He peered at her with skepticism. "The sarcasm is more searing than usual," he said. "Is there some occasion?"

Cinder shrugged and became quiet. "I'm restless. Alban, do you ever wonder what else the world has within it? There must be so much beyond Braemuir Kingdom. Wonderful things. I just don't know... how to reach them. Or even what they might be."

"I have heard tell of some of the world's wonders," he said. "Castles big as cities, music and paintings that move the hardest of men's hearts. Flavors of food that do the same. Unlikely things people build, cities made of stone, carved into a hillside, a wall so enormous it crosses entire countries. Oh, and a beautiful white palace constructed of gemstones, built by an emperor. Nobody ever lived in this palace; it is a mausoleum for the emperor's beloved wife."

"Are such things real?" she asked.

"I have not seen them myself," he said. "If anyone shall see the world's wonders someday, it is you, my friend."

She looked into his eyes. She believed what he told her, or at least she wanted to. She longed to touch his face again, or his hand, perhaps by mistake. She caught her own breath, then turned toward the Morisar Sea, and let the wind wash her face.

"But," he said, "the wonder you most wish to see is the island that holds your own mother's remains."

She glanced at him. "Yes," she said. "It's out there somewhere. That island. It calls to me sometimes. Do you think me mad to say that?"

"No," he said. "Sometimes the stables call to me. They say, 'Alban, clean the stalls. They can be smelled on the far side of Braemuir.'"

"Not like that, silly," she said. "I feel it. In my bones. Some part of me is out there...in a place I can't reach. But I will go there one day. I will find the hazel tree my mother is buried beneath."

Alban studied her. "What was the name of the island?"

"St. Kiana," she said. The island's name was like music to her, and she loved to speak it out loud. "Have you heard of it?"

"I have heard it mentioned," he said. "Nobody lives there now, I believe."

"My father grew up there. He told me it was a strange little place, like a large rock. There is a small village, brown sheep and a few crofts. My mother went there to care for an old woman, and then she met my father. He rowed the dory that brought her there and fell in love with her the moment he saw her."

"He gazed upon her," Alban said, "and told her, 'I built this boat myself and someday I shall build tall ships that will travel the world. Will you please be my wife?'"

"I suppose I've told this story before?" she said.

"Once or twice," he said. "But why is your mother buried out there?"

She shrugged, frowned, looked even harder into the distance. "She was ill. My father took her away on a ship to seek healing springs that they thought could help her. But Mother died on the ship before they could reach the island. They were close to St. Kiana, so my father brought her there. He wanted to bring me to the island to say goodbye to her. Only, he never did."

Alban looked at her. "I'm sorry."

"I wish..." she started. "I wish I could see her one more time. I would tell her that I miss her." Suddenly, she felt that she had opened her heart too wide, had told Alban too much. She wanted to change the subject. "Alban, will there be another war?"

"Why do you ask?"

"Foreign soldiers camping in town," she said. "They make themselves quite at home, and still, no word from the King."

"Their mission is mysterious but not hostile," he said. "An emissary from King Mathieu is residing at the castle. I do not believe he poses any threat."

"If we did go to war," she said. "Would you have to fight in it?"

He considered his words before he spoke them. "Quite likely, my friend," he said. He spoke the next words slowly and carefully. "Although, if we avert war and the prince marries, and I think he will, there is a good chance my work would take me away from here. From you."

Her heart ached at the thought. She did not know how she might continue living this hopelessly mundane life without believing that on any given day, Alban might be waiting for her out on Sayre Cliffs.

"I know," she said. "I think I have always known."

"And if that happens," he started, and he took her hand in his and looked at her with concern in his eyes. "Well, when that happens, I should want you to know—"

Her heart beat fast at his touch. Her head swam. Suddenly, she thought it possible: the two could wed. They could build a small house and start a farm. She would bear children who would help in the fields and the kitchen.

"Alban—"

The moment she said his name, she understood none of it was possible. She had no dowry and no possessions, no title, no land. And Alban worked in the king's stables; someday, he would find a noble lass to marry, the pretty daughter of the queen's lady-in-waiting.

Cinder felt the world was full of beautiful things, and none of them would ever be for her.

Suddenly, a voice came from the hills below them. "Hey-o!" a man called. She looked down the side of the hill and saw someone waving. "Hey-o!"

"Oh dear," Alban said. He released her hand. "I am needed at the castle."

"That man is with you?" Cinder asked. "That's a relief. I always worry that one of the king's guards will find me here and accuse me of trespassing upon the king's lands."

"Don't worry about the King," Alban said. "If anyone tries to put you in a dungeon, come find me straight away. I'll settle things."

"Will you?" she said.

"Well," he said. "I *would* tell the king we are acquainted. But I don't know your name."

"I am the girl from beyond the cliffs, nothing more," she said.

"I have a feeling you are a great deal more than that," he said.

She looked into his eyes one more time. *How I wish I could be more than that,* she thought.

"Hey-oh!" came the call from the hillside again.

"I must leave." Alban stood up and reached down to Cinder to help her up. "I guess one of the dreadful princes needs a horse groomed."

"Take an apple for your supper," she said. She tossed him one from the basket and he caught it. She collected herself and smiled. "For my part, I go forth reassured that war is not immediately upon us as Prince Finn is this very moment selecting flowers for his wedding."

"Indeed," he said, smirking.

"Alban, do come around more," she said. She chose her words carefully, for she did not want to reveal how open and fragile was her heart, like a newly formed pearl. "I've missed you."

"Soon," he said. "I will try to come soon."

"If you come soon, Sir, then I shall see you soon," she said, curtsying. "And I shall look gladly forward to it."

Chapter Four

Alban mounted his horse and rode down into the dale to meet the man, Jakob, who was also on horseback. As he went, he replayed what had transpired between himself and the young woman. He could not say why he had kissed her hand. He never had before, nor could he recall considering doing so. His action had been so sudden, he was relieved she did not slap his cheek. Why, it was only a mannered gesture, he thought, and nothing more. Countless times had he kissed the hands of women in the court.

No, he thought. It was more than that; much more. He reminded himself that he had always cared for that girl. Ever since he first met her. He remembered the touch of her hand on his cheek, and wondered if she could sense how much he cared for her. Now he longed to tell her the truth, that he would soon marry a duchess and after that, he would never meet her again.

He pulled back the reins to slow the horse as he approached the man.

"Your mind is occupied, my liege," said Jakob. "I can see it on your face."

"Good day, Jakob," he said. "Indeed. I am untangling matters of the heart."

"I see," he said. "Well, I wouldn't interrupt, Prince Finnian, but your parents wish to see you. There may be news from Spitzbergen."

"My gratitude to you, my friend," he said. "For this notice and...for telling me she was here."

"You are welcome, your majesty. Few things can be left to chance, and meeting a pretty girl is not one of them. Any luck learning her name?"

"None," said the prince. "But it doesn't matter anyway."

Jakob nodded. "No, I suppose not."

As the two rode back to the castle along the coastal road, Finn recalled the first time he'd met the girl. Many years earlier, the king's sentry had seen a child alone at night, roaming a remote section of the cliffs. Finn was twelve years at the time, little more than a child himself, and he took it upon himself to investigate. Late one night, he ventured out to where the child had been seen. He was surprised to find a girl, and more surprised to discover that she had made a home for herself in a cave by the surf. He'd approached her gingerly to inquire whether she was all right; was she lost or injured? Did she need assistance getting home? Did she need food or water? No, she told him quite confidently, she was well and in need of nothing.

The ruse had started here: Finn worried he'd frighten the girl if he told her he was the king's eldest son. So, he told her he was Alban, a stableboy from the castle. And she had refused to tell him her name or where she lived. And still never had.

After that, he met her on the cliffs a few times a year. He'd watched her grow and become a beautiful young woman. They began the tradition of the Fairy Tree as a way to leave notes to each other, notes made of acorns, twigs and moss.

But now that his marriage time was approaching, he was beginning to realize how much he thought about this young woman when they were apart.

And then, the kiss.

Yes, he cared for her. And more than that. He longed for her. But he had been promised to another since he was born, and he knew that a strategic marital union was one of the crown prince's responsibilities. Sons of kings, he had been taught, did not wed for love. They married for the benefit of the kingdom. But he knew he would always consider the mysterious girl from the cliffs his first love.

When they reached the castle, Prince Finnian alighted from his horse and handed the reins to the groom, then went inside to change his clothes. Once properly outfitted to meet his parents, Richard, the king's gentleman-in-waiting, brought him to the small dining chamber where his parents sat at a table bedecked with candles and platters of food.

Prince Finnian entered the room and kneeled to greet his parents. As soon as he rose, he could tell something was wrong.

"Son, sit down," said his father. "We have news."

King Humphry the Bald was a large man, tall and imposing. He was an excellent soldier, but his temper was generally on the verge of combusting. In matters of the court, he was quick to decide, and ruled with strength and authority. His voice boomed when he spoke, and people throughout the castle jumped when he sneezed, so reverberant was the sound. And true to his name, there was not a single hair on his head.

"This is important, Finn," the queen said. Queen Eleanor's nature was kind and compassionate, but she was also smart, and understood the complexities of politics.

Finn noted the stern looks on both of their faces and how they each leaned forward. "Where are my brothers this evening?" he asked. A servant placed a dish of food before him, roast meat and carrots, bread with cheese, and apple-rosemary sauce.

"We invited the school master to dine with them," said the queen. She picked up a small envelope from the table. "Finn, we received a message from Spitzbergen."

"The duchess ran off with a rogue," the king said.

"You mean, she wed?" Finn asked.

"Yes," said Finn's mother. "And now she and her betrothed are in hiding, likely to avoid the consequences of this union. Her family does not know where they are."

"Or, if they know, they are not telling us," said the king.

Finn dragged his fork across the plate. This was a strange turn of events; he had talked with the girl about this only a short while earlier. It seemed to him now the girl's words had walked out of the air and come true.

"I have no stomach for food," the queen said, and pushed her plate away. "Humphry, how could your cousin allow his daughter to do such a thing? These two have been promised since they were infants. Duchess Agnatha has joined us for festivities her whole life; she was like a daughter to me."

"If she was my child, I would have dealt with the suitor," the king said, pounding his fist upon the table. "Swiftly, in a manner that left no question of this course being attempted. And long before their interest in one another caused disgrace to another family."

Finn knew he was supposed to feel angry and betrayed, but he felt strangely relieved. He did not blame the duchess. He envied her. "Perhaps, the duchess fell in love," he said.

The king and queen both looked at Prince Finn with surprise and doubt, as though his words made no sense and they'd forgotten he was there.

"It's possible," Finn said.

"Peasants marry for love," the king said. "After that, peasants raise their peasant children in their peasant homes, then they work until they are buried in peasant churchyards." He swallowed a piece of meat then pounded his chest to let free a burp. "The cost of power is responsibility. The actions we take in this family matter. Our actions will be recorded and remembered for generations. We cannot act on impulse or love or revenge or any other singular emotion. A king marries to bring land and wealth into the kingdom, or to create an alliance. Preferably all of those."

"We planned this union long ago, to unite Braemuir with Spitzbergen..." the queen said.

"I have spent my life building this kingdom," the king said. "Mark my words: whether through peace or force, I will add Spitzbergen to our realm."

"Then again," said Finn. "I have wondered what kind of a queen Agnatha would make. Her mouth sometimes ventures forth without the presence of her mind."

"I have observed this," the queen said, sighing. "At the Feast of the Fatted Cow, the duchess seemed nurturing of a...shall we say, headstrong personality."

"She threw cheese at a servant," Prince Finn said. "And declared war upon the castle dogs who were nipping at her ankles."

"Prince Heath admitted he tucked chicken bones into her pockets," the king said, chuckling. "Oh, that boy."

"I had forgotten about the flying cheese," the queen said. "The duchess does have a hearty interest in ale, not unlike others in her family."

"People like ale," said the king.

"What concerns me is the temper, not the ale," said the queen. "Speaking of ale, I would care for a bit of wine." She gestured to the servants who fetched it for her and some for the king as well.

"We are speaking about territory," the king said, taking a gulp of wine. "If we are at odds with the Spitzbergens, we lose access to the west. The tribes beyond the strait could invade by crossing through the Black

Woods. We stand a chance of resisting if my men can infiltrate those woods. But if we are denied access by the Spitzbergens, then we are at the whims of the forest folk. And they are...unpredictable at best."

"Cannibals, some say," the queen said.

The king growled. "And difficult to secure their loyalty."

"Is invasion imminent?" Prince Finn asked. "Is there some news?"

The king and the queen exchanged looks. "The threat of invasion always looms," the queen said slowly, carefully.

"I understand," Finn said. "But also, what of Gallia? Why do those soldiers camp in the town center?"

"Gallia is immaterial," the king said. He sat back and crossed his arms. "Theirs is some matter regarding succession."

"This is all you know?" asked the queen. "After talking with Monsieur De Fontenay all night and into the early morning last week?"

"We played dice," the king said gruffly.

"While draining the royal whiskey coffers and gambling," the queen said. "Admit it."

The king coughed and grumbled. "Monsieur De Fontenay cheats," he finally said.

"And you cheat right back, I am certain," she said.

The king smirked. "If the king does it, it is not cheating."

The queen sighed. "Gallia is not our present concern. If Finn is not to marry Duchess Agnatha, as we have been planning for more than two decades, then how should we proceed? The crown prince's first job is to marry a proper wife."

"True," the king said. He leaned forward upon the table and interlaced his fingers. "When people learn that the line of succession is uncertain, rebels start meeting in the public houses. Relatives begin plotting and making count of their friends and horses. Mark my words, this matter needs to be settled."

"What other options have we?" asked Finn.

"No obvious choice comes to mind," said the queen. "There's the princess of Moravia, yet a toddler, or Princess Thomasina of Greece, she's six, I believe. There is a lord's daughter in Sarvarre, a country endowed with a wealth of natural resources. She is not royal, but she has an acceptable dowry. An alliance with Sarvarre might prove very useful."

"There are fine, suitable young ladies right here in Braemuir," Finn said. "Why couldn't—" He opened his mouth as though to speak but then stopped and shook his head.

"Yes?" his mother said. "You look like you have a thought."

"I do," he said. "But I fear it will be dismissed outright."

"Speak your mind, son," she said. "If you are to become king, you must learn to do so…"

"And speak with force," the king barked, pointing his finger at his son. "As though you are only right and anyone who disputes you is a traitor deserving of death. Speak as though your word is the only one that matters."

His father had honed that skill well, but Finn was not sure he would ever have his father's confidence. Still, he gathered his courage and took a breath and spoke the words he was thinking. "Might I be allowed to… choose someone?" the prince said. "The duchess seems to have done so."

"Do you have someone in mind?" asked the queen, sipping from her wine goblet.

"There's a girl…a young lady," he started. "She's a commoner. And… that's almost all I know about her. Including she has never told me her name."

"You do not know this girl's name? " the queen asked. "And yet, you have come to care for her?"

"Yes," he said. "A great deal."

"What exactly *do* you know about her?" asked the king.

The prince looked into the candle's flame. "Her hair glows like sunshine in a jar of honey," he said. "Her eyes are green brown. When she laughs, they are decidedly green and when she is sad, the brown takes over. She loves the sea. She loves apples when they've just been picked. She's very talented at taking a few strands of grass and twisting them around a twig into the figure of an animal or a tree. This is harder than it sounds, by the way."

"Son," said the queen. "We need to know something about her character, her upbringing. What education has she had? And what of her family, are they wealthy of coin, or only land?"

"Neither," said Prince Finn. "Her parents are deceased, and she is the ward of her father's second wife." He tried to think of what else he knew. "She has a very old cat who sleeps with her beside the kitchen fireplace."

The king laughed. "She's an orphan," he said. "The Crown Prince of Braemuir shall not marry a pauper."

"Humphry, wait," the queen chided. "Finn, there must be something more you can tell us about this young woman."

Finn considered what he knew. "Nothing else of consequence."

"Well," said the queen, "you seem to know everything about her except the important information."

"Clear the dishes," the king boomed, gesturing at the servants. "How exactly do you know this girl?"

"And how long have you known her?" the queen asked. "Where are you encountering people about whom we know nothing?"

The servants removed the dishes, including Finn's untouched plate. Finn paused. He wasn't sure how much he wanted to divulge to his parents.

"We have crossed paths through the years," he said.

"How can you wed someone you know nothing about?" asked the king.

The queen cleared her throat. "What exactly did you know about a certain young lass when you chose your own wife?"

"She was a beautiful maiden," he said, taking her hand in his and kissing it. "There was nothing more I needed to know."

"And you," said the queen, "were a young soldier. Handsome and strong. You were no king then, and there was no promise you would become one."

"The battle had raged through the night. My leg was badly injured, and I was in desperate need of drink and kindness," he said. "A pretty girl took my head upon her lap. She poured water into my lips and stroked my wounds. I felt I'd come home."

The queen smiled at the memory. "But you did not know my name, my king," she said. "And neither I—nor my father—knew yours."

"Yet, here we are today," the king said.

The queen smiled. "Indeed." She looked into her husband's eyes another moment. "I suppose we should remember that marriage is not exclusively a matter of names and titles."

"Names and titles matter greatly, my queen, when land is at stake," he said.

"What matters land when you have not the trust of the people in your kingdom?" the queen responded, her eyebrows arched in disbelief. "Let us consider...the story of a future king marrying a common girl would tell the people we stand with them and for them. People would feel loyal to such a family."

The king grunted and stared at the ceiling as he thought it over.

"Humphrey?" said the queen. "What say you?"

"I cannot see how we might summon this girl when we do not know her name," he said.

The queen searched the ceiling as she thought this over. "Perhaps," she suggested, "we assemble all the young ladies of the kingdom. Offer them a benefit of some sort."

"Such as?" asked the king.

"A festival," the queen said.

"A picnic," the king declared. "A day of jousting games at the castle."

The queen put a finger over her mouth as she thought. "A day of sport would not draw out the young ladies. They would prefer an elegant event. A dance, perhaps," she said. "A ball. A matchmaker's gala. We could invite all the young people of the land. We would offer music, food, dancing. Merriment."

"But still..." King Humphry's face darkened, and he looked at his son. "Finn cannot marry a peasant."

"A local girl," the queen said.

"Call her what you will, but she is a young lady with neither name nor land, nor coin," he said. "We shall miss an opportunity to benefit the kingdom." The king sighed deeply, and looked at his wife and son. "I wish to learn what the council thinks of all this."

"Oh, yes," the queen said. "Ask your chancellor, ask the council. Then do as always, ignore them and enact the opposite of what they suggest."

The king chuckled and burped quietly. "That plan always works for me," he said. "And while I gather their counsel, you may plan some event. Even if they advise against Finn's idea to marry a, what you call, local girl, the people of the region might enjoy an evening at the castle."

"Marvelous," the queen said, clapping her hands. "I have many ideas. We have a good bit of work to do."

"Thank you, mother," Finn said.

"But Finn, if we meet this young lady and deem her inadequate for marriage," Queen Eleanor said, staring her son in the eye. "Your father and I must find a more suitable maiden. You should adapt to this idea ahead of time."

"I understand," said Finn. "But once you see her, you will forget all others."

The queen smiled. "I do not know whether we will," she said. "But I can see you already have."

Chapter Five

When Cinder awoke the next morning, the sky over the sea was slate gray and unmoving. It had rained the night before, and once again, the leaking chimneys had snuffed out the fires. As always, Cinder built the kitchen fire and mixed the day's bread and fed the chickens. When the sun's glow broke through the clouds, they revealed a world where the trees were bare of leaves and the only green that remained was evergreen needles. On the way to the henhouse, Cinder passed through what had once been her mother's gardens. All the flowers she used to tend had long since died, and now, even the ivies were brown and crumbling. Fall was fading; winter was on its way.

The bells from the upper rooms began to ring in the kitchen: first, Mother Rhona's chimed, then Liisi's, then Orla's. Cinder sighed, and trudged up the stairs to make fires and deliver tea. Finally, when all in the household were warmed and fed, Cinder returned to the kitchen to continue the day's chores: chop wood, mend shoes, clean the floors. Once those were complete, there was more to do. Just as she was considering where to begin, someone pulled the bell at the door. Cinder wiped her hands on her apron and went to answer: in front of her stood a tall man standing slightly stooped, his dark hair thin and graying at the edges, but his dandy new clothes were tidy and pressed.

"Good morning, young lady," he said, slightly tipping his hat to her.

"May I help you?" she asked.

"Lord Warin Fitzalan come to call," he said.

Cinder remembered that name, and stumbled slightly backward at hearing it. Lord Warin was a mysterious man with some connection to Mother Rhona's first husband. He had visited Bowmore House once or twice when Cinder's father, Sir Gerik, was alive. Her father had had no time for the man's nonsense and had shown him summarily to the door. They had not seen Lord Warin for some years. And nobody had missed him.

"You must be here to see my stepmother."

"Your stepmother?" he said, glaring at her. "You're not a house wench?"

"I suppose I am that," she said. "But I am also the daughter of Sir Gerik, the shipbuilder, second husband, though deceased, to the lady of the house."

"Ahh, yes, Sir Gerik," he said curiously. "Storm at sea, or some awful thing, if memory serves."

"Yes, sir, five years ago now," she said.

"Terribly sorry for the loss," he said. He looked at the doorway and suddenly seemed flustered. "Do you intend to invite me inside, girl, or am I doomed for eternity to view nothing beyond the lintel above the doorway?"

Cinder said not a word but stepped aside and allowed Lord Warin to enter.

"Good. Now, fetch your stepmother for me. And make haste, for I have other matters to attend." He pulled a pocket watch on a chain from his jacket, regarded the time then snapped it shut. He studied the entranceway. "My, this Bowmore is a fine example of architecture. I have always longed for a cottage by the Morisar Sea."

"Have you?" she said. "I would think city-living would suit you better, sir. Or town-living." *Or simply,* she thought, *somewhere-else living.*

Lord Warin hmphed, and Cinder started up the stairs to fetch Mother Rhona, but Lord Warin stopped her before she alighted the second step. "One moment, girl," he said. He walked up to her and stroked her cheek gently with the back of his hand. "You're a pretty little thing. How old are you finding yourself these days?"

She turned her face away from his hand. "Age is but a number, they say," she said. "And there is no number that puts me in the mind that I might deserve your lordship's attention."

Lord Warin laughed slightly. "Well, you needn't belittle yourself."

"It's not myself I was disparaging," she said, again quietly. Then she cleared her throat, hoping he might not hear her words. "Pardon me," she said, and dashed up the stairs as quickly as she could.

She knocked upon the door to Mother Rhona's room. "Come in," came a voice. Inside, Mother Rhona was sitting at her desk, staring at a ledger of the house accounts, her head perched in her hand.

"Lord Warin Fitzalan has arrived," she said. "He awaits you in the vestibule."

Rhona sat up straight and frowned. "That buzzard. It's like he knows I'm looking at the numbers. He smelled my despair and came to feed upon it."

"Shall I tell him you're ill?" she asked.

"No," Rhona said. "He would only return another time. I shall collect myself. Tell him I will be there presently. Have we any biscuits, Cinder? Nay, I know we do not. Prepare tea, then, and bring it to us in the parlor."

Cinder nodded, then slipped into the corridor and found Liisi standing there. The two of them peered over the balcony into the foyer below, where Lord Warin was wandering around. The girls watched him approach a painting of some fine gentlemen. He straightened it then took out a handkerchief, spat, and dusted the edges of the frame.

"Why is he here?" Liisi said, looking disgusted.

"I don't know," Cinder said.

Liisi nodded vaguely, a shadow of a sneer upon her mien. "He used to visit my father. He'd bring candy for me and Orla like he was trying to lure us into his tangled web. He'd inquire whether we were being 'properly educated on the womanly arts.'"

"The womanly arts?" Cinder asked, vaguely grimacing. "What does that mean?"

"I do not care to know," Liisi said.

"Oh, no," said Orla, suddenly appearing beside them. Her face at once grew dark, as though a shadow had fallen upon it. "I didn't realize we had company."

"Look, Orla," Liisi said. "Your favorite person has arrived."

"Does Lady Mildred accompany him?" Orla asked.

"He arrived alone," Cinder said.

"Orla believes," said Liisi, "quietly, mind you, that Lord Warin had some connection to the fire that burned our house down."

"He had been staying with us for some weeks," Orla said. "Strange how he escaped from our father's study that night, but our father did not."

"Strange indeed," Liisi said.

"After we escaped the house, I saw him slinking about, avoiding us," Orla said. "He told some story about trying to drag our father from his study, but the fire grew too fast and he had to save himself." She shuddered. "Do you remember that, Liisi?"

"Regarding that night, I remember as little as possible on purpose," Liisi said.

"So, I am the lone keeper of this memory." Orla looked down below. "I feel suddenly quite ill. Please excuse me."

Cinder watched Orla go back into her room then turned to Liisi. "So, why is he here?"

Liisi sighed and crossed her arms. "Our mother owes him a debt. One amassed, so he claims, by my father's worst habits: gambling and drinking...and likely other unsavory hobbies as well."

"The debt was not forgiven upon your father's death?" Cinder asked.

"No debt is forgiven when the one who procured it expires," Liisi said. "Debt is passed down, Cinder, just like wealth."

Rhona emerged from the bedroom wearing her long, black dress, her hair pulled in a neat, tight bun. She smoothed her dress, preparing herself for battle. Liisi and Cinder watched her slowly descend the stairs.

"I must also retire to my room to lock the door behind me and see to some urgent matter," Liisi said. "Cinder, you may want to find some task that keeps you at a distance. I fear the house will soon fill with the stench of something long deceased."

Rhona heard their voices. "Cinder, I asked you to make tea."

"Yes, ma'am," she said.

Liisi retreated to her bedroom and closed the door behind her, and Cinder lingered upon the balcony to watch the scene below.

First, there were pleasantries. "Lord Warin!" Rhona exclaimed. "What a lovely surprise."

He bowed to her and presented her with a small bouquet of autumnal wildflowers. "I found these along my route here and thought kindly of you."

"Are there still blossoms to be found in this chilly season? Delightful," she said. Rhona set the flowers, tied together with a pretty ribbon, upon a table in the corridor and gestured for him to follow her into the parlor. She spotted Cinder upon the balcony and frowned. "You may bring the tea in here, Cinder."

"Yes, ma'am," Cinder said. She came down the stairs to gather the flowers, then paused for a moment to listen at the door.

"Does the fair Lady Mildred accompany you today?" Rhona asked as she led Lord Warin into the parlor.

"Ahh, so you do not receive news from your late husband's family?" he said.

"I have two late husbands," Rhona said. "And I do not receive information, nor any other thing, from the families of either. Is Lady Mildred unwell?"

Lord Warin cleared his throat. "Around six months back, Lady Mildred and I took our tea, at four o'clock, as we had each day for many years, and after, she began to feel poorly. She went to rest, and, sadly..." He sneered and smacked his lips. "She never awoke from her respite."

"Oh, Lord Warin, my deepest sympathies," Rhona said.

"Her life ended quickly and without prolonged suffering," he said. "I find relief in this only."

Cinder watched his lips curl up in a vile, sinister smile as he delivered this news. No, she did not trust this man. She knew she did not have the authority to show him to the door as her father once had, but she needed to pay attention.

Rhona stood and approached the door. "Cinder," she said. "What are you doing?"

"Gathering these," she looked at the bundle of weeds on the table.

"I requested tea," Rhona said, her teeth clenched in anger. "Do not make me ask one more time."

"Yes, ma'am," she said.

Rhona closed the doors to the drawing room so Cinder went down the corridor to the kitchen and put a pot of water upon the fire to boil then set a tray with a teapot and tea cups. Once that was set, she skittered back up the hall and tiptoed into a sitting room that adjoined the parlor. The room was dark, and she concealed herself behind a screen that separated the rooms. Lord Warin was pacing, inspecting portraits on the walls while Mother Rhona sat, perched upon the settee, gripping her own hands. Cinder watched Mother Rhona's face; her stepmother was making a grand effort to show no emotion.

"Rhona, do not try to distract me. You have not made a payment in many months," he was saying. "I have written you regarding this matter. And from you, no response."

Rhona nodded. "Finances are rather tight at the moment."

"I don't believe this is my concern," he said.

Rhona forced a smile. "Oh, Lord Warin, I am certain you would not penalize a poor widow caring for three girls in the wake of the loss of the man of this house. You understand, none of us can earn a wage and we have each shed all pleasantries of life. I know you will find it in your heart to, if not forgive this debt, one I did not amass, grant me a recess until I can find new situations for these young ladies—"

Lord Warin cleared his throat to interrupt her. "These three ladies you speak of, they are all of marriageable age, if I recall."

Marriageable age. The words sent a chill down Cinder's spine.

Rhona glared at him with dark eyes. "You have no right," she said sternly.

Lord Warin stood at the mantle and lifted a small bowl fashioned of painted enamel, which Cinder's father had brought home from his travels. "Shall I remind you, my good lady," he said as he studied the bowl from all angles, "of a certain letter given to me by your husband some years ago..."

"It is a forgery," Mother Rhona declared. "You know this."

He pondered that for a moment. "No. I do not believe so," he said, and he set the bowl down. "Your husband gave it to me as payment for a lost bet. Which one, I cannot recall, for there were many." He turned to Rhona and Cinder could see his smug expression. "You know the letter of which I speak, do you not?"

Rhona glanced away.

"The letter's author is the Constable of London. He wrote to Archie to make him aware that his new bride was naught more than a pauper run-away in possession of jewels once given by the King of Gallia to his wife's sister."

Cinder listened carefully. What was he saying? He was accusing Mother Rhona of stealing jewels that once belonged to the King of Gallia.

Sir Warin coughed into a handkerchief, then continued. "An odd case, for this woman had been found murdered a few months earlier. Her daughter disappeared entirely. So, the question arises: how did you come to acquire these jewels? Perhaps your paths crossed in travel, and you, upon learning what the girl possessed, injured her, perhaps killed her, then stole the jewels?"

Cinder quietly gasped. *My stepmother stands accused of murder.* She was shocked and a little impressed to learn that her stepmother might not have been the paragon of perfection she presented herself as.

Mother Rhona's face grew pale. "I was charged with no crime," she said. "The girl's body was never found, and no death ever proved."

Lord Warin put the bowl down and smiled at her. "And yet, it's an odd situation, is it not? Perhaps you care to explain how you came into custody of these jewels?"

"I owe no explanation for a crime I did not commit," she said.

"I surmise that the people of this region would be interested to learn the sordid and possibly quite scandalous history of the matron of this family."

Mother Rhona stood up and walked to the edge of the room, concealing her face from Cinder.

"You wouldn't," she said.

"Allow me to repeat my original question," he said, and cleared his throat. "In this house you have residing three young ladies. All of marriageable age. Do I have that information correct?"

"Yes," she said.

"One daughter is maimed, and I won't trouble you about that one," he said, dismissing Orla with one gesture. "But another is quite pleasant of appearance."

Mother Rhona turned, and Cinder could see her twist her hands. "My younger. I wish her to find a husband of noble blood."

Lord Warin held his hands behind his back and wiggled his fingers, as if he believed he'd proven himself victorious. "Why, by coincidence, I myself am of noble blood," he said. "On my mother's side, going back many generations."

Cinder gripped her hands into fists and glared at Mother Rhona. Would she really sell her own daughter to settle a bet? The expression on her face was like an animal with a foot in a trap: terrified, desperate. "Indeed?"

"Then again," he said, "perhaps you prefer to wed your daughters to those with no familial connections…"

"Y-yes," Rhona said, stuttering. "This is the case."

"There is a girl living in this house who is not a blood relation of yours. Am I again correct?"

"Lord Warin, no—"

"In fact, I believe she opened the door for me," he said. He clicked his tongue to express remorse. "So, terribly disconcerting for you. Have you no house staff at all, Rhona?"

"I have made accommodations in the face of difficult circumstances," she said.

"I would hate to deprive you of a house girl," he said. "But you understand, we must settle this debt. This may be a solution worth considering."

"Sir, my stepdaughter, she—"

Cinder could no longer hold herself back. She burst into the room.

"Cinder," Mother Rhona said, looking surprised and nervous. "Where is the tea?"

Cinder swallowed. "The water hasn't boiled yet."

"Ahh, this is the one about whom I was speaking," Lord Warin said. He stood and put his face close to hers. His body had a smell to it that reminded her of the putrid odor of bed pans needing to be cleaned. Cinder held her breath. Lord Warin pulled a lock of her hair out of her kerchief and rubbed it hungrily between his fingers, a slight line of spit seeping from the corner of his mouth. She was desperate to flee but could not make herself move.

"Now I remember you," he said. "You were but a child when last I saw you. My. You have changed."

"Sir, if I may," Cinder began. She pulled away so her hair fell out of his hand, but did not know what to say next. "Please forgive me, but I was cleaning, and I happened to overhear some words of your conversation. Sir, I have a meager request— "

"Cinder, go to the kitchen this moment," Rhona said. "I requested tea."

"My dear girl, speak it," said Lord Warin, smiling contentedly. "It would be my sincere pleasure to satisfy... any need you may have."

Cinder looked at her stepmother and the snake who stood before her and swallowed. "In my efforts to improve my station," she began, "I have been attempting to educate myself. On the subject of..." She tried to think of some subject she might have tried to learn. "Mathematics."

"Mathematics!" exclaimed Rhona.

"Interesting," said Lord Warin.

She nodded. "I understand Mother Rhona's first husband owed you a debt, and that she has been paying it off since he perished. I wish I could see a true example of arithmetic in daily life. So, might I review the figures for this debt?"

Lord Warin's self-assured grin turned slowly into a sneer, and he sat back down. "The figures?"

"If you please, sir," she said, trying to seem effervescent with curiosity. "I am certain you have been tracking these." She looked from Mother Rhona's face, which held an expression of infuriated surprise to the face of Lord Warin, which seemed caught in abject bewilderment. "My father used to keep his business ledgers in a book of accounts. He tracked expenditures and receipts, of course, as well as debts he owed and debts owed to him. Sometimes I double-checked his sums."

Lord Warin coughed effusively. "Nobody likes a girl who has an opinion."

"Cinder," Mother Rhona said sternly, "this is not the time—"

She was telling the truth about the sums. Her father had wanted to train his daughter to someday help him with his business. And she liked numbers; she delighted in working with them; they were a kind of puzzle. "Even a small error compounds itself if not caught and corrected in a timely fashion. I am certain you would agree that this is true. Therefore, may I?"

"May you... what?" Lord Warin said.

"See the ledgers regarding this debt," she said. "Just a list of what was initially owed and what has been paid. Have you been tracking compounding interest, for example? And if so, at what rate?"

"Compounding..." he exclaimed.

"It would be helpful for our household finances to know specifically what is yet owed." She glanced at her stepmother; the woman looked like a red tea kettle about to boil over. "Don't you agree, Mother Rhona?"

"I do not," she snapped. "I requested tea..."

"It's not that simple, girl," he said. "You could never understand something like this, this sort of calculating is way too complicated for a *girl*." His forehead was beginning to emit tiny beads of perspiration, which he patted away with a small white handkerchief.

"Oh, sir, beg pardon," she continued. "I would never deign to think I might understand such a thing. I am only a silly kitchen maid. But this is why I am trying to improve myself."

"Why bother with any of it, silly girl? All you shall ever do is marry and birth sucklings," he said, tucking his handkerchief back in his pocket. "Trouble yourself not with numbers, which may add lines to your pretty forehead. This would not please your husband."

His words stirred Cinder's stomach, and she felt she might be sick. "Of course," she said. "But still, I am at the mercy of my own curiosity."

"I do not know those numbers in my head and you're a fool if you think I carry those books around with me from place to place," he said. "You know nothing of the ways of the world or men's work..."

Cinder laughed out loud. "Indeed, kind sir, I do know something of the world," she said, standing up straight with a strange, and sudden confidence. "I know that neither I nor my sisters can be offered as payment for this debt."

"Cinder," Rhona said. "Excuse yourself now. And be gone. This moment."

Cinder looked at her stepmother. She knew she had stepped too far. "Pardon me, Lord Warin," she said. "I must fetch tea."

"No need for tea," he said, standing. "I shall be taking my leave."

"My sincere apologies, Lord Warin," Rhona said, and she also stood and followed after him to the door. Cinder dashed down the hall to the kitchen, then, and stood with her back against the kitchen table, breathing hard. She was certain she had foiled Lord Warin's plans to secure herself as his bride, but she also knew she'd provoked the ire of Mother Rhona. In short time, as she expected, Mother Rhona walked into the kitchen like a storm on the horizon.

"Exactly what did you think you were doing back there?" she asked, fuming.

"Has that walking mound of bile departed?" Cinder asked.

"You will show me respect. This is a matter between adults," Mother Rhona exclaimed. "It is none of your concern."

"How can you say that?" Cinder asked. "He was talking about me and Liisi as though we were sides of meat."

"I did not invite you to listen," Rhona said. "Nor participate. You think you are smart and perhaps you are. But you do not know the ways of such men."

"And you do?" Cinder asked. "Had I not intercepted, you might have handed me into that man's bondage."

"I would never have done so!" Rhona exclaimed. "I would never have done so," she repeated, calmer. "Cinder, stay out of matters you know nothing about."

"What letter does he possess, Mother Rhona?" she said. "Did you really kill someone?"

Rhona turned to her, then slammed her hand on the table. "This is none of your concern," she said. "I warn you, girl, inquire upon this no more. And when I ask for tea, I expect you to deliver a tray then depart without comment. Nothing more. Am I properly understood?"

"Yes, ma'am," Cinder said, her eyes cast down.

Mother Rhona walked curtly out of the kitchen while Cinder watched. Once she was gone, Cinder sighed quietly with relief and went to her cat and scratched behind his soft ears.

"Well, Henry," she said. "It seems that my perfectly perfect stepmother has a nefarious past. What do you think she's hiding?"

Henry purred.

"My suspicions as well," she said.

Chapter Six

After Lord Warin departed, a dreary pall remained over Bowmore House, made drearier by rain that fell in sharp, cold pinpricks, pushed by the hard wind. By afternoon, the rain had stopped, leaving in its wake a steel gray sky. Cinder went into the yard to sweep the leaves and sticks scattered upon the front walkway. Suddenly, there arrived by palfrey a second visitor for the day, a messenger dressed in the king's crest. The gentleman alighted from his horse, bowed to Cinder, and, without a word, handed her an envelope printed on vellum. He tipped his hat, returned to his horse and rode off.

Cinder watched him ride away and wondered vaguely whether Alban had suited that horse. *Alban*, she whispered to herself. *Alban*. What had happened the previous day? His kiss upon her hand had changed her like a magic spell. She felt as though a veil had been lifted away from her eyes, and suddenly she thought of him as she never had before. How strange was time, she thought. The day before, she'd considered Alban only a friend, and now, one small kiss had awakened a warm desire in her heart. There was no possible future that held the two of them together, but that morning, she'd been unable to keep from thinking upon it as she had built the morning's fires. She could almost picture them, walking upon the cliffs, fingers intertwined, or sitting beneath a tree on a sun-drenched day, eating apples, and laughing. What would it feel like, to be so connected, tangled, indivisible, lives, bodies, souls? She could only imagine.

She shook her head. Such lofty ideas would come to nothing. And still, she wondered about time. Time had transformed her parents, one moment alive, the next, lost. How did time work, exactly? Could it be an element, like a road? Could she ride that road forward to gain a glimpse of what would become of Alban? Or, if time was a road, could she ride backward to her last moment at her mother's side? She longed to tell her mother the words she had not been able to say on the day they parted: *I will love you forever.*

A burst of wind came up and over her, startling her attention back to the walkway of Bowmore House. She looked at the envelope. It bore the king's coat of arms. She wondered if it contained more dread news.

"I saw the messenger from the upstairs window," said Liisi, suddenly appearing through the front door. She reached out a flat palm and gave Cinder a pert smile. "Hand it over."

"I have been instructed to deliver all mail directly to your mother," Cinder said.

"You may pass that one to me," Liisi said.

"How do you know it is not something terrible like a court summons or a tax bill?" Cinder said. "So far, the tides of the day have brought only things foul and bleak."

"I will tell you how I know," Liisi said, and she snatched the envelope from Cinder's hand. She lifted it to her nose and inhaled. "The paper is fine, costly. And this is the full coat of arms, used only for celebrations. Also, the size is wrong, much larger than a tax bill. This, Cinder dear, is an invitation. We have finally been invited to the castle. Watch."

Cinder watched doubtfully as Liisi cracked open the wax seal and lifted the flap of the envelope. Cinder didn't want to care, but if Liisi was wrong, she needed to be on hand to make some derisive comment.

Liisi loosed the card from its casing and read the words printed within. She gasped as she read it. "It *is* an invitation! To a ball at the castle!"

"At the castle?" Cinder repeated.

"We're going to a ball!" Liisi exclaimed, and she ran up the stairs to her room. "Mother!" she shouted before she reached the top of the stairs. "Mother, Orla, come see!"

Rhona and Orla emerged and all went into Liisi's bedroom. Liisi sat on her bed, gazing at the invitation. Cinder slipped in quietly after them.

"It's a ball, mother, at Glengoe Castle," said Liisi. "A match-makers' ball! All the young people of the kingdom are invited. Orla, we must both go. And we shall dance through the night. And eat the most marvelous things. We shall meet the princes!"

Rhona took the invitation from Liisi's hand and read it herself. "Well," she said. "I did hear that the crown prince's wedding had been called off. Perhaps this is the reason for the ball, to find the prince a bride."

"The crown prince?" said Liisi. She sat up, eyes wide. "It shall happen. I will become a princess. And someday a queen." She pressed her hands to her chest, her heart overcome at the very idea.

Cinder smiled at Liisi and looked at Orla. Orla could not keep from laughing, which she disguised by coughing.

"I'm so happy for you, my sister," Orla finally said.

"Cinder, bring us tea and toast," Rhona said. "This ball is in two weeks. There's not much time. We need to make plans."

Cinder left to make tea and when she returned, the three were perched on Liisi's bed. Rhona and Liisi were feverishly exchanging ideas about costumes and hairstyles. Cinder put the tea pot on a small table and poured them each a cup.

"Orla, dear," Rhona said. "The ball is so soon. I hope you shall feel well enough to attend."

"You must," Liisi said, and she clutched her sister's arm. "I couldn't bear if my sister was not with me on the night when I would meet my betrothed."

"I shall try," Orla said. "But what about Cinder?"

"What about her?" Liisi said. "She wouldn't be interested in something like this. Oh, I hope not, she'd only embarrass us horribly."

Cinder winced but refused to show how much Liisi's words hurt. "You have nothing to worry about, Princess Liisi," she said. "I do not intend to ruin your fairy tale."

"The invitation does state," said Rhona, "that all the young people of the kingdom are invited. If you can find something suitable to wear, Cinder, we should not stop you from attending, if you so desired. Of course, we wouldn't introduce you as Cinder. Remind me, dear, what name do you tell people outside of the family?"

The question made Cinder freeze. She did not care to remind Mother Rhona of the name her true mother had given to her. "Thank you for the offer, Mother Rhona." Cinder held her head high, her shoulders back. "I feel certain the crown prince will not object to having one less girl to meet. Now, if you'll pardon me, I must go feed Henry."

Down in the kitchen, Cinder prepared Henry a plate of scraps from breakfast and a dish of fresh milk, which she warmed in the fire. She patted the old man's black and white fur as he ate. The only thing worse than marriage to Lord Warin would be a ball at the king's castle. Who could bear such pomp? There would be a huge ballroom, bedecked in gold and filled with candles. There'd be an orchestra as well, and it would be ear-numbingly loud, with thousands of people attending, all pushing and shoving for the chance to glimpse the king and queen. Worse still, there would be a thousand young ladies, each elbowing their ways through the crowd to reach the princes.

And dancing? Of course, there would be dancing. But Cinder did not know a single step. And even if she did know how to dance, or could stomach the absurdity of all the posturing and pretension, she had nothing even close to suitable to wear.

"A ball at the king's castle, Henry," she said. "It sounds dreadful."

Then again, she wondered whether those in the king's employ would be invited to attend. Would Alban be there? It could be nice, she thought, to have an evening with him. Just to talk.

She laughed to herself and told herself that Alban's action–his kiss– had only been a gesture of common courtesy between a young man and a young woman. She was best off casting the matter out of her head. She knelt down before the dwindling fire and fed it a few twigs and small logs. She recalled how Mother Rhona had demanded Cinder's real name. Rhona knew it once; had she forgotten? Cinder still remembered all those years ago, when her father introduced her to the imposing black-haired woman.

"This is my little Marguerite," he'd said to Rhona. "She's high-spirited, but she will be glad for sisters."

"Marguerite, so nice to meet you," the strange woman had said.

Cinder remembered how she hated hearing her name on the shrew's lips. How could this woman with the sharp features and eyes the color of mud think that she might take her beautiful mother's place? If Mother Rhona had forgotten Cinder's real name, that much the better.

Suddenly, Liisi burst into the kitchen. "Is that cat still alive? He must be a hundred years old by now. Meow, Harry."

"His name is Henry," Cinder growled.

"All this planning for the ball has made us very hungry," Liisi said. "Bring us a plate of bread and cheese, Cinder. Have we any of the good cheese left? I do so love good cheese."

"You finished the last of it two days ago," Cinder said. "I can pick more up at Kilderbrae market, but it's quite costly."

"Oh, bother," Liisi said, making a sour frown. "When I become princess, my favorite cheese shall always be in the castle kitchen. And if I care to sup in the middle of the night, I shall order castle servants to bring it to me in bed. Along with fresh bread and the best wine."

Cinder almost burst out laughing but stopped herself. "You have very big ideas, Liisi," she said. "You will have to put in your best effort to get the prince's attention at this ball. What shall you do with your hair? I could arrange it for you."

"Oh," said Liisi. "What would you suggest?"

"Your hair is so lovely," said Cinder, and she reached for Liisi's flaxen locks and held them atop her head. "We could plait it, then twist and curl the braid so it beams like a giant torch atop your head."

"A torch, you say?" asked Liisi.

"And then, we could paint it with mud and clovers and entice a hive of honeybees to come and nest within." she said. "When the bees swarm, all the other ladies shall run away and you will be the only one left. And we'll put a small spigot on the side of your head so everyone can draw honey."

"Stop it, Cinder! You are terrible," Liisi squealed in terror. She scrambled to push Cinder away from her head and, panicked, batted her hands at imaginary hive of bees.

"You'd get a great deal of attention," Cinder said, as she sliced bread.

"Watch your step, sister," Liisi said, her hair now tousled and unkempt. "One of these days, you will find your beloved feline skinned and roasting on a spit over the fire." She licked one finger. "The house will fill with the aroma of roasted cat. Yum, yum, yum."

Cinder took the knife she was using to slice the bread and raised it over Liisi's head. "Don't you dare threaten Henry. If you touch his smallest toe, I will cut your head clean off your body while you sleep."

"Put the knife down this instant," Rhona said, appearing suddenly behind her.

"I didn't touch her," Cinder said, lowering the knife. "She threatened Henry."

"She wants to put bees in my hair!" Liisi shrieked.

Rhona walked up to Cinder, grasped her wrist and took the knife from her hand. "Go to your room, Liisi."

"But Mother, I–"

"To your room," she repeated. Liisi turned and sulked out.

Rhona's dark eyes beamed like embers in a fire's core. "I will not tolerate such behavior in my house. Learn your place, girl. Do not intervene in my conversations, and do not threaten your sister with a knife. To the tower."

The breath went out of Cinder's body. "But ma'am, I didn't– "

"The time is late for excuses," Rhona said. "I do not want to hear your voice nor see your face again before morning. Now, go."

Cinder fumed and glared at her stepmother. Then she scooped up her cat and turned and walked away.

Cinder's father had commissioned the builders of Bowmore House to install a small tower atop the roof like a squat lighthouse or a castle turret. At the top was a six-sided room with windows on every side. He'd envisioned a place where his wife and daughter could stand upon a landing and watch him sail away, then keep watch for his return. The landing had long since crumbled, but the tower and its interior room were still intact. To reach it, Cinder went through a door in the kitchen to a small pantry room she used to store grains, potatoes, jams and pickles, then climbed a long spiral staircase built of stone. Cinder loved the spot, but the winds off the ocean made the room too cold to linger for more than a short while, especially at night. Indeed, sometimes the wind blew so hard she could feel the tower sway, an unnerving sensation, like being onboard a ship.

When Cinder reached the room, carrying her beloved cat like a baby, she felt the shame and pain of being the only daughter who would be issued a sentence such as this. Why was she sent away while Liisi's bad behavior was indulged time and time again? It was not fair. She looked out the windows that surrounded her; the wide sky unfurled like a flag and gray clouds pulled apart like tufts of wool while the ocean churned below it, containing so many secrets.

"Not a bad place to spend some time," she said out loud, though she knew full well that once the sun set, the room would become pitch dark, and bone-chillingly cold. Cinder looked out over the cliffs at the Morisar Sea. She searched the horizon for some sign of the island of St. Kiana. And this time, like all the other times, no matter how hard she looked, she could see no sign of a small island jutting out of the ocean surface, no sign of the tree that guarded her mother's grave. Only a few rocky outcroppings, the empty horizon and beyond that, nothing.

She remembered the day a ship had borne her mother away. Her mother had been ill for so long. Cinder's father had decided to bring her mother to a warm, southern country, known for its healing springs. The crossing would be difficult, so Cinder was to remain home with the nurse. Before she left, Cinder's mother had removed an amber trinket from her own neck and placed it upon her daughter. It was no priceless jewel, only a leather string with a brown teardrop upon it, and inside that was trapped a peculiar winged insect.

"I received this gift when I was young," her mother said, her voice weak. "It stands for courage, strength and kindness. You have all these inside you, my love, and you must cherish them. But I have seen your blood run hot. I worry you may speak or act in ways that cannot be undone. Stay strong and you shall always find the answer."

Cinder had worn the trinket every day since, and now, as she remembered, she touched the amulet. Strength, kindness, courage. Sitting in the cold tower, Cinder could not say for sure whether she had cherished those qualities. All she knew was, Liisi was downstairs, warm by a fire that Cinder had built, while Cinder herself was freezing alone in the tower.

When the time had come to bring her mother on board the ship, Cinder kissed her mother's face, but could not make herself say goodbye. She had believed that if she did not speak the words, her mother would be compelled to return. Cinder ran home, straight to the tower, and watched the vessel's northward journey until it disappeared over the horizon's edge.

Some weeks later, her father returned alone. He told Cinder that her mother had died on the journey, and he'd buried her on the island of St. Kiana, a place she had dearly loved. Cinder had wept hard and ran to the cliffs and hills around Bowmore House, shouting at the ocean until her voice was hoarse. She had searched the horizon that day, hoping to see the island that bore her mother's grave. She had been searching ever since.

Since then, something in Cinder's heart had never settled: she had not told her mother a proper goodbye, and she had not told her mother how much she loved her. This fact haunted Cinder, and she held on to it like a hard stone in her pocket, its edges sharp, its weight heavy.

After her mother died, her father hired a series of nurses. None could keep Cinder inside and make her tend to her studies. But the final one had locked the child in her bedroom. Cinder had beaten the door hard with all her might, shouting loudly. By the time her father let her out, her hands were bloody and her throat hoarse and inflamed.

Her father fired that nurse summarily. And when Mother Rhona arrived, he'd made her swear not to lock the girl inside any room. For whatever else she had done or forgotten, Mother Rhona had kept this promise. Even now, Cinder knew the door to the kitchen was not locked. She remained in the tower on her own accord; she did not agree with her punishment, but she would endure it.

After a while, the sun began to sink and the room grew colder. Cinder rubbed her arms and blew on her hands. Then she noticed something she had not seen earlier: a trunk, in a shadowed corner of the room. In the fading light, she looked at the insignia on the top: her father's family crest, a circle with a tree in the middle, and around it, the waves of the ocean. She opened the box carefully. Sitting on top was a thick, white-yellow sweater, warm and woolen, and slightly greasy from lanolin. She put it on; it was a man's sweater, large on her, but very warm. She inhaled the wool; the aroma was peat smoke and something sweet and familiar: it smelled like her mother. Suddenly, she felt her mother's embrace, across time and ocean.

"Mother," she said, tears beginning in her eyes. "I miss you."

She left on the sweater and pulled out the rest of the clothes, examining and inhaling each dress, stocking, skirt and blouse. Once again, she thought of time, and how she wished she could slip through a window to a place where her mother was alive, wearing this sweater against the chill winds off Sayre Cliffs. Her mother had fallen ill so suddenly. Cinder recalled the sour smell of her mother's sickroom and how cold the ocean winds blew that year. She recalled her mother's colorless skin, her lifeless eyes.

In the bottom of the box, something caught Cinder's eye. A stack of papers. She lifted the stack out of the box and studied the first page. The paper felt fragile, like it might crumble if handled roughly. In the tower room's fading light, she squinted to make out the writing. It was a note in her father's hand:

Dear Sir,

I seek your assistance. My young daughter is in need of motherly guidance after her mother died some years ago. I have hired nurses, several in succession. None have been able to rein my daughter in.

She is not a bold child; she is always polite and gracious, but she follows her interests, no matter whom it suits or suits not. I believe she is haunted by grief for her mother, and well so, as her mother was a treasure upon this earth. In her headstrong ways, I suspect my daughter takes after her own father, myself. Furthermore, I believe firmly that the spark in her is not something to be extinguished but guided and directed.

I seek a woman, preferably handsome of face, and preferably with her own children, who would marry me and live as my wife. Furthermore, she must understand that I am a builder of ships and sometimes captain of them, and shall at times take leave from this house for large stretches of time, leaving her in charge.

Please contact me forthwith if this request puts you in mind of any individual.

Always your humble servant,
   Gerik C. Barclay

Cinder put the letter down. Her stepmother had joined their little family from nowhere, and now Cinder realized that this was not because, as she had been told, her father had fallen suddenly in love, but because the woman had been sent to him. Her stepmother had been little more than an employee.
Rhona.
Cinder had always thought it uncanny that her stepmother's first name was the same as her mother's. An odd coincidence. There were no other similarities between the two; indeed, they could not have been more different. Cinder's mother had been slight of figure, light-haired and gray-eyed, with a childlike spirit. Stepmother Rhona was tall and imposing, dark in hair and eyes, which were full never of wonder but only worry. Cinder's mother had been quick to smile and laugh, her laughter like music, like magic; it danced in her eyes like candlelight. There was no better moment than when she could make her mother laugh, especially when her mother was sick. Stepmother Rhona never smiled, never laughed. The best Cinder could hope for was a flat-mouthed grin, and even then, her eyes were unmoved.
How peculiar, these two Rhonas her father had married. Her father had been a sailor, always looking to the stars for wisdom. When he met his second wife and learned her name, did he perceive in it a message, maybe sent by the first Rhona? Cinder would never know, for her father's secrets had sunk into the ocean along with his bones and the payload he had invested all his capital into.

She turned back to the stack of papers. The next page contained a contract related to her father's shipbuilding business, and it was followed by three or four letters about goods sold and exchanged. After that, several more pages of accounting notes. And under them all, a stack of handwritten pages. Cinder paused to read the first page.

To my sweet daughter,

I am ill. Tumors have filled my lungs and they are not diminishing, only increasing. I have been weak and wasting for some time. Today the doctor spoke to me with terrible honesty. I now know that I should abandon any hope that my health will improve. Indeed, the day when my pain is ended will be the day when I cease to breathe. That day, my eyes shall no longer see your face, which is the loveliest thing I have ever known.

My daughter, there are truths I must tell you about who we are, who I was and who you are in turn. I must impart them before I am too weak to remember or record. Your father does not know these stories, so if you press him, he will claim ignorance. Believe him. These secrets have been mine alone, and I have kept them for many years, with good reason. Once you read all I intend to put down, I hope you will understand.

Cinder's hands shook. "Henry," she said. "We found her; we found my mother." Henry stretched and yawned in response. Cinder flipped through the pages, but could barely see her mother's handwriting in the fading light. She could not bear to know that soon she would lose the light entirely. She squeezed her eyes and tried to make out the words.

My story begins and ends with you, my girl. You are a wild thing. How you fight your father and me, and how you venture off on your own, exploring the noble hills and vales that surround our home. Oh, and the ocean! Many times, I have lost my breath worrying about you and how long you had been away from home. I have spent many worrisome hours fearing you had followed a mermaid song into the water. My God, I prayed, please bring my girl home. You were always delivered back to me, thus relief, and yet, you refused to stay in one place, thus, more worry. You have kept your mother occupied!

But I know this: you never walked into the ocean past your ankles. Not because of anything I told you to do, for you never had much regard for your parents' advice. You stood upon the shore and observed that the rocks at our coast are many and jagged, and the water there pounds hard, the temperature nearly ice, and the water's depth drops quickly. You observed, you experienced, you considered, and you chose safety. Not because someone instructed you to, but because you assessed the world yourself.

This is where I put my faith: you, my daughter, are smart. There are many skills you can learn, but nobody can teach you how to think. You came upon that on your own.

Cinder held the pages with tears in her eyes. Why had nobody told her about this letter? Perhaps nobody knew. Perhaps her father had packed her mother's things after she died, and unknowingly tucked this letter away.

But now, the sun was close to the horizon and would soon plunge below in a burst of pink and gold. Cinder had only one minute to read, two at the most.

"Please don't disappear," she said. "Oh, world, stop turning and leave me with enough light to read by."

But the world continued on its travels. A few seconds later, the sun reveled in its exhibition, filling the sky with colors and clouds. Cinder despaired. Ahead of her was a long, cold night.

Then, a sound came from down below. She could hear footsteps of someone approaching upon the stairs. Cinder stood and saw Orla, climbing slowly.

"Cinder?" came Orla's voice, shaking, tentative.

"Orla," she said. "You shouldn't be here; it's so cold."

Cinder hid the pages in the trunk and went to meet Orla at the top of the stairs. A lantern hung over one arm, and in the other hand she balanced a blanket and a dish with a napkin over top.

"You're carrying too much," Cinder said, and she reached out to take the plate and the blanket.

"One blanket for you, the smaller is for Henry. I brought you bread and butter. Oh, you found a sweater!" Orla said. She sighed with relief at having reached the top. "I'm glad. I hated to think of you freezing up here."

"I found it in this trunk," she said. "I think it belonged to my father."

"Oh, yes," Orla said. "Mother had the errand boy cart that up here a year ago. She said it was filled with needless old things."

"Did your mother ever review what was inside?"

Orla frowned. "Not that she mentioned," she said. "I believe she opened it once and saw old clothes. Perhaps she decided to keep them for you. Did you happen to find any coin? Pirate doubloons, maybe, hidden away by your father some years ago?"

"No pirate treasure of any sort," Cinder said. "This sweater, though. It's quite comfortable."

Orla smiled and placed the lantern on top of the trunk and gazed out the windows at the sunlight's last gasp. "The view from up here is lovely," she said. She eased herself onto the floor. "Please, eat. I supped already." Then she winced.

"Are you all right?" Cinder asked.

"Yes, yes, just weary," she said. "Cinder, I'm sorry. I know Mother is...can be...difficult."

Cinder did not answer her, but spread the butter upon the bread and took a small bite.

"The only thing she knows to do is fight," Orla continued. "She's had to struggle for everything she's ever received."

"I know what that's like," muttered Cinder.

The lantern light flickered in the draft and cast dancing shadows upon the floor. Breaking waves down below swished in and out and the calls of the night gulls swept through the darkness. Cinder set out the small blanket for Henry. He stood and stretched, and looked first at her, then at Orla, then took a stroll around the room's edge. He decided this was sufficient exercise then returned, kneaded the blanket with his claws, curled up and resumed his rest.

Orla gazed upon the eastern sky, and the one or two stars that had begun to shine. "She rarely speaks of her childhood. She confided in me only because I am the elder. I suspect your father never even knew about her past."

Cinder recalled the references made about her stepmother's life earlier that day. What had Lord Lizard accused her of? There was a letter, he'd said. The constable of London had accused her of...what? Theft, at least. Murder, possibly.

"What do you know of her past?" Cinder asked.

"My mother wishes everyone believed she was born into affluence and status," Orla said. "But it's not true."

"Go on," Cinder said.

"I cannot say more," she said. "It is my mother's private business."

"To whom would I disclose?" Cinder said. "I never speak with anyone outside this house."

Orla sighed. "Do you promise? Even Liisi does not know these things."

"You need me to promise to keep a secret from Liisi?" Cinder asked. "Consider it done."

Orla smirked. "My mother's parents died when she was an infant. She was raised by distant relations who treated her as no more than a servant."

"Relations who treated her as a servant?" Cinder said. "Sounds familiar..."

"Oh," Orla said. "I guess her lot in life is similar to yours. When our father told his family they were to wed, they forbade the union. They desperately wanted him to marry someone related to the nobility."

Cinder looked upon her stepsister with confusion. "This is so contrary to the tale your mother tells. Or, implies, I suppose."

"This is why our mother insists that Liisi marry a husband with status," she said. "She wishes us to rise above *her* birth. She wants our children to ascend through the ranks of nobility until she and her origins are mere and puzzling footnotes in history."

"How strange it must be to live that way," Cinder said. "Always pretending. Always wondering who knows or suspects what. But what is enough to secure her favor? It seems impossible."

"Don't be short with Liisi," Orla said. "That would help."

"But she pressed me!" Cinder protested.

"Perhaps she did," Orla said. "Perhaps she does and will each time. But when she begins something, you must end it. It might not be fair, but fair is only a myth, is it not? Something wonderful they teach children but isn't real, like golden eggs and fairy godmothers."

The moon was beginning to rise in the western sky, where the horizon was already dark.

Cinder considered then what she never before had: that justice was a myth. The fact that this truth was spoken to her by a maiden who would have been the comeliest in the house had she not been so brave as to walk into a burning house made Cinder think it was likely so. Sometimes, Cinder tried to imagine what Orla would have looked like if her face had not been maimed, her body not so broken. Orla certainly would have been married by now, nursing her own babes.

"Orla, were you afraid that night?" Cinder asked. "When you...went into the house?"

"The fire?" Orla asked. "What makes you think of this?"

"What you said, that nothing is truly fair," Cinder said. "You know best of all."

She sighed deeply and was quiet for a while. "I awoke to the sound of our dogs crying in terror from their kennels, three floors beneath ours. Our bed chamber was full of smoke. Liisi and I went to the hallway and met a confusion of activity. My mother and two servants rushed us down the servants' stairs through smoke. It was so hot. We reached the yard then stood there, watching our home burn. When I found my bearings, I thought, someone is missing. Precious moments passed before I realized my father was not among us."

"It must have been awful," Cinder said.

"I realized he was inside and needed help," Orla said. "So, I ran in. I never could have reached him through the fire, but I did not have the sense to know that. A burning beam fell upon me. I remember being pinned in place, and struggling to breathe. The gardener risked his life to rescue me. Had he not been there, I would have certainly endured the same fate as my father."

"Orla, I am so sorry," Cinder said. Then she too was quiet a while and only gazed out at the dark ocean. "Orla, I am desperate to see the world, accomplish something, become someone. I feel it in my bones, these days worse than ever."

"You are someone, Cinder," Orla said. She leaned forward. "There is no lock on the door to this tower. You can leave. You could walk away from Bowmore House and never think about us again."

"I love this house," Cinder said. "I was born here. How could I walk away from this place?"

"My sister, this I say with love: I would be so happy to wake one morning and have nobody bring us tea, and nobody start our fires," Orla said. "Mother might search for you and find only an empty kitchen, and then I would know, ahh, yes, Cinder has begun her journey."

Cinder gripped her warm sweater around her. "Orla, how do people change?"

"I'm not sure," Orla said. She pointed toward the window at the silvery orb. "The moon knows about change."

"Yes," Cinder said. "The moon. She becomes someone new every day."

Orla flinched, then smiled sadly. "I can't imagine what it's like, planning for life beyond Bowmore House. I don't think I shall ever live anywhere else." She grimaced and gasped.

"Oh, my dear," Cinder said, reaching for Orla. "What happened? Are you suddenly in a great deal of pain? The cold's not good for you."

"It comes and goes. But suddenly, it has arrived."

"Let me help you down the stairs," she said. "You can lean on me."

"No, my sister, I can descend on my own," she said. She took Cinder's hand and pushed herself up. "My parting advice? Do not let Mother or Liisi provoke you. They aren't worth the trouble."

"You're right, Orla," Cinder said. "I will listen to you. You're much smarter than I am."

Orla unwrapped the blanket from around her, folded it and left it on the floor. She went to stand up to go back down the stairs when something caught her eye in the lantern light. "What is this?"

"An old dress of my mother's," Cinder said. "It was in the box. I suppose I forgot to put it back."

Orla lifted it up. "It's simple, but I like the material."

"It's coming apart," Cinder said, pulling it out so Orla could see where it was fraying.

"You could fix it," Orla said. "Cut the sleeves to a more fashionable length, and embellish the cuffs. Cut back the bust, show a bit of skin—"

"Orla!" Cinder said.

"I'm only suggesting," she said, "with a bit of work, we could get this dress into dancing condition. Into *ball* condition."

"I can't see how that would be possible without throwing it into the fire and asking a seamstress to start over," Cinder said. She sighed. "And no dress would change the fact that I don't know how to dance. I'm not going to that ball."

"Well, Cinder," Orla said. "The invitation was addressed to *all* the young people of the kingdom." Orla's eyes twinkled as she gently replaced the dress. "By decree of His Royal Highness. Truly, Cinder, I'm not sure you have a choice."

Chapter Seven

After Orla left, Cinder nibbled another slice of bread. Henry slept soundly upon his blanket, stretching and changing position every now and then. When he poked his head up, she fed him small pieces of bread, which he slowly chewed. The wind had calmed but the air was cold and she was grateful for the sweater and the blanket. The moon was high now, illuminating the ocean so it appeared like molten metal. The sea churned quietly, and the clouds had cleared. Now the sky was filled with more stars than she'd ever seen.

Suddenly, she remembered the letter from her mother and realized that Orla had left the lantern, so now she could read. She scrambled to the trunk and withdrew the letter. In the dim lantern light, she quickly reviewed what she had already read to the new section, then read with fervor, almost holding her breath.

> Of all the experiences in life I shall miss, I mourn none more than the opportunity to tell you my story in person. This is a strange tale, an unlikely one, a dangerous one, and you may not believe everything I write. I myself did not believe all these things when they happened. But I assure you that I shall only write the truth. What you make of it is up to you. After my heart stops beating, this world is yours only.
>
> While you slumber, I write by the light of the lantern and the fireplace. My energy wanes, though, and sometimes the pain wrecks my body and batters my head. But I trust that my quill and these fine pages of parchment will be good company in these dark hours.

First off, introductions. You have always known me under the name Rhona. This is a name I accepted at the age of sixteen years when my life was in danger. I donned this name like a cloak and while it preserved my life, it was never my own. My mother called me Ailen; I think of this as my name, even though I never returned to it. But the third name I mention will be the first I received, as it was the one my mother gave me when I was born. It will sound familiar when you hear it: Marguerite Bertrade de Valois. Your name is almost the same.

But I am getting ahead of things. Let us begin with a secret birth somewhere deep in the darkest woods of the country of Gallia. I was born to replace the lives of two siblings, one murdered, one stolen, and I, the third child, was eased into the world by my own unlikely midwife —a sorcerer of sorts. Let me explain.

My mother, your grandmother, used to tell me the story of my birth over and over, like a terrible fairy story. Her name was Leontyne, and she was a Gallic beauty with flowing red hair, green eyes and long, slender features. She was beautiful like a princess. After I was born, she brought me to this country of Dalkeith and raised me in Dunford Town, a place of modest size beside a vast woodland. My mother ran a millinery shop where she made the most delicate and beautiful dresses for the fine ladies of Dunford. I was a small child with light brown eyes and pale-yellow hair. My mother used to tell me I was ill and kept me indoors, away from the other children. Whether I was truly sick, or if she wanted to protect me from other perils, I do not know. But I spent most of my childhood isolated from the outside world.

Each night, my mother would bring me from my bedroom into her own and fashion some small, odd meal over the fire. She'd pour herself a glass of local whiskey, her only indulgence. I smelled its sharp, smoky aroma from across the room. She handed me a cup of milk, sat me down, and told me this story:

"When you claim your birthright in Gallia," she would say, her accent thick. "A servant will bring you fine chocolates on a silver tray every night."

"Gallia is so far from Dunford Town," I would say.

"Yes," Maman would whisper. She gazed into the fire as though watching the story unfold before her. "It is many days to walk, easiest by horseback. That's how I brought you here when you were a babe. I clutched you tight to my breast. My dress was black. I hate to wear black, so drab." Maman would sometimes go to the window and stare into the dark, letting herself remember those nights.

"The horse brought us far enough away to a place where she would not find us," Maman would say. "She seeks us now, the Queen of Gallia. I feel it in my bones. She knows that somewhere in the world there is a child who would rightfully inherit the throne of Gallia. She wants you dead. I feel that too."

"Why would someone want to hurt me?" I always asked.

"You have nothing to fear, my child," Maman said. "I know her tricks, I have seen them all. I will die before I let her touch you."

By now, the fire might be raging, but even so, I shivered. My mother wrapped a blanket around my shoulders and kissed my head.

"There were two before you," she said. Her face changed and grew still darker, for this was the heart of her grief.

I would only say, "Yes, Maman."

"Two before you," she would repeat. "They were stolen from this life before I could choose their names. The first born in winter, a cold, snowy night. I sent my servant for the midwife. She came, but slowly and made me endure terrible pain alone. My servant, I never saw again. When the baby was born—a beautiful boy! I was never so happy. I believed I was holding in my arms the future king of Gallia. The midwife took him from me, and put his small, perfect head in a bucket of water. Tiny bubbles came from his nose as my infant drowned. I tried to fight her, but I was weary from giving birth and she was much stronger than I."

I shivered as my mother spoke.

"A second child, born in summer. This time, I thought I had learned my lesson," she said. "I took care to know who would help me, a midwife with excellent credentials, with connections to the King's supporters. Perhaps she was good, perhaps honest. But the queen—" She sighed. "She had so many spies. My daughter nursed at my breast, and fell asleep in my arms. While we slept, someone came into my cottage and stole her from me."

Maman's voice broke; she was trying to hold back tears. "Sometimes I wonder if the girl is out there still. She would be a sister for you, my pet!" She stared into the fire. "No, the queen killed my first daughter, I know this in my bones. The queen's heart is black and hot, like the center of the fire, a place too terrible to look into."

Each time she told this story, I became so weary. I could feel myself being wished dead by an evil queen, my bones drifting into ash, scattering among the fireplace embers.

Maman looked at me. "And then, my pet, you crawled into my belly." She would come and sit on the floor before me and put her head upon my knees. "This time, Maman was smart. When I knew you were coming, I became..." she put a single finger to her lips. "Silent. Cloaks covered my belly. And I did not speak a word. When you began stirring, whispering to me in the night that you would soon come, I knew I needed help. I called out to the stars only, but told no human of what was to come. The night I gave birth, I was visited by a witch who emerged from the woods. She helped me."

This part scared me most of all.

"It was the fall season, but cold, with snowflakes flurrying. I found a cottage in the woods where the wicked queen and her informers would not see us. The one who appeared? I never knew how she found us, but I was glad she did."

"The earth-witch," I muttered. "Nula."

"She said her name was Nula-na-Nekon," Maman said. "She promised to guide and protect you through all your days. She made a prophecy: she told me you would have an extraordinary life, and your story would be told through many generations. She instructed me to bring you away from Gallia. She promised we'd find safety, not forever, but for many years."

"Did she really ask you if she could follow me?" I asked.

"She said there would be times when—what were her words? They were so strange, I memorized them—the bending of time might assist in the unfolding of what would be," Maman said. "I did not understand her words, and still do not. But this I know and believe: you are the chosen one, my beautiful girl."

This is when I grew most frightened of all. I put my fingers in my ears or closed my eyes tight and wished the story to end.

"Princess Marguerite Bertrade de Valois," my mother would say. The words sounded musical when my mother spoke them, as though they were a line of Gallic court poetry. "This is your true name and your birthright. Now, you speak. Say your secret name."

I never wanted to. I was Ailen and I wanted to go to bed. Maman would stand tall and strong, as though she believed her voice could be heard past the town's borders, beyond the woods, and past the borders of the country of Dalkeith. "Speak your name, your real name, the name given to you by your mother, your king and God Almighty. Say it."

That name was a great mouthful for a small child, and a heavy load to bear. "Princess…"

"Louder," Maman demanded, thrusting her own chin up proudly. "Speak with pride. You deserve this name. You came into the world to claim this name. Speak it."

I'd try again. "Princess Marguerite Bertrade de Valois," I said slowly. "Maman, I want to go to bed."

"Good night, my love," Maman would say, kissing me on the cheek. "Sleep with the angels, wake with the chickens, and a good day awaits you."

I left Maman's room to let her drink her drink, recall her memories, and make her plans. I did not believe any of her stories. But one day, I would learn they were all true.

This is all I can put down this night. I just went into your bedroom where you are sleeping soundly. I pulled your blanket up around you, you sighed, mumbled and turned over. To know that you are safe, warm and happy makes my heart so very glad. And with that gladness, I shall now put this quill and these pages to bed and then, also, my own self. Good night, my sweet. Sleep with the angels.

Cinder's body shook from the chill, and she pulled the blanket around her. Tears fell down her cheek. Here in her hand, upon mere parchment pages, she had found her mother's voice, her mother's story. A story she never imagined existed and words she had no idea had been written.

"Goodness, Henry," she said, bringing a corner of her apron to her face to wipe away the tears.

There were so many strange details on this page, she did not know how to begin to think about it. Her mother was from Gallia, not Dalkeith. A witch had attended her mother's birth? So strange, so unlikely.

And her mother's name. All these years, Cinder had thought it a strange coincidence that her mother and stepmother had the same name, but now she knew, it was a ruse.

"Why have you been hiding, Mother?" she whispered.

Suddenly, a gust of wind burst in through cracks in the window with a roaring howl. Fear gripped Cinder's body, and she acted without thinking, pulling Henry close and wrapping the blanket around herself. The gust blew the lantern out. Cinder watched in horror as the pages of her mother's letter were snatched out of her hand and sent sailing all around the stairs and through the tower.

The gust retreated, and the tower was once again cold, dark and silent. But now, the pages of her mother's letter were scattered. Cinder squinted to try and see the pages by the light of the moon. Three or four sheets landed beside her, so she gathered those up. Several more landed on the steps of the tower, and she gathered those as well.

She had no means to light the lantern again, and in the moonlight, she could not make out a single word. Instead, she held on to her mother's letter and gazed out the window, listening to the wind. When she heard the church bells begin to chime, she knew it was midnight. The second chime was a hard tone that shook the air then faded, like circles traveling through water. As they reverberated, Cinder felt the air around her change. The night's quiet emptiness seemed to crackle and stir as though it had come alive. Another bell chimed, then another and another.

"Oh, Henry," she said. "How would you change who you are? Or not, who you are but how you are?"

The sixth bell rang and Cinder felt a nameless sense of wonder brewing inside her. The seventh bell rang, then the eighth. "Perhaps the change could begin with me, inside me. It would begin with the decision for change."

The ninth bell. Cinder held her head high and spoke to the moon. "Hear my voice, Lady Moon," she said. "I no longer accept the role they cast me in. I shall not be the wearisome cur of the house, waiting for the last scraps."

The tenth bell. "What happens begins next, and I shall decide it."

Eleven. She placed her fingertips upon the surface of the window glass; it was cold as ice. With the darkness as her witness, she said aloud, "My name is Marguerite Bertrade de Valois Barclay, I am the daughter of Marguerite Bertrade de Valois. At the stroke of midnight on this day, I hereby declare, I shall walk through the world as one who matters. They may put me in a tower for a night, but I shall not spend my life in prison."

The power of her words and her intention sent a chill down her back. She didn't know how she would carry out this pledge, nor precisely what she had vowed to do. She only knew that she was ready for change.

"This, I decide," she said.

After the midnight bell, the world became quiet again. Cinder looked around; she half-expected some fiery, winged figure to appear in the darkness either to validate the spell or refute it, but the room remained dark and silent. Cinder did not understand what kind of magic might accompany the changing of one day into another, an invisible shift that she would not have noticed but for the church bells. But there had been magic in the air, she'd felt it. The vow she had spoken mattered.

She looked through the window down to the shore below. Emerging into the beam of moonlight was the hooded figure who sometimes crossed through their yard, the one she had seen with Orla just the day before.

"Greetings, Watcher," she said quietly.

She did not know if she imagined it, but she thought she saw the figure turn and wave toward the tower. She waved reluctantly back, certain she could not be seen in the darkness at this distance. The Watcher turned back and continued their journey.

After that, Cinder grew weary. So, with the pages of her mother's letter in her hand, wrapped in her mother's sweater and the blanket Orla had brought her, Cinder sank to the floor, lay down beside Henry and rested her eyes.

Chapter Eight

Cinder awoke on the tower room floor when dawn's first gasp of light spilled over the line of the Morisar Sea. Clutching her mother's letter as a child holds a doll, she sat up and looked over the glossy, rose-colored surface of the ocean.

"Night is done," she said, and she kissed Henry's head. She tucked the letter in her apron pocket, then gathered Henry and her things and walked down the stairs. The still, silent house was much warmer than the tower, and Cinder was relieved for it. In the kitchen, she built up the logs in the hearth and made a fire. She boiled water for tea, and in short time, her hands were wrapped around a cup of the hot elixir, which warmed her from the inside.

She put her mother's letter on the table and examined the stack of crumpled pages. In the dark, she had collected every scattered page.

"How shall I put you back together?" she asked out loud.

The only answer, of course, was to study each sheet and try to assemble it, like a puzzle. Cinder took a sip of tea and picked up the page on top. She scanned the words: *"And then I was truly alone,"* she read. *"In that small village...the first time I saw the ocean..."* And then the words that stopped Cinder's eyes: *"I am Gerik; I was paid to bring you across."*

Gerik. This must be her father. Cinder realized this must be the story of the moment her parents met. She looked at the time on the clock. She had some minutes before her stepmother and sisters awoke.

She would put off sorting until later. She could not resist the invitation to read about the first time her mother saw the ocean, and also her father. And so, though she did not understand what events preceded these, Cinder read:

> I had never been so afraid in all my life. I climbed into the back of the wagon, and the goatherd hitched up the horse. I pulled my hood over my head to conceal my face, and sunk down among the baby goats, whom the goatherd was transporting to his family's farm in the northlands. The goats comforted me: their deep grassy smell, their soft fur, their warm bodies. By the time we reached the small village by the coast of the Morisar Sea, some hours later, I was out of tears. The goatherd helped me out of the tangle of hay in the back of the wagon, and left me there.
>
> And then, I was truly on my own...

Over the next few paragraphs, the goatherd delivered Ailen to some quaint village and she saw the ocean, the Morisar Sea, for the first time in her life.

> I sat upon some craggy rocks by the water's edge and listened to the crashing waves. Gulls sang, the sky grew darker, and, in time, the stars blinked into being. I did not know what would come next and I was so afraid. My only comfort was the sound of the waves breaking upon the shore. The ocean, I believed, understood my despair. Perhaps the ocean could carry some of it for me. Yes, I was sure it could.

After that, Ailen found sanctuary, a tavern that served her a meal and gave her a warm bed for the night.

> In short time, I slept, though not soundly. I was haunted by dreams of my mother's murder, and the terrible knowledge that in her final moments, I had not been able to go to her, to ease her pain, or comfort her. Each dream ended with a vision of the queen walking calmly away, my mother's blood staining the bottom of her swollen white gown.

Cinder stopped for a moment and reread those words: *haunted by dreams of my mother's murder*. Again, she shuffled through the pages to see if she could find the answer: who had murdered her grandmother, and why? How had her mother escaped this attack? There was no quick answer. She'd have to organize the pages and read the whole thing in order.

For now, though, Cinder continued where she was, and watched her mother stand on her own for the first time. In the morning, Ailen was to meet a boatman who would bring her to an island: St. Kiana.

> I imagined the man I sought was the age of the rocks themselves, his head circled by a few strands of unruly white hair, a voice like the grinding of sand against stone, eyes with no need of light, for he navigated by the sound of the ocean, and time-hardened hands that bore upon them a map of the sea. I walked to a spot by a dock where a bench sat beside a thicket of flowering golden saxifrage and kept watch for my own ancient mariner.
>
> My boatman made me wait quite some time. Indeed, by the time he appeared, the sun was high in the sky and shining like a pearl, and the village fisher-folk were halfway through their work day. Worse still, the boatman might have been the great-grandson of the one I imagined: he was only a few years my senior, in fact, with scruffy brown hair, outfitted in a heavy, dirty-yellow sweater.
>
> "You, Rhona?" he shouted to me, like I was a work animal.
>
> "Yes," I said.
>
> He came over and observed me with some disdain. "I am Gerik; I was paid to bring you across," he said. "Wait here. I'm to fetch the post."

Cinder smiled. Ailen had met her Gerik.

> So, I waited. And again waited quite a long while. When this Gerik returned, he bore with him a large sack full of parcels and letters for the island's residents. He also had a smaller paper sack of buns, and offered me one. I was angry with him for taking so much time, but I was too hungry to refuse a bun. When Gerik announced it was time to depart, he helped me into the boat; it was my first time in a boat, and the first time a young man touched me. The brush of his skin upon mine released inside me a burst of warmth. I looked into his eyes. They were a lovely dark blue, like nothing I had seen short of the sea itself.

Cinder smiled. She knew what it was to be touched by someone, and have that touch release a feeling inside that felt like a door opening. *Alban,* she thought. *Come and seek me out this very day and all the days in all the world.* The steady ticking of the wall clock reminded her that the day was moving forward. No, she was not ready. She wanted to linger in her mother's world just a little longer.

"Steady now," the young man said. "Bottom of the boat's soggy, so mind your skirt."

I gathered up my hem and took my seat. The boat bobbed and swayed below me. I gripped the sides; the water terrified me.

Gerik saw my face. "Don't worry," he said. "The day is fine and fair, and we shall have only smooth waters."

I smiled in response, then Gerik took the oars and pushed us off the shore. The sun peeked in and out of the clouds. As we drifted away, I watched the village grow small. I supposed it would be my last view of land for some time.

After some moments, I noticed Gerik looking at me.

"Did we meet another time?" he asked. "Have you kin on the isle of St. Kiana?"

I shook my head. I was too shy to speak.

"All right," he said.

A few moments later, Gerik said, "This is my boat. I built it myself. Have you ever built a boat?"

I shook my head. It seemed a ridiculous question.

"My father taught me how," he said. "I carve each plank, then steam the boards to curve them. If I piece the parts together tight, it floats. Ever been on a boat before?" I shook my head. "Been to the sea?" I shook my head.

"Welcome, then, Miss Rhona," he said. "If you start to feel peaky, lean over the side and let it all out." I gave him a dubious look. "Happens to everyone. The motion of the boat does it."

I nodded at him in thanks. Still, he was right: my stomach felt unwell and a sour taste had come into my mouth. I breathed in the salted sea air, and hoped it would pass. But I was so cold, I could not keep from shivering. Gerik noticed and handed me his woolen jumper.

"Your lips are blue," he said. "You need this more than I do."

The sweater hung over me like a tent, but oh, it was the warmest thing I ever wore. The fibers were rough and oily and smelled of ocean and fish, and something else, a pungent person smell.

"Keep the jumper. It gets fierce cold on St. Kiana," he said. "You don't look like you packed for the elements."

I nodded in gratitude and clung to the sweater.

As we went along, the boat dipped and wobbled through the water, sometimes rising up over small waves and crashing back down.

"Almost there," Gerik said. "See that dark spot yonder? That's where we're headed."

I turned to look in the direction he was pointing and saw a stretch of land.

"My new home," I said.

"She speaks!" he said. "Yes, your new home is a large rock. If you stand in the middle, you can see the sun rise in the east and set in the west from the same spot. How many places in the world can say that?"

I smiled. I could not forge a guess.

"I've lived on that rock my whole life," he said. "You'll find the Barclay house in the middle of town. It has a yellow door that gleams bright as a lantern."

"A yellow door?" I asked.

"My mum makes us kids paint it every time one of us makes her cross," he said.

I laughed. We rowed a bit more and Gerik's expression changed. He looked like he had something to say.

"Miss Rhona," he finally said. "I have a plan for my life." His voice stuttered with uncertainty. "I shall build ships. Not rickety rowboats like this, tall ships, a fleet of them. And I shall train men to sail them to lands far and wide. My crew and I shall travel the whole world."

I smiled. It sounded so wonderful.

"I shall need a wife to assist me in seeing my plan through," he said. "And I need a woman to bear sons who can build boats alongside me."

I nodded. Of course, he would build ships with his sons. Of course, he needed a wife to help with this business.

"Would you consider becoming my wife?" he asked. "Not now, but someday?"

I did not anticipate these words. I felt my eyes grow wide, and my cheeks burn. I pulled the sweater over my hands. To my silence, he said, "I'm sorry. Sometimes I think growing up on an island robbed me of the ability to speak to people. Forget my words."

"Please, Gerik," I said. "I won't forget. Ask me another time, promise me you will. For today, I want only to see a place where you can stand in the middle of a rock and from the same spot see the sun rise by morning and set by evening. Take me to St. Kiana. Let us speak of other matters another time."

He smiled and the look he gave me, I cannot explain: it was as though he looked into my heart, into the essence of me. I would never have to tell him of all that had happened to me, for somehow, he knew. He had always known. He had been waiting for me, rowing little boats for years, certain that one day I would alight in one. "I shall," he said.

I suppose by now you have guessed the ending: this Gerik who lived on the isle of St. Kiana in the Barclay house with the yellow door was the same Gerik Barclay who would become your father. Seven years would yet pass before you were born, my sweet! But in that moment, I knew I would marry this boy, this Gerik. He knew it too. I shall always be grateful to him for recognizing that our future was each other, and for waiting for me.

Cinder imagined her mother sitting in a rowboat, her father rowing the oars, both of them so young, neither knowing what to say. Cinder could hear the water lapping at the sides of the boat. The splash from the sea jumped out of her imagination and right on her hand. She blinked; the wet was not from her mind's eye but from beloved Henry, who was licking her hand.

"Ahh, yes, you are due a bowl of warm milk after your cold night in jail," she said while she scratched his ears. Cinder poured milk into a pan and set it over the fire to warm. While she waited, she took the clock off the wall and wound the key.

Suddenly, she saw something she never had before: in the middle of the clock, where the bobbin held the base of two golden hands, a face took shape and seemed to peer at her. It was a woman, aged, with scraggly strands of hair flanking her thin face. Cinder gasped. And though her first instinct was to drop the clock, instead, she studied it.

The face looked familiar, but Cinder could not recall a name. She thought the face was trying to speak but she could not make out the words. Then the face changed and blurred, becoming a dark, shapeless mass. Cinder thought the vision had ended, but from the fog beyond the kitchen, she spotted the nameless hooded watcher, whom Cinder had seen the night before.

She sank onto the bench. A breeze wafted through the kitchen with the same crackling energy of the tower room at midnight. The night before, she had looked over the sea as the moon spilled into the water, and promised to change. What did any of it mean? She could not know.

Then she turned her attention back to Henry. After she set the warm milk down for the cat, a bell rang. Mother Rhona was awake and calling for fire and tea. Cinder sneered at the bell board. She picked up her mother's letter again and tapped the pages to straighten the pile, then she hid them in a drawer of a dresser that held table linens. She looked at the drawer for an extra moment.

Mother, wait for me. I shall come back.

"I didn't...know if you would be awake yet," came a voice in the doorway. Cinder turned to see Liisi, wrapped in a shawl, her fair hair braided.

"I have been summoned to build a fire for your mother," Cinder said, avoiding Liisi's eyes. "And then I shall do Orla's and, of course, yours as well."

"Cinder, I—Orla reminded us, last night, you are not our domestic staff. You are our family."

"Kind words from Orla," Cinder said.

"And I shouldn't... I mustn't be awful to you," Liisi said. "I am not sure why I am so. Although you really were terrible suggesting you'd put bees in my hair..."

"In jest only," Cinder said.

"Well, I didn't know that," Liisi said, her hands on her hips. "I suppose I wish to tell you that I regret suggesting terrible things about your cat."

"You should," Cinder said.

"Yes, well," Liisi said. "I ought to try to be a better sister to you, that's what Orla says."

Cinder nodded.

Liisi smiled flatly, and something about her expression made Cinder think she'd forgotten everything she'd just said. "All right. When Mother is cared for, you may bring my and Orla's tea to us and come and build our fires," she said. "Last night was quite cold, so make haste."

Cinder sighed. She remembered the vow she had made the night before, in the midnight moonlight. *I shall walk through the world as one who matters. They may put me in a tower for a night, but I shall not spend my life in prison.* She was not sure what it meant, but she sensed in her bones that it started now.

"Mistress Liisi," she said. "May I remind you, four of us live in this crumbling house. Nothing about life here is perfect, far from it, but we are protected from the elements, we have some sustenance and we are each in mostly fine health. Indeed, I am not the domestic staff. Tasks such as boiling water and building fires might be beyond your abilities, but you might consider *requesting* my assistance instead of expecting it. And once these tasks are complete, you could express gratitude."

Liisi nodded slowly. "I could try," she said tentatively. "Cinder, would you be so kind as to bring tea to me and Orla? And when you arrive, please fix the fire. I, and Orla as well, would be eternally grateful."

"I shall," Cinder said. She smiled and turned her attention to setting up tea trays, putting out the pots, cups and sugar bowls.

Liisi sneered and crossed her arms. "You probably hate me. Now I fear you should poison my tea."

Cinder spooned a few leaves into each small pot.

"Do not fear, pretty Liisi," Cinder said. "Go lie in your bed as you always do and I shall bring tea as soon as it's ready."

"And you won't add anything dreadful?" Liisi asked. "Nothing terrible or vile?"

Cinder smiled slightly. "Why would I do so? You are my sister."

Liisi looked perplexed, then, and turned on her heels and rushed up the stairs.

Henry sat by the fire, still lapping his sweet, warm milk. Cinder went to him and pet his head. "After all, Henry, if Liisi died by poisoning, I who made her tea would be the first the authorities would suspect," she said. "You're right, Henry, it's best to rise above it. I should always listen to you."

Chapter Nine

Through the morning, Cinder quietly performed chores while Rhona and her daughters deliberated over what they would wear to the ball. By afternoon, Cinder had completed her tasks, and while the others were busy, she put on the sweater she had found in the night tower. She believed it must be the same one her father gave her mother when he rowed her to the isle of St. Kiana. She tucked her mother's letter into a sack and stole out of the kitchen. When she reached the cliffs with her pile of apples, she lay on the ground with the letter and continued reading.

Gerik brought me to a small, white croft house, the last along a path. This was the home of Miss Marrah, the elderly widow who summoned me, or rather, my friend, Rhona. Gerik knocked, and the door creaked open and there appeared a small, tight face like a frightened animal.

"That's the girl?" the woman said. "I was told it was a tall one, dark hair, big teeth. Not afraid of killing rats."

My stomach churned with dread. "Hello, ma'am," I said. And now I realized I would have to lie, and claim the details of Rhona's life as my own. "My name is Rhona, I was sent here from Dunford Town. I worked in the household of Lord and Lady MacMargeson since I was a child. And I..." I hesitated, swallowed. I had never lied before. Could I truly kill a rat? I did not know. "I can take care of rodents, ma'am, and do anything else you need."

> The woman was small in stature, her light blue eyes wide, thin white hair pulled back. Her teeth were askance and brown. She sneered and looked me up and down. "Not the right girl," she said.
>
> My heart froze. I assured her I could help her with cooking and cleaning and anything else she needed done.
>
> Miss Marrah sneered again. "She's thin and frail." She pinched my cheekbone. "One winter storm will toss this waif such like she were a child's toy."
>
> I put my feet together and pushed my shoulder blades out to make myself seem taller. "I am stronger than I look, miss," I said.
>
> She studied me for a bit, then finally said, "Since you're here, may as well stay. Remember the terms of your contract. If I am not pleased after one month, you go back where you came from. Understand, girl?"
>
> "Of course," I said. "One month."

Cinder kept reading. The woman gestured for Ailen to enter the cottage, and when she opened the door, some number of cats ran out. The letter explained that Miss Marrah liked to feed the island's feral cats, so that was now Ailen's job.

For the next five years, Cinder's mother, Ailen, but under the name Rhona, lived in St. Kiana and came to be like a daughter to Miss Marrah. She learned all manner of household skills: milked cows, collected eggs, caught and cooked fish, baked bread and churned butter. Each day, she kept the fires that protected the small croft house. Together, the two women sought refuge from the cold island winds that blew constantly, howling like a lost animal.

> My happy days on St. Kiana ended when Miss Marrah passed. We buried her in the churchyard with her family. After that, my heart experienced an unexpected pang: I could not leave the croft house. I could not leave St. Kiana. Families had been departing the island in large numbers, seeking a better future on the mainland. By that time, only a few remained. Even Gerik and his family had left. Gerik begged me to come with him, but I couldn't abandon Miss Marrah's home.

Who would feed the cats if I was gone? Who would weed the garden, churn the butter, and lay wildflowers upon Miss Marrah's grave?

For weeks, I remained alone in Miss Marrah's cottage, but a dark season was approaching. On a misty morn in late autumn, Gerik knocked on the door. He stood fast in the doorway and would not come inside. He stood so tall, it was as though he had become a proper man in our time apart.

"Miss Rhona, you must leave here today," he said. "The season of storms will come soon. I cannot allow you to remain upon this bare rock."

His directness surprised me, and so I responded directly. "You have no post to let me do or not do anything."

Now he looked surprised. "As I transported you to this town, I am responsible for your safety," he said. "By my decree, now you must leave."

"By your decree?" He was addressing me as though he was a constable.

"Rhona, you are not safe here on your own," he said, his demeanor softening. "I won't always be able to bring you supplies. You could get hurt or ill and nobody will be here to help you. Please, Miss Rhona."

Your father was right. I knew it and I despised him for that. My eyes filled with tears at the prospect of leaving. I had not expected this would be the day when I would leave St. Kiana, and yet, it was.

"Will you bring me back here sometimes?" I asked. "Just to stand in one place and watch the sun rise and set?"

"Of course, yes," he said. "I would do anything for you."

I would do anything for you. For all these years, I had been serving Miss Marrah with a child's love and loyalty. But now, here was Gerik, pledging to do anything for me. In that moment, I realized Miss Marrah was gone, and though I would always care for her, she no longer required my presence. Now, I needed to leave and walk toward the next adventure in my life.

And then, I was ready to depart the home of my second childhood.

I sought the burlap sack, the only thing I had brought with me to this house, and I found it, hanging upon a peg. The sack had some weight to it; strange, though, for I had not stored anything inside it.

Do you know what was within? A kitten, a wee thing dressed in a black and white striped suit. I laughed. He was mewing for help, but he was so tiny, I had not heard him.

Ailen took out the kitten, and Gerik fed it warm milk from his fingertips while she gathered her things. Then it was time to leave. But before they went, Ailen and Gerik and the kitten took one last walk around the island.

I looked across the Morisar Sea at the view I'd seen every day for five years: skerries and eddies, tiny, distant islands, packs of seals and the vast, roiling ocean. I loved it, but I was melancholy for I did not know when I would see these things again. Gerik brought me to the top of a small hill where grew the only tree in St. Kiana, a single hazel tree. Island residents said the tree was magic, visited by the fey. We stood a few moments and watched the clouds drift past while we breathed the cold wind.

Finally, Gerik spoke. "Miss Rhona," he began. "When you alighted my boat for the first time, I asked you a question. You were lovely of face when you arrived but that was all I knew of you then. Over these years, I have come to know you as someone who is kind and gentle, unafraid of storms, and wise in so many ways. And your face is lovelier today than ever. And so, let me ask again…"

He took my hand and held it to his heart. "Miss Rhona," he said. "Will you be my wife?"

I did not need to consider my answer. "I would be honored, Master Gerik of St. Kiana."

And so, we wed. I never told your father my true name nor any of the other details of my childhood or heritage. After those years in St. Kiana, I felt that what came before and who I had been no longer mattered.

We named the kitten Henry. He has grown into a beloved house cat whom I can now see upon his cushion by the fire, licking his paws. He adjusted well to life upon the mainland, and he has dutifully kept our home free of mice.

And what fortune befell my friend, the true Rhona? Did she find a way to London? This I never learned. If you ever happen to find her—you will know her by the dark of her hair and eyes—please thank her for saving my life. Indeed, she saved my life two times. More than that, she set me on the road that brought me to the next part of my life. I owe my friend so much.

Alas, my body was not one to birth a hundred ship-building sons, only one child, a daughter, you, my dearest. Perhaps you will grow up one day to help your father build ships. I pray only that you find happiness and magic in this world.

It is strange to conclude this letter knowing that if you are reading these words, my mortal body has surrendered. If that is the case, know that I have found peace. And no matter whether my bones are above the earth or below it, I love you for as many waves flow through the Morisar Sea.

My daughter, no matter what my name is or has been—curiously, I have had many—the only name that matters to me is the one you called me, Mother. You are the dearest part of me.

I love you, loved you, will always love you.
    Your Mother

"I love you too, mother," Cinder said. And once again, she looked out on to the horizon over the Morisar Sea, seeking an island she could only imagine.

She re-read these words:

And what fortune befell my friend, the true Rhona? Did she find a way to London? If you ever happen to find her, you will know her by the dark of her hair and eyes...

Cinder looked out to the ocean and thought about it. *Rhona, dark of hair and eyes.* This described her own stepmother, but she did not know how it would be possible.

Cinder knew the answer to this mystery was somewhere in these pages. Who was the first Rhona, and how had she saved her mother's life? Could it be that the true Rhona, dark of hair and eyes, was her own stepmother?

"What, reading on the job?" Alban said, plopping beside her like something a seagull had discarded.

Cinder's heart surged at the sound of Alban's voice, but she made sure her face did not reflect this. She carefully tucked the pages in the sack she'd brought them in, then weighed it down with apples. "Two times in one week, then," she said. "The awful princes must be traveling."

"The awful princes are in their usual spots," he said. He looked at her face. "Are those tears, my friend? Has someone hurt you?"

"Oh, no," she replied, wiping her cheeks. "The wind is gusting so hard today. It burns my eyes."

"The wind?" he asked. "Are you sure?"

Cinder dabbed her face with her apron. She had not realized she was crying. She looked at the concern in his face, and remembered the words her mother had written about her father. *It was as though he looked into my heart, into the essence of me. I would never have to tell him of all that had happened to me, for somehow, he knew.*

Cinder suddenly felt her breath stop and she had to gasp to restart it, to keep herself from floating off the surface of the earth. "I am," she said. "But thank you for asking."

He looked at her and smiled slightly. He seemed about to say something, but then he stopped and helped himself to an apple. "What mysterious document were you reading, which was not making you cry?"

"Oh, family history," she said. "Of no interest to anyone but myself. Well, tell me everything. What has happened since I saw you last?"

"I was wondering," he started, his demeanor nervous and hesitating. "Have you heard about this... nonsense, really... apparently there's to be a ball at the castle."

"Ahh, yes. My sisters are as eager as pups on the chase," she said. "Well, one is. The other is a bit more measured."

"And what of your sisters' sister?" he asked. "Do you plan to attend?"

"Me?" She laughed. "Attend a ball at the castle?"

"All the young people of the kingdom are invited," he said.

"Invited is not the same as expected."

"But you will go, won't you?" Alban said. "I am required by duty to attend, and if you are there as well, perhaps we will see one another."

An invitation. Alban wanted her to attend the ball. "Alban, I have not been raised as others. I cannot dance," she said. "I have nothing fine to wear and I know no formal manners. I would not begin to know how to address a prince were I to meet one, not to mention a queen or a king."

Alban laughed.

"Why do you laugh?" she asked.

"I don't have this, and I can't do that, and I can't and I won't and I shan't and I quit," he said. "This is how you sound. Attendance at this dance is the King's decree, you know."

She stood up. "My friend, I hope you have a deliriously wonderful time at the ball and meet so many pretty girls you don't know what to do with them." She took the apple out of his hand and helped herself to a bite. "I shall await the invitation to attend your wedding."

"I would send you an invitation, yet I do not know your name, nor where you live," he said. "I have heard that the king expects every young person to attend."

"Oh, and if I stay home, will he send the calvary for me?" she asked, handing back the apple. "My absence will be noticed by nobody. Except the pastry chef, as there will be one extra cream puff which I will not eat. Everyone else may divide it amongst themselves."

"Yes, there will be food!" Alban declared. "Marvelous cakes and puddings, plus roast meat and bread and cheese, all cooked in the king's kitchen by the finest chefs of our land. You must come, if just for the pastries."

Cinder glared at him. "Alban, thank you for inviting me. The event, nonetheless, is a ball, and I cannot dance."

"Dancing is a skill," he said. "Easily attained. You learn, you practice, and then, you dance."

She sighed. "Well, fine then," she said. "When I have a spare moment and with my extra pocket money, I shall find a teacher and get straight to work."

"Like magic, the teacher has arrived," he said. He took one final bite of apple then threw the core into some bushes. He stood before her, his posture straight, his left hand extended up as though perched on a shoulder and his right hand curved around the waist of an unseen partner. "Yes, please then, miss. Don't keep the teacher waiting. Take your place."

Cinder laughed. "What, they teach the stable boys to dance, do they?"

He clicked his tongue twice. "We don't have all day, then. Take your place, miss."

"You are impossible," she said.

He grinned slightly but did not look away. "Opinions. Still waiting for you to take your place, now. There are other things to be done this day, Miss, so let us waste no further time."

She was struck by how strong he looked in that pose, how composed. "What, here? Now?" she asked. "There is no music."

"The only thing required for dancing is feet. I notice that you have two, which is the correct quantity." He clicked his tongue twice again. "Time slipping away, miss."

She walked over to Alban. "Young man, if you click at me once more like I am a horse, I fear there should come a sharp slap to your cheek. All right, I am here. Where do you want me?" He inched closer and put her arm on his back, wrapped his arm around her and took her other hand in his.

She quietly swooned at the touch of his arm upon her back. She looked into his eyes; she only wanted for him to hold her. "And?" she finally said, trying not to reveal how fast her heart was beating. "There's to be some movement, is there not?"

He glanced down, and shuffled his feet slightly. "We walk in a square," he said. "You go backward and I go forth. Start with your right foot."

"Like this?" she said, taking a step backward. He stepped forward at the same time.

"Good. Then left," he said. She completed the step. "Then you slide the right foot to meet the other. You can count to keep in step, like this. Here, watch me." He did the steps himself and counted as he danced. "One, two, three, four. One, two, three, four," he said. "Like that."

She came over to him and resumed the position. "Which foot first?"

"Left for you, right for me. Keep your eyes on mine. And simply walk."

Cinder started with her right foot and bumped into his, then did that three more times. "My feet do not speak this language," she said, laughing, embarrassed.

"Let us try again, slowly," he said. He took her hand and counted off. "Left...two...three...four. Right...two... hree...four. Better?"

Focusing on the steps kept her from thinking about him. "I didn't step on you that time," she said.

"See, there's hope," he said. "Keep your back straight and don't look down."

"How can I not look down?" she said. "I will trip."

"You know what your feet are doing, just keep moving," he said. "Left, right, together, turn, right, left, right, together, turn."

She tripped and laughed. "This will not work," she said. "My feet will not follow instructions."

"Try this," he said, then, holding one hand on her back, he twirled her slightly away then pulled her back to him.

"I feel silly," she said.

"Try again," he said. He locked her eyes with his. "It takes practice. One, two, three, begin."

She stepped forward with her left foot and he did the same with his right foot, tangling the two together. "Sorry, sorry," she said.

"Try again," he said. She stared down at her feet. "My eyes, look at my eyes. Your left foot goes back and my right foot goes forward. One, two, three, begin."

She looked into his eyes, and kept her focus there. This time, she got it right and squealed with joy. He continued to count. If she paid strict attention to his words, she could complete the steps without getting tangled or stepping on his foot. She was amazed at how well Alban could dance, like he had been doing this his whole life. She wondered how a stable boy had had time and opportunity for so much dancing.

"You're improving," he said.

"I'm still upright," she said. "That's a start."

"We can practice as much as you like," he said. "Out here. Just like this."

"I'd like that," she said.

Before the afternoon was over, she learned to lose herself in the rhythm Alban kept, forgot about the motion of her feet and simply trusted the touch of his hand on her back. Her feet started to learn what to do without her brain having to remind them.

When his hand was on her back and her hand was in his, she felt like they had taken flight. His eyes focused on hers, and their feet kept the rhythm of music they did not hear, dancing in the sunlight on a cool day above the cliffs over the Morisar Sea. Cinder wished the dance lesson would never end.

They danced around a wide circle, and when they reached their starting point, Cinder, breathless, pulled away.

"You are a very quick study, Miss," Alban said. "You've made wonderful progress."

"You're quite a good dancer yourself," she said.

"Thank you, Miss," he said. "Shall we again?" She took one last breath, then nodded and took her position. He took her hand in his and placed his hand at her back. As she waited for him to begin, she looked into his eyes. But then, she got lost in them, and forgot how to move her feet.

"Alban," she said, quietly.

She did not know how it happened, only that it did: their faces came together, so easily, and their lips met. Then, for a moment, a gentle but certain kiss. Cinder felt suddenly filled with joy, as though she was a kite dancing among the clouds through rays of bright sunshine.

But then, she remembered herself and pulled away, touching her fingers to her mouth. She didn't want it to stop, but she could not let it continue.

"Forgive me," he said. "I do not know if that was invited."

"It was," she said. She felt her breath come in shallow, her body shaking.

"I have cared for you for so long," he said.

"And I you," she said.

"I wonder then, would you ever consider..."

She stumbled backward and put up her hand. "Do not speak another word," she said. "There is no future that includes the two of us together."

"Why not?" he asked. "If we care for one another."

She searched his eyes. "It's not possible," she said. "You have said this yourself."

"But, if it was— "

She felt breathless. "How can you not know? You must know. Do not be so cruel as to make me speak it aloud."

"I do not even know your name, and yet, when I am with you, I am the truest *me* there is," he said. "Am I selfish to wish my whole life could be like this?"

"I have nothing, Alban," she said. "No dowry, no family, no name. I thought I was entitled, at least partly, to a parcel of land, but even that is now in question."

"None of that matters—" he started.

"Of course it matters," she said. "Your parents, I'm sure they are also under the employ of the king. And they likely have already chosen your wife. You shall marry some daughter of a nobleman or a land-owner or a foreign dignitary. Women are currency in this world, and marriage is how the purchase takes place."

"No, you don't understand—"

"What I understand is that I am an orphan with no worth," she said. "I am not complaining. I am stating reality."

"Let me only speak a moment—"

"Alban, I have loved you since the first time you found me on the cliffs," she said. "Do you remember? My father had died and I felt like I was a ship adrift on the ocean. A thousand times I have dreamed of our lives together. But someday I shall lose you; I have always known this. If there was some hope of a love between us, and then it was lost, carried off in the wind...a part of my heart would die forever. My soul would die."

She put her hands to her face; for the second time that day, hot tears fell.

Alban looked at her. "I wish you would tell me your name."

"I have no name."

"Come to the ball, at least," he said. "Dance with me. Promise."

She wiped the tears from her cheek. "If I come to the ball, it shall be my farewell," she said.

"You have made up your mind about that," he said.

Her heart felt devastated at having revealed the full truth of what was inside it. "Farewell is our only future."

"Everyone's future is farewell," he said. "Promise me you will come to the ball."

Cinder sighed. "I will try, Alban, I will try."

"Good," he said.

Suddenly, they were interrupted again by a call from the man in the valley. "Hey-oh!"

Alban took her hand in his, gently lifted it and once again kissed it. Cinder's heart ached with yearning.

❧

"Sorry to disturb, Your Highness," Jakob said. "Your parents sent for you; they have urgent matters to discuss regarding the ball."

"Of course," said Prince Finn. "No need to be sorry; it is your job to find me."

"How is the young lady, Your Highness?" Jakob asked.

Finn did not want to speak of the kiss that lingered still upon his lips. "I do not know if she will come to the ball," he said. "And I do not know how to persuade her without alarming her."

"Sir, does the young lady know the responsibilities involved with being a princess, a queen?" he asked. "It could be quite a shock, you know, to go from being a simple croft girl to queen of the land. This might be especially complicated for a girl who has never ventured past the boundaries of Braemuir."

Finn looked over the hills as he considered it. "An intriguing point," Finn said. "Made more interesting by the fact that she does not know I am royal."

"Doesn't know—"

He peered at Jakob. "When I first met her, I told her I was a stable boy named Alban. After that, I didn't want anything between us to change."

Jakob grinned. "I suppose it could be challenging to find true friends when you are the king's first-born son."

Finn nodded. "I often disappoint people by not being princely enough."

"Never, Your Highness," Jakob said.

"I'm not strong and handsome like Eiran," he said. "I'm not a quick study like Heath. I'm not a brave warrior like my father."

"Prince Finn, don't be so hard—"

"It's all right, I know these things are true," he said. "Someday, I shall inherit the throne. But the truth is, Jakob, I dread it."

Jakob nodded.

"Sometimes I wish I was like Eiran, bold and confident. My brother is often impatient with me; I think him jealous of my station. I wish I could tell him, take the crown, the position, the power, take it all. He would like the king's life. The ceremony, the pageantry. I think I would like a life of freedom, roaming the world, with…"

"With her by your side?" Jakob said.

Finn looked sheepishly at Jakob. "Do you know the two happiest days of my life?" he asked. "The first, that day I was in your cottage while a tempest blew outside. Your wife gave me tea and biscuits, and I spent the day by your fire. Do you remember that?"

"You'd been out hunting, Your Highness," Jakob said. "A terrible storm came up fast. I brought you to my home to keep you safe from the torrents."

"I felt such joy there," he said. "More so than I ever have in the castle."

"And your other happiest day?" Jakob asked.

Finn smiled, looked away. "This afternoon, with her. Just the two of us together, her eyes, so bright and beautiful."

"Your Highness," Jakob said. "I believe you might be in love."

Finn knew Jakob was right, but he did not want to admit it.

"When will you tell her?" Jakob asked. "The truth, I mean, of who you are?"

"I'm not sure," Finn said.

"You have to tell her before the wedding," Jakob said. "We can't have our future queen faint from shock on the day of her nuptials."

Finn laughed. "I wish that was the only obstacle," he said. The two began to canter and soon they reached the stables. Finn and Jakob handed their horses off to the real grooms. Finn's brothers were returning from a ride at the same time. Once they were all three relieved of their horses, they headed up to the castle together.

"Hello, brother," said Eiran, a tall, golden-haired young man with broad shoulders and a wide smile. He gave Finn a powerful pat on the back. "How, pray tell, has your day been?"

Finn's conversation with the young woman was still weighing on his mind. "Uneventful," Finn said. "And yourselves?"

"Quite well, quite well indeed," Eiran said. "Heath and I have been hunting. We started at the lodge, then followed a group of foxes down to the southern end."

"We caught a few," said Heath, a young lad of fourteen and the most scholarly of the three brothers. He was taller than his older brothers but weighed less, which was why his father called him the Royal String Bean.

Eiran continued, "We took the coastal road back to the castle, and from the bottom of that valley we looked up to Sayre Cliffs and were treated to a most delightful performance. Weren't we, Heath?"

"Hardly delightful," grumbled Heath. "It reminded me how much I hate dancing."

"Ahh, yes, a dance performance," Eiran said, nodding at Heath. "Upon an outdoor stage. Lovely dance, brother. I had no idea how skilled you were. You should join the ballet company."

"All right," Finn said. He hoped the dancing had been all his brothers had seen. "Glad if you enjoyed yourselves."

"I hate that we should have a ball," Heath said. "Mother said I must have extra lessons ahead of it. But the dance-master is old and smells of castor oil."

"So, was that the girl?" Eiran asked, draping his arm around Finn's neck.

"What girl?" Finn asked.

"*The* girl!" Eiran said with an air of exasperation. "The one we're doing all this for?"

Finn felt his face grow hot, and he shrugged Eiran's arm off.

Eiran whooped and laughed. "Brother, your cheeks are very bad at keeping secrets."

"That's true, Finn," Heath said. "You look like a grape."

"Can't you two find someone else to bother?" Finn demanded.

"It's more fun to bother you," Eiran said. "The girl is pretty."

"And she looked like a good dancer," Heath said. "Better than me, anyway."

"Yes?" Finn asked, grinning slightly.

"I think you quite liked dancing with that young lady," Eiran said. "What was her name again?"

Finn looked away, searching his mind for some other direction to point the conversation. He started to mumble something about having been summoned by his parents.

"Sorry, brother, maybe you didn't hear me," Eiran said. "I asked what name she goes by."

"I don't know her name," Finn finally said.

Eiran laughed. "That is what Father told me, but I did not believe it! How can you marry someone whose name you don't know? Finn, get serious. The fate and the future of the kingdom depends on who you choose for a wife. And you have chosen a girl who will not reveal her name? You know she's someone's house wench. She likely has no name."

"She is not—" Finn said.

"Think about it, Finn," Eiran said. "There must be some reason she will not tell her name. Her employer would be furious if they knew she was sneaking out and failing to tend the chamber pots. Or perhaps she is a...wagtail, of sorts—" Eiran pursed his lips and sent pretend kisses into the air.

"Hold your tongue," Finn demanded.

"Maybe she's a spy," said Heath. "And she's using the ball to plan her infiltration."

"Really, anything is possible, Finn," Eiran said. "You cannot be careful enough."

"Let me worry about my own affairs," Finn said, stopping. "You two occupy yourselves with your own matters. If you cannot find any, I shall speak to the schoolmaster about extra lessons."

Eiran laughed. "We were only teasing, brother," he said. "The future of the kingdom rests on your shoulders, but there's no need to be so serious."

Chapter Ten

Cinder went home that afternoon and cooked a stew of meat and the season's last vegetables from the garden. Within her, Cinder felt something bubbling: she was quick to smile, quick to laugh. She even caught herself humming and trying to recreate the dance upon the kitchen floor, though when she was alone, she could not recall the steps.

That afternoon, dancing with Alban, it had made her...what was the word? Which emotion felt like warm sunshine and butterfly wings? Ahh, yes, this was happiness. The realization made her giggle and swiftly cover her mouth.

And the kiss. She touched her lips in memory of it. And their talk after. As she recalled it, she suddenly wondered with horror if she had revealed too much. Now that he knew her feelings, would Alban keep his distance from her? She couldn't imagine such a thing. After all, his feelings seemed to mirror hers. They might not have forever together, but at least they'd had one day, this day.

She stroked her cat's head. "Henry," she said, "another gentleman is in my heart. You will like him. He might be more accustomed to dogs, but we shall win him over."

Henry purred. Henry could win anyone over.

While the stew simmered, Cinder checked the parlor; Rhona, Liisi and Orla all sat in there, content in their afternoon activities: Rhona and Orla played a game of cards while Liisi practiced playing the harpsichord.

She was trying to match her flat voice to the round notes, and each time she got a note wrong, she slammed the keys and shouted. With them all occupied, Cinder knew she could steal a few uninterrupted moments with her mother's letter. First, she ordered the pages she had not yet read, carefully matching up the last word and sentence on each page to the first on another. Then, having corrected the pages' order, she began to read the story closer to where her mother intended.

> I grew up in Dunford Town, a place not so unlike Kilderbrae, the town you know best for it is closest to our beloved Bowmore House. In Dunford, muddy roads were flanked by simple cottages, and there was a market where one could sell and acquire goods of all sorts. We had apples in the fall and flowers in the spring, snow by winter, and in the summer, cherries, berries, flowers and birdsong. By morning, the baker would walk up and down the street, calling out for all to take hot buttered buns, a sack for a half penny. By evening, the lamplighter walked down the same street, reaching his wick over the tops of the lamps then drawing the starlight down from the heavens and fixing it over our lanes.
>
> I could name all the people who walked those streets every day, for, every day, I watched them through my window.
>
> Maman made a home for us in the rooms above her dress shop. She designed my bed chamber to be a magical place, a deity's home away from Heaven: the window hung with cream-colored silk curtains adorned with gold thread and embroidered rosebuds, fabric remaining after Maman made some gown. The floor was lined in ruby-colored velvet, left after Maman fashioned someone a cape. It was rich and soft, though slippery and not very practical as a rug. My own bed was covered with a quilt of many fine fabrics.
>
> The rooms where we lived had once been the home to a gentleman scholar named Professor Godfrey Bovington who'd left behind a pile of beautiful books. I spent many hours reading. My favorite book was a volume entitled, "Great Insect Beasts of the Northern Hemisphere." Maman thought the book ghastly and ill-suited for a young lady, but I loved the pictures of creatures and beasts so wild I never could have imagined them. They were fiends from other realms, replete with pinchers and claws, prickly spikes, eyeballs at the ends of their antennas,

hairy needle feet, skulls like a soldier's helmet, and mighty, marvelous wings.

Of course, wings! Wings of all sorts, long, stout, wide or tiny, in pairs or foursomes, decorated like a flower garden or fully translucent with gossamer thread edges. Wings gave even the most bulky, hideous creatures the one power I wished I had: flight.

Oh, my girl, how much and how hard and how painfully I wished I could fly! I dreamed of soaring over trees, reaching the ocean, the mountains, experiencing all that existed for me only in books and dreams. But I, a nervous child, even at eleven years old, had not the ability to fly, spin a web or dig tunnels. So, I lay in my small room on the third floor, and waited patiently and obediently for something to happen.

And then, one day, it did. A friend stumbled into my life. My friend, Rhona.

Cinder stopped here. *My friend, Rhona.* It was such a peculiar coincidence that Cinder's mother's friend had the same name as her stepmother. At that moment, she heard her stepmother's laugh ring out from the other room. If her stepmother had been friends with her mother, how could nobody have spoken about it? Did nobody know? And why had her mother assumed her friend's name? She hoped the letter would provide answers. And until she understood the whole picture, she would not speak of it with anyone.

Cinder continued reading...

On an early spring morning, I watched two women walk down the lane. One seemed only a few years older than I, and this would become my own Rhona. The other was an ill-tempered woman, whom I learned later went by the name Mavis.

Cinder's mother described the two women, dressed like servants, one older, one younger. From her bedroom window perch, she watched them bring goods down the lane from the market. As they walked, the older one berated the younger. Without warning, the younger servant slipped in the muddy lane. The older woman's scolds increased, and the girl disappeared from view.

My mother's shop below suddenly filled with ladies' voices, gasping in panic. Then I heard pounding footsteps in the hallway. When I opened my door, the young servant suddenly burst into my room. Her face was streaked with tears and mud, and her eyes had the look of a lost animal.

I closed the door. Then we two stood, wordless from the shock. In the hallway beyond my door, I heard voices, the pig-squeal voice was talking to my mother whose tone, as always, was controlled and measured.

I looked at the girl, and she at me. Ought we try to hide? Such efforts were futile. Best thing to do was allow our elders into the room and address them directly. When Maman knocked, I opened the door.

"You see, children always find each other," Maman said to the other woman.

The woman noticed Rhona, and how covered she was in mud. "Miserable thing," she said. "You're spoiling where the nice girl sleeps."

"It is only earth," said my Maman. "It will cause no harm. I shall fetch a cloth for your daughter."

"She ain't my daughter," the woman protested. "She's the kin of my employer is all. Her mother left her at the MacMargeson house when the child was a bairn. Lady thought she could assist me now that she's older and such. Only she ain't no help, she un-does everything I does."

"I said I was sorry," Rhona mumbled, her voice low. She pressed herself flat against the wall, as if she hoped the wall would open up and consume her.

I looked to my mother. She put her hands upon her hips; I could tell she was scheming.

"You know, madame," started my mother. "My daughter has been secluded in this room since she was young. Now that she is older, she is so shy, she does not go out. Perhaps the young lady could...stay for a spell."

We all looked at the pig-faced lady. She seemed to consider it, but dismissed the idea. "We have work to do. And now we need to get back to the market for our second shopping. I hope we have enough coin. Come along, girl."

I looked at Maman to see what she would do next. "Where are my manners today?" she said. "We have not been properly introduced. This is Ailen, my daughter."

I smiled a little, then waited for the girl to say her name but she only smiled meekly back. Finally, Maman asked her. "Do you have a name, Miss?"

The girl looked at us then finally spoke. "Rhona," she said.

"I'm Mavis," the other woman said. "And you're Madame Leontyne, you don't need to tell me so, whole town knows about you."

"Yes," Maman said, smiling slightly. "Miss Rhona, would you care to join us for tea? I have biscuits also, although, I only have two, I am afraid..." and she gave Mavis a side-look.

Maman stooped slightly. I sensed she was trying to see the girl's eyes, hoping to gauge her thoughts.

"She can't stay for tea," Mavis said curtly.

"Child," Maman said, "you are welcome in this house. Lady Treasa MacMargeson is a customer of mine. But if she needs you to work, then by all means, please, visit us another day."

Rhona remained quiet.

"Come along home, Rhona, and stop wasting these peoples' time," Mavis said.

"Miss Mavis," Maman said. "If the girl, Rhona, may remain here now or return later, I could pay her a shilling each visit. Perhaps, perhaps she could teach my Ailen to read."

"Read?" Mavis shouted. "That's a fast one; this girl don't know to read."

Rhona glared at Mavis with furious, hurt eyes. I grabbed one of my books from a pile and thrust it in front of Rhona. The bug book. Rhona opened it up and looked puzzled. She found a page with only pictures. I nodded her on.

"Tell us what you see on the page," Maman said gently.

Rhona swallowed and finally spoke. "Bugs is...creatures...they live in the wood. They love dirt and sticks and things. Some fly. Some crawl." She looked at us all again, her confidence increasing. "Ladybugs...are not ladies. And dragonflies aren't dragons. Damsel flies are...almost never in distress."

"'At's not reading," Mavis said, scowling. "Her's just talking, looking at the pictures, making things up."

"No, this is what is on the page," Maman said. She took the book from Rhona and handed it to Mavis. "See for yourself."

Mavis turned a few pages. The ones in the front were filled with complicated words that even I never read. Mavis glanced at them, thoroughly flustered. "It's a book about creepers; any fool could see that."

Maman took the book from her and placed it down upon the stack. "Miss Mavis, let the girl stay. I shall pay the shilling directly to you to make up for any disruption in the MacMargeson household."

Mavis didn't like this suggestion, but she could not pass up the chance to earn an easy shilling. "I suppose...if she can teach the girl to read, she'd be of service."

Maman smiled; she was very pleased with herself. Then she brought Mistress Mavis down to the shop and offered to make her a corset to bind her bosom and ease the pain in her back.

Then, Rhona and I were left alone in my bedroom, each of us so shocked by all that had happened that we had no idea what to say to one another.

"Cinder?" came Liisi's voice at the doorway. Her sharp tone made Cinder jump. "Were you going to serve dinner tonight or did you want to wait until tomorrow?"

Cinder shook her head to bring her mind back into the Bowmore House kitchen. The stew hadn't burned yet, but it would if left for much longer. She jumped up to pull the pan off the coals.

"Almost ready," she said. "Really, Liisi, don't be so impatient."

"I am not the one who is impatient," she said, wandering into the kitchen. "You are the one who is late. What have you been doing anyway? What are those papers?"

Cinder gathered the pages together and tucked them away. "Old recipes," she said. "I found them in a drawer."

"Recipes?" Liisi said. "But where did they come from?"

Cinder shrugged. "I suppose Mrs. Brodie wrote them down," she said. "Before Mother Rhona sacked her."

Liisi groaned. "I couldn't bear that woman," she said. "She stank of fish. I could taste it in everything she cooked. Even the chocolate cake."

"A natural consequence of being wed to a fisherman," Cinder said.

Liisi looked side-long at Cinder. "Might I see the recipes? Perhaps there are some that you could make. Without the dead fish aroma. Strange, I have lived by the sea all these years, and I never developed a taste for the flesh of aquarian beasts."

Cinder squinted at Liisi. "As it happens, these recipes are for all manner of fish preparations," she said. "Not a word about chocolate cake."

"Of course not," Liisi said, sighing loudly. "The things I care for are never included. Well, Cinder, finish your own cooking, as we do not wish to wait until next week for tonight's dinner."

"Of course," she said. "It will be ready in some moments."

After Liisi strolled out of the room, Cinder scrambled to fill bowls with the stew. As she sliced the bread, she turned the one question over in her mind, the possibility that her mother's Rhona and the Mother Rhona of her own life were one and the same. Her mother's friend had been a child working as a servant in the home of her relatives. What had Orla said about her mother, that night in the tower? She'd been raised by distant relations who treated her as no more than a servant. The two descriptions echoed one another so closely, it seemed impossible she might be wrong.

Cinder did not know how she might go about learning the truth. She carried the tray into the dining room, where the three women sat at the table.

"Ahh, look everyone, dinner," Liisi said. "And served within the same day on the calendar as our other meals. What a miracle. "

Cinder was growing weary of this line of taunting. But she managed to not respond, and for this, she was quite proud. She placed bowls of stew in front of each of them.

"What a wonderful flavor," Liisi exclaimed. "I'll have to hire Cinder as the castle cook when I become princess of Braemuir Kingdom."

Cinder glanced at Liisi but decided against goading her. "I am certain you will employ someone who has more skill in the kitchen than I have."

Liisi continued chattering; and Cinder's mind was still upon her mother's letter. She had been thinking about this too long for the next thing she heard was, "Cinder?" Rhona said. "Have you fallen asleep?"

She blinked. "Asleep? No, no, simply lost in thought. Pardon me."

"Please join us at the table," Mother Rhona said.

"Also, Mother, I must hire a dressmaker," Liisi said. "I tried to make decorative ruffles on my own, but I cannot get them right. All the girls are wearing them these days. Is it not practical to hire someone to help embellish? It will take me twice the time to do something half as nice, and that sounds wasteful to me."

"My daughter, the answer remains no," Rhona said. "Every young lady in the kingdom is seeking someone to help them with their dress. Dressmakers may charge however much they like. People will pay."

"Basic economics," Orla said. "The supply has not changed, but, because of the ball, the demand has increased significantly."

"It is so very unfair, Mother," Liisi said.

"I have heard of a dressmaker," Cinder blurted. All three turned toward her. "In Dunford Town."

"Dunford Town?" Mother Rhona said, as though she was trying to hold back laughter.

"But Cinder, that's a day's journey away," Orla said.

"There was a dressmaker there once," Cinder said.

Orla shrugged. "A dressmaker in Dunford may not have much business from ladies in Braemuir."

Cinder nodded. "Precisely."

Rhona looked at both girls. "We shall not hire a dressmaker from a pathetic little hamlet like Dunford," she declared. "It would make more sense to bring someone up from London."

"Oh, Mother, London!" Liisi exclaimed. "We simply must–"

"Liisi, both options are thoroughly impractical. We cannot near afford a seamstress from London."

Cinder sighed. Rhona's response had been less than helpful. While she ate, she let her mind wander off to the cliffs and all she'd experienced that day, and how she and Alban had danced. She recalled the feeling of his hand upon her back, strong and confident. His eyes upon hers. Alban had been close enough that she had breathed in his smell. What did it remind her of? Leather and horse. And something else, a slightly lavender, soapy scent. And the salt of the sea, and the sweet, crisp smell of apples.

And a kiss. That kiss would remain on her lips for the rest of her life.

"Why, for the love of the devil, must she grin at me?" Liisi exclaimed, glaring at Cinder.

"Grin?" Cinder said. "I was not even looking at you."

"Mother, see how she laughs at me," Liisi said. "She takes nothing seriously. Put her in the tower before she hurts someone innocent. I have nightmares of waking in the morning to find that she cut off my hair in the night. Please, Mother!"

"Cut off your hair—" Rhona cried.

"Liisi!" Orla exclaimed. "Cinder said nothing. Nobody has cut anybody's hair."

"But she could," Liisi said. "See how the very idea makes her smile."

"You do seem to be beaming quite a bit, this evening, Cinder," said Mother Rhona. "What is the source of this...exuberant bliss?"

Cinder put her hands over her mouth. She had not realized she was smiling.

"I have something to say," Cinder finally said, pressing her shoulders back. "I'd like to attend the king's ball. A young man invited me, and though I told him I had no interest, he pressed me. If it suits you three, perhaps I may ride in your carriage?"

"Wonderful!" Orla declared, clapping.

"Which young man?" Rhona said.

"Exactly what do you intend to wear?" Liisi asked, crossing her arms. "Not one of your mother's old rag-piles, I hope. You have to find something appropriate for the occasion or you shall embarrass us terribly."

"How did you know about my mother's dress?" Cinder asked.

"I told her," Orla said. "I said it might be nice to help you fix something so you could join us."

"Tell the truth, Orla," Liisi said. "You laughed and said, 'you should see the moth-eaten shreds of her mother's frock; she could never wear that to Glengoe Castle.'"

Cinder's face fell and she looked to Orla for an explanation.

"The way Liisi speaks it is not what I intended, Cinder," Orla said. "Your mother's dress would do well with a bit of mending and some ornaments. I told Liisi that she and I must have some baubles we could give you. I never meant my words to mock."

"Cinder," said Rhona, "I am sorry. Truly. But if you do not possess a proper gown, you may not attend the king's ball. Am I to take it that you never had such a garment? Even when you were younger?"

Cinder considered it. Of course, her mother had made dresses for her when she was a child, but she had long since outgrown those. After her mother died, her father once had a seamstress make her a pretty dress; she wore it the first time she met the woman and her two daughters. Afterward, she tore the frock off and threw it in the fireplace.

"I have nothing," she said.

Mother Rhona looked upon the girl with pity. "Please understand, this is an important opportunity for the older girls. We do not receive invitations to the castle every day and we must present ourselves as best we can."

"I am not skilled at stitching," Cinder said. "Could we not spare just a little money? It doesn't have to be ornate—"

"Mother!" Liisi exclaimed. "Why does she get a brand new dress and we do not? It's terribly unfair."

Rhona held up a hand to silence Liisi. "More to the point," she said, leaning back in her seat. "Who exactly is the young man who requested your presence?"

"Oh, yes," Liisi said, also leaning back. "We'd like to hear about him."

"This matter has nothing to do with us," Orla said.

"Let Cinder speak for herself, Orla," Liisi said, smiling in a most unfriendly way.

But Cinder well understood that these were questions to which there was no correct answer. Whatever small bit of information she offered would be twisted past recognition. She tried to think how to quiet their inquiries, but her throat went dry.

She swallowed. "He's nobody. Just someone I know."

"Someone you know," Rhona said. "How could you be acquainted with some young man with whom the rest of us are not?"

Liisi stood. "It doesn't matter," she said, her voice growing increasingly shrill with every word. "Mother, she doesn't have a thing to wear. We already decided. She cannot go to the castle ball. This discussion is pointless."

Orla looked at Cinder with an expression of commiseration. "I'm sorry," she said.

"No, Orla," Mother Rhona said. "I am sorry. Due to our circumstances, we truly cannot spare any extra expense right now. We must reserve what we have. The two older girls have dresses, which they themselves will adorn, mend and wear to the ball. Cinder, if you have no proper frock, you may not attend. Believe me, I am truly regretful."

But her voice did not sound so. As she delivered this news, her stepmother's face bore a glimmer of smile, and the smile on Liisi's face was more than a glimmer, more like a stiff, smug smirk. Only the face of Orla, her unexpected betrayer, seemed to understand how Cinder felt being left behind. Again.

Cinder held her head high. "That suits me fine," she said "I'd rather stay home. After all, I don't even know how to dance."

Cinder turned on her heels and went into the kitchen and closed the door behind her. There she wept silent tears.

Cinder's tears were interrupted with the sound of someone pounding upon the front door. The hour was late for visitors. She dried her eyes on her apron and hastened to the door. There, a messenger stood holding a notice. He gave it to her curtly and instructed her to deliver it to the Widow Rhona Barclay. Cinder took it and glanced at the seal. She did not recognize it, but the notice was small and without ornament; she sensed it was not another invitation. The messenger returned to his horse and rode away, and Cinder went into the dining room and handed the notice to her stepmother. Mother Rhona wiped her mouth with her napkin and took the message. She glanced at the seal for one moment, and then an extra moment. She gave her daughters an overly happy smile, and said, "Please, continue eating."

"What is it, Mother?" asked Orla.

"Oh, business, only," she said. Cinder noticed that Mother Rhona's hands shook as she broke the seal. Mother Rhona pulled out the notice and read it. Then, she gasped.

"Are you all right?" asked Orla.

Mother Rhona stood and smiled an artificial smile. "Please excuse me," she said. "I am suddenly very tired, so I shall go upstairs and rest." She stood, then clutched her chest and her whole body collapsed.

"Mother!" Orla and Liisi both cried. They reached and caught her before she sank to the ground. The note fell out of her hands onto the floor.

"You two help her up the stairs," Cinder said. "I shall bring tea and a bit of buttered bread."

"It's naught but an ache in my head," Rhona said.

"You need to lie down, Mother," said Orla.

"Thank you, dears," Rhona said. "I can walk. Cinder, please bring me a cup of tea. With a bit of rest, I should be good as new."

Cinder waited until all three were on the way up the stairs before she collected the notice from the floor.

The scrawled handwriting said: "One month to this day. If the balance of the debt is not paid, Bowmore House shall be transferred into my ownership."

It was signed with one letter: W.

Liisi and Orla assisted Rhona up the stairs and fussed over her as she dressed for bed. Cinder delivered tea and bread, and also the notice. Rhona sat in her chair and stared at the fire and sipped her tea. The girls departed, and Cinder stoked the fire one last time, then turned to leave the room.

"Can he do that?" Cinder asked. "Take the house. Has he a legal right to do so?"

Rhona sighed and rubbed her head. "I don't know."

"Is there anything I can do to prevent him from doing so?"

"Something you can do?" Rhona said. "Yes, go back in time and silence your interference in my conversation with him. I would never have allowed that devil to marry Liisi or you. But you...you made him look the fool. Now his pride is insulted. Cinder, you know nothing of the ways of men. Their feelings are fragile and they can be so cruel."

"I'm sorry," Cinder said.

Rhona swallowed the last sip of tea from her cup. "I know you do not care for me, Cinder," Rhona said. "But sometimes, you must trust me. I want the best for my daughters. You included."

"Now that the snake is awakened, what will we do?"

Rhona shook her head, slowly, sadly. "I will think of something," she said. "But for now, Cinder, please leave me be. I must think. Do not mention this to the girls."

"All right," Cinder said. "But if you need me to make a plan—"

"For heaven's sake," Rhona exclaimed. "No more plans. The least you can do is make no more trouble."

Cinder departed then, and finally, Rhona was alone. From under her bed, she pulled out her secret flask and filled her teacup with whiskey. The hot, sweet elixir burned her throat and numbed her nerves. She stirred the coals in the fireplace and added another log, then sat, gathering her thoughts.

She glanced at the notice on the tray. She did not need to look again at the message; she knew what it said. It said that Lord Warin had set his sights on taking their home.

He had no right to it, she knew this. But if Lord Warin brought the matter to the courts, no magistrate would rule in favor of a penniless widow. And she had no money to hire a barrister to argue their position. Even if the man could provide no evidence of a debt, she would lose her case. Men won. Every time.

She held her hand against her mouth; angry tears fell down her cheek. She wanted to throw the cup against the wall, just to break some other thing instead of being broken. The collateral for his blackmail attempt was a letter, which she knew was a forgery. But that mattered little. If she demanded legal action, the matter would become public, and then the whole world would learn the story he was promoting, that she had robbed and likely murdered a young woman. Rhona would be found guilty of murder in the minds of the people. And that was a sentence from which she would never be released.

The letter claimed she had killed her dear friend, Ailen. Ailen had given her the jewels, which turned out to be a burden, not a boon. And she knew Ailen had survived that terrible day, for she herself had sent Ailen away from the real danger. Though Rhona had never heard from her again, she hoped her friend still lived, safe and happy, somewhere in the world.

Dunford Town. How strange that at supper, Cinder had mentioned this place. What did she mean, she knew a seamstress in Dunford? Lord Warin must have prodded her. *Ask her about her past*, he had perhaps said. *Ask what happened in Dunford.*

Rhona rarely let herself think back to those days, but she would always remember Ailen, the light-haired girl who had taught Rhona to read. What a miracle it had seemed, all those years ago, to learn that those marks on the page were alphabet letters, pieces of sound that joined with others to create words, render meaning, form sentences and paragraphs, and tell stories. When Rhona learned to read, the whole world opened up for her, like a secret box, or the most exquisite flavor of food, which she had never before known.

She took a sip of whiskey and listened to the wind batter the windows. In London, all those years ago, she had tried to sell one ruby ring when she was desperate to buy food. The scoundrel who agreed to buy it informed the sheriff of London that she, nought more than a small-town wastrel, possessed a jewel engraved with the royal seal of the throne of Gallia. How had she come by it, the sheriff demanded, and what did she know of the murder of a dress-maker in Dunford, and the woman's disappeared daughter?

Rhona claimed ignorance. She'd found the ring, she said, caught between the cobbled stones of some back alley. She knew nothing of anyone's death nor disappearance, nor of the land of Gallia. She was just a beggar seeking coin enough for a few bites of gruel and perhaps a blanket.

The sheriff had kept the ruby ring, for evidence, he said. He never learned about the other jewels she concealed: a diamond necklace, an emerald ring, a golden ring and an ivory brooch embellished with diamonds. She had always hoped that one day she would see Ailen again and hand them back to her.

The jewels. Their worth was a sum that could change someone's life, but since she could not sell them, they were worthless as sand. What could she now do? This house was barely standing, but it was a place to live. If Lord Warin claimed it and ejected their little family, where would they go? Into town, perhaps, to rent some foul, leaking fisherman's cottage. After the fire, she and her daughters had had no place to live. For a while, she'd brought them to live with this or that relative of her husband's, but in time, the family's good will ran out. For weeks after, they wandered about, carrying all they owned, sleeping and eating only when someone took pity upon them. Rhona had hated seeing her daughters live like that.

Their saving grace had been a man who needed a wife to raise his tempestuous daughter: Gerik Barclay. Rhona knew right away that his daughter was not such a problem, she was simply a girl who had her own ideas. At least she had thoughts, which was more than one could say for Liisi. But then again, the girl hadn't thought through her ruse regarding Lord Warin's accounts...

Still, there was one source of hope: the king's ball. Perhaps one of the girls might receive an offer of marriage. Orla was unlikely, but perhaps Liisi could. If she did, they might secure support from the family of Liisi's suitor. This family might even have the means to provide them with a place to live. A young man would have to have a very wealthy family and be quite in love with Liisi to be moved so.

Rhona had an idea; she stood and went to her bureau and eased open the bottom drawer. The back of the drawer was concealed with a piece of wood. She pulled it away and found a small wooden box. She brought out the contents: a necklace, a gold ring, an emerald ring, and a brooch with diamonds. Jewels from the throne of Gallia. How ridiculous was fate that she would possess such things.

Liisi was the last pawn Rhona had to gamble. The girl would have to walk into that ball, shining like a princess. She would have to be thoroughly charming; even if she did not secure a proposal of marriage from the crown prince himself, Liisi would show the other men in the room that she was the boon to strive for. Liisi was pretty enough, but she would have to be perfect.

Rhona would make sure Liisi was glittering. After all, the jewels should be used for something. Why shouldn't her daughter wear one to the ball? All of Rhona's hopes were stacked upon her younger daughter. In one night, the night of the king's ball, everything they had would be won or lost.

Chapter Eleven

Through the night, Cinder did not sleep. Her thoughts were upon the note delivered during supper. She could not believe the possibility that Lord Warin truly had the power to take their home. Bowmore House belonged to her, and she to it; it was as much part of her as the Sayre Cliffs or the Morisar Sea. Nobody could take from her the ocean or the cliffs. Someday she would leave Bowmore House, but not because someone forced her. Particularly not that reeking, seething vulture.

Long before sunrise, Cinder sat up and surrendered to her insomnia. She lit a lantern and stoked the fire. She glanced at the time: five o'clock. Her mind turned to the letter. She felt compelled to read it, as though somewhere within her mother's words she might find wisdom and direction to help her know what action she should take. So, with Henry snoring quietly beside her, she pulled out her mother's letter and continued reading where she had left off.

The two girls were now in the bedroom of Ailen, Cinder's mother, the letter's author. Cinder's grandmother, Leontyne, brought tea and cookies. The girls told each other about their lives. Ailen learned that Rhona's father had died of the fever and that her mother had brought her to live in the house of his kin, promising to return. But she had never returned, nor sent word of where she was, so Rhona had grown up in that busy house alone, working hard to earn her keep.

> Rhona visited me one or two days each week and I taught Rhona to read. She learned so fast! By our third day together, she had memorized

the alphabet and was sounding out words. The people in her house berated her for lacking intelligence, but I thought her very smart. Rhona's aunt was Lady Treasa MacMargeson, one of Maman's best customers. She ordered a new gown for each season, and each season she found an occasion to host some revelry. I could not imagine what it was to live amidst so many fine things and lovely rooms and warm fires, and people always coming and going. I begged Rhona for details, but she was always on the outside of the excitement. The family was unkind to her: they never treated her as kin and the staff likewise did not treat her as one of them. In that big and busy house, Rhona was terribly lonely.

One morning, before the sun rose, a tap came to my window and woke me. I wondered if a bird might have caused the sound, but a moment later, there came a second tap. This time, I sat up. Was the evil queen in the street, throwing darts at my window? At the third tap, I finally rose. There, standing in the first ray of morning's light, stood Rhona, a burlap sack over her shoulder.

I opened my window and looked out. Rhona's face was upset. "I am leaving," she said. "Come with me."

"I don't want to run away," I said.

"Then walk with me to the edge of Dunford. You can go home after. I would be glad for the company." She gasped, holding back tears.

"All right," I said. I closed my window and dressed myself, then, while my mother slept, I quietly made my way past her bedroom and down the steps to the front door. Slowly, carefully, I unlocked the door and slipped into the street. I had never before left our home without my mother. I tried to seem unaffected, but I was terrified.

I asked Rhona what happened.

"Promise me," she said, trying to scrub the tears off her face with the back of her hand. "If you ever have a daughter or a servant, and they make a mistake, even in front of the most important people in the world, never laugh at them."

I took her hand in mine. Rhona's household had given a lavish party the night before. I knew this for Maman had been working very hard making last-minute alterations and embellishments to many fine gowns. I had even helped, sewing flowers, lace, buttons and trim of all sorts on to ladies' gowns.

"Promise," she insisted. And yes, I agreed, I would never laugh at another person. And I have kept that promise.

Rhona planned to stop at the house of the tinker, deep in the woods. We decided I would go with her that far then return on my own. It seemed a fine plan. Maman might awaken and find me missing, but I would be home before supper. As we walked along the dark morning streets of Dunford Town, each step I took was the furthest I had ever walked past my mother's shop without my mother; I was buoyant with joy and terror. But I had to keep vigilant. Though I doubted its truth, the story my mother had told me—over and over—of the evil queen who murdered my siblings had worked its way into my consciousness. The queen's spies, I believed, could be anywhere.

"But Rhona," I said, scurrying to keep up with her. "Where shall you go after the tinker?"

"There's a town called Bridge of Thorngill," she said. "Those in the household talk about it. Girls can get jobs and learn to make things of leather, shoes and saddles and such. They live together in a house and a house matron feeds and cares for them. " She shrugged. "They say anything can happen in the city. Perhaps I would find my fortune. Maybe I would even meet my mother."

"You think she's in Bridge of Thorngill?" I asked.

"She's not here," Rhona said. "So, she could be anywhere."

"Oh," I said, quite amazed. "But Rhona, why do they treat you badly at House Ara Dun?"

She glanced at me with angry eyes. "Aunt Treasa and Uncle Tomfat, they have their smart, fair-haired sons, and I, a stupid dark-haired girl, have no place there."

"You're not stupid," I said.

"Mavis says, not everybody can be expected to be treated kindly. Is that true?"

"I believe everyone deserves kindness," I said. "Will they be angry when they discover you gone?"

"I don't know," she said. "And neither do I care."

The town seemed strangely silent as we walked, like the world was holding its breath. As we walked down the lane, the space between houses grew larger, evidence that we were approaching the ancient wood.

"Greetings children!" called a lady who was gathering herbs in front of her cottage. "It's a fine morning, and a fine day. Enjoy your picnic!"

Rhona waved and nodded in thanks, and on we continued. After that, the path grew narrow, and the sun hid behind a cloud. We pushed past a tangle of thicket, then we were in the heart of the woods. Hinter Hollow.

Rhona and I stood for a moment, taking in the majesty of the tall trees, a stream whose water rushed over stones and pebbles so it sounded like fairy bells, tunnels of boulder stones covered in green moss, craggy trees that clawed the sky, and squirrels skittering about. And birdsong! I cannot imagine an orchestra could sound so grand. Everything around us felt alive.

"Is this real?" I asked, suddenly aware of how childish my question sounded. "I have never seen any place more lovely."

"Have you never been to the woods?" Rhona asked.

"I saw pictures in Professor Bovington's books," I said. "But I never dreamed it could be so magical." I closed my eyes and inhaled. I tried to work out the names of the things I smelled, a perfume of moss and muck, rotted logs, wild herbs, flowers, grasses. I walked with my neck craned up and tilted backward so I could watch the trees and branches overhead.

"Ailen, keep your eyes on the path," she said. "There are many dangers in the woods. Some you do not notice until they are upon you."

"But, Rhona, look," I said, pointing at a tree filled with wood sparrows. "They sing like a chorus of angels. Is the world always this beautiful?"

"No, Ailen," she said. "Not always."

And then it happened: while I was looking in the wrong direction, my toe stuck in a tree's root. I heard a crack as my foot twisted, and I fell flat on the ground.

Rhona ran to me. "Are you all right?" she asked. I could not respond; I could barely breathe, and a terrible pain throbbed in my ankle.

Once I caught my breath, I tried to stand. "My foot can't hold me up."

I sat back down and Rhona tried to take off my shoe. I cried with pain.

"I will take you home," she said.

"Please, no," I said. "I want to meet the tinker. I want to see the woods."

"But you're hurt—"

"We have come this far. Rhona, I don't want to go back," I said.

We argued for a while. I was polite as always, saying "no, thank you" and "if you please." Finally, I raised my voice and declared, "Rhona, I will not go back."

"All right," she said. "Then we must fix you up to walk." Rhona reached out to the bottom of her apron and tore off a strip of fabric. She wrapped it tight around my foot then found a large stick. She helped me stand and showed me how to use the stick as a crutch. The pain was still there, but I could take a few steps.

"You're a doctor," I said. "Thank you."

"I am certainly not that," she said. "But I know how to keep going forward."

We continued on, more slowly this time, and now I kept my eyes fastened to the path ahead instead of the sky. I did not love it any less, in fact, I was dizzy with joy, and after some minutes, I forgot about my foot.

The fine day did not last. The sky began to darken, and a cold drizzle began to fall, soaking us. But soon we came upon a small cottage built of stones with a thatched roof. This was the tinker's home. Rhona knocked on the door, and a skinny old man with long, gray hair and a face that crinkled as he spoke answered the door. He wore a small cap upon his head, and wisps of brownish-white hair poked out from under it like animal whiskers. His eyes were wide and watery.

"Visitors!" he exclaimed, clapping his hands together. "Young Rhona and companion, you are welcome here. Please, come out of the rain, my dears."

He ushered us inside, then addressed Rhona. "Have I something to repair for House Ara Dun, Mistress Rhona? My memory is not so clear these days."

"Today is a social visit, only, Mr. Collins," she said. "Here's my friend, Ailen."

I curtsied, and a shaggy gray-haired mutt stood up to greet us. I thought it was a wolf and I recoiled in fear. Mr. Collins laughed. "Why it's only old Hammer. She looks a brute, but in truth, she is fierce as a bowl of porridge." She sniffed at Rhona and wagged her tail in greeting. Rhona laughed, and it cheered my heart to see her happy.

"Is Mrs. Collins about?" Rhona asked as she scratched Hammer behind the ears.

"She took the wagon to town to visit relations," he said. "But I make tea just as well, and there is bread from the morning. And a pot of jam somewhere. Come, warm yourselves by the fire."

Outside the window, Cinder noticed that the sun was beginning to rise. She decided to get a start on the day's chores. She braced herself against the cool morning, and carried the letter with her to the barn. She propped the pages up on a board so she could read while she sat on her little stool and milked the cows, Mistress Cheddar and Mistress Camembert.

On the next page, Rhona told Ailen and Mr. Collins that at the banquet the previous night, she'd been carrying a large, ornate cake and her aunt's son stretched out his foot, causing her to trip. The cake crashed to the floor, destroyed. The guests laughed; her aunt was horrified.

Cinder could picture it: a grand party, guests dressed to the nines, everyone watching the girl carrying that big cake. And in a moment, a mischievous deed reduced the cake to sludge. Then laughter, then heartbreak. Cinder could imagine the girl's embarrassment, and how she would feel so knocked down, she might never stand up again.

Cinder stopped milking for a moment. She pictured Mother Rhona's face, her dour expression, eyes that seemed always watching ghosts. Cinder herself had known a parent's love; she'd had a home, and places where she felt safe. A child who grew up without those, and was teased and laughed at, might never let joy into her heart. More and more, Cinder considered the possibility that the girl in the letter was her own stepmother.

She went back to reading.

By afternoon, the rain had stopped. Mr. Collins told us we could stay the night, but Rhona insisted on bringing me home.

"We will go back the way we came," Rhona said. "And then I suppose I shall return to Ara Dun. I cannot seem to get away from that place."

That was when I noticed her face had grown pale. I thought it was because of her disappointment.

"If you're not staying then, girlies, out the door with you," Mr. Collins said. "I will not be still until I know you are safely homeward. If Mrs. Collins had not taken the wagon, I would drive ye."

I gathered my makeshift crutch and Rhona and I thanked Mr. Collins and scratched Hammer's ears one last time. Then we ventured into the wood.

"The walk back is not long," Mr. Collins called after us. "But in the dark and damp, even familiar things look strange. Make haste, good friends! And when you have two paths to choose from, take the one that rises higher, for that way is the most direct. Travel swiftly!"

"We shall," I called out. The air took on an uneasy breeze that felt like a warning. I turned to my companion and noticed her colorless face. She was shaking. I asked if she was all right. She put her hand to her head, as if steadying herself. "Why should I shiver when I am so hot?" she asked, laughing nervously. "Some in the household took ill last week. Perhaps..."

"Oh, dear," I said. Drops of rain were beginning to fall. "Come home with me, Rhona. Maman will let you stay with us. You could help in the shop and live with me. We would be like sisters."

"I do not belong in Dunford, not at your mother's shop, nor anywhere. I will come this night, only because of this storm. On the morrow, I shall leave again for Bridge of Thorngill alone," she said. Then she regarded me sadly. "I wonder if I should ever belong somewhere."

I took her hand. "You're my friend. You belong with me."

The rain started to fall, and the breeze increased. I hobbled upon my stick and Rhona walked slowly beside me. Rhona began to cough. After we'd been walking for little while, she stumbled.

"I can't," she said and she went to a tree and leaned against it, slid to the ground and closed her eyes. "I must rest a few moments."

"Not now," I said, shaking her arm. "Please, Rhona, come with me. I cannot carry you home. Please don't sleep."

But my friend did not move. Her eyes closed. I felt her forehead; it was hot, and her face flushed red, even in the cold rain.

I feared that my friend Rhona had been afflicted with an illness not unlike the one that claimed her own father's life. I refused to let Rhona die. But I did not know what to do, especially with my hurt foot. I couldn't see which direction we'd come from since the tinker's cottage, and anyway, I would not leave Rhona alone to go back for help.

The wood, which had been so radiant that morning, had become a place of despair and we were imprisoned within it. No matter for Rhona's dreams of reaching Bridge of Thorngill and never looking back, but would either of us see the sun rise the next day?

I wanted to cry, but I knew my helpless tears were folly. I took my friend's head in my lap and gently begged her to wake.

The rain came down harder and then thunder clapped, and a bolt of lightning exploded. I sensed that evening was quickly falling, turning the world a dark, dank gray. We needed shelter. I searched the landscape and noticed a thicket beyond the trail that might offer some protection. My foot ached, but I ignored it. I lifted Rhona's arm to my shoulder; she awoke enough to lean on me and I pulled her along. We reached the thicket and squeezed through a small opening to find a tiny cavern inside a shrub.

I lay Rhona down, and put her bag under her head for comfort, then placed my cloak over her. It was damp, so offered her little comfort. Rhona's head was hot, but her hands were cold. I held them in mine and tried to warm them. The rain came down harder and the thunder continued. Our shelter would not protect us if the storm got worse.

When Cinder had finished milking, she tucked the letter into her apron then started back to the house. She could not read while she walked, for she carried two pails of warm, fresh milk, which she did not want to risk spilling. She brought the pails into the kitchen and carefully set them on the counter. The time was six o'clock, at least an hour before everyone else would wake. Cinder was desperate to learn what became of the girls in the storm. She tucked herself away in the pantry, the small room at the base of the staircase to the tower room, and closed the door half-way so she could hear the bell. She threw some onions out of an almost empty crate and tipped it down-side up, then sat upon it and continued reading.

Through cracks in the shrub around us, I could see a stream nearby. If the water rose much, it might crown over the banks, flooding all in the area. With Rhona ill and I injured, I knew neither of us would be able to escape a flood. We needed to leave.

"Rhona," I said, shaking her, now almost frantic. "You must wake. Please, Rhona, we have to go back to town."

"Pain in my head," she whispered, her eyes still closed. "I must lie a bit longer."

"You can't," I said. "This place isn't safe; we must home, lovely Rhona. Please."

But Rhona did not stir. I looked out through the thicket; the water in the stream grew higher every moment. A great clap of lightning and thunder shook the ground below us and flashed in the darkness, lighting the world like a summer's morning.

It startled me so, I screamed. But in the brief blaze, I spied through the slits in the shrubs something I had not noticed before...behind us, a cottage. It was small and secluded behind a grove of trees. I did not know how I missed it earlier. Then, I saw a light in the window; somebody was inside.

Again, I shook Rhona, this time more forcefully. "I found shelter," I told her. "A true shelter; we must reach it."

"Where?" she asked, her voice still weary.

"Near," I said. "Come."

I slung Rhona's arm around my shoulder and was stabbed by the sharp pain in my ankle. I buckled, then pressed on. I managed to bring Rhona out of the thicket, and braced her against the weather. The two of us, both soaking wet, hobbled to the cottage door. It opened almost before I could knock, and then there before us appeared a figure whose face was concealed by a hood and a heavy gray-blue robe.

"Bring her inside," said a voice that was vaguely feminine. A hand pointed to a bed beside a lovely fire. "It's a terrible time to be out in the hollow."

Cinder stopped reading. *Face concealed by a hood...a heavy gray-blue robe.* She glanced up at a shelf of jars of pickled courgettes. The description reminded her of her own Watcher.

Chapter Twelve

The moment Cinder looked away from the letter, she thought she heard some sound on the other side of the door. She went to it and saw Mother Rhona standing by the fire.

"Good morning," Cinder said tentatively, slipping the letter back into her apron.

"Cinder, where have you been?" Rhona asked. "I have been calling and calling."

"I was in the pantry," she said. "Did you ring the bell?"

"No bell, not today," Rhona said. "The notice from Lord Warin has upset me terribly."

"You are not alone," Cinder muttered.

"Please, Cinder, the last thing we need is more schemes from you," she said. "I am the adult; leave the planning to me. Am I quite clear?"

"Yes, ma'am," Cinder said.

"Good," Rhona said, and she pressed her hand to her forehead. "I woke up with pain in my head. I need a cool compress. I wish to look upon some different corner of this house, so I shall take my tea in the parlor. And Cinder, there is terrible banging noise in the attic. A gull must have gotten in through the roof."

"Oh, not again," Cinder said. She put her hands on her hips. "I covered up a hole in the roof some months ago, but perhaps there is a new one. You'd like a fire in the parlor, I presume?"

Rhona rubbed her arms and sighed. "That room will be freezing.

But it's quite warm in here. You must have been up for some time. Perhaps I shall take my tea in the kitchen instead."

"If that would please you," Cinder said. To herself, she sighed, for she certainly could not read the letter while her stepmother sat right in front of her. Then she had an idea. Rhona sat at the table and quietly watched the fire while Cinder boiled water, warmed slices of bread and prepared a compress, then she set out a tea pot and tea cup, and dishes of jam and butter. Once it was all set and Mother Rhona had all she needed, Cinder took a bucket that contained scraps of discarded food and declared, "Time to feed the chickens. I shall return in a few moments."

"Can that task not wait?" Rhona asked. "The girls could wake soon. Especially with all the noise."

Cinder glanced at the clock. "They will sleep for at least another half hour," she said. "I shall return." Cinder did not give Rhona a chance to respond but quickly slipped into the yard and closed the door behind her. She looked back at the door.

"You know, Mother Rhona," she said quietly. "In a world made of paper, your twin lies feverish in a strange cottage. If this is you, I suppose you survived. And if it is you, I wonder what you know about my mother."

The closed door offered no insight, so Cinder turned to go to the hen house. There, she freed the chickens from their cages and tossed the food scraps to the ground. Then, with the pages buckling in the wind, she continued reading.

> I was relieved to find shelter, but I remembered my mother's warnings never to speak to strangers. But we were desperate; I had no choice. The person took Rhona's limp body and set her upon a bed by the fireplace.
>
> I gathered all my courage. "May I ask, who are you?"
>
> "A friend," said the figure, the voice low and hollow-sounding.
>
> "She needs blankets," I said.
>
> "Yes," was spoken, though I could not see the mouth that spoke it. The individual brought blankets out from a chest. I used one to dry Rhona as best I could, and then I wrapped another around her.

The person in the cloak was not foreboding of stature, but there was little else I could detect. Male or female, I was not certain, young or old, I could not tell. Color of skin and hair were likewise concealed. While I tended to Rhona, this person stirred the fire and pulled dried herbs from a braided garland that hung around the hearth, then put them in a pot with water spooned in from a bucket nearby.

I took Rhona's hand in mind. "We have found shelter," I told her. "We shall wait here until the storm clears."

Her eyes closed, Rhona mumbled something I did not understand. A moment later, she insisted, "What house have we come into?"

"I know not," I told her. "But we are warm and out of the rain."

"Ailen," Rhona said, her eyes still closed. "Some say there is a witch in this wood."

My hopes that we had found a safe haven to pass the night dropped. I glanced over at the resident. "How will I know if it is a witch?"

"Come to me," Rhona said, managing to weakly pry open her eyes. "I can barely stay awake. Be polite to her. Perform any task asked of you. But whatever you do, do not speak your name. If she learns your name or mine, she can force us to do her bidding."

I swallowed. "What if my name is requested? What do I say?"

"Tell the wrong name," Rhona said. "Some other name. Any name you can think of. Even now, between us, do not speak names. We do not know if she can hear us."

Rhona stopped speaking, seized by pain, and I gripped her hand. "Please, please, do not die tonight," I said. "You are my best friend."

"A healing tea," said the resident, bringing a cup of hot liquid to Rhona's bedside. "Made from roots and leaves of the earth. These plants ingested the light from sun and the stars, and sustenance from the earth below, where the remains of all living dissolve and foster new life." A hand came out from the cloak's sleeve. It lifted Rhona's back and placed a small cup inside Rhona's grip. "Drink," said the voice. "The earth heals."

"She needs rest," I said.

"This will help her slumber," came the voice.

I regarded the figure, then dipped into my heart. Did I trust this stranger? I was nervous, but I did not feel that our host meant to harm us.

Finally, Rhona took a sip.

"More," the figure said.

Rhona drank again, and then her eyelids seemed too heavy to remain open.

"Is my friend all right?" I asked, careful not to speak her name.

"She shall rest," the figure said. "And awake at daylight."

A bolt of thunder crashed outside. "Is it night now?" I asked, shuddering. "The darkness is not only from the rain?"

"Yes," the figure said. The person stood in the cloak, face concealed, hands calmly clutched. "Your mother seeks you. She worries that you are alone in the wood."

"My mother," I said, and suddenly, a pang of guilt stabbed me like a knife. "I did not tell her where I was going. Nor that I planned to return."

"She is home now, driven inside by the storm," the figure said. "But she shall wait by the door through the night. She is afraid for you, but she is safe."

I wandered across the cottage to the small window by the door and looked out into a world which was thoroughly dark. I could no longer see the rain, only hear it upon the cottage roof. *Maman*, I thought, wishing I could send her a message with my mind. *I will come home. Don't lose hope.*

"We have things to discuss," the figure said. "Come to table."

I did as I was asked. The figure—I say the figure, the resident, the individual, for I had not yet learned a name, nor anything of the identity—they offered me stew from a pot in the fire. As soon as I smelled the rich, fatty broth, hunger raged inside me. I took a few bites then regarded the individual who sat opposite me. "Thank you," I said.

The figure nodded. "You are welcome," it said.

The humble cottage was similar to the tinker's, constructed of stacked stones, containing a fireplace to cook and keep warm, lanterns for light, hooks on the wall for clothing. Sausages and dried flowers and herbs hung around the hearth. But the individual who inhabited the place was peculiar. All I could discern was the voice. And that was strange too, the tone was not high nor low, though possibly it was both. I finally decided: the voice was multiple. The voice was many voices, each with a different tone, cadence, sound, register.

What sort of being has many voices? I could not recall one from any fairy stories I ever read. I peered at the figure, hoping for a glimpse of some face beneath the hood. But I could see nothing, and devised no other conclusion from our surroundings. Everything around us made sense except for our host.

"Daughter," said the figure, and this time I heard the many voices for sure. "Place your fear to the side. I will hear your questions."

"I am not your daughter," I said.

"In fact," said the resident. "Of a sort, indeed, you are."

I stood up straight then, offended. "My own mother is Leontyne. She waits for me now."

"Is not the one who catches you from your mother's womb a kind of mother?" the resident said.

"The one who..." I muttered. "I don't understand."

I heard then the strangest sound I have ever heard. The resident laughed, and all those voices laughed sounding each so different, each unique in pitch, tone, speed, volume, as though a different person spoke each.

"What shadow are you?" I demanded. "If you are the witch of Hinter Hollow and you intend to eat me and my friend, tell me now. Do not tease me as though I am a mouse and you a cat."

The resident laughed once more, then stopped, and seemed to sigh. "I wish to tell you a story."

Then I saw the strangest thing I'd ever seen. The individual pushed one sleeve away and stretched up its hand, fingers poised as though they were holding something. A wondrous vision appeared from those fingers: circles, spheres, different colors, rising and bouncing just above the fingertips. They reminded me of something I had seen in Professor Bovington's books, luminous stars and galaxies. I was transfixed.

"Once upon forever," the resident said, "there was neither light nor darkness, neither warmth nor chill, and there was nothing to distinguish one from another. This season lasted for a moment, a heartbeat, or possibly millennia—the span cannot be measured for there was no time. But then, the universe chose to be created. An explosion, then mass and motion were brought into being, and those birthed weight, distance, gravity, fire. Those assumed their roles in governing the newborn universe. And the law they ruled by was time."

I felt myself shaking. "What kind of magic is this?"

Its fingers continued to move. The vision changed from stars into planets, all different colors, different sizes, some with rings and moons, some without, all turning at different speeds, and bouncing above the resident's fingers like a child's toy. "Time begat beginnings and ends, and being and not being, and change that was constant. With one exception..."

I stared at those planets so hard my eyes hurt. "What exception?"

Suddenly, a small clock chimed, and a little wooden bird popped out and chirped "coo-coo." My daughter, when I tell you I nearly jumped out of my chair, this is true. Indeed, I nearly fainted.

The resident again laughed that great, strange laugh that was many voices laughing.

"One small piece dropped outside of time, and received no shape, no rules, no limits. Earthbound, yes, timebound and shape-bound, no." The resident closed the hand, and the vision of the planets disappeared.

"I do not understand your words," I said. I was growing impatient. "What game is this? I demand you tell me who you are and what you want from me."

The resident leaned slightly toward me. "We travel now to midnight. In that darkness, one day dies and the next stands in its footprints. The new day is not yet strong enough to resist those things that hide from the glaring light of your closest star."

A terrible thought turned my blood to ice. "If you are the Queen of Gallia," I said. "Or from her, if you seek to end my life, do it now. Please, no more games."

"I know you are frightened, but the sanctuary I offer is true," it said in that strange multiple voice. "Child, you are safe this night. I promise you now, and I promised you the moment of your birth. When the clock strikes midnight, I shall explain more."

"Midnight?" I asked.

The figure's concealed head nodded. "But for now, tea."

Cinder looked around to make sure that nobody was seeking her out. The chickens ate the last of the slop, and she went to the low steps leading up to the coop and sat and continued to read.

The specter rose and went about pouring water into a black pot that hung over the fire. They selected some leaves from dried herbs that surrounded the hearth. I sat in my chair, my back rigid, hands clasped together in my lap. Rhona stirred in her sleep but rested soundly, and I was glad for it. The storm still raged outside, but the claps of thunder and lightning had lessened, and this was a comfort.

After a while, the resident presented a pot of tea, and cups for us both, and then we sipped and waited. I think I had fallen slightly asleep, and startled awake when that little bird popped out of his doorway, announcing the first of a dozen coo-coos.

"Midnight," I said. "You promised you would explain. Who are you?"

"After the final chime," said the resident.

I watched the bird as it poked in and out of the little door. When it was done, I looked to the resident. "Now?" I asked.

"Now," it said.

One hand reached to the hood of the cloak and slowly pulled it back. A face was revealed then, one whose hair and eyes shone. A woman's face. My impression that the voice had been many matched what I beheld—her face was multiple, and each face transformed, glistening and glimmering, shifting with every fluid moment. My eyes could not make sense of it.

The faces were, I finally realized, moving through time. One face seemed an infant, then child, then adolescent, adult, through the stages of middle age to a shrunken and wrinkled old age.

After that, the face appeared drawn and drooping with death, then a shadow of what seemed to be the dust of bones blowing away. In the next moment, the face was fresh and soft like a newborn.

Then the cycle continued.

"I am one who lives in all times at once, both ahead and behind," she said. "I know all of what has happened and what is to come. This is my way in the world, free from the limits of time. Formless, shapeless, timeless, almost nameless."

I swallowed. "So, what name?"

"Nula-na-Nekon." Her face lit up a little as she spoke her name, as though a flame had quickly grown and bubbled.

"Hello," I mumbled, and still, as Rhona had instructed me, I did not speak my own name.

"Humans find the fact of me puzzling," she said, her eyes opening wide. "But I embody the natural law that all things which seem opposite are in fact a single string continued in a circle."

"I don't understand," I whispered.

"The moment a person is born, they are dying," Nula said. "So, birth and death are not opposite, they are one. In the deepest silence, there is sound. In the blackest darkness, there are the far reaches of light. A newborn infant is a future grandparent, they are young and old at the same time. Life continues through cycles, and all cycles connect; this is the way of the world, the way of all worlds."

A bolt of thunder clapped outside, and Rhona mumbled something.

"The girl is sick and well at once," Nula continued. "And you? Frightened and brave, princess and pauper. Queen and commoner both."

"I do not understand," I said, nearly crying. "I wish the rain would end so I could go home."

"The rain," Nula said. "Has already ended. And it shall never stop falling."

"I cannot bear any more riddles," I said.

"No more riddles," Nula said. "But a single revelation. This one, your friend?"

"Promise me she will survive this night," I said. "She is my best friend. My only friend."

"She shall survive," Nula said. "And she will marry your husband. She shall raise your daughter."

"Stop speaking," I said, pressing my hands to my ears. "Please, I don't understand."

Cinder stopped and read those words out loud: *She will marry your husband. She shall raise your daughter.* The prophecy had meant nothing to her mother, but now, so many years later, Cinder understood that this strange Nula had known all along how this story would unfold. Indeed, the prophecy felt like it had been placed there for her to read. For what reason, she could not decipher.

"I can stop," Nula said. "But my silence has no meaning, for these events have already happened. And they are still to come. And they will take place again, one million times over."

"I am so weary," I said. "I have no more wit for games."

"I play no games, child," Nula said. "I roam the earth only as a guest and a witness. Let me tell you a story."

"No more stories," I whispered.

Nula stared at me with those eyes that shifted through time, disclosing an entire lifespan in seconds. Once again, Nula reached to the sleeve of the cloak and pulled it back, and her hand stretched out and up like a claw. The fingers danced, like they were playing a musical instrument, and suddenly there appeared a small cottage, not much different from the one we were in. I heard a woman's voice inside; she was calling out in pain. I recognized it to be my own mother's voice.

"Once upon a time, a young woman was ripe with life, about to push a babe into the world. She was afraid, for she knew that the queen of the country she hailed from wanted to end her child's life."

This story sounded familiar. "The queen?" I asked.

"The door I opened that night could have led to any place at any time, but it led me to your mother's side," Nula said. In the scene that played out atop her fingertips, I watched a hooded figure enter the cabin. My mother's screams grew louder.

"I comforted her and calmed her, and when you were born, it was into my arms you came first. I saw your face even before your own mother did. And... I buried you on an island under a hazel tree."

The more she spoke, the less sense her words made. I wanted to flee that cottage and never look back. I couldn't, though, so I listened only, and tried to remember what I heard. As I write these words, I realize I am transferring to you some prophecy that never made sense to me. Perhaps it will to you.

"Why are you saying these things?" I demanded.

Nula stood up and turned her face slightly toward the fire so the light of the flames shone in her eyes. Her great, mysterious voice spoke: "I am the seed and the great tree hidden inside. I am the wood split into logs on a pile. I am the embers glowing and I am the ashes. All in the same body, the same moment... the start, the conclusion, the return, forever."

Suddenly, in my imagination, I could see all those—seed, sapling, tree, log, embers, ash—and I understood I was in the presence of something eternal, outside the boundaries of human life. Something I could never understand.

"And you," Nula said, turning toward me, "you, dear child, are the princess, the true queen, a promise that will be recognized over generations."

I was so weary, I almost wept. "I don't understand."

"You understand more than you realize," Nula said. "Your friend instructed you not to speak, so I shall tell you your name: in the place called Dunford Town, you are known as Ailen, but your true name is Princess Marguerite Bertrade de Valois. You are the daughter of King Mattieu of Gallia."

These words struck in my heart like a lightning bolt, for this was what my own mother had told me all my life. I could not respond; my gaze fell upon the fire that burned warm and easy, the only familiar thing in the cottage.

"I don't want to be a princess," I said.

Nula smiled slightly, and all the faces from all the ages smiled along. "You already are one," Nula said. "And you never shall be."

At those words, a terrible pain started in my head. Nula had pushed me one riddle too far.

"I wish to lie beside my friend now," I said.

"Yes," Nula said. "First, a gift." Nula reached to the mantle over the fire and brought down a box made of dark wood. Her hand took out a length of leather, and suspended from the middle was something dark and reddish, shaped like a teardrop. Within was an insect, its gossamer wings barely visible against the golden matter.

"Amber," Nula said, and placed the string over my head. "A piece of time preserved. The color translucent, like honey. See how it filters the light. And the creature within. You can see the earth remembering its history."

I held the amber up. Each time I moved it, a different shade of gold lit up within it, like a slow-moving flame. "Why are you giving me this?" I asked.

"Ailen, Princess Marguerite of Gallia, you have been brave this night," Nula said. "I have shown you things most people never see. You have glimpsed into the very soul of time. Because I watched you move between the realms, from unbirthed to birthed, you and I are bound. I am always nearby. I cannot change beginnings or endings, but I am witness to all. No matter what befalls you, this amulet shall remind you who you are."

"Nula," I said. "What sort of being are you?"

"Well," Nula said, that strange face lighting up again, smiling a little. "Your kind has many words for me. Fairy, witch, sorcerer, shape-shifter. Others too. None are precise. I am the passage and flattening of time. I am part of nature and outside it." She curled her fingers, and once again the planets appeared at her fingertips. "I was formed when the planets started their feverish spinning, burning scoria flung off from a wild, burning star. I walked the surface of this place long before humans grew legs and stood upright. And I shall remain until time shatters and scatters in a hazy dust of gravity, fire and oblivion."

I sighed. "I was only trying to work out whether you are good or bad…"

"What do you think, child?"

I shrugged. "If you were going to hurt me, I think you would have done so already, and saved your energy in speaking all these strange things."

Nula laughed. "Rest, child," said the specter, and Nula rose and led me to the bed where Rhona slept, and tucked me in beside her. I fell asleep then, holding on to the amber.

Chapter Thirteen

The chickens pecked at Cinder's feet, and she looked up. This chapter of her mother's story was the strangest yet. She looked back at the words on the page. What had the specter said of Rhona? *At once, friend and foe. She will marry your husband. She shall raise your daughter.*

A chill went down her spine, then, for she understood: the prophecy had come true. And it was not the only one. What else had Nula said? *I saw your face even before your own mother did. And I buried you on an island under a hazel tree.*

I buried you on an island under a hazel tree.

"Cinder!" came Rhona's impatient voice from the house. "Cinder, where are you?"

"I am coming," she called back. Cinder tucked the letter back into her apron pocket and breathed the cold morning air. She looked at the chickens. "Enjoy the morning, girls," she said.

She went into the kitchen. Rhona awaited her there, and began chattering that the clock now showed the seventh hour, and the girls would be up soon. Cinder may as well begin preparing the tea now, so they wouldn't have to wait.

"And then, please come to my chamber and fix my fire," Rhona said. "I must return to bed and close my eyes for a while."

Cinder looked at Rhona and her mind flattened time: in her stepmother, she saw a young girl who'd been berated by her own family her whole life and now lay sick and feverish in a strange cottage, stranded in the woods in the middle of a storm.

"Has your discomfort improved?" she asked.

Rhona looked at her with an odd, suspicious expression. "Yes, the pain in my head has subsided some."

"Good," Cinder said. "I'm glad."

Rhona returned to her bedroom and Cinder remained in the kitchen alone, relieved for a moment of solitude. She stoked the fire again and put on a kettle of water, then set out the tea pot and cups. Henry uncurled himself and stretched; Cinder poured fresh milk into a small pot and warmed it, then poured it into his bowl. He ambled over and took a few sips. Cinder patted his back and considered the day's chores: bake bread, sweep the floors, fold and iron the clothes she had washed the day before, and others.

But her mind was full of echoes from her mother's letter: who was this Nula who dallied with the planets and stars as though they were toys? Had she really aided in her mother's birth?

Her mother described Nula as a hooded figure with a concealed face—was she Cinder's Watcher? Had her face appeared in the clock? If she was the very soul of time, she might have an affinity for clocks.

And Cinder's mother had been the daughter of a king. Had Cinder inherited her mother's royal blood? Of course, she had inherited the blood itself. Some claim to a throne? Impossible.

Cinder smiled. "Henry, you mustn't let me think such foolish thoughts," she told him. "I am best when rooted in the solid and the real. Don't you agree?" Henry ignored her and continued lapping his milk. "Yes, I knew you would."

While considering time, she took down the clock to wind it. She recalled what had happened the previous day, and she watched the clock face carefully, nervous to see whether it would again take on the guise of a human face. Then, before her eyes, a cloud slowly formed around the numbers on the face of the clock. Just under the numerals ten and two, a pair of eyes emerged, and the clock took on the ghostly face of a woman, wrinkled with age.

Cinder gasped. She reached to the center of the clock as though touching it might help her understand, then quickly withdrew. She did not want to dissolve the spell, but she also did not want it to speak to her. Still, something about the face seemed familiar. She examined it more closely. It was a woman's face. The nose was sharp, lips thin, and the eyes, gray green and rheumy, pointed in different directions. Cinder realized she knew a woman who resembled that vision, but she had not seen her in many years.

"Miss Nollie," she whispered. "Is that you?" But the face only hovered and watched her. It did not speak.

Now she was certain: this was the face of Miss Nollie Washbucket, a lady who resided at the edge of Kilderbrae town. Cinder had only spoken to her once, after her mother died. She had been seven years old. Her father had sent her to the town bakery for butter cookies. That day, Cinder took a different route and passed a cottage she had never seen before. It sat back against the woods, as though emerging from the forest. The yard was encircled with a fence of rough-hewn logs. Behind that, she spotted a cur on a line. The dog was small in size, and had a gray and black coat, spotted white. He sat in the yard and watched her, and did not bark or lunge or show his teeth. His eyes were deep brown, and his face was so ugly, she fell in love instantly.

She went up to the fence and stood before it. "Hello," she'd said out loud.

The dog cocked his head and looked at her, his pointed ears straight up.

"Are you lonely, boy?" she asked. He whined in a way that seemed to be answering, yes.

She looked to make sure nobody was around, then slipped behind the fence. The dog let her pat his head and scratch his ears.

"Who tied you up?" she asked. "If I was stuck by myself in a yard, I'd be miserable. You and me, we're the same. We like to wander and roam. It makes us feel less lonely."

The rope was tied to the dog's neck with a simple bowline knot. Cinder's father had taught her how to tie and untie every knot, for that was essential education aboard a ship. In a moment, the dog was free. "Promise me you will take care," she said to the dog. "Do not get hurt or eaten. Have wonderful adventures. Go, now, and find fun, enough for both of us."

The dog licked her face and ran off into the woods.

She watched him go, then continued her walk feeling she'd done a good deed. But in town, she was stopped by an old woman who wore a kerchief around her head like a pirate. The woman's eyes pointed away from each other and Cinder did not know which she should look at.

"You're the child that visited my house," the woman hissed. "What business have you with other people's animals?" Cinder tried to protest, but the woman continued. "You loosed my dog into the wood. Did your mother not teach you manners?"

Young Cinder could barely speak. She did not understand how the woman could know this unless she'd watched from inside the house. Cinder was terrified the old woman would kill her with her staring eyes.

"Your dog had a roaming heart," she said. "You cannot lock up creatures who have roaming hearts. It hurts them. It hurts the same as pain of the flesh."

Mistress Washbucket crossed her arms and looked at the girl. "But tell me this," she said. "What is to become of a dog loose in the world who would seek to become friends with foxes, bobcats and bears, all them what would gobble the poor hound in one bite?"

"I told him to be careful," she said.

"That counts for little if a dog meets a bear," said Nollie. "Forty times his size, with biting teeth and tearing claws."

Cinder held her jaw tight and looked Nollie in the eye. "There are no bears in Kilderbrae Wood."

Mistress Washbucket squinted and snickered. "Child, you never know what mysteries lurk in the heart of the forest. There's things out there hungry for blood. Maybe even a child's blood."

Cinder was nervous but she held her ground. "You don't frighten me."

Mistress Washbucket regarded Cinder and nodded slightly, a mysterious smile upon her cracked lips, then stood back up.

"Listen now, child, some things need only be said once. First, don't let free other peoples' animals. They're safe when they're held in place. They eat, they nap, they are loved." She crossed her arms and looked about, then continued. "And if ever you need help, come find Nollie Washbucket. Could be Mistress Washbucket knows how to fix a bit of this and that. Do you understand?"

Cinder had been confused and surprised. Why would Mistress Washbucket offer to help when Cinder had just sent her dog off into the woods, possibly never to return? She would have been less surprised if Mistress Washbucket had set a curse upon her head.

So, why would the woman's face appear suddenly in the kitchen clock two days in a row? Cinder patted Henry as he snored softly in his bed by the fire. Mistress Washbucket had been ancient back then; was she still among the living? If she was, what kind of help could she offer? Everybody believed Mistress Washbucket was mad; but maybe she knew of some magic that could fix an old dress. Cinder supposed it was worth the time to suit up Duncan, the horse, and take a ride into town.

―❦―

But Nollie Washbucket was not so easy to find. Cinder started her search at the woman's cottage outside the town borders, tucked neatly in the woods on a road that twisted up a hill. She found the place quickly for it appeared the same as it did when she was seven. No dog lay in the yard, but chickens clucked happily in their coop.

Cinder went to the door and knocked, but no answer came. Wisps of smoke rose from the chimney. Nobody was home now, but someone inhabited the house.

Then Cinder rode Duncan into town. At the market, she asked the bread baker, the cheese-maker, and a washer-woman whether Mistress Washbucket lived still. Each said they had not seen her recently. Finally, Cinder came upon the fishmonger and asked him.

"Oh, she's around. Unless she died within the past hour," he said, as he sliced the skin off a fish as though slipping a sweater off a child. "I just saw her at the public house, in the corner, playing chess with Widow Irvine."

"The public house?" Cinder asked. "Are you certain?"

"She elbowed me ribs as I walked past, just to pester me," he said.

Cinder hated the public house. After her mother had fallen ill, she'd needed to go there sometimes to find her father when he was conducting business with his ships' captains. The place was always crowded with loud, boisterous men. A young girl in the public house was almost invisible, but those who happened to notice her bore terrible smiles, eyes wide and hungry at the sight of her, like wolves seeking supper.

Each time she passed through, she made herself brave by believing she was.

This time, too, she tried to assume a mask of courage, though she was taller now, and on a sunny morning, the public house was not as busy and frightening as it had once been. The place still reeked of sour ale and stale smoke. Sunlight streamed through the windows, and in the far corner of a back room, she saw them at a table, two ladies, each as old as the moon, playing chess and drinking tankards of ale. Their cackles rang out from across the room.

Cinder walked up to the women, but suddenly, her throat became dry and all possibility of words escaped her. She stood silently beside the table, watching the chess game. The women seemed not to notice her but continued to laugh, until finally they stopped.

"How, now," said Mistress Washbucket. Her hair was as it had been all those years ago, tucked into a kerchief wrapped around her head, straggly tendrils falling loose around her long, thin face. And as before, her eyes seemed to roll about in their sockets independently of each other. "We have a visitor, Widow Irvine."

Widow Irvine's silver hair was pulled back neatly in a chignon. Her face was soft and circular like a round of dough, and she wore upon her nose a pair of spectacles with a tarnished frame. "Indeed, we do, Mistress Washbucket," she said, her voice higher and clearer than her companion's. "Just as you said we would. How do you do that? You always know what will happen. I don't know why I play chess with you. I can never win."

"Aye," Mistress Washbucket said, tapping her long fingers on the table. "But I pay for the ale, and we do have quite a laugh, don't we, Widow Irvine?"

"Indeed, Mistress Washbucket," she said. "And if you promise to always pay for the ale, I promise to always let you cheat."

Mistress Washbucket lifted up her tankard. "It's a deal," she declared, and the two women laughed, then toasted and drank.

Finally, Mistress Washbucket noticed again that Cinder was yet standing there. "Take a seat, anyway, girl," she said to Cinder. Cinder looked at Mistress Washbucket's face, three large teeth stuck out in the front and her cheekbones were high, her skin hanging upon them like a wet sheet, and spotted like chicken flesh. Her eyes seemed a color in motion from dark green to translucent gray. But if her vision was at all compromised, it did not impede her ability to play chess.

Cinder pulled a chair over to their table, sat down on the edge of it and pushed her hood aside.

"It's the Barclay girl, dear," said Widow Irvine, as she moved a rook forward three squares. "How nice to see you, miss. I knew your parents. So sad what became of them. First the mother, then the father. Oh, so sad."

"Don't be too happy to see this one," Mistress Washbucket said as she leaned over and moved a knight. "Years ago, this urchin liberated my dog."

"I said I was sorry," Cinder muttered.

The Widow Irvine moved her rook ahead three spaces. Then Mistress Washbucket studied the board, lifted a bishop and considered which way to move it. "You said many things, child, but none of them included the word, 'sorry.'"

"Well, I was," Cinder said. "And I still am."

Widow Irvine chuckled. "Mistress Washbucket had the loveliest old hound, a mongrel named Albert," she said. "His coat was black and gray and spotted. He died last year. He was such a love, he'd melt with joy when anyone scratched his darling pointed ears."

Cinder glared at Mistress Washbucket and crossed her arms. "He sounds like the twin of the hound I met in your yard years ago."

Mistress Washbucket looked up sheepishly. "After you freed him, Albert had the good sense to come home," she said. "Actually, he was home before tea. Good thing, for some bear would have made a neat snack of him."

"There are no bears in the Kilderbrae Woods," Cinder said. "Mistress Washbucket, ma'am. Apologies for the interruption, but I must ask you a question."

"One moment," she said. She moved a black queen, topped with a tiny crown, and knocked down the opposing white king. "Check mate."

Widow Irvine sighed. "Oh, good," she said. "I have earned my ale and now I can go home for a nap. Grand game, love. Same time tomorrow?"

"If I am still alive, I'd like nothing more," Mistress Washbucket said.

"Lovely to see you, Miss Barclay," Widow Irvine said.

"You as well, ma'am," Cinder said.

As Widow Irvine walked away, Mistress Washbucket began to carefully put the chess pieces away in a small box. When she had one last piece, she held it up to show Cinder.

"It's the queen, this one, the most powerful piece in the group. See the delicate crown?" She touched the top of the piece. "Nothing delicate or frail about any queens I know. I once knew a queen who killed her own sister. By daylight. Left the woman's daughter, the queen's own niece, almost an orphan. Orphan enough, for she did not know her father."

"That's tragic," Cinder said.

"The girl fled to safety," Mistress Washbucket said, fixing her strange, changing eyes on the queen. "She changed her name and found sanctuary. The queen's soldiers never found her." She turned the piece as though ensuring that Cinder could view it from all sides. "Oh, the queen looked everywhere. Tore up houses to see if the girl was hiding within. Her soldiers bludgeoned anyone suspected of knowing where the girl was. But she was in a rowboat being taken to an island by a lad she would someday marry. And that girl, in her childhood name, at least, was never heard from again."

Cinder peered at the woman. "This resembles my mother's tale," she said. "Did you know my mother?"

"Only in passing, my child," Nollie Washbucket said. "This is not what you came to ask me, is it?"

"No," Cinder said. She bolstered up her courage. "Mistress, why has your face been appearing in my clock?"

Nollie Washbucket shrugged. "How am I to know where my face appears and where not? Faces sometimes go places by themselves like stray cats, yeah?"

"In my experience, they rarely do," Cinder said.

"Then we've had differing experiences," she said. She packed up the rest of the game and stood to leave. "Don't waste my time, love, I have chickens to tend. If you have a real question, speak it. If not, I wish thee well."

Mistress Washbucket began to walk away from the table, and Cinder swallowed and took a breath. "Please," Cinder said. "All those years ago, when I freed your dog? You said that if I needed help, I could ask you. What did you mean? Are you a—I mean, are you able to cast spells and such?"

Mistress Washbucket turned. "Girlie," she exclaimed. "I won't have my time wasted. You deign to come in here and interrupt my game, and then dance around like I am made of time?" She smiled, and revealed her gums, almost empty of teeth. "You want help, ask the real, right question."

Cinder felt her breath become shallow. "I want... I very much want...to go to the king's ball, but I need help. I need a dress. And shoes, I suppose. Mistress Washbucket, I can't do it by myself, and my family will not help me. Can you, are you able to help? Tell me no and I shall waste not another of your earthly moments."

Nollie fixed her drifting eyes upon Cinder. She reached to the table, lifted her ale tankard and drank, then let the tankard fall to the table with a thunk. "Hate to leave a finger of drink behind. I might have a spool of thread rolling about my cottage somewhere. If I find it, I will send it to Bowmore House."

Cinder stood and began to take leave. "I will tell you the same thing

I told my father when I used to fetch him from this place," she said. "Ale makes your breath smell like goat's piss. Good day."

"By the by, girlie," Mistress Washbucket said, grabbing Cinder's arm. "You should take care. You seen the soldiers marching around town? They're from Gallia. They are on the hunt."

"Who are they seeking?" Cinder asked, wrenching her arm away. "An old lady with a crooked smile? If they ask me where you are, I'll send them to the public house."

Cinder went to her horse and rode him back along the main road to the house. As she went, a light rain began to fall. Why would someone send their face to appear in a clock and then offer no help, no clue, no suggestion for what to do next? Magic is folly, Cinder thought. Hope is folly.

Miss Nollie had been Cinder's last hope. Now, she was alone with her undertaking to find or make a gown. The cost of failure was to miss the ball, miss the chance to dance in the king's castle with Alban.

Alban. He'd seemed to genuinely want her there. That afternoon dancing at Sayre Cliffs, warm sunshine upon their faces, soft clover beneath their feet, might have been one of the happiest episodes of her whole life.

It was beautiful before they had kissed. But the kiss had awakened something inside her. She wanted to feel that again. She longed for it.

When she reached home, she examined her mother's old dress as if searching for clues. She wished she could revive it, but she did not know how she might when the frock was so worn and ancient in style, and had never been a grand frock to begin with. One moment, she thought it might be possible to breathe life into the old thing, the next she thought the dress better used if shredded for rags.

Think not on the ball, she told herself again. *It is simply not my fate.*

Chapter Fourteen

Two days before the ball, by afternoon, Finn was in the courtyard of the castle training on the arts of swordcraft with Sir Godfrey, one of the king's knights. Finn held the sword up with both hands over his head to assume a high guard position.

"Legs apart, stand strong," Sir Godfrey ordered, standing the same way. "Begin."

Finn advanced and swung and Sir Godfrey lifted his sword to defend against Finn's and hopped backward.

"Arms up," Godfrey directed. "Quick. Quicker!"

Finn drew his sword back and thrust it at Godfrey, and they continued in the mode of strike/counterstrike.

"In battle, your life depends on your ability to think and act swiftly and without doubt or fear," Godfrey said. "Speed is your father's specialty."

"I have heard this," Finn said. "From my father, my mother, and every bard who comes to sing of the great king's conquests." Finn grunted as he swung.

"I have stood beside your father in battle," Godfrey said. "Many times, he dueled an opponent who I thought would be his last. But King Humphry always proved me wrong. He has a fleet mind and a strong arm, and those two saved him every time."

"Fights my father started," Finn said. "What glory is there in achieving victory when advancing against small principalities? People die, and in the end, it is only a matter of glory for the sovereign."

Godfrey blocked Finn's swinging sword over their heads and held it in place. "Why young Finn," he said. "The things you describe are the essence of what it means to be king."

Finn rested his sword. "Some days, I am not sure I was cut from the right purple velvet cloth," he said, wiping his forehead with the back of his sleeve.

Godfrey raised his sword over his head. "When the time comes, you shall be a fine leader. Lift your blade. We fight to the death."

Finn lifted up his sword and repeated the exercise of swift, thrust and parry.

"Better," Godfrey said. "Much better." They dueled for a while, then Finn pointed his sword tip point down.

"Ahh, the fool's guard. Well chosen, my prince," Godfrey said. He lunged, and Finn countered him by propelling his sword up and over, and ended in a position that might have punctured his tutor's throat had the blade not been blunted.

"Outstanding," Godfrey said. "You are learning."

"Pardon, Your Highness," came a voice, and Finn pulled his sword away and looked at the speaker. One of the king's servants stood nearby. "The majesties have requested your presence in the ballroom."

Finn glanced at his teacher. "That's fine, we're done for today," Godfrey said.

Finn was breathless, for he and Sir Godfrey had been sparring all afternoon. He took a cloth and wiped his forehead and neck, and poured water from a pitcher into a cup and drank. Then he followed the servants into the ballroom and found his parents meandering through, surveying preparations for the ball. Lamps circled the room, each fitted with fresh candles. Workers stood on ladders, cleaning the chandeliers. Long tables had been built and set against one wall, and servants were outfitting them with fresh, white cloths.

"Greetings, Finn," the queen said, stretching out her arms. "Arrangements are coming along well, don't you agree? The last task will be polishing the floor so it gleams. Artisans are creating lovely topiaries and flower arrangements. The cooks are preparing a feast and baking cakes. The orchestra will arrive tonight to practice."

"It will be wonderful, Mother," Finn said.

"Did Thomas find you?" the king asked. "Grand news from Spitzbergen."

"I have not seen the earl today," Finn said. "What brings him west?"

"He came as an emissary for his grandfather, George, Duke of Lorne," the king said.

"The kingmaker?" Finn said. Suddenly, he understood that something important had happened. "What has occurred?"

"How does Finn not know?" the queen asked the king. "You promised you would tell him."

"I had not seen the lad until now," the king said.

"Finn, the duchess was located and her marriage annulled," she said. "The Duke insists that your marriage to her proceed as planned."

Finn felt his face fall.

"Son," the king said. "Do not sulk. This is very good news."

His mother took his hands in hers. "It is," she said. "For all of us. But take heart, we shall not cancel the ball. In fact, we will use the event to announce your upcoming marriage."

"The political alliance this union shall create is one we cannot do without," said the king.

Finn mused. "But…we spoke of my choosing a bride. One of the people."

"I know you are taken with this young lady," said the queen. "But you will marry Duchess Agnatha. In time, this other girl shall fade from memory. And no doubt, if she is as attractive and captivating as you say, she shall find a husband in due course."

"Have I no choice in this matter?" said Finn. "We are discussing the person with whom I shall spend my life."

"Yours is to prepare to become sovereign of Braemuir," said the king. "The woman you marry has nothing to do with the heart. After Agnatha bears you sons, you may take a lover—"

"Pardon me," said the queen. "*Your* wife is standing just beside you."

"*I* never would, my queen," he said. Humphry took his wife's hand and kissed it. "I am simply saying that this is an accepted practice."

"It is not accepted by me," she said.

"You treat my choice of bride as though it is no more than a clerical matter," Finn said.

"Finn, you must accept that this girl was an illusion," the queen said. "She wasn't real. You do not even know her name. You must accept the role you were born to claim. And this begins with a marriage that serves the kingdom."

Finn tried to believe that he had imagined the girl, that he had been dreaming out on the cliffs all these years. But that kiss had been no illusion. He had not dreamed his love for her. "What about my heart?"

The king and the queen exchanged a long look. "If this girl attends the ball, you must tell her goodbye," the king said, gravely.

Finn regarded his parents adorned in their fine regalia. What was the meaning of all this pageantry? The king in his castle, the queen on her throne, a family leading a region, defending their power through battle, fostering alliances, marrying for strategic placement. The work of fighting and planning to hold their place on the chess board had no end. And his heirs would spend their lives fighting, marrying, producing heirs and dying to protect the throne and their family name. The endeavor for power was constant, seeking to win and defend for no other reason than to record their names and deeds in history books. Suddenly, he wasn't sure how important these pursuits were.

"What if I do not?" he said.

"What if you don't—" asked the king.

"Say goodbye to her," said Finn. "What if I choose her?"

"Finn, you seem to not realize how important this is," the queen said.

"The crown prince must abide by certain principles," said the king. "If you cannot uphold these…"

"Finn knows his responsibility," the queen said. "He would never consider—"

"Abdicating?" Finn said. "Is that what it is called?"

"Oh, Finn," said the queen, her face twisted with concern. "This girl cannot be worth losing everything."

Finn thought for a moment. If there was a future to pursue that bonded together him and the girl—he would someday learn her name—taking a chance to seek that future was not a task he likened to losing.

The day before the ball, Rhona gained a terrible pain in her belly, and a pain in her head bloomed to match it. She knew it was likely from her endless worrying about the ball and the fate of their home, but she could not stop her mind from its torturous churning. She walked about the house with her hands on her midsection, quietly wincing and sighing. She made a tea with dried mint and comfrey, but a few sips only made her sleepy. What would she do if Lord Warin took their home? She could not put the girls through that. Especially Cinder—the house was her legacy, and Rhona could not bear the possibility that she might lose it.

Throughout the day, everyone at Bowmore House was in a frenzy preparing. Orla and Liisi had woken early to complete the finishing touches on their gowns, and Rhona had helped. After that, Rhona played the piano so Orla and Liisi could practice dancing. Orla took the lead and Liisi the follow; Rhona judged their efforts to be adequate, perhaps more procedure than art—Liisi frowned and counted steps with her mouth as she performed them—but neither girl would be entirely lost on the dance floor. By afternoon, both girls retired to their rooms to rest, and finally, Rhona had the chance to work on her own dress: long black satin, a widow's gown.

After years of mourning Gerik, could she relinquish the black? No, her heart still mourned: the loss of her first husband, the loss of her second husband, and her daughter's fading life. The loss of a carefree life, which she had never known. And she dreaded that Lord Warin would reveal a crime she never committed and in doing so, make public the truth about her beginnings: she was an orphan from nowhere, abandoned by her own mother, and not worth the shoes on her feet nor the dirt underneath them.

She had worked to convince the world otherwise by holding her head high. She judged the worthiness of others so she could act elite. And the charade had succeeded: she'd procured a well-heeled first husband and a second husband who'd had adequate means, at least while he was alive. The mask she carried bore a terrible weight. Perhaps, she thought, black was the only color she had any right to wear.

As she sat in her bedroom beside the boarded-up windows, repairing a dress that she had repaired many times, Rhona worried about what was ahead. I should set this house on fire, she thought. At least then, Warin will not gain a benefit from this game.

After all, Rhona had lived through other fires.

She shook her head to free herself of these dark thoughts. She wanted to think about the ball. The music would be exquisite; the food magnificent. What would it be to meet the king in person? She chided herself; the royal family would not have time to greet everyone. And what of it anyway? They were only ordinary people with golden crowns upon their heads.

She stopped her needle to gaze upon a ray of sunlight spilling through a crack in the window boards. They would not be the first royals she had encountered. Ailen had been a princess. After they parted ways that day so long ago, she never learned her friend's fate. In lonely times, of which she'd had many, she imagined what it might have been like if they'd both remained in Dunford: they might have each married and raised children in nearby houses. They might have stayed friends.

She wished she had a friend now, another adult who would allow her to share her troubles, a woman, perhaps, who had experienced some of the difficulty and confusion of raising children.

She'd never had another friend like Ailen. She'd never had another friend.

Rhona went back to sewing and pricked her finger on a pin tucked into the dark fabric.

"Oh, bother," she said.

She put her finger to her mouth so the blood would not stain her dress, but her bleeding continued. She put down her needlework and walked to the kitchen seeking water to rinse the wound and a clean rag.

"Cinder?" she called. "Cinder!"

But Cinder was not in the kitchen, nor any other room. Perplexed, Rhona went outside and walked around the yard, calling. Cinder was not there.

How could she ramble off on this day when there was so much to do? "That child," she exclaimed.

Rhona walked through the yard and pressed her arms around herself in the chill wind. The chickens pecked about her feet, and Henry the cat, who was older than some hills, slept in the sunshine, unbothered by the hens.

"Where does that girl disappear to? You probably know best of all," Rhona said, addressing the sleeping cat. She nudged him gently with her toe and he raised his head to peer at her with sleepy eyes. "And who is this rogue who dares ask a young lady to the ball without consulting her family?"

Henry, who was quite deaf, only put his head down and curled back up. The cat's indifference and the chickens' lack of interest frustrated Rhona more. Pain stabbed her from inside then, inspiring her to rage. She went inside and donned a thick pair of woolen socks and her sturdiest shoes and walked into town, determined to find the girl. As she marched upon the dusty road, tall Rhona in her housedress, her face made severe by time and worry, was quite a spectacle for the carriages and wagons that happened to pass. The one or two who called to her received only a stony glare.

Once Rhona arrived in town, she did not know where to begin looking. She wandered toward the market and suddenly heard a high voice. "Afternoon, Mrs. Barclay," said a woman.

Rhona blinked and had to look around before she saw the doughy face that was the source of the words. "Mrs. Etwall," she said without smiling. "How lovely to see you."

The short woman pushed a small wooden cart with the words "Etwall Hand-Pies" painted on the side. "Won't you have a pasty, you look terrible thin. They're hot and quite good today, if I do say so myself," Mrs. Etwall said. "My husband used to say, you make a tasty pasty, Mrs. Etwall. I didn't call him a liar that time."

The smell of meat pies made Rhona hungry. "That would be very kind, Mrs. Etwall," she said. "If you have a small one, I would relieve you of it. But I haven't any coin with me..."

Mrs. Etwall handed Rhona a steaming pastry wrapped in newspaper. "No coin needed, my dear." Rhona ate, and ate heartily. The pain in her belly began to subside.

"Well," said Mrs. Etwall. "The whole town's got the fever, everyone eager for the ball. Your girls must be terrible excited! Getting ready is half the fun. No king ever gave a ball at the castle when I was a young lady. But I would have loved it. Oh, to be a young person today..."

"Mrs. Etwall," Rhona said. "I am seeking my stepdaughter, Cinder. Have you seen her?"

"Not today," Mrs. Etwall said. "But I have of recent. When was that, again? Not yesterday, I don't imagine. Two, perhaps three days ago. Then again, yesterday perhaps. I saw her enter the public house."

"The public—" Rhona exclaimed. "What on earth was she doing there?"

"I shouldn't know. I didn't follow her inside," she said.

"Thank you for the pie, Mrs. Etwall," Rhona said. "Please, excuse me."

Rhona marched across the market square to the door of the public house, flung it open and walked inside. She tried to appear calm as she searched for her ward, but her fury was so palpable, the whole room grew silent. At the back of the establishment, Rhona spotted two biddies tucked in a corner table, drinking ale and playing chess, cackling like chickens. Rhona guessed that those two passed many hours in the public house, so she went straight to them.

"Good day, Mistress Washbucket, Widow Irvine," Rhona said.

"Well, look what the weather blew in," Mistress Washbucket said, and she sucked on her cigar.

"Mrs. Barclay, how nice to see you," said Widow Irvine. "Would you care to join us?"

Rhona had strong opinions about people who had nothing better to do than spend the afternoon in the public house, but she strained to keep her opinions silent.

"Thank you, no," she said. "I am seeking my late husband's daughter, a girl we call Cinder. Have you seen her?"

"Have we?" Widow Irvine asked, looking sidelong at Mistress Washbucket.

"Why do you seek her?" Mistress Washbucket said, as she gestured with her fat cigar. "Has she failed to complete her chores?"

"I was told she came in here recently," Rhona said, holding her hands together at her center, her head high. "I wish to learn what business she had in a place like this."

"On that note, Mistress Washbucket," Widow Irvine said, "what business do *we* have in a place like this?"

"Nobody gives us the boot, so we keep returning," Mistress Washbucket said, and the two laughed and lifted their tankards to each other.

Rhona looked back and forth between them. She would not stand for these two drunks mocking her. "If she was here..." she said, and her voice sounded fierce and breathless even to her. "If she was meeting a young man, I must know."

"I noticed no young man," said Widow Irvine. "Did you, Mistress Washbucket?"

"Come now, Mrs. Barclay," said Mistress Washbucket. "The public house is full of men, young, old, past their prime, wrapped in swaddling blankets and all the stages in between. Can't imagine the lady was here and didn't see one of them. Unless her eyes stopped working."

Widow Irvine gasped. "Wouldn't that be a tragedy though? With one so young. Oh, my dear, I hope that did not happen."

"That is not what I am asking," exclaimed Rhona. Now she was furious. "Was Cinder here? Did you see her? Was she meeting a gentleman?"

"Oh, my, now this one's angry," said Widow Irvine. "Mistress Washbucket, what was the name of the girl that was here the other day? Is she the one this lady is asking about?"

Mistress Washbucket fixed one of her wandering eyes upon her friend. "I can't remember exactly," she said. "Someone was here, but my brain isn't..." She tapped her head and gave Rhona a dubious look.

"Pretty girl, she was," said Widow Irvine. "Hair, reddish brownish. Slender. She had a look of fiery determination in her eyes. Don't you recall?"

Mistress Washbucket tipped her face down and glared at her friend more. "Memory fails, dear."

Rhona looked back and forth between their faces, then nodded. "I see," she finally said. "You're protecting her. Let me be clear: if she came here to meet a young man, your lying to me does not help. My duty is to keep her safe. I cannot have her knocking about the public house, convening with strange men. Not now, before the king's ball. Nor any day. You two have provided me no help at all, so I decline to bid you gratitude and only wish you both an agreeable day."

Mistress Washbucket glared at the dour woman as she pushed her way out the door.

"Well, that lady was rude," said Widow Irvine, as she looked over her spectacles at the chess board. "Whose turn is it, dear? I've lost track."

Mistress Washbucket smiled vaguely and took a puff from her cigar. "My move comes next," she said. "Actually, Widow Irvine, I was planning to let the chips fall where they might on their own. All paths find their way with me or without me. But now I'm bothered."

"Move a piece is all, dear," Widow Irvine said in exasperation. "Make some motion. You shall win all the same. You always do."

"Well, truly," Mistress Washbucket said, lifting her rook and checkmating the Widow Irvine's king. "This is one puzzle I'll have to consider with my eyes open. Luckily, the one thing I have is time."

Chapter Fifteen

That same day, Cinder had spent the morning helping Liisi and Orla put the finishing touches on their dresses. After that, the girls had their own dance lesson in the parlor, which Cinder watched for a moment. Liisi held her body stiff and glared straight past Orla's face, counting as she took wooden steps. Cinder had the impression that both girls had learned to dance from reading a book. Then, the girls and Mother Rhona retired to their rooms to rest for the afternoon, so Cinder journeyed to Sayre Cliffs. She hoped to find Alban. She wanted to tell him in person that she would not attend the ball. And not only this, she needed to release him forever. She needed to tell him goodbye.

She wondered how much of her life she would explain. Should she tell him how deeply she cared for him? Would she say how she wished she could be with him every day, that her body ached for his touch? That she would never forget his lips upon hers?

After so many goodbyes in her life, she did not think she could bear to say those words to Alban. She ached with longing for the world to turn back to a time when her friend might happen to appear on the cliffs, and their talk would be a light in Cinder's heart for days to come.

Why couldn't there be some dial that would bring her back to other times, relationships the way they had been? She wished the world kept pockets of time, like chapters in a book, so she could return to them.

Despair hung over her heart, heavy like mud. The day was chilly and the breeze off the water blew cold. As always, she searched the horizon for some sign of St. Kiana. What had her father told her mother? The island was little more than a rock in the sea, and you could stand in one spot and see the sun rise in the morning and set at night.

When Alban did not appear, Cinder brought her mother's letter from her pack. She was ready to read the final piece.

Rhona and I awoke the next morning in a guest bedroom at Ara Dun, she tucked into a warm, soft bed, and I, on a small cot upon the floor, my foot wrapped in clean strips of cloth. To this day, I cannot explain how we arrived there, nor who called the doctor. Neither of us had any memory of it. All I can report is that we each recovered and the amber was still draped around my neck. Were it not for that trinket, I likely would have believed I dreamed my encounter with Nula-na-Nekon.

After I went home, my mother had words for me—more than a few, none complimentary, many delivered in a loud, high tone, some in her native Gallic tongue. She'd been so very worried, and I hated what anguish I'd put her through. After that, Rhona was no longer welcomed in our home, and Maman enrolled me in manners school. I was old enough, she said, to mingle with the fine daughters of Dunford Town and learn to conduct myself like a proper lady.

I made new friends at school. I did. But I never made another friend like my beloved Rhona.

Five summers passed in Dunford Town, and five winters too. Rhona remained at Ara Dun, but what else occurred in her life, I never learned, for we kept our distance. On a day in spring when I was sixteen years, something happened: in a clearing off the town square, there appeared burlap tents, more than a dozen, housing soldiers from a foreign land. The soldiers meandered in the clearing, some drinking from tin cups, others cooking over a fire pit, others practicing sword fighting. I hid behind a tree and watched. Two walked past me and I heard them speak. It was my mother's Gallic tongue.

I rushed home and found Maman in her shop with the young ladies who helped her in her dress craft, sitting in a circle, laughing and gossiping. Maman instructed me to greet each lady with a small curtsy, but when I finally told her there were soldiers from Gallia in town, she stopped chattering and stared at me, her face drained of color.

The ladies informed Maman that they'd heard the soldiers were searching for someone, and the Lord Mayor had assured everyone that this matter did not regard the residents of Dunford Town. The ladies thought it quite wonderful that soldiers from a foreign land were encamped in the square. One giggled and wondered if she might find a husband among them. Another rubbed her pregnant belly and said she was set in that department.

I quietly asked Maman what we should do. She chewed her lip and rubbed her forehead. I had never seen my mother so worried.

"Is there some chance it's not—" I asked.

"No, my dear," Maman said. "It is."

The moment my confident, brave Maman became afraid, the whole world changed. The situation was dire. Maman looked up, smiled and clapped her hands as though inciting a band to begin playing.

"Thank you, friends, this is enough for today. We have worked hard this week, yes? Take tomorrow as a holiday."

The ladies laughed and smiled, delighted to be granted a break. They tidied up their projects, and Maman clicked her tongue and told them to bring their work home with them.

"But Madame," one said. "We like coming here to sew with you."

My mother's eyes filled with tears, and she went to each of them and took their hands, then kissed them on both cheeks. She paid them for their time and sent them into the lovely spring day. Once they were gone, Maman's smile disappeared and she closed the shop door.

"If the king is dead and she lives, this is the worst for us," she said. "But he cannot be dead; I would have been told. Perhaps he is away, on campaign or such. She must have found us."

"What if you're wrong about all of it, Maman?" I asked. "Perhaps I am simply Ailen from Dunford Town and you are Lady Leontyne who runs the dress shop. Maybe the soldiers are here on some other errand entirely."

Maman came to me and touched my face, then embraced me. "We cannot waste time," she said, sniffing. "Go to your room. Pack things, warm clothes, a book, one only. I will sew jewels into the hem of your dress. I am sorry, my sweet. I thought we would have more time. I prayed we would."

"Maybe we can outrun her," I said. "Let us leave now. We will find a new home, start a new shop. Please, Maman."

"If she has found us here, there is no place else to hide," she said. She wiped a tear from her eye then pushed me toward the door. "We had our chance, my sweet, and so many lovely years. I cannot run, but you shall. Hide your satchel outside the shop, behind the bush in the front. Make sure it cannot be seen. If the time comes when you need to flee, take it and go. Do you understand?"

"How will I know if I need to leave?" I asked.

"You will know," she said.

"But Maman—where shall I go? And how will I find you after?"

This question saddened her the most. "You will not have to seek me out. Your beloved Maman will become part of the sky, and I shall watch you from Heaven," she said. "No person has as much time as they would like with the ones they love. And we have had even less. But we must be grateful for the time we have had, my pet."

I would learn later that at the same time, things were changing at the grand house, Ara Dun. The lord and lady of the house had told Rhona that since she had come of age, they would soon send her away. She dreamed she might finally be sent to a city of possibilities, maybe Bridge of Thorngill, maybe further, even London. Then, one day, she was summoned to the office of her Uncle Tomfat, a brusque man of law and business who did not waste time on kindnesses.

They had found her a station. However, they were not to send her to some bustling city but to a cold, isolated island: St. Kiana. They were sending her to work in the service of an elderly woman. They were sending her to the end of the earth.

My friend's heart was broken. It was the last cruel blow of a family who had offered her shelter but never warmth; four walls, but no home. She had always felt as though the family was punishing her for the crime of being born.

Her uncle told her to pack and say her farewells for she would depart on the morrow.

That same evening, I packed what I could carry into a sack, and prepared to travel to—where? I had no idea. Stockings, clothing, my book of bugs and my fairy stories. (I defied my mother and brought two books.) I did not need to pack the teardrop that Nula-na-Nekon had given me, for that was eternally around my neck.

My mother spent that night sewing, but this time, she was concealing jewels in the hems of a simple frock for me. When the hour was late, Maman kissed my head and tucked me in as always. Before she blew out the candle, she and I both looked around my room, wordlessly saying goodbye to our home and to one another.

In the morning, I rose and went to school, and the sight of the Gallic soldiers in the town square filled me with terror. I was clumsy and distracted through my school day, and glad when it ended, though I dreaded going home. And yet, if there was to be a confrontation with an evil queen, I was anxious for it to begin. I wished to see this monarch who had haunted me my whole life. I wanted to look her in the eye. I wanted her to take on a physical shape and explain herself to me. I was Ailen, small and quiet. Why would anyone want to hurt me? How could I be a threat to her? And my siblings, those murdered infants. What danger did they pose? I wanted answers.

I made my way home and entered through the door of Maman's shop as always. The place was silent and cold. Maman faced away from me, touching the clothes and notions as though she was seeing them for the first time. She wore an unusually ornate gown, gleaming white and so bulbous it almost lifted her off the ground. Her arms were covered with white gloves to her elbows and her hair was also strangely extravagant, braided and coiled around her head, powdered pure white. Ribbons hung upon her wrists, bedecked with jewels.

Had I understood who I was looking at, I could have turned and fled and this story might be quite different. But I did not.

The woman turned slowly like a wooden ship, not quick and graceful like my mother. Her powdered face had little red circles painted on her cheeks and a small heart painted upon her lips. Her lashes were caked in black and her eyelids glistened with blue jewels when she closed and opened them. Finally, I understood: this was not my mother.

She looked at me and spoke in a thick Gallic accent, "You must be Marguerite. We have not met. I am your aunt, Queen Deutaria."

My legs lost all feeling. I never believed this woman was real and here she was, standing before me.

"Come, sit, child," she said. "I have looked forward to meeting you."

I sat down. I was so terrified, I could barely breathe.

"Won't you say hello to your beloved auntie?" she asked, smiling.

"Hello," I said, not meeting her eyes. My hands were at my sides, gripped in tight fists. I felt myself drift into silence, felt my eyes grow and widen. I was becoming the little girl who spent days in bed, wordlessly watching life unfold through my window. I wanted to make myself invisible.

"I am the queen, yes?" she said, her accent much thicker than Maman's. "You speak, Your Highness."

"Hello, Your Highness," I whispered. My mouth was as dry as lost bread. The next thing I said was the phrase I'd heard my mother speak so many times in her shop. "How may I help you?"

"We have matters to discuss," the queen said, and she continued to slowly wander the store, her skirt rustling as she walked.

I looked around. Where was Maman? Had the queen murdered her while I was at school? I saw no sign of blood or body.

"I wonder what your dear mother told you about your auntie," she said. "Did you ever wonder why she never brought you to Gallia to visit your family?"

I shook my head. I never did wonder.

"Allow me to explain," she said, her eyes narrowing, her smile widening in a way that was devious, deranged, and slightly amused. "You come from one of Gallia's great noble families. I was the first born, and I was promised as a bride to the king. When I was of age, I wed King Mattieu of Gallia. Do you know what a queen's job is? She has only one. Let us see if you are smart enough to guess what it might be."

I had a few guesses, but my mouth was dry as chalk and I could not make words come out of it.

While I sat, the queen brought something out of a small white purse that hung from her gloved arm. She put a small glass upon the table beside me. She was so close now, I could smell her, an aroma of mineral powder and something charred.

As I write this, I wonder why I only sat and did not run away. Why did I perform every task she commanded me to do? I cannot say. I suppose I was mesmerized, dazzled. I was a bug in a spider web, my autonomy disappeared. I had no choice but to do as told.

I offered no guess, so the queen answered her own question. "A queen's job is to bear a child, an heir to the throne, preferably male, preferably many. This is how the king's royal lineage gets passed down. Me, I could not have a child. My body only birthed small teacups of blood. Who did I turn to for help? My own, precious sister."

The word "sister" was hissed through her teeth, boiling with hatred. Then she brought from the little purse a corked bottle containing clear liquid. She pulled out the plug and poured the liquid into the glass.

"She could have helped me. She might have saved me," the queen said. "Instead, she claimed what was not hers. Glories intended for me she took for herself."

Finally, I found my voice. "But Your Highness," I said, trying to smile. "These things do not matter. Maman and I left Gallia. You can find another child and say it is your own. Nobody would challenge you."

The queen looked at me with pity, as though my stupidity was difficult to believe. "What she stole was his affection, his desire. After she left, he changed. He longed for her. I was nothing to him. So, I vowed to the gods of justice: my niece shall never become queen."

"I do not want to be queen," I said.

She took a vessel of white powder and tipped it into the glass. "Well, then," she said, as she stirred the mixture with a small, silver spoon. "We agree on something. And you want to ease your beloved aunt's mind, do you not? I have a task for you that is so simple, even you cannot make a mistake." She lifted the glass and handed it to me. "Drink," she said. "Drink from this glass and your pain will end and my pain will end and we shall all live...happily ever after."

My body shook from the inside. Where was Maman? If she was already dead and I would never see her again, perhaps I should drink, knowing the contents would end my sorrowful life. The queen stood, walked over to me and handed me the glass.

"Here, my little cantaloupe," she said. "So easy. Just drink."

I took the glass. The queen's eyes were filled with a cold, stinging fury that came from the core of her broken soul. I lifted the glass to my lips.

"Ailen, drop that," came a voice from the doorway. Maman came into the shop. "Now. On the floor. Smash it. Hard."

The voice of my real mother broke the spell. I threw the glass to the ground and went to Maman.

"Leontyne," the queen said. Her lips pursed into the shape of a smile, and the little red heart upon her lips squeezed red, but her eyes were still filled with ice. "How nice to see you after so many years."

"Deutaria," Maman said. "I have been searching for you. I thought we could discuss matters like adults."

"There is nothing to discuss," the queen said. "I have come to settle the score."

"Settle the score?" Maman asked. "You killed two of my babies then hunted me like an animal. And now you try to kill my one surviving child? The score is mine to settle."

"Now, Leontyne, so much drama," the queen said. "Why did you tell this insolent child to throw that glass upon the ground? Now I must mix the tincture again. Luckily, I brought extra." She opened her purse and again pulled out a glass, a vial of liquid and a small vessel of powder.

Maman turned to me. "Ailen, this is the moment. You took care of something yesterday, yes?" I nodded. "You know what to do. The time is now."

"The child is not excused," the queen said. "I am making a fresh drink. Wouldn't you like that, my darling rutabaga? You look thirsty."

"She will not chase you," Maman said to me quietly. "She cannot. Go, and do not look back."

"But Maman—"

"My love," Maman said, kissing my head. "The soldiers will do as she commands them. Run."

"She shall not leave," the queen growled. "I have not given her permission to do so."

"Your grievance has nothing to do with her," Maman said.

The queen stirred the substance in the glass. "See, it is ready now. The girl must drink, or why did I bother making it?"

"Where should I go?" I asked.

"Any place, far from here," Maman said. "Do not look back."

"Soldiers!" the queen shrieked. "Now!"

> "Maman, I love you," I said to my mother, kissing her cheek one last time.
>
> "I love you more than the world and the moon and the stars," Maman said. "No matter where you go, your Maman will always be beside you. Do not be afraid. Now, leave us, my girl."

Cinder stopped reading and looked out at the cliffs, the Morisar Sea churning in the distance. The words her mother had spoken to her own mother reminded Cinder of the jagged stone she carried in her pocket, the fact that she had not told her own mother a real goodbye, nor told her how much she loved her. She winced as she remembered her child's idea that if she withheld the words, her mother would have to return, if for no other reason than to collect her goodbye.

What a fool I was, Cinder thought.

She looked back at the letter. Suddenly, she thought how strange it was to read this, to find herself an audience at the final words between her mother and grandmother. She almost envied her mother; at least she'd had the chance to say goodbye.

> I left the shop and went to the loose brick under a box of flowers in the front where I'd hidden my sack. I pulled it out, and walked quickly away. I heard shouting in the shop behind me, but I did not look back. I pulled the hood of my cape over my face. I could see nothing but my own tears. I knew I would never see my mother again.
>
> I turned a corner, then, and looked up, and my eyes found a safe haven: Rhona. Her dark eyes were red and swollen, and she also wore a cape and carried a sack. I stopped her and put back my hood.
>
> "Ailen, I was searching for you," she said. We embraced, each of us desperate for a friend's touch.
>
> "I'm leaving Dunford," I said.
>
> "I as well," Rhona said. "They're sending me to a strange island."
>
> A line of soldiers marched toward us, and I pulled Rhona into an alley.

"The family sold me," she said. "To work for an old lady. I do not know how I will live on a rock in the ocean. I think I will die."

"I am sorry, my friend," I said. An idea started to form in my mind. "Rhona, how will you reach this island?"

"I am going now to meet the goatherd. He shall bring me to the coast, then tomorrow at sunrise, some boatman shall meet me," she said. "Uncle Tomfat arranged everything. He was so pleased with himself when he told me he'd paid my way. As though he'd done me some kindness. I know it's time for me to leave Ara Dun, but why would they send me to the ends of the earth where there is no way to improve my station? It's cruel."

"Rhona, where would you rather go?" I asked. "If you could choose."

"Some city," she said. "I believe I could find my fortune in a city."

"Well, let it be so, then," I said. "I will go to your island. You go to London. Here, I have money." I pulled out the purse my mother gave me, and handed Rhona the dress with the jewels sewed in the hems. "Take this, too. I shall take passage to the island."

"But why are you leaving, Ailen?" she said.

I tried to explain, and I could barely squeeze the words from my throat. "You must never tell another," I said. "I am...I am the daughter of a king."

"You—?"

I nodded, and explained as much of the story as I could manage. Rhona's eyes grew very wide and she curtsied.

"Please don't," I said. "I do not feel like a princess."

"Where is your mother?" Rhona asked.

"If she is not already dead, she soon will be," I told her. "Send me to the goatherd. Find your city, Rhona."

"You would do that for me?" she said, her voice breathless with amazement.

"This is something *you* are doing for *me*," I said. Just then a line of soldiers from Gallia marched past the entry to our alley. "They seek me. I must leave."

"I will bring you," she whispered. "For your part, tell the goatherd your name is Rhona. That is the name of the girl he seeks, and you are that girl, so that is your name. From this day forward, your name shall be Rhona. The queen shall never find a girl named Ailen. Understand?"

"Thank you, my friend," I said.

"Hard to imagine I'm friends with a princess," she said.

Her words made me so very sad. "Please, Rhona. It is only a title, and one I never desired," I said. "And it's brought me nothing but grief. I have lost everything I care for because of this title. Do not think of me as a princess. Remember me as a friend."

We embraced, then Rhona took my hand and led me on a strange route through back alleys, narrow passageways, cramped twitchels and damp, dark tunnels. Though I'd lived in Dunford my whole life, I had no idea these routes existed. I will never forget the putrid smell of muck and oozing death that surrounded us We stumbled over gaps in the path, squeezed through soupy narrows, past rats and vile insects.

I could not tell where we were or what direction we were going in. At one point, I heard voices on the other side of the wall and stopped. It was my mother's voice, speaking Gallic, desperately arguing with another woman, likely the queen. I could not see her, nor could she me. I could only hear the voices quarreling, their angry tones ascending over the other. The queen's voice made some declaration, and those words were followed with popping musket shots. Then silence.

I ran against the damp tunnel wall and placed my palms against the stones. "Maman," I cried. But I knew she was gone.

"Oh no," Rhona said, pressing her hand against her mouth. "Madame Leontyne. Ailen, we cannot dally. You must come now."

The queen had ended Maman's life. I remembered so many evenings by the fire when Maman recounted the story of my birth, and the two stolen infants. Now, my mother's life ended as she knew it would, at the word of a wicked queen. My only comfort was to think that my mother had gone to Heaven and would meet her first two babies there.

I, her third child, would have to continue without her.

Rhona tugged at me, but I could not walk. I could not make my legs move. My mother's body lay on the other side of the wall, surrounded by people who did not know her or love her. I longed to go to her, but I knew I could not.

"Mourn tomorrow, when you are safe and far from here," Rhona said. "Now, you must leave Dunford."

I knew she was right, so I followed her through the final passageway. I was relieved when we fell into daylight. In a certain square in the town of Dunford, a wagon waited, filled with hay and half a dozen young goats, and a young man to drive it.

"Hello, man, are you bound for the north coast? To the village where one can gain passage to St. Kiana?" Rhona asked. The young man had a scruffy beard and small eyes, and looked himself somewhat like a goat. He grunted an affirmation. "Here is Miss Rhona, your passenger."

"In the back, then," he said, gesturing to his wagon. "You ride with the stock."

"Can't she sit up front with you?" Rhona asked.

"I was paid to transport animals," he said. "If she wants the first class seat, costs extra."

"That's just like Uncle Tomfat, paying the livestock price," she said to me. Then to the boy, she said, "Make sure you bring her all the way. If anybody asks her name, you tell them this is Miss Rhona."

The curly-haired youth gave Rhona an understanding gesture and commanded me in the back. Rhona and I embraced.

"Safe journey, Rhona of Dunford," she said.

"Safe journey to you," I replied. "I wonder if we should ever meet again."

"What did the witch prophecy? All those years ago," Rhona asked.

I had forgotten about Nula-na-Nekon, and that strange night, and her face, which seemed to cycle through time, and all she had told me while Rhona slept, exhausted from fever. What had she said?

"The strangest prophecy of all," I said. "That you should marry my husband, and raise my child."

Rhona clucked and crossed her arms. "Your fortune teller's spyglass was broken," she said. "Someday you and I shall meet again. If we believe this, it shall be so."

"I hope we shall," I said. We embraced again.

I climbed into the back of the wagon, and the goatherd hitched up the horse. I pulled my hood over my head to conceal my face. As the wagon pulled away, I watched Rhona, her visage finally disappearing when we turned a bend. I could not make sense of all that had happened, all I had lost and how suddenly it had all disappeared. My home, my mother, even my name, had all been left behind. Now I was on a new journey. And I had no idea where it would take me.

With these words, Cinder knew she had come to the part of the story where she had started. She turned to the last page of the letter and read these words again:

My daughter, no matter what my name is or has been—curiously, I have had many—the only name that matters to me is the one you always called me, *Mother*. You are the dearest piece of me.

I love you, loved you, will always love you.
    Your Mother

Cinder looked out at the wistful, drifting clouds. *I love you too, Mother*, she thought. *And some day, I shall lay flowers beneath a tree on the isle of St. Kiana. I will find you.*

Cinder's mother had pushed through so much uncertainty to find her destiny. And Cinder? Her life felt so hopeless. She needed to leave, and like her mother, she did not know where she would go. The love she had lost sank her heart like the last beam of sunshine failing the day. Leaving Alban behind would hurt, but this would happen whether she stayed at Bowmore or did not. But then, if her mother's story was true, was she the granddaughter to a king? It seemed unlikely. But perhaps she too was sought by a queen who was desperate to end this branch of a family.

Cinder was beginning to believe that Mother Rhona had rescued her mother. And she was the actor, though powerless to resist, in Nulana-Nekon's strange prophecy: *She will marry your husband. She shall raise your daughter.* Yet, Mother Rhona seemed to have no idea that Cinder was Ailen's daughter. Would she tell Rhona of the connection? She did not know.

Bowmore House is not a prison, Orla had told her. *You can leave at any time.*

She turned and looked toward the house in the distance. "There is no way around it," she said. "I must depart. Tomorrow night, when everyone is at the ball."

Cinder would travel to some place she'd never seen, just as her mother had. And perhaps she'd change her name, as her mother had. She would be brave, leave behind everything she knew and begin a new life on her own. If her mother had done it, so could she.

Rhona went home and found Cinder in the kitchen, making supper.

"Oh, you're here," she said, trying to subdue her anger. She removed her kerchief and hung her cape upon a hook. "I went to town in search of you."

"Town?" Cinder said. "No, I have been here. I finished my chores, so I went for a walk down the lane—"

"Of course," said Rhona coolly. "Down the lane. Just like every afternoon. You're quite adept, as it happens, at finishing all you need to do and walking out of the house without a word to anyone. Then we hear a young man is requesting you to accompany him to the ball."

"But ma'am, he's not—"

"You do not speak," Rhona demanded. "Now is my turn."

Cinder sank down on the bench. "I haven't done anything wrong."

"Silence," she said. "I learned you recently visited the public house. Several people saw you."

"And this is against the rules?"

"Common sense, child!" Rhona exclaimed. "I have two daughters older than you. How will they find husbands if their sister runs about like a common harlot? Do you know what people think of young ladies who venture into the public house? Do you know what happens to maids who linger too long in such places?"

Cinder's face went pale and she became silent. "How could you think that of me?"

"It matters not what I think," Rhona said. "What other people see matters. Until I decide otherwise, you are forbidden to leave this house alone. If you must go to the market, you shall bring Liisi with you."

"This is not fair!" Cinder exclaimed. "You promised to never keep me captive."

"You do not understand the gravity of the situation," Rhona said. "Your father could not keep his ship upright, and so it falls upon me alone to protect this family's good name. Our name is the only thing we have left, and I will not let you tarnish it."

"I will not submit to being your prisoner," Cinder said. "One day, you shall wake up, and I will be far from here."

Rhona stuck her chin out. "Leave if you will," she said. "I, for one, would not miss you."

The girl's face took on a strange expression, a sort of knowing smirk. "You might miss me," Cinder said. "We have quite a bit in common, you and I."

If Rhona was already angry, she was infuriated that this insolent girl would suggest that they were somehow equals.

She glared at the girl's face. "Rest assured," Rhona said. "You and I have nothing in common. Not a thing. Are we understood?"

"I understand more than you realize," Cinder said quietly.

Chapter Sixteen

That night, Cinder fumed at Mother Rhona's attempt to restrict her travels. She worked hard and she believed she deserved at least the freedom to roam as she pleased. She spent most of the night tossing from side to side. After a time, she sat up and stared at the embers in the hearth, throwing in sticks just to watch them ignite and burn away. Finally, she drifted to sleep, and it seemed only a moment had passed before she awoke to the sound of bells coming from all the bedrooms of Bowmore House.

Thus began the day of the royal ball.

She stood and donned her apron and tied back her hair. "Henry, this is our final day at Bowmore House."

Henry mewed in response.

Wispy clouds sifted across a blue sky. First, Cinder brought everyone tea and stoked the fires, then she cooked a hearty breakfast. Next, her other household duties kept her busy until it was time to prepare lunch. After this, the girls and their mother took an afternoon rest.

Once all was quiet, Cinder scooped Henry up and gazed out the window at the trees that danced in the wind. She thought of all the things she would miss about the house when she left. She'd loved having the cliffs and the sea to herself. And all her memories of her parents were from this place. She supposed that now she would never tell Rhona of the connection she'd discovered; she could not see why it mattered. Rhona might have been her mother's first friend, but she was not a friend to Cinder. She would miss Orla, and to a degree, Liisi. But there was one she would miss above all others.

"Alban," she whispered aloud. "I am sorry I will not dance with you this night. I hope you find someone wonderful who well knows the steps. Tonight, and for all the nights to come in your life."

She scratched Henry's head. "You would have liked Alban," she said. "You are lucky to be a cat. You will never know how deeply wounds a broken heart."

Cinder considered what to pack. She would bring her mother's sweater, for that was warm and useful. She could not bring the clock on the wall, for that was too fragile, and she was just as happy to forget that she'd seen Nollie Washbucket's face appear there.

She would bring Henry, but she needed to fashion some kind of a sling to carry him in. She packed her things into a square of fabric, which she folded into a bundle and tucked out of sight until the next morning.

Not so different, she thought, from how her mother had hidden her things away the night before she encountered the wicked queen.

All too soon, the girls awakened and the time came for final preparations. Cinder kept cheerful as she fixed their hair, for she saw this as an act of kindness between sisters, among the last she would undertake. She braided Orla's brown hair and twisted it around her head then inserted decorative pins to hold it in place, careful to arrange her locks so they hid the scars on her neck. She curled Liisi's long, flaxen hair with a tool warmed gently in the fireplace, then twisted it around and up, and held her creation in place with more pins and bows, teasing out a few locks so charming curls spilled out on the sides.

Liisi studied her hair in a mirror. "Cinder, are you certain you didn't conceal a tarantula underneath, or some other horrible thing?"

Cinder smiled. "I'd have to go to a great deal of trouble to find a tarantula," she said. "And spiders don't care for narrow, foul-smelling environments."

Liisi frowned and opened her mouth as though she was about to snap back, but Cinder laughed before she could speak. "Only a jest," Cinder said.

Liisi smiled. "I know. Of course I do."

Then the girls began to get dressed. First, they put on corsets, and Cinder pulled hard on the laces to tighten them, then Cinder helped the girls step into petticoats, fluffing and straightening each layer of stiff fabric. After that, while Mother Rhona watched, Cinder climbed a ladder to place their gowns over their heads, carefully pulling the layers down over the undergarments. Cinder and Mother Rhona fussed about each girl until each detail and adornment was perfect.

"You look beautiful, Liisi," Cinder said while Liisi pulled long white gloves over her elbows. "You will have so many invitations to dance, you won't know how to choose."

"I have a plan for that," Liisi said, tugging on the gloves to make them smooth. "I shall choose in order of importance. Royal first, nobility next, then dignitaries, then handsome village boys. Anyone who is not in one of those categories, I shall not respond to."

"So, sewer rats and mangy mudlarks shall receive no acknowledgement whatsoever?"

"Of course not," Liisi said, as she studied her hair in a mirror.

Cinder smiled. "Liisi," she said. "May I ask a favor?"

Liisi's eyes narrowed. "What would you ask of me, Cinder?" she replied. "I shall not sneak cake out of the king's castle..."

"I have no need of cake," Cinder said. "Two favors, really. One, if you happen to meet a stable boy named Alban, who is a very skilled dancer, please tell him that the girl from the cliffs sends her deepest regrets."

"Oh," said Liisi. "Is he the one?"

"More importantly," she said. "Make sure Orla enjoys herself tonight."

"Of course," said Liisi. "I'm certain she will have a nice time."

"Not just nice," Cinder said. "I wish for her night to be...magical."

Liisi studied Cinder. "I shall do my utmost," she said. "You have my word."

"Thank you," Cinder said. Then she noticed something she had not seen before, a piece of jewelry pinned to Liisi's dress just above her dress' neckline at the top of the bodice. It was a brooch made of ivory and encircled with small, luminous diamonds. "Oh, my," she said. "What a lovely trinket."

"Mother gave it to me," Liisi said, placing her gloved fingertips upon it. "She said it makes my eyes shine."

"Indeed," Cinder said. "I did not know your mother possessed anything so grand."

Liisi laughed. "I am certain it is made of glass," she said. "Mother would certainly have sold it by now if it was real."

"Is it from your father's family?"

"Mother did not say," Liisi said.

"Well," Cinder said. "It looks nice. And you do look beautiful."

The girls dabbed spots of perfume from Gallia upon their necks. The two sisters looked at each other; they were transformed.

"Liisi," Orla said. "We have become princesses. I can barely believe it."

Liisi smiled. "We are beautiful, Orla," she said, barely able to contain laughter and tears.

Orla looked at Cinder and touched her shoulder. "Thank you for all you have done for us," she said. "Cinder, I wish you could—"

"Think not a moment of me," Cinder said. "I hope you both have a beautiful night."

Mother Rhona emerged from her own room in her long dress. The girls went to her and they all complimented each other, giggling with excitement. Cinder smiled too. The old house had not seen ladies decorated so lavishly in many years. And if the next owner would be Lord Foul Fitzawful, there was no telling whether it ever would again. When all else was ready, the three women followed Cinder, who carried a lantern, to a carriage that waited outside. She watched the three climb inside. They called out goodbye; the driver shook the horses' reins, and with a rumble of wheels against the road, the carriage brought them off into the night.

Then, Cinder was alone. A salted breeze blew off the sea, through the dark yard of Bowmore House. Cinder watched the carriage disappear down the lane. It had finally come, the night of nights, the King's Ball. Alban had invited her–Alban had kissed her. And though she had tried to find a gown, she had failed. So, she would spend this night alone, donned in her usual rags, face unpainted, hair disheveled. She wished he would appear before her now, her Alban, having somehow figured out where she lived, and deciding himself to forego the ball. He would bow to her and offer his hand. She would curtsy and take it. And with her hand in his, and his other hand upon her back, they would dance in the garden by moonlight. It would be a hundred times lovelier than the ball.

Yet, she knew this would not come to pass. By daybreak, she would leave Bowmore House and she would never see Alban again.

The night air was cold, for the autumn season was upon its last breath before winter, and the smell of wood smoke hung in the air. Clutching the lantern, Cinder pulled her cloak around herself and looked into the sky. Clouds concealed the stars. She walked around the house to the back garden. The flowers had long since died and all that remained were a few hearty herbs, bitter winter greens, and some scattered squashes and gourds, most of them rotted and rodent-bitten. She sat upon a stone bench. She had known no other home but this one, and now she knew Bowmore House was not her destiny. What had her father told her mother about St. Kiana? The island was not their future, it was only their past. Cinder was never meant to be a servant in this place, sleeping by the fireplace, covered in the ash of other peoples' fires. If she could muster the courage to walk out the door, she might find her fate.

But if she never took that step, nothing would change.

"Oh, stars I cannot see," she said out loud. "I am ready to learn what you have planned for me."

Then, a great sadness took root in her heart. She had tried to do better, to rise above the matters that caused her pain. She had tried to live with Rhona and her daughters, to consider them family, to care for them and make Bowmore House a good home. She had tried to be good and obedient. Why had her best efforts failed? She did not know. Disappointment spilled into one last, lonely, falling of tears; possibly, she thought, the last she would shed in this house.

"Dry your tears, child," came a gentle voice. Cinder looked up, surprised, for she had thought she was alone. She raised the lantern and saw standing in the shadows beside her a person whose face was concealed by a hood.

She gasped. The Watcher had come to her at last.

Cinder stood. "You..." was all she could say. "It's you."

"There is no time for sadness," the figure said. The voice was strange and muffled, like many voices speaking at once.

And suddenly, Cinder understood the identity of the one who stood before her. "Nula-na-Nekon," she said. "You saved my mother in the wood. And you have been with me all these years."

"Years, minutes, seconds, eons," said Nula. "I have always been with you, my daughter, and I always shall."

"And you never will be," Cinder whispered.

"You read your mother's words well," Nula said.

Cinder felt suddenly nervous; she understood that she was in the presence of an entity that was not exactly human, and she was not sure what kind of protocol she should follow. "I am honored to meet you," Cinder said, and she bowed her head in reverence. She thought to remark that the timing of the visit was not ideal, but she suspected that

Nula-na-Nekon knew more about time than she ever would. Instead, she asked, "What inspires your visit this night?"

"You asked me if I could help you attend the ball..." Nula said.

"I asked you–" she said.

Nula pushed back her hood and revealed her strange face. Cinder tried to remember how her mother had described this vision. *Faces moving through time...seeming very young, then childlike then adolescent, adult, then elderly and through to a shrunken and wrinkled old age.*

Now she saw the same thing. Then another emerged from the blur of faces. The visage she had seen in the clock: Nollie Washbucket.

"Mistress Nollie," Cinder said, amazed. "But how..." She was so confused, she did not know what to ask.

The voice of Nula/Nollie began to speak. "I embody the natural law..."

Cinder remembered this from her mother's letter. "...that all things which seem opposite are in fact a single string continued in a circle," she said. "Yes. And your form, it changes according to what time and place you choose to visit. Now I understand. You are a shapeshifter."

Nula nodded. "You always were such a smart girl," she said. "Indeed, there are no bears in Kilderbrae Woods."

Cinder smiled. "Still, better to leave other peoples' dogs where they are," she said. "This I have learned."

Cinder looked at Nula's face as it cycled through all the stages of life. She had never seen anything like this before. She felt the same way her mother described, amazed at Nula's visage, and curious—but not afraid. To Cinder, it made sense that one person might encompass all of these stages. She felt it about herself, too: she was at once a babe, newly born, and a child who did not know better than to roam the cliffs over the ocean at night, and a young woman whose heart yearned for the touch of a certain young man.

And she was the daughter of a mother who had lived, once upon a time, and whose life had ended too soon. "Nula," Cinder said. "You are a sorceress whose realm is time. Are you able to...could you set the clock backward?"

Nula laughed, and as her mother's letter described, all the Nulas through time laughed simultaneously, the effect haunting.

"Time for me is not a measure of thread stretched like a spider's web through space," she said. "All the nows in all the places are always occurring."

"But can you send me to another moment?" Cinder asked. "Could I visit the past? Not to live forever, but to...correct an error?"

"Alas, child," Nula said, her voice sympathetic. "I cannot transport a mortal through the doors of time. What moment would you visit? Ahhh, I understand, your mother is the one you seek."

"When she left me," Cinder said. "I did not say goodbye. I did not tell her I loved her. I...I failed. And then she died, not knowing."

"Ahhhh," Nula said, and her voice was like the wind through the trees. "I am beside your mother now. She lies in pain, on a cot in her husband's quarters on the ship. I am with her now upon that ship when her heart ceases to beat. I am alongside her now, as sailors lower her body into the soil of a hill upon a small island. The only thoughts in her mind, the only words on her lips, are of you. She asks each person she sees to make sure you are cared for, comforted and nurtured. To make sure people understand you as she did. She knew you would feel her loss deeply; she knew you needed freedom. She wrote you a letter..."

"You know about the letter?" Cinder asked. "Did you orchestrate my finding the letter?"

Nula smiled and a sound like breath, like air moving, went through her.

Cinder studied Nula's constantly changing face. She was starting to understand that her mother's guardian had been watching her for a long time, perhaps since the day her own mother died. Cinder did not understand what kind of magic was afoot now. But if she could find a way to correct her error, she would do all she could.

"Nula, do you mean you are...with her now?"

"Ahhhhh," Nula said, and her voice wafted through the yard, again like the wind.

"Please, tell her I love her," Cinder said. "You will say she knows and has always known, but give her the words from me, as concretely as she handed me this amulet."

"That amulet," Nula said. "I gave to your mother because it is a whisper from the earth's past. It is time, flattened. You have given it to your first daughter. And she has no children, so has given it to her niece."

A chill went down Cinder's spine. "The generations continue after me?"

"Of course, my child," Nula said. "I can see them now. And your mother? She knows you love her. She knows you cannot speak the words. Child, words do not matter. Your mother wishes that your heart would be healed. She wants you to claim what belongs to you."

"She knows all that?" Cinder asked. "In some moment that is past for me, and is somehow present for you, she knows how much I love her?"

"She knows this in all the moments," Nula said. "My daughter, let go of that weight. You must walk into your own future."

Cinder closed her eyes for a moment and breathed in the night air. She imagined the moment when her mother lay upon her cot next to the ship's dock. She remembered then that until the ship was ready to sail, she had been holding her mother's thin hand.

Then she remembered the sensation of tears streaming down her face. She'd been weeping. Of course, she'd been unable to speak, her throat was choked with tears. Her mother had known all she had been unable to say. Her mother had always understood.

Cinder felt relieved. Something like a stone fell out of her pocket and into the night's darkness, never to be seen again. Cinder breathed.

"I want to walk into my future," Cinder said. "Tell me what to do, Nula."

"My daughter, I am glad. But tonight, there is a dance," Nula said. "And a young man very much hopes you will attend."

"A dance? Oh, the ball? Nula, I...have no will for that now," she said. "The others have already departed. A dress and shoes would be useless now."

"Faith, child," Nula said. "Time can be an ingredient of change. Each of us is all things at once: the ancient one within the seed, the child not yet born, and the grandmother whose end approaches. The infant, the bride, the middle woman, everything in a state of blooming, becoming, decaying, and starting again. We begin as seed; we end as soil."

"Your words puzzle me," Cinder said. "As they did my mother. Please, come inside. Warm yourself by the fire. I can make tea and you can tell me stories all night long. This would cheer me greatly."

"Daughter," said Nula. "We have work to do."

"There is no more work," Cinder said. "I have already made my decision. By daybreak, I shall leave this place. Tonight, I stay home and tend the fires one last time."

"You asked me for help," Nula said. "If you no longer need assistance, I shall take my leave. At least we have put one matter to rest.

Good night." And Nula-na-Nekon turned and began to walk slowly away.

Cinder watched Nula depart, her long cloak fluttering by her feet as she went. Cinder was content letting her guardian drift away, as she always had. But still, the thought occurred to her: what if Nula could conduct some kind of magic? Cinder ought to at least see what it was. If nothing else, she might at least witness something wonderful.

"Wait," she called. "Do you truly have the means to help?"

Nula did not turn, but called over her shoulder. "Only if you care to attend the ball."

"Please, Nula-na-Nekon, mistress of time," Cinder said slowly and carefully. "If you command some sorcery that can dress me suitably, and if you can deliver me to Glengoe Castle, I would be honored to attend the king's ball."

Nula turned and smiled. "Good," she said, and all of her faces smiled. "We must make haste. First, I require some vegetable, a sturdy cucurbit should do. And a creature to act as driver, another for a footman. Then, more animals to pull."

Cinder smiled in puzzlement. "A squash of some sort?" she asked. "And animals? I wonder if perhaps you do not fully comprehend the task we have at hand."

"Do you doubt me, girl?" Nula asked.

"No," Cinder said. "I would just seek to ensure that you understand, the hosts of this ball are the king and queen. I need a gown of some sort..."

"Ask no further question," Nula said. "Find me a vegetable, large and plump. And animals, any size or shape will do."

Cinder nodded. She fetched the last unbroken pumpkin from the garden, then found four mice in a trap and brought all to Nula. Cinder watched as Nula-na-Nekon reached her hands out of her sleeves and wriggled her fingers. This, Cinder imagined, was the same gesture she had made when she was showing Cinder's young mother the planets and the stars. Now, the motion caused a change in the air that Cinder only sensed but could not see. Suddenly, the pumpkin was surrounded with a bubbling cloud, much as the clock had been before it took on Nollie's face. After a moment, the vegetable emerged, transformed into a beautiful carriage. The mice also were obscured from vision then changed into four grand horses.

Cinder gasped in shock. "How is this possible?"

"Every small thing has something extraordinary and grand deep inside," Nula said. "I invite the transformation. Two more animals, please."

Cinder found a small chipmunk who had been curiously watching the strange show from a hole in a tree. Nula once again fluttered her fingers, and he was transformed into a carriage driver.

"Another," Nula said. Cinder was so shocked she could not move. "Time is precious, girl."

"Of course," she said, and she dashed into the house. She woke Henry from his sleep and brought him to Nula.

"Please, be careful with this one," she said. "He's my dearest friend."

Nula held the cat up and looked him in the face. "You need only look into his eyes to see the memory of the kitten he once was," she said. "How he romped and played, and stretched in the sunshine. How he chased and caught birds. Back in your day, the mice quivered in their socks when they knew you were about, did they not, friend?"

Henry lifted his head to look about sleepily.

"I see other parts of him too," she said. "In another form, another time. But that is not a story for this night."

Then, Nula's fingers twitched, and in a moment, Henry the cat became Henry the gentleman, dressed as a footman. Cinder was overwhelmed to the point of tears.

"Henry," she said, and she wrapped her arms around the fellow whose gray hair bore one stripe of black and one stripe of white. He hugged her back with the warmth and kindness he had always shown her. "You are every bit as handsome a man as you were a cat," she said.

Henry smiled warmly, but did not speak.

"Forgive me for doubting, Nula," said Cinder. "This is all a miracle. However, I would still need a proper gown or I shall be quickly turned away."

Nula looked at Cinder. "Oh, yes," Nula said, and took a deep breath. "Now, let us truly bend time. Someday, my girl, you shall be a great queen. It is not from me; it is your birthright."

Cinder laughed slightly. "My mother's letter spoke of how she was descended from the king of Gallia."

"You doubted this as well," Nula said. "My daughter, you have walked in the world believing only what was in front of you, and this has served you well. But now, I beseech you, entertain some faith in what you cannot see. You shall attend the ball this night, outfitted as the princess you will someday become. First, you must do as I ask. Tell me your name."

"My name?" she asked. "I am Cinder."

The strange multi-aged voice said, "That is not your name, child."

"It is what those who live in this house have called me for many years," she said.

"No," Nula said. "That name is a moniker devised by the ignorant to assist themselves in forgetting who you are. You have also forgotten. Speak your real name, child, the name your mother gave you. The name that is borne upon your soul. The name you spoke over the ocean's eternal waters at midnight's stroke. Tell me that name."

"I do not speak that name to others," Cinder said.

"It is the name of the woman you will become, the name of the babe in your mother's arms," Nula said. "Say that name."

Cinder hesitated. There was about her a strange, crackling feeling of magic in the air, as there had been that night in the tower cupola. The garden seemed changed, full of a strange light, as though all the stars in all the skies were twinkling around her at once.

Cinder took in a deep breath of cold air.

"My name," she said, "my true name is Marguerite." She held her breath and squeezed her eyes tight. But nothing happened. She opened her eyes and looked at Nula.

"Say the whole name," Nula said. "Speak it as though you believe it."

Cinder nodded and stood tall. "My name is...Marguerite Bertrade de Valois Barclay." And suddenly, a strange light enveloped her body, so extravagant it blinded her. The light was intensely hot but did not cause her pain. For a few moments, she could not tell what was happening. When the beam retreated, Cinder saw that she was bedecked in a gown of green and gold, adorned with bows and ribbons and strands of pearls. Her hair was swept up, curled and arranged atop her head, flowers tucked into the strands, and a golden tiara on top. Her hands and arms were fitted with soft gloves, white as snow.

When the haze of magic dissipated, Cinder gasped and blinked. She had never seen such a dress. The gown's structure made her hold her back straight, her shoulders down, her head up. She had never felt so noble. Her body took a woman's shape she did not know possible. The skirt of the gown made a soft rustling sound, like a fire softly cracking.

"How can this be?" Cinder breathed.

"My dear, how beautiful you look," Nula said. "Your mother would have loved to have seen you this day. Your father as well."

"Everything about me is changed," Cinder said. "Only because of a dress."

"No person can wear a gown like this without believing they matter," Nula said. "You matter, my daughter. You always did. And you always shall."

"Thank you, Nula. Oh, but...my shoes are the same." She lifted the dress. "Perhaps nobody will notice."

Nula laughed out loud, and all the Nulas from all the ages laughed at the same time. "The shoes. Yes, yes." One last time, Nula's fingers danced, and suddenly upon Cinder's feet appeared beautiful, gleaming slippers. They seemed to be spun from enchantment, woven into a fragile sheen, sheer like diamonds, and sparkling blue.

Cinder held up the bottom of her dress and looked at her feet. "What are they made of?"

"Glass," Nula said.

"Oh," Cinder exclaimed. "That seems impractical. What if something falls upon them? Or if I trip?"

Nula chuckled lightly. "These shoes shall not break. The only danger is that they may run off without you."

"I hope they do not," Cinder said. "Nula, I do not know how to thank you."

"One last matter, and this one very important," Nula said. "As with all things in miracles, we can twist time to serve our needs, but at some point, it will untwist on its own. At the clock's last midnight strike, you will change back into the girl you were when the sun rose this morning." The voices became stern. "Heed my advice. Do not lose track of time or time shall lose track of you. Midnight's last strike. Do you understand?"

"Yes," she said.

"Now you are ready, my girl," said Nula. "You shall walk into that castle wearing a gown made for a queen, glass slippers upon your feet, and everyone will see you and wonder. But only one will recognize you, and he will do so for he knows your heart."

"Alban," Cinder said, blushing slightly.

"Yes," Nula said. "But even with these dressings, you may feel small, mired in the belief that you are merely some urchin, a keeper of fires, an orphan with no business in a place so grand. But you do belong, my girl. And not because of whatever spell I have cast this night. You belong because of who you are and who you were at the moment of your birth."

"I will try to believe it," Cinder said.

"Go now, my girl," Nula said. "And do not forget about midnight. I cannot change the progress of the hands of the clock. Only bend them a little."

"I shall not forget," she said. "But please, may I ask one last question? Why have you helped me?"

The face of Nula-na-Nekon changed, and she looked into Cinder's eyes. "When I acted as midwife for your mother, you and the generations after became my kinfolk. You would have found your way without my assistance, but sometimes we all need a little help from family."

Chapter Seventeen

Cinder made her way to the carriage, stepping carefully in shoes that seemed almost too delicate to support her weight, but practically lifted her into the air. Henry gently took her hand to help her step in. She turned to thank him and felt like she was looking into the face of an old, dear friend. She took her seat in the carriage and inhaled a vaguely grassy vegetable smell.

"I am ready," she said out the window. "Does the...chipmunk know where we are going?"

Henry made a sound to indicate he wasn't sure, but a moment later, the carriage lurched forward and began to roll. *This is impossible,* Cinder thought. *This must be a dream.* They drove through the cool night, and Cinder looked out the window. Bowmore House stood like a soldier beside the sea. It was dark but for the fires left burning, which she could see glowing faintly through the windows. The carriage brought her down the lane from the house and up the road into town; the shops were closed and dark, but the public house was bright and busy. She could hear the rousing music, and people clapping and whooping. She waved one gloved hand toward the public house; if Nollie Washbucket was inside, Cinder hoped she felt her gratitude.

Once the town was behind them, the night was quiet again. She knew she would never forget this night, the ride beneath the stars, the sea wind blowing clean and cold, magic breathing through and crackling around her. In almost too short a time, the carriage arrived at Glengoe

Castle. Its towers were illuminated with torches and every window was filled with light; she could hear glorious music even before the carriage crossed the entranceway. The castle awaited.

The chipmunk-driver steered the carriage to the door where the king's footmen waited. The carriage stopped, and Henry helped Cinder step out of the carriage on to the threshold of a grand door that opened on to a marvelous ballroom. The room was full of people, all of them beautiful, laughing and perfectly performing the steps of a country dance. Cinder stood at the doorway alone, peering inside. Suddenly, her courage failed. She was no lady, and she had no place in the king's castle among the nobility and royalty. She turned back to the carriage, but Henry closed the door and gestured toward the castle.

"Henry, I can't do this," she said. "Please don't make me."

He said nothing, but looked at her with the same deep green eyes that had been gazing at her her whole life. His expression, though sweet and filled with adoration, made it clear: he would not open the door.

"I don't know what to do here," she said. "I'm not meant for this."

Henry only looked at her again, and very patiently gestured toward the castle door. Then she remembered Nula's words: *You do belong, my girl. You belong because of who you are.*

This time, she understood. She braced herself, then breathed, nodded, and turned toward the door. Before she entered, she looked back once more.

"Stroke of midnight," she said. "Do not be late. Can cats tell time?"

Henry smiled and gestured toward the door, raising his eyebrows as if to say, "the night will end soon enough. Get yourself along now."

Cinder gathered the bottom of her dress so she would not trip on it, and carefully crossed into the castle receiving hall. Nula's words echoed in her mind: *Every small thing has something extraordinary and grand deep inside.* She wasn't sure if this was true, but she tried very hard to make herself believe it.

The king's footmen stood in a line on both sides of the room and gestured toward the ballroom in invitation. She walked past them, and suddenly she was in the largest, brightest room she had ever seen. Every detail was painted gold and ivory, lit by a million candles whose light was refracted through crystalline chandeliers. And music like nothing she had ever heard rang through the hall. It was a scene from a fairy story.

She scanned the room, searching for four people: Mother Rhona, Orla, Liisi, and, of course, Alban.

At first, though, she had to let her eyes adjust to the spectacle of people. So many people! They stood on the sides of the room, eating, drinking, visiting, and in the middle of the room, dancing. The dancers seemed to glide on air; everyone knew the steps perfectly and performed without a single misstep or stumble.

Then she saw a familiar face: Liisi. She was dancing right in the middle of the floor, tossing back her head to laugh that certain Liisi-way. Cinder judged her dancing a little less wooden now; Liisi must have found a partner who inspired her more than her own sister had. Cinder held her gloved hands to her face and peered through her fingers for Orla and Rhona; they would not be far. But who was Liisi dancing with? The young man's face was turned so she couldn't see him. Then, finally, she did.

It was Alban.

The moment she saw this, her heart sunk. Nobody would want to dance with her once they had seen Liisi. Now Cinder truly wanted to go home, and she decided she would. She turned and began toward the door, but a throng of people filled behind her and she couldn't push through. Then the music stopped. She looked toward Alban; he seemed to be searching for someone. He released Liisi's hand, and she was flirtatiously protesting.

Cinder stood where she was and watched him. He looked fine this evening, his clothes clean and crisp, a red sash across his suit. She thought the sash curious; the king must have decreed such royal uniform even for those who were employed at the castle. Alban turned and spoke to some people, then walked away and disappeared into the crowd. Her heart fell again; she felt very alone in this room that was bursting with people.

A moment later, a voice spoke behind her. "Beg your pardon, my lady," said a young man's voice.

She turned. "Alban," she said, breathing with relief.

"I didn't know if you would come."

"I didn't want to miss it," she said. "You look wonderful. So dressed up for a stable boy."

"You look like you are made of starlight," he said. "I almost didn't recognize you."

She blushed and looked away. "As lovely as all this is," she said. "I'd rather be at Sayre Cliffs."

Just then, the music began. "Well, let us go there now," he said. "My lady, may I have this dance?"

She tentatively offered her hand, and they took their positions. "I don't know if I can do this," she said. "I'm so nervous in front of all these people. I fear I will forget everything you taught me."

"What people?" he asked. And when he gazed at her with his eyes the color of early hay, something inside her swooned. "You and I are here at Sayre Cliffs together, just the two of us."

"Alban—"

"Look into my eyes," he said. "Nowhere else." She nodded. The music began and their feet started to move. "See, the ocean is just there." With his head, he pointed toward a crowd but she saw the churning sea on a day when the sunshine illuminated the white, frothy peaks that whipped up among the waves. "See the cliffs over the ocean," he continued. "We shall sit on the edge later and eat a pile of apples, snapped off the tree only a few moments ago."

Yes, she could see those too.

"Look over there," he said, glancing over his shoulder. "Can you see the dolphins playing in the surf?"

She laughed. "I can see them," she said. "And over there, the forest. When I walked through those trees to this place, I felt I was entering a dream."

"It is like a dream, isn't it?" he said.

"Yes," she said. "And after a time, a man will stand at the bottom of the hill and cry out 'hey-oh!' And the dream shall come to too quick an end."

He smiled. "Can you smell the sea air?" he said. "Feel the sunshine, hear the waves crashing?"

She closed her eyes, and she could feel it, she could hear it. And now they were Cinder and Alban, just the two of them, dancing together upon the cliffs. The less she thought about the steps, the more her feet in their tiny slippers knew what to do. She would wonder later whether the shoes themselves knew the steps, or perhaps contained some kind of magic that made her dance like the breeze. The light but steady touch of his hand on her back made Cinder's heart swoon.

"You're doing it," he said.

"I can't believe it, really," she said, laughing.

Suddenly, the music stopped, and everyone clapped. Another girl approached where they stood; she had her sights on Alban, but he turned to Cinder and said, "May I have the honor of another dance?"

"You may," she said. The music began again, and he took her hand in his and they began again.

This time, Cinder scanned the edge of the crowds. "My stepmother and sisters are here but they do not know I am. I'd like to find them so I can keep my distance."

"You didn't come together?" Alban said.

She shook her head. "My stepmother forbade me to leave the house."

"Oh, dear," he said. "What did you do this time?"

"It's a long story," she said. "Oh, you danced with one of my sisters earlier. The girl with the blond curls. That was Liisi."

"Oh, yes," he said. "She giggled a lot."

"She does that," Cinder said. "Oh, who is that? Is that the crown prince?"

Alban looked where she was gesturing. "Ah, no, that is the prince's younger brother, Prince Eiran."

Prince Eiran was also dancing with a lovely maiden. "He's handsome," Cinder said.

"A matter of taste, I suppose," Alban said. "Over there is the youngest, Prince Heath."

Cinder looked to where he was gesturing and saw a youth dancing with a girl who looked the same age. He seemed not as adept a dancer as his brother, and was somewhat leaping about, pulling his poor dance partner along with him.

"Where is the crown prince?" she asked. "Did he sneak off to play chess? That scoundrel."

Alban looked around. "He's here somewhere."

"Oh, and the king and queen," Cinder said. "They must be here as well."

Alban gestured toward the dais at front of the room. "Indeed, they are," he said.

Cinder squinted at the two seated figures, bedecked in crowns and royal sashes. Strange though, she felt the king and queen were looking straight at her and Alban. "I think they're watching us," she said. "Actually, I suddenly feel like everyone is watching us."

"Are they?" he asked. "I hadn't noticed. I thought we were alone out here on the cliffs."

Cinder was beginning to feel uneasy, as though she had missed a point of information. "The room suddenly feels quite warm," she said.

"Let us dance over here." And he navigated her through some doors, out upon a terrace overlooking the garden. They stepped out together into the night and under the stars. "This is better," he said. "Unless it's too cold. Are you all right?"

"I'm fine," she said, looking into his eyes. "I don't feel a bit cold. Oh, look at the stars, Alban. Can you believe that anything so beautiful exists in this world?"

"I do believe it," he said.

"See, you've changed me. Now I don't want to stop dancing." She laughed, and he gave her a gentle turn.

"I knew you could dance if you tried," he said. "You could probably do anything."

She looked doubtful at that. "That's not quite true," she said. "Actually, I should tell you…I'm leaving. I have decided. I will not find my destiny if I stay where I am."

"Really? Where will you go?"

She shrugged. "I'm not sure. My hope is that if I take the first step a plan will make itself known."

"You're shivering," he said. "Let's go inside."

"No, I don't want to go back," she said. "I don't want this moment to end. I might never see you again after this night."

He took her hands in his. "I must confess, my heart would be pained if I never saw you again."

"Leaving you was the hardest part of the decision," she said.

"When shall you depart?" he asked.

"I was planning to leave tonight," she said. "But I'm hardly dressed for adventure. And these shoes are not fit for travel. They're barely good for walking."

"Then come, dance with me," he said. "But come out here with me later. I have something important to tell you."

"Tell me now. Do not make me wait," she said.

He started to speak and then he stopped himself. "No," he said. "Later."

They returned to the ballroom. Alban showed her a table of food where people were helping themselves to plates of roasted meats and fresh bread and cream puffs for dessert, but Cinder was too excited to eat. She searched the room; finally, she spotted Mother Rhona at the opposite side, talking and laughing with some man. The two approached the table and just then, Cinder saw Orla standing nearby, watching the dancers. Cinder turned to Alban and said, "My family approaches. Shall we dance?"

But they did not move quickly enough and suddenly Liisi rushed ahead and stood beside Alban. "Save the next dance for me, won't you, Your Highness?"

Cinder stood beside Alban and turned away, covering her face with her gloved hand. What had Liisi meant, *Your Highness*?

"I'm already promised," he said.

"You cannot dance with the same girl all night, it isn't fair," Liisi said. "Even your partner would agree. Aren't I correct, Miss?"

Cinder cleared her throat and looked directly at Liisi. "The gentleman should choose for himself," she said, trying to change the tone of her voice.

"Well," said Liisi. "If you will, Your Highness, save at least one more dance for me. Please?"

"I will try," he said, bowing slightly at her.

Liisi walked away but glanced back over her shoulder at the couple. Had she truly not recognized Cinder? Or was she pretending? No, Liisi had no wit for pretense. If Liisi recognized Cinder, she would have called the guards. And worse, her mother.

The music started again. "Why did she address you as *Your Highness*?" Cinder asked. "I thought only those who were royal would be addressed this way."

Alban only shrugged. "Perhaps she addresses all people associated with the king this way," he said. "Miss, may I have this dance?"

"You may," she said. But now, Cinder was curious. As they danced, Cinder looked about the room, seeking the actual prince. "I still have not seen Prince Finnian," she said. "You must point him out; I would not know him from sight alone. I have only ever seen him from far away, in parades and such."

"I'm sure he's somewhere," Alban said.

She looked at Alban. She had noticed his attire that night, but she had not thought about how it appeared compared to what others were wearing. Now she looked more closely. He was dressed more formally than any other man in the room. His waistcoat was decorated with elaborate insignias, many pressed in gold. She glanced over at the young men whom Alban had told her were the younger princes. Their attire was similar, only with...less gold, fewer ornaments.

She studied his eyes, his face. Could Alban be—no, Cinder decided. That would be absurd. The young man who held her now in his arms—was this Finnian, the Crown Prince of Braemuir, the first-born son of the king?

The idea was ridiculous. And yet...

Suddenly, Cinder's feet stopped moving and she looked into Alban's eyes. "Your Highness," she muttered. She could not look away from his face, his hair, perfectly combed, the insignias that were so polished, they almost glowed.

He seemed to sense the pieces she was putting together. "Let us return to the balcony," he said. He took her hand again and danced her out the door. Once they were well beyond the crowd, in the chill night, she released his hands.

"You're no stable boy," she said.

"I'm sorry," he said, his face serious.

Cinder stepped backward. "Why did you bring me here and make me guess?"

"I did not do this to hurt you," he said. "I care for you more deeply than you shall ever know."

"I'm such a fool," she said. "Why did you not tell me?"

"When first I met you, you had taken to the cliffs for sanctuary," he said. "You were a child. I wanted you to trust me."

She felt panic grow in her chest. "That was nine years ago," she said. "In nine years, there are opportunities for one friend to tell another who they are."

"Yes," he said. "But...people change when they realize they are in the presence of the king's son. Suddenly, everything becomes formal; mistakes are endlessly apologized for, or people beg some favor that only the king can grant. Nobody sees *me*, the person I am. Except you. You were my friend because of who I am, not because of my birth order or my father's identity."

Cinder understood. She looked into his eyes and saw inside the young man a little boy with an open heart.

"Ahh, but if you are the Crown Prince, this explains the man who was always appearing to summon you."

"That was my man, Jakob," he said. "You might be angry that I attested to a false identity, but you have still told me no name at all. Perhaps now, we can both speak the truth."

"Think not on my name, for it is of no consequence," she said.

He smiled sadly at her. "My friend," he said, "no matter what name you know me as, I shall always be the boy who danced with you at Sayre Cliffs."

"And I shall always be the girl whose heart you lifted as if on seagull's wings," she said.

Their faces once again drew near, and Cinder's heart beat hard and fast. Their lips nearly brushed one another, then Cinder pushed away. "Alban, Finn, my name has no meaning now," she said. "I am leaving in the morning."

"Why?" he asked. "What about our hearts? What about what we want?"

She turned from him and stood by the balcony balustrade, gazing onto the royal gardens below and lines of boxwood topiaries lit by flaming torches.

"You were hard to find when you were a stable boy," she said. "But if you are the Crown Prince? Our feelings do not matter."

"They must," he stated. "Feelings must matter."

His words made her almost want to laugh. "No, they don't," she said. "You see me now as a lady of substance and beauty. But it's a trick of light and magic. Don't you see? It's an illusion. The light will shift and the magic will end, and I shall go back to what I only am: an orphan with no title. What my future holds is a mystery to me, but I must seek it out. I will never forget you. But Alban, Finn, you must forget me."

"I never will," he said.

Suddenly, a man in a military uniform walked briskly toward them.

"Your Highness," he said. He did not look at her, but bowed his head to the prince. "The king is making an announcement and he'd like you to stand beside him."

"Once again," she said, "our time is interrupted by some royal summoner."

Finn's expression changed, suddenly irritated, and he turned to Cinder. "I'm not sure what he will announce," he said. "But if my father's words cause your heart any pain, wait for me to explain. Please? Promise me?"

She nodded, and the minister rushed Finn off. Cinder followed calmly behind, then joined the crowd to listen to the king.

"Welcome, everyone," the king said. "And thank you for joining us on this glorious evening." The king expressed gratitude to everyone for making the event possible, praised all the young people of the land, and lauded the character of the people of Braemuir.

"I have a wonderful announcement: my son, Crown Prince Finnian of Braemuir..." He grasped his son's shoulder. "Shall this summer wed the Duchess Agnatha of Spitzbergen. The kingdom of Braemuir shall rejoice!" The crowd erupted with cheers, so loud, the king could barely be heard when he said, "Until then, I wish you all health and happiness, and very glad tidings. Now, enjoy the dance!"

A throng of people crowded around Finn, shaking his hand and hugging him in congratulations. Cinder's eyes met his. She smiled at him sadly. Cinder had always known that neither Alban nor Finn would marry her, but the king's announcement hit her like a dagger in her heart. She did not need to worry about her glass shoes breaking; her heart was shattered.

Then she glimpsed Liisi. When she heard the king's words, her sister's face went from giddily joyful to thoroughly crestfallen. But it did not last long, for she turned to a handsome young man who was standing beside her and a moment later, both were laughing. She was glad to see Liisi flirting with someone; for Cinder, there would be no other love.

Cinder remembered that Finn had asked her to wait for him to explain his father's words; he must have known something of what his father was going to say. She might have waited for a moment, at least, to say goodbye and thank him for the dance, but then, she heard the sound that stopped her heart: the clock, the first toll of what she knew would be midnight. She remembered Nula's words: *when the clock strikes midnight, you will return to the girl you were when the day began...*

She looked at Finn again. People were still consuming his attention. He tried to gesture at her to wait, but she shook her head, and blew him a kiss from both of her hands.

"I have to leave," she said, though she knew he could not hear her.

At that, she turned toward the ballroom and began to push her way through the people, and rush as fast as her fragile shoes and cumbersome gown would allow. She almost reached the door when she realized Finn had freed himself and was coming after her.

The third toll. She kept her eyes on the doors and continued toward them. Her tiny glass shoes felt like they might break or fall off. She jostled past Mother Rhona and looked her right in the face.

"Pardon me," Rhona said, her tone exasperated.

"Apologies," Cinder muttered.

The fourth toll.

"Please, wait!" Finn called. "At least tell me your name!"

"It doesn't matter anymore," she said, breathless. "None of it matters."

She crashed past the castle doors and into the cold night air. She did not see the carriage. She turned and found herself at the top of a great staircase, and spied the pumpkin carriage at the bottom of it. She grasped her skirt and fled down the steps as fast as she could. When

Cinder reached the bottom, she realized one of her shoes had fallen off. She did not have time to go back and fetch it, for the sixth bell was ringing.

Cinder could hear Finn calling for her as she fled toward her carriage, but she pressed on, tears in her eyes. Finally, she reached the carriage where Henry the footman waited faithfully, holding the carriage door open for her.

Chapter Eighteen

While the bell still tolled, the carriage departed, and dashed through the night as fast as its mice-horses could take it.

"Can you go any faster?" Cinder asked the driver, who, she thought, being a chipmunk, might know something of speed. Yet, they proceeded at the same rate. The moment the sound of the twelfth bell finished, everything stopped. There was no flash of light, no puff of smoke, only a haze in which all things returned to their original conditions. Suddenly, Cinder was herself again, sitting on the road in her housedress and apron. Once the dizziness passed and Cinder could see her surroundings, she found herself in the woods just past the castle. Mist surrounded the trees and stars hid themselves behind clouds. The carriage was, once again, a pumpkin and Henry, once again, a cat. The grand horses became mice, and the chipmunk-driver reverted as well. The chipmunk and the mice stood dazed for a moment, then looked at Henry. When the rodents realized their peril, they scattered into the darkness.

Henry mewed affectionately and snuggled against Cinder. "Hello, old friend," she said. "What a wonderful dream. Thank you for your help."

She looked in her lap; there, upon her apron, sat the last glass slipper.

"The other one ran off without me, but you remain," she said, smiling. "I shall bring you home and tuck you away forever in my own trunk of memories."

She lifted the shoe, but the moment her fingers touched it, the slipper dissolved into sand and blew away in the breeze.

Cinder felt like she might cry from the shock at the sudden end of this last remnant of magic. "Well, then, no mementos for me. The clock has turned back for all of us. A glass shoe becomes sand. What a fickle friend, time."

She watched the last of the sand blow away, then she stood and shook the grains from her skirt. "Cold, still. And we're far from home. I suppose from here, we walk." She tucked Henry under her arm and kissed his head. "It's too far for you. You transported me earlier, now I carry you."

Cinder abandoned pumpkin, mice and chipmunk, and began to walk. She was grateful that she had been restored complete with her mother's sweater and a pair of proper shoes, but she soon realized that the carriage had only progressed a little past the castle. In fact, it had only gotten to the far edge of town, which was still a long way by foot from Bowmore House. After she walked for a while, Cinder stopped under a tree, seeking shelter from the wind and a place to rest her eyes. Henry nestled happily in her lap.

When she awoke later, she knew by the lightened sky that daylight was close. Her family was surely home by now, she realized, and if they'd arrived expecting to find her, excited to tell her about the ball, they now knew she wasn't there. Now she had a new worry: what distress would she walk into when she arrived home? She had no idea, but she knew she had to pick up Henry, carry on and face it.

The magic was over, the ball had ended, Alban was Prince Finn and the prince would marry a duchess. There was nothing for Cinder in this land anymore. She might rest for a day, but then she would do what she had planned: leave.

Prince Finn woke in his bed with a start, jostled by the impact of some dream. He could not remember the scenario, but he was ready for action. He raised his head and noticed on the table beside his bed a small pillow placed there the previous night. There upon it sat the most delicate shoe he'd ever seen. He looked at it now, glistening in a ray of morning light; he could not tell what it was made of. Enchanted gossamer spider webs, maybe, perhaps a moonbeam encased in ocean water. In any case, it was perfect.

He'd found the shoe moments after midnight, when the girl—she had still not told him her name—abruptly fled away. He couldn't blame her for leaving. He had failed in the courage to tell her his identity; she'd figured it out on her own. Then his father, unbidden, announced that Finn would marry the duchess. Finn knew his father was making a grand gamble: once he'd made the announcement public, he hoped his son would just play along.

But King Humphry did not know how much Finn cared for the girl. How could he? Finn was still realizing it himself.

The night before, he had stood on a step outside the castle and watched the girl ride away in her carriage. His heart fell as he watched the carriage disappear down the lane and around the bend. That's when he happened to glance down and notice the shoe sitting abandoned upon a step. Carefully, he'd picked it up. In a ballroom full of faces, he sought one out: kind Jakob. In a corner of the room, he'd handed the shoe to Jakob and asked him to bring the shoe to Finn's chamber.

"And whatever you do," he'd said. "Do not drop it. It may be my only link to her."

Jakob had looked at the shoe in puzzlement. "Do you expect to try to find her using this?" he asked. "Will you visit every young lady in the land and ask each to try the shoe?"

Finn had smiled. "No need of that. I know this young lady. But if I have missed my chance and never see her again, this might be all I have to remember her by."

After that, he'd spent the rest of the night thinking about her. He longed for her. When she was in his arms, everyone else in the room melted away. He remembered their time at the cliffs over the ocean, laughing easily, dancing on an afternoon when the sun shone and a slight breeze blew across the Morisar Sea, whispering love songs from long ago. When she looked into his eyes, he was the man everyone wished he would become, and he was completely himself. He knew now: she was the only woman he wished to spend his life with.

Finn sat up. The party had not concluded until early morning, and now his head ached and his eyes burned. He needed to decide what to do next. More than anything, he needed to find her.

He set the shoe back on its cushion. Then he remembered: he had not discovered the girl's name, but he had learned where she lived. The tittering blonde girl was her sister—what was her name? Liisi. After the girl left, he danced again with Liisi, (leading her on somewhat, which he knew was wrong and would apologize for later) and Liisi revealed their address to be Bowmore House, a stone-built manor outside of town, near the coast.

Only a short walk from there to Sayre Cliffs. Of course. It made sense.

If he could find the house, he'd find the girl, and then he could ask her to marry him. What would he do if she said no? For this, he had no answer. Before that, there was yet another puzzle piece to contend with. He needed to talk to his parents.

When Cinder reached Bowmore House, the sun had broken, and the first rays of golden light spilled upon the roof. She saw the house standing near the coast like a lonely sentinel, enveloped in misty sunrise. The house mirrored her character: solitary, steady, and strong. Soon, she would walk away and never again see this house.

She walked across the yard to the kitchen entrance. Before she opened the door, she looked out at the cliffs and the sea. She hoped she might catch a glimpse of the Watcher, but she saw nothing.

"Thank you, Nula-na-Nekon," she whispered. "The night was perfect. Completely perfect."

Then she opened the back door into the kitchen, and carefully set her sleeping cat in his soft bed. She was surprised though, for the room was warm and cozy, the kitchen fire already lit. Cinder turned and saw Mother Rhona, sitting on the kitchen bench beside the table, a pot of tea and a cup beside her.

"Where have you been?" Rhona said.

The woman's voice sent chills down Cinder's spine. "Good morning," Cinder said. "I have never known you to start a fire."

"I am capable of doing many things," Rhona said. "Now, explain yourself."

Cinder put on her apron and tied her hair back in a kerchief, then threw two more logs upon the fire. "I went out for a walk," she said. "But I grew weary and fell asleep on the ground."

"I forbade you to leave the house," Rhona said, her tone hard. "Did you think that merely a suggestion?"

Cinder was too tired to argue. "I did not," she said, and she poured a ladle of water into the pot over the stove. "Would you care for tea?"

"Where did you go, exactly?"

Cinder paused and looked quizzically at her stepmother. "You have nothing to worry about, Mother Rhona," she said. "The family name remains in fine standing."

Rhona stood up to address her stepdaughter. "I know where you were," she said. "I saw you. Where did you get that dress? Who helped you? If I find out you stole from the house purse—"

"I did not touch the purse," Cinder said. "I never would. Check it yourself— "

"And how did you travel to the castle? Did that boy bring you?"

"That boy?" Cinder replied. Then she smiled to herself, and chuckled slightly. She would have liked to tell her stepmother who "that boy" turned out to be. That information would stop her tongue in its tracks. "It doesn't matter. None of it matters. It was a fairy tale, can't you see? A beautiful dream that ended at the stroke of midnight. The dream even had a handsome prince, but he is promised to another, so the dream is ended. I remain the invisible cinder girl in the back kitchen."

"What are you talking about?" demanded Rhona. She crossed her arms, and her face bore a look of disgust.

"Nothing, Mother Rhona," she said. "After today, I shall burden you no longer. I am leaving Bowmore House."

Rhona laughed. "And where do you think you will go?" asked Rhona.

"I haven't decided," Cinder said. "Someplace far from here."

She went to her secret spot and brought out her sack. It contained, among other things, her mother's letter. She took out the letter and looked at it, the pages ragged with age, corners scuffed, handwriting scrawled across in lines, some of them neat, some drifting down and across the page. Cinder placed the letter on the table before her stepmother.

Rhona looked at her. "What is this?" she demanded.

"I am weary, Mother Rhona, and I cannot play games anymore," she said. "My mother wrote me this letter when she was dying. It was secured in a trunk, which was stored in the tower room. I believe you sent it there."

"Your father's trunk," Rhona said. "It contained only old clothes and papers."

"Yes, a stack of my father's papers. And under those, this letter," Cinder said. "I found it when you sent me to the tower room a fortnight ago."

"If your mother wrote you a letter, that is no matter to me," Rhona said.

"My mother," Cinder said. "My mother, Rhona, wanted me to know who she was. As it happens, her name was not Rhona. Her name was Ailen."

Rhona's face seemed to suddenly drain. She sank down upon the bench and touched the letter with only her fingertips. "Ailen?"

"She grew up in a town called Dunford. She had a dear friend whose name was Rhona," Cinder said. "I have been trying to figure out if you are the same. I tried to trick you into volunteering the information, but you are impenetrable. So, now, tell me. You once knew a girl named Ailen, didn't you? You were her friend. I can already see it on your face."

Rhona's mouth was agape and her eyes red. "What are you saying?" Rhona pointed at the letter with shaking hand. "May I?" she whispered.

"Of course," Cinder said.

"Mercy, Ailen," Rhona whispered, her hands quivering as she lifted the pages. She wiped tears off her cheeks. "How is this possible? What did she write about me?"

Cinder looked at Rhona and felt a pang of sympathy. She suddenly realized: her stepmother was a broken woman, and had been since long before she came to live at Bowmore House, maybe her whole life. Cinder sat down on the opposite edge of the bench and gently took the letter from Rhona's hands.

"She wrote how she met you," Cinder said. "When you slipped in mud and went into her room. How you became friends and she taught you to read. She wrote that you brought her into the woods, and she twisted her foot and you contracted a fever. And then you were rescued by a mysterious spirit."

Rhona held her palms together and put her shaking hands to her face. "There was a terrible storm. We did not know if we would survive the night," Rhona said. "I was so weak. The figure in the hood gave me tea so I would sleep. We did not know if she was some witch of the woods. But that spirit saved us."

"That spirit has been keeping watch over me for some time. Perhaps since my mother died," Cinder said. "And she came here last night, as well. Her name is Nula-na-Nekon. I cannot explain how she did so, but she transformed me so I could attend the ball."

"Your mother's guardian must have transferred to you," Rhona said.

"The last time you saw my mother," Cinder said, "was the day my grandmother was murdered. My mother fled. She met you, and you told her to take your name, Rhona, and you sent her to the island of St. Kiana."

Rhona nodded. "St. Kiana, yes."

"My father was born and raised on that island," Cinder said. "Did he ever tell you that?"

Rhona looked at Cinder with dark eyes. "He never told me anything about his life," she said. "Aside from our wedding vows, the man barely spoke to me before he set sail."

"Of course," Cinder said. "Because you weren't so much of a wife as you were an animal-tangler hired to settle the shipbuilder's unruly daughter."

A wave of unspeakable grief went over Rhona's face. "We needed a home, and your father believed you needed the care of a mother and older sisters. But there was nothing I could do to comfort your grief."

"He told you about the nurse who locked me in my room," Cinder said. "Do you remember?"

"Yes," Rhona said. "And I vowed never to do that to you."

"And you never did. For that, I thank you," Cinder said. "But after my father died, I became a servant in my own home."

"He left us with nothing," Rhona said.

Cinder smiled slightly. "You knew we would endure, because you have always done so," she said. "I know I fought you, Mother Rhona. The moment you came here and every moment since."

"Every moment," Rhona said, putting her hand to her head.

"You were three strangers invading my home," Cinder said.

Rhona stood up. "That is never what I intended," she said. "All these years, something in your face looked so familiar, but I could not place it. Now I understand. My Ailen. You have been with me all this time and I did not know it."

Rhona took Cinder's hand in hers. Cinder was surprised, and realized, then, in all these years, the woman had never touched her. "I am so sorry, my girl," Rhona said. "My dearest friend put you in my care and I failed at every point."

Then, Rhona let her hand go and sank down onto the bench. "But, child," she started to say. "Does your mother's letter tell you about her heritage? Her lineage?"

"That her father was the king of Gallia?" Cinder asked. "Yes, the letter speaks of it. I do not know what to make of this, though I doubt it has any meaning for me. I thought perhaps I would go to Gallia, and see if anyone there remains who remembers. And if not, at least I can view the great hanging gardens of Gallia's City of Light."

"City of Light?" Rhona said. Suddenly, Cinder felt like Rhona was searching out a conversation that was only in her head. Then she turned toward Cinder and glared at her.

"Oh, my word," Rhona finally said, breathless, almost shaking. "My girl, you need to do exactly as I ask of you, though I cannot explain it. Would you do so?"

Cinder pulled back. "Mother Rhona, are you all right?"

"You must..." started Rhona, still thinking. "You must fetch something from the store room at the base of the tower. We keep flour in there, do we not? Extra bread this day, yes, we must bake extra bread and so will need flour. The girls and I, and you as well, shall be very hungry from all of yesterday's activity. Would you do that, please?"

"All right," Cinder said, though she could not understand why their conversation was being interrupted with the need for flour.

"Now, my child," Rhona said. "Make haste."

"All right," Cinder said, then she went to the store room at the base of the tower. Rhona followed her in and stood beside her as she searched for bags of grains.

"Flour," Cinder said, and she took a wooden box from a shelf. She opened it and sniffed. "This should be more than enough, though I do not know exactly how much bread you believe we need..." she said. Suddenly, the door behind her closed and she heard a loud, metal click.

"My dear, I am sorry," Rhona said. "I must go find someone. And you must stay here."

Cinder tried to open the door, but it had been tightly fastened. "Mother Rhona, let me out," she shouted.

"I have never locked you away until this moment," Rhona said. "And mark my words, I shall release you. But I haven't much time. I will be back, my girl."

Cinder heard her words, but continued to push against and shake the door. "Come back!" she called.

A few minutes later, she heard a sound from outside the house that resembled a whinny from the horse, Duncan. She ran up the stairs to the tower as fast as she could to see out the windows. Rhona had bridled the horse and was riding away.

Cinder placed her palms on the cold glass and looked. "No," she muttered. Her stepmother had betrayed her. They were connected through her mother, this she now knew, but this woman, her father's second wife, could never be trusted.

Rhona had once known Cinder's mother, but she was no friend of hers. And she never would be.

Chapter Nineteen

Before he set out from his room, Prince Finn washed his face and combed his hair, then dressed in his most princely regalia, complete with a fresh pressed shirt, sash, and all the medals and ornaments required during events of great ceremony, some of which he had worn the night before. Finally, he donned a pair of freshly shined shoes. He looked in the mirror. There he saw obedient Prince Finn, reporting for duty. He walked out the door to his bedroom, certain that the next time he came back through that door, his whole life would be changed.

When he stepped into the corridor, the castle was quiet. He could hear the soft rustle of people roaming distant hallways, likely servants, but he did not see them. He walked past several doors until he came to the one belonging to his parents' chambers. He knocked and when his mother called, "Come in," he did so.

Inside, his parents were in bed drinking tea, as they often did after large, late parties. When they saw their son and how he was bedecked, they both sat up straight, as though they were attending a meeting that had been called to order.

"Good morning, son," said his father, the king. "You're up early."

"Yes, father," he said, bowing his head.

"Are you going someplace this early?" asked the queen. "Finn, why are you dressed so formally—"

"Mother, father, Your Majesties, I hope you will someday forgive me," Finn said. "I am here this morning to tell you, after everything, I do love the girl."

His father sighed, deeply and loudly. "This again," he growled.

The queen pushed the covers away and got out of bed and put on her dressing gown. "What of the duchess?" the queen demanded. "She has been promised a king."

"Yes," Finn said. "And all the pieces were in place for years. I waited for her to come of age, for our families to decide the time for marriage. I never challenged this or grew impatient. She changed the plans. She chose to marry for love. Now that she has changed her mind again, I, who have always done as asked, must sacrifice what I desire."

"Nobody promised you life would be fair, boy," the king grumbled.

"When we first learned that she had married, we considered whether there was another lady I could wed to benefit the kingdom," Finn continued. "Had we identified one, I would have performed my obligation without question. Since the moment of my birth, I have always taken my station and my responsibilities seriously. I never questioned that I was to marry the duchess or whoever was chosen for me. I never demanded anything for myself. Until today."

Finn thought then about the small shoe. He remembered the girl, how beautiful she had been the night before, how beautiful she'd always been. But last night, her hair, the color of warm honey, shone in the candlelight, and when her green eyes locked upon his while they danced, he felt a bliss he'd never known. He could not now remember the color of her dress, only that he had never seen one so fair. He had loved dancing with her, on the cliffs over the ocean and in the ballroom watched by all the people of the Braemuir Kingdom. He longed to dance with her again, to spend his whole life dancing with her.

"When the duchess changed her mind," Finn said. "My choice was revoked. When I had the opportunity to choose, I chose *her*. And now I am willing to take whatever action deemed necessary for me to retain that choice."

The queen crossed her arms and sighed. "Finn, you cannot mean–" she said. "Stop this. Once you walk through this door, you will not return."

"You have two other able-bodied sons," Finn said.

King Humphry lunged, pointing. "You are a king's first-born son," he exclaimed. "Your duty is to act as sovereign. You cannot forsake your duty because you've fallen for some harlot."

"She is no harlot," Finn stated.

"Finn, you are the crown prince," the queen said, stepping in between father and son. "You know a prince marries for country. This is your duty."

"If choosing her means walking away from the throne, then today..." He took a deep breath. "I shall take that walk."

A whisper went out of the room, the sound of something long hoped for quietly dying. The king roared and threw a chair against the wall. It fell apart in bits and splinters.

The queen paced and held her hand to her head. "Did you learn her name, Finn? Or anything about her family or background?"

"No," he said. "After Father made his announcement, she fled, leaving behind only her shoe. But I learned she lives at Bowmore House near Sayre Cliffs. This morning, I will go there. I intend to ask for her hand in marriage. I do not know if she will say yes. And I do not know what I shall do if she says no, but I must take the chance."

"Oh, Finn," said the queen. "I am a mother without words. I am happy to think of you seeking your life, but my heart aches to think it will not be in the post we raised you to accept."

"Eiran will be a fine king," Finn said. "He is confident, and smart. We two brothers were born in the wrong order."

"The first true thing you have spoken," grumbled the king.

"Hush, Humphry," she said. The queen looked Finn straight in his eyes. "I do not believe that. If the girl does not accept your marriage invitation, come home to your family."

"What does he care for family?" the king growled. "That he would do this to us, embarrass us and show me to be a liar. That he would walk away from his responsibilities without a second thought."

The queen sighed. "Perhaps, my king, it is our duty as parents to acknowledge that Finn has explained his feelings. He never came to us insisting on a love marriage. In fact, he's right, I cannot recall a time in his life when he asked for anything, much less put his needs above those of the crown."

"Until now," his father said.

"And what other matter is so deserving of sacrifice than love?"

"You're taking his side?" he said.

"Your son is not sneaking off in the dead of night like the duchess did," the queen said. "He's not failing to realize that his choices affect the entire kingdom. He is standing before us, bravely explaining his reasons. For this, I am proud of my son."

Finn smiled meekly at his mother.

"And because of these things," she said, projecting her chin forward and taking on the posture of a queen. "Allow me to make a proposal. Let Finn marry this girl he loves, if she will have him. Eiran may marry the duchess. Eiran may also presume the title of Crown Prince and Heath shall be next in line until the princess bears sons. Finn, however, will be acknowledged as a member of the royal family as...the Prince of the People."

The king stood in front of the window with his back to Finn and the queen. "And he would never be king?"

"He would remain a part of our family, and the family of the country," the queen said. "Perhaps we could bestow upon him a role such as...something like...Prince Tribune."

The king turned slowly and stared at his wife with an expression that Finn could not read.

"You are the king, my highness," she said, bowing her head. "Your word is, of course, law. Perhaps Braemuir does not have to lose Finn as a countryman or counselor and we do not have to lose a son. Well? What say you, good and fair King Humphry?"

Finn and Queen Eleanor waited while the king glared at them, arms crossed. He paced the room once, then a second time, and Finn thought he could feel the weight of the king's heavy footsteps upon the floor. Finally, the king sat down on a chair beside a small desk and pressed his hand into his head. "I don't know," he grunted.

At that, the queen smiled and turned to Finn. "He will consider it," she said. "It's the best we can hope for. Now, go, find the girl. Make it known that you shall not become king, for if there is a chance that that is why—"

"She didn't know who I was until the moment she ran away," he said. "I had always told her I worked in the castle stable. I wanted her to know me as me, not the king's son."

The queen looked at her son. "Truly?" He nodded. "My son, you might be the most humble soul I have ever known. Nonetheless, do tell her. You learn a good deal about people from how they react to such things. If she says yes, then, if the king allows it, we shall plan a wedding and...we shall try to figure out what a Prince Tribune is."

"Thank you, mother," he said. "If by the grace of His Highness it comes to pass, I shall try to be the best Prince Tribune you have ever had. Now, if you will excuse me, I must find a foot."

At Bowmore House, Liisi awoke to the sensation that she required a chamber pot. She took care of this then donned her dressing gown and stroked her hair. She'd only had a few hours of rest, but she was wide awake, her mind so full of all the wonderful memories from the previous night: the king's luminous castle, wonderful music, pastries and confections. And the dancing! Now, she stood before her bedroom window and looked out at the ocean, but what she saw was the incandescent ballroom; what she heard was the beautiful music. She began to hum, then swished her skirt and stepped in time with the music in her memory. She had danced with several young men, each noble to some degree and quite handsome. Better still, she had danced with the prince. Though he would wed someone else, her heart still raced with the thrill of it.

The sun was just over the horizon and the sky was a perfect shade of blue. It would be a fine, fine day, she thought. Then she remembered— the prince had asked where she lived. And she had told him. Perhaps he would seek her out, and invite her to become his very own kept woman. Oh! She wouldn't mind that as long as he kept her in jewels and beautiful gowns and sumptuous meals.

Yes, she thought. She would make a very fine courtesan.

This idea delighted her so much, she clapped her hands, and squealed with joy, then spun around and danced and swayed again in front of the window. *I shall leave this house behind*, she thought. *I shall live in the castle, perhaps I shall gain employ as the queen's lady-in-waiting.*

She waited for her mother or Orla to come and wake her; she could not wait to tell them the marvelous news. Her mother was desperate for her to marry a respectable gentleman, but the possibility that she might become the king's sovereign lady was horribly scandalous and terribly glamorous. It suited her better, she thought. History would take note of her. Songs would be written about her captivating beauty, and plays would be performed that displayed her devastating wit.

After nobody came to find her, Liisi went in search of her sister and mother. She expected to find both in her mother's bedroom, but the room was empty and cold. How mysterious. She went down the stairs and peeked into the kitchen. The fire was lit but nobody was about. When they arrived home from the ball the previous night, all the fires were out and the house was cold, dark and quiet. Her mother searched and called for Cinder, but there had been no response. Orla once again brought up the tedious topic of how Cinder should have attended the ball, and Liisi and Orla should have helped her. Liisi had been unable to hear this tired story again, so she went to bed.

"Mother," she called out now. "Orla? Is anyone here?" Orla stepped out from behind a corner. "Oh, you surprised me. Where is Mother? The house feels too quiet."

"Mother is on some errand. Come over here," Orla said, and she gestured to Liisi to come with her to the door of the store room. On the floor beside it was a pile of old, rusted keys.

"Liisi is here," Orla said to the door.

"Good morning, Liisi," came a voice from the other side of the door. "I trust you enjoyed yourself last night."

"Cinder?" asked Liisi. "What are you doing? Did you lock yourself in there? Why would you do such a thing?"

Orla pointed to the padlock. "Mother locked her in," Orla said. "And then rode away on the horse."

"The horse?" Liisi said. "She hates to ride. Oh, I cannot bear any intrigue this morning. Cinder, come out and make my tea. And my room is freezing; please come make the fire."

"Did you not hear me?" Orla said. "She is locked inside. She cannot get out. The kitchen fire is hot, go boil water and make your own tea."

"Oh, truly locked in?" Liisi said. "I don't understand. Why?"

"Cinder went for a walk last night and came home late," Orla said. "Mother was in the kitchen waiting for her. And then Cinder told her that she had learned the oddest thing..."

Orla paused and looked toward the door.

"Yes, well?" asked Liisi. "What oddest thing?"

"Your mother and my mother," Cinder said from the other side of the door. "They knew one another when they were children."

"They were not only acquainted," Orla said. "They were friends."

"Rhona and Rhona, how charming," Liisi said.

"My mother's name was not Rhona," Cinder said. "Your mother told her to call herself that so she could escape peril."

Liisi sighed and put her hand to her head. "I cannot absorb these details before tea," she said. "Where is Mother now?"

"We do not know," Orla said. "I have been trying every key to open the door, but none of them work. Liisi, do you know if there is a key to this lock somewhere?"

"Me? Certainly, I haven't any idea," she said. "I didn't even know we had such a lock. Cinder usually knows these things."

"I directed Orla to every key I could think of," Cinder said from behind the door.

"I'm sure Mother will be back," Orla said. "She cannot mean for you to rot in there."

"Oh, Orla!" Cinder said, her tone suddenly urgent. "Check the table in the kitchen. Is there anything upon it?"

Orla went to the kitchen and called from there. "I see a board for cutting," she said. "And a knife, and a heel of bread. I believe we left those out when we arrived home."

"What of pages?" Cinder said. "Do you see a stack? A pile of papers?"

"No," Orla said.

"Please look carefully," she said. "It is the letter my mother wrote me. This is how I learned of the history between our mothers."

"Oh dear. You can search too," Orla said to Liisi. "Where should we look, Cinder? I don't see anything."

"I don't know," Cinder said. "It is a letter of several pages. Your mother was reading it...and she sent me in here then locked me in."

"I don't see any sign of pages," Orla said.

"Not a single one?" Cinder asked. "Perhaps they scattered about the room in a gust of wind."

Liisi could hear tears in Cinder's voice. She had never heard that before.

Both sisters searched all corners of the kitchen but found nothing.

"Cinder, we cannot find them," Orla said. Then, slowly, Orla and Liisi looked toward the fireplace; the fire inside burned hot and bright. Orla looked at Liisi, her face twisted in despair. "If Cinder found a letter from her own mother, it would be the most precious thing she possessed," Orla said quietly. "To destroy such a thing would be cruel beyond words. Mother would never...would she?"

Liisi looked into the fire. "I do not see bits of paper floating about," she said. "That's a good sign, right?"

"Do not speak of this to Cinder," Orla said. "She has enough concerns." They returned to the door. "I'm sorry, Cinder. We found nothing."

"Perhaps your mother took it," Cinder said. "But why would she do such a thing? Your mother has finally gone mad."

"You might be right," Orla said.

"Orla, can you do one last thing for me?" Cinder said. "Henry needs breakfast. I always warm his milk over the fire. Not to boiling, just enough to remove the morning's chill."

"Yes, of course," Orla said.

"Orla, Liisi," Cinder called. "There's something more I need to tell you. I am planning to depart Bowmore House."

"Leave?" asked Liisi. "And go where?"

"I haven't decided," she said. "Until this moment, I have never been a prisoner in this house. But now, I am even more resolved. The moment this door opens I shall be out the front door and I will never return."

"Oh, Cinder," Orla said. "I should miss you."

"And I will notice your absence," Liisi said. Orla kicked her and Liisi winced. "I mean, I will miss you too."

While Orla warmed milk for the cat, Liisi went upstairs to dress. The room was cold. The hearth contained a few bits of hot coals, and Liisi tried to enliven them by tossing in sticks, as she had seen Cinder do, but they did not catch the flames. She knew it might help if she got closer to the embers and fanned them, but she did not want to. She did not care to get so close to fires; after she watched her home burn down all those years ago, she hated them. She had always appreciated that Cinder tended the fires and was fearless about it.

Yes, she supposed she appreciated many things Cinder had done for them.

Liisi dressed then admired herself in the looking glass. She took the fan she'd carried at the ball and held it up so it covered her face. "Oh, Your Highness," she said, giggling. "You are so very strong and handsome. Why yes, I would be honored to stroll the gardens with you. Oh, Sire, you must not look at me like that while your wife stands right there!"

Liisi laughed. *I really do have the most marvelous ability to daydream*, she thought.

Just then, the bell at the door rang through the house. She flinched; who would visit so early? She went down the corridor to the top of the stairs. Orla stood in front of the door, looking through the keyhole.

"I think it is the prince," Orla said.

Liisi gasped. "What prince?"

"The one you danced with last night," she said.

"Finnian?" Liisi whispered. "Prince Finnian?" Orla nodded, and Liisi was paralyzed with thrill. It wasn't just a daydream, it was all true, she thought. *The prince loves me and my life begins now, today. Of course! He asked where I lived and now, he has come for me.*

"Good morning," came a man's voice from the other side of the door. "Might we speak with someone inside?"

"Hello, kind sir," Orla said through the closed door. "I regret to tell you, we are only two ladies alone here and cannot open—"

"Don't tell him that," Liisi said. She rushed down the stairs as fast as her legs would bring her. "He'll go away and he won't come back." She stood in front of the door and fluffed her hair and pinched her cheeks, then straightened and brushed her clothes. Thank goodness she'd taken her time with her appearance.

Today, her real life would begin.

She touched her hair one last time and smiled widely, then opened the door. There standing before her was Prince Finnian, flanked by an older man and a boy.

"Good morning, my ladies," said the man. "Allow me to present..."

"Speak not another word, sir, for we are well acquainted. Your Highness, Prince Finnian." Liisi curtsied deep and slow, and signaled to Orla that she should also do so. "We are honored to have you visit our home. You are always welcome, but how mysterious that you would arrive so early. Have you properly recovered from the ball? Are your feet not weary from so much dancing?"

"It was a lovely night, Miss Liisi," he said. "One I will remember for a very long time."

"Please, come inside," Liisi said. "We…gave our servants the day off, for they deserved to rest after working so hard to help us prepare for the ball. But my sister can make us tea, if you please."

She turned to the side to welcome him in.

"Forgive me, Miss," he said. "May I also present my man, well, my friend, Jakob, and his son, Bard."

Jakob and Bard nodded in greeting.

"Hello," said Liisi. "And, if you please, this is my sister, Orla."

Orla curtsied again and bowed her head.

Prince Finn cleared his throat. "How do you do, Miss Orla?" he said. Liisi noticed that he was looking into the house beyond her. "Miss

Liisi, we are searching for a young woman. Is there by chance another who lives here?"

"Another?" Liisi asked, perplexed. "Are we two not enough?"

"Actually—" Orla started, but Liisi shushed her.

"Orla and I are sisters, and we are our mother's only children," Liisi said.

"I see," Finn said. "Miss Liisi, I am so very sorry. I was led to believe that a third young woman resided here. A young woman who claimed that you were her sister."

"Oh, that's peculiar," Liisi said. "What name did this young woman go by?"

Prince Finn looked at his companions. "I never learned her name."

Liisi looked at Orla in confusion. "You met her last night?" Liisi asked. Finn nodded. "And she told you she lived here?"

"That's right," he said.

"I see," Liisi said. Her daydreams were dissolving like soap bubbles. "Why are you seeking her now?"

"I wish to learn her name," he said. "And more, I wish to ask her hand in marriage."

Orla gasped and put her hands over her mouth.

Liisi frowned. "What of the duchess? The king announced last night that she was your intended."

Prince Finn smiled. "My father has his own ideas," he said "And the woman I danced with last night is someone I have known for many years."

"Not very well, though, if you never learned her name," Liisi scoffed.

"She is a pauper, I know this," he said. "She is an orphan. Still, I realized last night that my heart belongs to her alone. My parents gave me a choice: if I choose to marry her, I must renounce the throne. Therefore, no prince stands before you now. I am but a commoner, a subject of King Humphry of Braemuir, just like any other. If this young woman is not here, I should take my leave and seek her elsewhere..."

Liisi did not let him end his sentence. "No longer a prince?"

"At this moment, no title at all," Finn said. "I am only a humble countryman."

"And that's," Liisi started, "permanent, is it? You couldn't return home and gain back your title? And marry the duchess and consider retaining a courtesan...of sorts?"

"I'm afraid I cannot, Miss Liisi," he said. "And were I given a chance, I would not."

Liisi chewed her lip as she thought about this. "Well, I hate to disappoint you," she finally said. "The only women who live here are my mother, my sister and myself."

Finn looked at Orla, but she would not meet his eyes. "Very well, then," he said. "I bid you two a good day."

"Thank you for the visit, kind sir. We wish you good fortune in your endeavors," Liisi said. She closed the door and Orla turned to her.

"Why did you do that?" Orla said in a frantic whisper.

"That was not Cinder last night," Liisi said, holding the door closed. "Cinder has no gown. She cannot dance. Someone lied to him."

"What if it was Cinder?" Orla said. "Liisi, what if it was? Perhaps someone taught her to dance and lent her a dress. We do not know. I thought that girl looked familiar last night."

"You always stick up for her," Liisi said. "Every time. What about me, what I want?"

"If Cinder was there and somehow charmed the prince, we owe it to her to tell her that he seeks her now," Orla said. "The one thing we know is that he gave up his title for whatever young woman he is seeking. This is no small sacrifice. If she is here, shouldn't we tell him?"

"What would we do anyway, Orla, bring him to a locked pantry door?" she asked. "Yes, Your Highness, or Your Ordinariness, or whatever, there is another girl here but our mother locked her up this morning so you will have to speak to her through the door crack."

Orla glared at her sister. "Maybe it is Cinder he seeks, maybe not," she said. "But after the way we have treated her all these years, we owe her the chance to speak for herself. We owe her the courtesy of acknowledging that she lives here. She is not an animal, Liisi. She is a human being."

When Orla spoke these words, something in Liisi's heart shifted. She let these thoughts sink in, and as she did, her hand on the doorknob grew limp and fell away. For the first time in her life, Liisi questioned herself.

"I shall go and speak to him," Orla said.

"If you do so," Liisi said. "You shall go alone."

Orla looked at her sister then pushed through the door and out into the yard. Liisi watched but did not follow her sister.

"Wait, Prince Finn," Orla called and ran across the yard to where the prince and his cohorts were preparing to climb upon their horses.

"Miss Orla," said Finn.

"The woman you danced with last night," Orla said. "You're sure she told you she lived here? And that Liisi was her sister? But she never told you her name?"

Finn looked at his friends. "I asked it, but she did not tell me."

"And if you found this woman, you would ask for her hand in marriage?" Orla asked.

He nodded. "I would."

"How amazing that you would give up the throne for this lady," Orla said.

Finn thought about this. "I would do it again, a hundred times over, if it meant I might be able to spend my life with her," he said. "I was never meant to be king. My brother, Eiran, is now the crown prince in my stead. And someday, he shall be a very fine sovereign."

"I'm sure he will," Orla said.

"May I show you something?" Finn asked. Orla nodded. He reached into a sack that hung across the horse's back and brought out an object wrapped in white silk. He pulled away the fabric and presented her with a shoe. "The girl I danced with last night left this behind. I do not know her name, but her foot will fit this shoe. If I cannot find her here, I will seek her somewhere else. I will not rest until I find her."

Orla touched the shoe gingerly. "You love this girl very dearly," she said.

Finn nodded.

"He has loved her for many years, Miss," the man, Jakob, said, putting a hand upon Finn's shoulder.

Just then, a sound came from behind them. "Finn!" someone called, and they turned. Cinder had been freed from her jail. She walked across the yard to where they stood. Liisi appeared behind her, and came and stood next to Orla.

"What did you do?" Orla asked. Liisi held up a bent fork. "Well done, sister," she said. "Oh, very well done."

Chapter Twenty

Meanwhile, from the chamber where she'd been imprisoned, Cinder heard the bell at the door. She listened to the murmur of Liisi's and Orla's voices speaking to someone—possibly a man's voice?—but she could not discern the nature of their conversation. She climbed to the top of the tower to see if she could make sense of it. But the view was designed to look out over the sea, and she could see nothing happening directly in front of the house.

Once again, she descended to the pantry. She banged on the door with the flats of her palms, shouting to be let out.

But the door was solid, and she could tell the sound would not travel past the kitchen. Why, she wondered, had her father designed this room to be a jail cell? She pressed her ear against the door. No matter how hard she tried, she could not hear words. She banged at the door again.

"Can anyone hear me?" she called.

Furious, she kicked the door then paced and tried to think of what to do. She pushed her back against the door, hoping she could crumble the lock, but the door did not move. Then she crashed against it with her shoulder, which only injured her shoulder. She searched the pantry for something she could slam into the door but found nothing.

"I should have stored an ax in here," she said. "Jams and pickles are useless."

She paced and banged and shouted for several more minutes. Finally, she heard a rustle on the other side of the door.

"Orla, is that you?" she said. "Who is at the house? Has your mother come home?"

"This is Liisi," came the voice. "It's not mother at the door. It's much more peculiar than that."

"Who is it, Liisi?" she asked. "Tell me what is happening!"

"You must come see for yourself," Liisi said. "I'm trying to liberate you."

"Did you find the key?"

"I heard a hairpin could open a lock," Liisi said. "But I'm not sure how to do it."

"Yes," Cinder said. "Insert the prongs of the hairpin into the keyhole. Then move it about until the prongs find the lock mechanism."

"I'm wiggling, but nothing is happening," Liisi said.

"Move the whole hairpin around," Cinder said. "Side to side. If it bends a little, that's all right."

"So you say," Liisi said. "I would rather not sacrifice a hairpin. They do not grow on trees, you know."

Cinder waited. "Is anything happening? Liisi, I cannot bear being stuck in here."

"You're terribly impatient," she said. "That's a character flaw, Cinder, you should work on that."

"Liisi!"

"I am trying my best, but it's not working," she said.

"Try something larger," Cinder said. "Could you find a utensil? A fork, maybe?"

"Let me see," Liisi said. "Hold on."

Cinder waited for a moment, and then another, and then another. "Liisi, are you still there?"

"I had to try different forks," she said. "The first one was too big, the second too small. Here's a third. And...it went in."

"Good. Now, move it about..."

"That is what I am doing," Liisi said. "Hold on. Oh! Something happened. Something clicked. I heard it."

Cinder realized then how strange and rare it was for Liisi to perform some task that resembled work, which would benefit someone other than herself. "Wait," Cinder said, stepping away from the door. "Why are you helping me?"

"I think it's done, now I just need to...Oh, the lock is so rusted it won't open. Where did Mother find this thing?"

"Lean on it, Liisi," Cinder said. "With all your weight."

"I am," she said. "I am almost sitting upon it." She emitted a loud growl, and Cinder heard a thud, and metal grinding. "Success!" Liisi said, and she opened the door.

"You did it!" Cinder said, gasping for air. "Thank you."

The two girls regarded one another. "Cinder, you asked why I helped you," she said. "I shall not pretend we have been the closest of sisters. When Mother brought us to this house and told us we had a new sister, I bristled. Our previous home had been so large, almost a castle, but in one night, it was reduced to ashes, along with our father. You had your father and your home, and you did not care about all that we had lost, all that we endured. You treated us like intruders."

"I never considered this," Cinder said.

Liisi cocked her head in that certain Liisi way. "To defend against my own sadness, I pushed you away," she said. "Whatever you were, I was determined not to be. You were wild, so I was polite. You worked and took charge of everything, so I was lazy. You did not consider your looks, so I cultivated mine. You were a wildling out on the cliffs, so I was a homebound princess. After your father died, we all lost our security. You became more you, and I pushed harder. Things might have been different if I had realized that...our situation was the same, and we all needed the same things. But I did not and neither did you." She paused for a moment. "So, there we are."

"Liisi, I did not know any of this" she said. "Forgive me."

"Yes, well, my father used to say, the only way forward is forward," Liisi said. Then her expression changed to shock. "Oh! We do not have time for prattle. Cinder, you must go outside."

"Why?" Cinder asked.

"You will see," Liisi said. "Orla is there speaking to some mystery party. None of it makes sense to me, but I do not know what life you lived out there on your cliffs. Go now. They might not wait forever, so make haste."

Cinder turned toward the front of the house and stopped herself. "Liisi, thank you."

"You are welcome, my friend," she said. "I promise never to threaten your cat again. Now, go find Orla."

Her curiosity piqued, Cinder rushed to the front of the house and stood in the doorway. Orla was in the yard, speaking to some men, three of them, standing beside two brown horses. Cinder's eyes needed to adjust to the light of day before she understood: one of them was Finn.

Or so it seemed. Unless her eyes were mistaken, or perhaps she was dreaming. Or, she thought, it could be a trick of the light, or her heart wanting so much for him to be in her yard.

She looked carefully. No, she was certain: the young man speaking with Orla was the friend she'd known for many years, the man she had kissed by the cliffs and the gentleman she'd danced with the night before.

The night before. Had it all been true, and not merely a dream? She would never understand how such things had come to pass, but she was sure the experience had been real: the miraculous transformation, and curious passage to the king's castle. And all of it orchestrated by one who wielded shape and time like they were a child's toys.

Cinder called to Finn, then walked out the door of Bowmore House and across the yard, the wind stirring her skirt and her hair.

"My lady," Finn said, and bowed.

"You found me," she said, as she approached. "I did not know if I would ever see you again."

"You left something behind last night," he said. "I have come to return it."

He brought out the shoe he had shown to Orla and presented it to Cinder. She gave him a wistful smile. "I should take it back," she said. "Your bride would not be glad for you to possess mementos from previous dancing partners."

"My bride?" Finn asked.

"The lady likely means the duchess, sir," the man said.

"Oh, the duchess," he said. "You should know, the whole world today is changed from yesterday. The crown prince of Braemuir Kingdom does not stand before you. At this hour, the prince likely remains in his bed, fast asleep. When Prince Eiran awakens, he will be told that he shall succeed his father as king for his brother has abdicated the crown in his favor. And yes, his wedding to the duchess will take place, perhaps soon."

"I don't understand," Cinder said.

"Plain Finn stands before you now, having made an important choice this morning. I was never suited to become king," he said. "But perhaps now I shall gain employment as a stable boy."

Cinder's heart raced, and she looked into the eyes of this young man, her dearest friend. "You gave up the life that was promised to you... for me?" she said. "Why?"

He smiled at her. "The young woman I danced with at the ball last night is someone with whom I wish to spend the rest of my life, if she would have me," he said. "You, my lady. You have held my heart for so many years. You knew me under a different name, but you have always understood what my soul is made of. If you would have me, I would be honored to share my life with you."

She looked into his eyes; she could not imagine how much courage he'd had to muster to walk away from his family and the role he'd been raised to assume. And he had walked away from it for her. She wanted desperately to say yes, a thousand times, yes.

"You have known my soul," she said. "The sight of you by the cliffs has always been a bright ray of sunshine in my darkest days. I always sought you, and when I found you, my thoughts after were only and ever remembering our encounters."

Finn gestured for her to sit upon an old bench behind her. He knelt before her and slipped the shoe upon her foot. It was a perfect fit. "It is you," he said, "If you will have me, I shall be yours until the end of time."

Cinder sighed. "Oh, Finn, last night was for magic of the most fleeting sort. But a glass shoe? That is only an illusion." She slipped the shoe off her foot, and it, like the first, held its shape for a moment then dissolved into fine sand. The grains fell through her fingers and blew away in the wind.

Everyone gasped.

"I cannot explain it; the spell had something to do with time," she said. "The glass was once sand, and so sand it becomes again. I am also changed since last night. Finn, if you are seeking a young woman who is lucent and fragile like a glass slipper, she departed the castle last night at midnight. She has not been seen since."

"You may not be the same, but you are even more lovely, here in the costume you wore every time we met." Finn said. "My lady, I have loved you since I met you that first night upon Sayre Cliffs. When I thought I might lose you forever, my heart changed. Today, I know what I want."

Cinder was silent for a moment. Then she put her own shoe back on and stood. She listened to the sound of the sea, lapping below the cliffs, and the songs of the gulls overhead. "But today, I am leaving this Bowmore House, and Braemuir," she said. "Do you remember all those things you told me about? Castles as big as cities, a city carved into a hillside. A wall that goes on for miles and crosses entire countries…"

"A palace made of gemstones," he offered.

"Where nobody ever lived," she said. "Built for an emperor's deceased wife."

"Yes," he said.

"Finn, I ache to see the world," Cinder said. "I do not want to marry because I could think of no other future, or because the world would offer me no other role. I wish to journey beyond this house where I was born, past these shores, past the borders of Braemuir and Dalkeith. I wish to see everything in the wide world."

"Wait a moment," Liisi exclaimed. "This man is proposing marriage. He is no longer a prince, but he is no less handsome. It is a marriage proposal; wouldn't you simply accept? And perhaps swoon, or at least pretend to faint a little?"

Finn laughed slightly. "This woman would never pretend to faint," he said. "And I know her vision of the world extends far beyond this place. She inherited her father's hunger for adventure. I have known these things for many years."

"Finn, we are so young," Cinder said. She grasped his hand. "My father fell in love with my mother the moment he saw her, but they waited years before marrying."

"Your father told your mother, 'I have a plan for my life. I shall build ships. And I need a wife to assist me and give me sons.'"

Cinder said, "And she told him, 'Ask me another time.' And he did. I have learned something amazing about time. It changes people. Time... changes everything."

"Finnian," Jakob said, setting a hand on the young man's shoulder. "I hear the sound of approaching hooves. Are they king's men?"

"I hear it as well," Finn said. "I can think of no reason why my father would send soldiers to this place."

"Nor can I," Jakob said.

"It might be Mother returning home," Orla said. "Though it sounds like several horses."

"She only rode one horse away from here," Cinder said. "Why would she return on more than one?"

"We will greet whoever is approaching when they arrive," Finn said. "For now, allow me to revise my offer. My lady, would you do me the honor of allowing me to accompany you and carry your maps on your journeys through the world?"

"Finn," she said. "You are my map. You are the stars I point my sextant toward, my north star and my southern cross. I have been lost at sea for years, and you are the one I always came back to. If you would venture away from this place with me, I would be honored. Please, though, ask my hand in marriage again, another time."

"I will, my love," Finn said. "I will."

Liisi grasped Orla's arm and whimpered. "She received a marriage proposal but she did not say yes," she said. "She told him to ask her later? Are ladies allowed to do that?"

Orla patted Liisi's hand. "Liisi, I believe we are witnessing a great and unlikely love story."

"Now that we are not betrothed," Finn said. "Will you finally tell me your name?"

Cinder laughed. "After all this, I forgot I have not told you."

"We called her Cinder," Liisi said.

"That is not really her name," Orla said. "She used to be called Marga."

"Marga, short for Marguerite," Cinder said. "My grandmother was descended from one of the noble families of Gallia."

"Hello, Marga," Finn said. "I am pleased to make your acquaintance."

Just then, the horses they'd heard approaching began down the lane to Bowmore House. They all turned to see six horses canter down the lane. One was the palfrey, Duncan, whom Rhona had ridden away that morning. She rode atop Duncan now, but she was sitting behind a soldier from Gallia, her arms grasping his middle, her eyes shut tight with terror.

Bard held on to the reins of the horses they had ridden, so they would not be spooked, and Finn and Jakob clutched the handles of their swords, in case defenses were needed. The arriving company stopped, and the soldier alighted from Duncan and carefully helped Rhona down.

"Oh, I don't care for horses," Rhona said, as she dusted off her dress. "Cinder, you're free. I'm glad."

Cinder took a step backward from her stepmother. "Liisi picked the lock," she said.

"Yes, someone would have had to do so, for I brought the key with me," Rhona said. She pulled a key from her pocket.

"Why would you detain me so?" Cinder asked. "And what of my mother's letter? Orla and Liisi searched the kitchen. If you threw it into the fire, I should truly hate you the rest of my days."

"No, child, I would never," she said. She reached into a purse she wore tied around her waist, pulled out the letter and handed it to Cinder. "You will find it all here, every page. I brought it with me to Glengoe Castle."

"Why?" Cinder said, taking the scroll. "You spare no opportunity to violate me."

"Please, child," Rhona said. "Let me explain. But..." Rhona turned and noticed the presence of Prince Finn and the other two men. "Your Highness," Rhona said, and she bowed her head and curtsied.

"He's not a Highness any longer," Liisi said. "He's simply a person." Rhona looked quizzically at her daughters.

"Please, mother," Orla said. "Tell us where you have been this morning. And why you imprisoned Cinder."

Rhona looked nervously at the faces around her. Then, a gentleman came to stand beside her.

"Monsieur De Fontenay," Finn said. "What business have you in this place?"

"I am the one to whom this lady presented the letter in question," he said. "Mademoiselle, please listen to what your stepmother has to tell you. There is sense to be made of things."

"My dear," Rhona said to Cinder. "When you told me about your mother, I was flooded with thoughts and feelings, and so many memories. So much so, I could not speak words. I could only act. You had declared that you were leaving, but I needed to keep you until I could speak with Monsieur, whom you see before you." She pointed at Monsieur De Fontenay.

"And you are the girl they call Cinder?" Monsieur De Fontenay asked.

"Yes," she said.

"I am honored to meet you," he said.

"Monsieur De Fontenay and the soldiers were due to depart Braemuir this morning," she said. "I had to make haste, which is why I rode the horse. But I will never keep you captive again. Nobody shall."

"I still do not understand," Cinder said.

Rhona took a deep breath. "Leontyne, your grandmother, was from Gallia," she said. "She had always told Ailen that her father was the king of Gallia. Your mother thought the story a fiction until the day the queen of Gallia herself appeared in your grandmother's shop."

Chills went up Cinder's spine. "My mother's letter told this story," she said. "This was why my mother left her childhood home. The queen..."

"Leontyne was a beautiful woman with hair as red as flames," Rhona said. "She always believed the queen of Gallia wanted to kill her and her daughter. And that day, the queen did murder Leontyne. But your mother escaped."

"She went to the island of St. Kiana," Cinder said. "Because you sent her there, and gave her your name."

"Your mother declared that those who sought a girl named Ailen would only find other people's memories," Rhona said. "And that was correct until this moment. Cinder, you are the daughter of Ailen, whose name was Marguerite Bertrade de Valois. You are the granddaughter of Leontyne and Mattieu, King of Gallia. You are the legitimate heir to the throne of Gallia."

"What?" Cinder whispered.

"My lady," Monsieur De Fontenay said, his accent thick. "Queen Deutaria was your grandmother's sister. Some months ago, the queen met her earthly conclusion, may she rest in peace. Her supporters now accept that the only way to continue the de Valois bloodline is to welcome you home. We have been seeking you for some time."

Cinder's mouth went dry. She searched her stepmother's face for any sign that this might be a joke, but her stepmother's face looked sincere.

"Do you know what this means?" Finn asked, taking her hand in his. "You shall travel the world. And everywhere you go, people will welcome and celebrate you."

"It is your birthright, child," Rhona said.

"If you accept," Monsieur De Fontenay said.

"If she doesn't, I will," Liisi said.

"Hush," Orla said.

"And for that matter," Rhona said. "This also belongs to you." She pulled from her pocket the brooch that Liisi had worn to the ball, fashioned of ivory, surrounded with diamonds. "Your mother gave me this, and a few other baubles, so I could escape Dunford. But then, I could not sell them, for the London constable identified them as property of the king of Gallia. It is well and right that I did not sell them; I held on to them for you."

"Is this the crime Lord Warin accused you of?" Cinder asked.

"This, yes, and your mother's murder," Rhona said. "I could not explain that I had not killed her for I did not know if the queen sought her still."

Cinder looked at the brooch. "I never would have dreamed these things."

"Mademoiselle," Monsieur De Fontenay said. "Your role as the heir to the throne of Gallia is yours to claim or claim not."

Cinder was nervous. She looked at Mother Rhona.

"It is your choice, Cinder," she said. "Only you can make this decision."

"I confess, I am somewhat shocked," she said. "If you told me I was descended from pirates, that would have made more sense."

Everyone laughed.

"But your mother told you," Rhona said. "She wrote it in her letter. Did you not believe her?"

"I considered it, but I never... I could not have believed that I would be the subject of a story of such proportions," Cinder said. "And if I had taken it seriously, I still would not have sought it out. I too would have wanted to avoid inspiring the queen's rage."

"I assure you, the queen's earthly fights are concluded," Monsieur De Fontenay said.

"Cinder, will you accept your title?" Rhona asked.

Cinder was silent a moment, and looked at each of their faces, wide with hope. "If I accept, everything in my life changes. I would leave Bowmore House, and Dalkeith. I would have to learn...many things, starting with the language of the country of Gallia, its history and customs, how to run a nation. I do not now know any of it."

"If you will have me, I will stay beside you," Finn said. "I may be able to help with some of these things, for I have some experience."

"Yes, Finn, you must," she said. "But what do I know of leading a country? Or anything of life beyond the kitchen of this house?"

"My sister," Orla said, and she took Cinder's hands in hers. "My lovely sister. I understand how you would be daunted by such a possibility. But you are well suited to rule. You have lived so many lives in such a short time. You know what it is to grieve the ones you love, to be cold and hungry, lonely and frightened, to be misunderstood, to lose everything and begin anew."

"But, Orla, I can't—" Cinder started.

"You have learned to think," she said. "You never once did as you were told only because you were told to do so."

"This is true," Rhona said.

Orla smiled at her mother. "And your ability for kindness has no equal. The stuff you are made of is compassion and courage, you have strength of mind, a quick wit, and a heart as wide as the sea. If there is more to being a ruler, I know not what it might be."

"My sister speaks the truth," Liisi said.

"That's right," Rhona said, tears in her eyes. "And my child, my child, I am sorry for how I treated you all these years. I did not understand. I could not see past my own grief. This morning, you told me about your mother's letter, and suddenly, I understood. In one moment, everything made sense. You truly are your mother's daughter, but you are also so different. If anyone in this world is qualified to assume the mantle of leadership, it is you."

"Thank you," Cinder said. She dropped Orla's hands and turned away from the crowd to face the sea. *Mother*, she thought, *tell me what to do.*

Her mother's voice spoke then in a whisper born upon the wind. *History is made up of kings, horses, and war. You could be queen, and in place of war, promote a mighty and courageous peace. Claim your birthright, my daughter. It was always yours.*

Cinder turned and looked at everyone, her heart beating hard and fast. "Promise me this: if Lord Warin comes here again, tell him...if he threatens this house, we shall send the royal cavalry and the navy. For Bowmore House is now under the stewardship of Marguerite, Princess of Gallia."

"All hail Princess Marguerite," Finn said.

"Hail!" they all said. And everyone cheered and clapped, and Cinder embraced first Orla, then Liisi then Mother Rhona. And then she turned to Finn. Their arms wrapped around each other, and she nestled her face beside his neck. She inhaled him; he smelled of horse sweat and earth and the sweet flesh of apples. She pulled her face away to look at his, and their lips came together as though their lips themselves had desired this for many years. They kissed for what felt like many moments though it was not enough. That day, Cinder learned the secret of a kiss: it fans a flame that is quick to ignite.

There was no doubt in anyone's minds: someday he would again ask her again to marry him, and that time, she would say yes.

"Perhaps," Monsieur De Fontenay said to Cinder, "Your Majesty will accompany me to Glengoe Castle. There, I can tell you about Gallia, our history and traditions. I will tell you more about your mother's family and legacy. And we shall make plans to bring you to Gallia and meet your grandfather. Would you care to join us?"

"Yes," she said. "I want to learn everything."

Finn looked at Jakob and Bard and laughed. "We set out this

morning not knowing where our journey would bring us," he said. "As it happens, our travels bring us to Glengoe Castle."

"You know what they say, Your Highness," Jakob said. "All searching leads to returning. In folk tales, this usually takes a bit more time."

"And I have learned that I must leave my house to find my true home," Cinder said. "Just like my mother before me."

"Just like your mother," Rhona said. "You are so much like your mother."

Chapter Twenty-One

After Monsieur De Fontenay invited Cinder—called now Marga—to Glengoe Castle, all decided she should go forthwith. But Orla rushed into the house and gathered the one item that could not be left behind: Henry. Orla wrapped him in a blanket so only his head was revealed and presented him.

"Finn," Cinder—now Marga—said, "meet Henry. He has been my dearest companion my whole life."

Finn leaned down to look the tabby in the face. "How do you do, sir?" he said.

Henry yawned.

"Don't try to shake hands with him," Orla said. "And sometimes, he's not very warm with strangers."

"Then, we shall have to get to know each other so we are no longer strangers," Finn said, as he gently scratched the scruff of Henry's neck. "I am pleased to meet you, good man."

She put her ear toward Henry and heard the quietest murmur of a purr. "He likes you. Still, don't try to shake hands. He never approved of such nonsense."

Then, with her beloved cat tucked safely in her arms, the young woman rode with Finn on the back of the horse he had ridden to Bowmore House. During that journey to Glengoe Castle, on winding roads through the king's land, which she had never traveled before, Cinder—nay, Marga—considered how she'd learned that day that Bowmore House was only where her story began. She'd been committed for so long to keeping and tending the fires in all the rooms, but this place was never meant to be her destiny. She had sensed and questioned this during her night in the tower when she looked to the moon and spoke her true name out loud. What power was in a name? She had spent years hiding behind the cover of a false name, as her mother had before her. Perhaps now that all names and relationships had been untangled, she might learn what more her destiny held. Marga—previously Cinder—dearly hoped that the next chapter would provide her and all of them peace. They all deserved it.

Marga felt the horse's hooves clomp and felt Finn's body behind her.

"Are you all right?" he asked.

"My mind is spinning," she said. "This day began last night a moment before midnight, when you were chasing me. This morning, I learned so many strange truths, and now, my entire life is changed. All because of a letter."

"When I left the castle this morning," he said, "I thought the most extraordinary event that might occur today would be finding you. Far from it."

She smiled. "When I arrived home this morning, I believed I would only pack my things and leave. How fast the world changes. In a single moment, the world reveals itself anew."

"Are you happy with all that has unfolded?" he asked.

"Happy? Yes," she said, and she leaned back into his chest. But she had many other feelings as well. She wondered what was ahead, what experiences life would yield, what kind of a person she would become. Someone entirely new, she thought, someone she did not yet know, who had yet to be created. Her new self would be built from all the people she had ever been: a daughter, a child, a person who felt and thought and loved and grieved, a friend, a sister, a stepdaughter. And one who started and nursed so many fires through the seasons of a house by the salty sea: a blaze-keeper.

Marga went to Glengoe Castle that day, and was presented to King Humphry and Queen Eleanor. Monsieur De Fontenay explained all that had happened and Finn explained that this was the girl he had told them about. They all agreed that if they had only known who she was to begin with, they could have avoided a good bit of trouble. The king and queen invited Marga to stay with them and prepare to make the journey to Gallia. Queen Eleanor requested her royal dressmaker to make her a closet of clothes, as Marga could not travel to Gallia and accept her role as princess while she possessed only the humble dressings of a kitchen wench.

After one month, Princess Marga and Prince Finn traveled together to Gallia along with Henry. When Marga met King Mattieu, the old man greeted the girl with a grandfather's warm embrace. Marga started to believe that she could call Gallia home.

If the ball at Glengoe Castle had been the first Princess Marga ever attended, it was certainly not the last. The king and his advisors planned festivities and dinners and picnics to present the princess to her new country's people. Marga now had to learn how to greet a crowd and to listen to peoples' concerns and figure out solutions. Over time, she found buried deep within herself talents and abilities she never knew she had.

By summer, Henry's eyes and ears seemed to weaken, and Marga knew his time was coming to an end. She wondered if he remembered that strange night when the mysterious Nula-na-Nekon visited Cinder in the garden and turned a cat into a footman. What did he make of it, and all the changes that came after? She suspected it mattered little to him, as long as they were together and dishes of milk were always delivered, sweet and warm.

Then, one morning, Marga touched the scruff of his neck. His skin was cold and he did not stir.

"My dearest friend," she whispered through tears. "I hope your hereafter is filled with so many mice to chase, and soft, sunny places for long naps. Henry, you have been so dear to me."

She explained to her grandfather that she desired that Henry's remains be placed beside her mother, on the island of St. Kiana, where the cat was born. King Mattieu believed it was time for the girl to finally journey to the island where her mother was buried.

Within the week, a ship had been commissioned and Finn and Marga, along with a small box containing Henry's remains, ventured to St. Kiana. After a day on the sea, they viewed the island, an archipelago surrounded by craggy stones, cliffs and hills swathed in green. In the distance, they could see a valley with a row of croft houses nestled within. Herds of small, brown sheep grazed on the hillsides, and over the tops of the tallest peaks, wisps of clouds hovered and flitted away. White gannets glided through the mist and around the summit, their calls and cries echoing high and lonely over the harbor.

"I see how my mother would love this strange, remote island,"

Marga said. "I feel like I have left the ordinary world and entered a dream."

"You likely have dreamed of this place," he said.

"Many times," she said. "But in my imagination, it looked no different from Sayre Cliffs. I cannot believe I am finally arrived."

Two sailors rowed Marga and Finn to the island. As the oars churned, Marga closed her eyes and felt the cold wind blow her face. It reminded her of so many days at the cliffs beyond Bowmore House, and days when she longed to see Alban. Now, though her eyes were closed, she knew her Finn was right beside her. But she took his hand in hers, just to make sure.

The rowboat hit the shore, studded with smooth, black stones, and the sailors pulled the boat on to the beach so Marga and Finn could climb out. The water receding over the stones made a high, tinkling music. Marga and Finn searched the landscape and spotted a trail that went through the jagged rock to the top of a hill. The two walked; first, they reached a village where a line of small, stone houses with black, thatched roofs sat empty.

"One of these must have been where my mother lived," Marga said. "My father's house had a yellow door." They examined the doors, but if any of them had ever been painted, they were now all scrubbed clean by wind and weather.

They continued their walk up another hill. From there they spotted a precipice in the distance that bore a single small tree, its leaves in full green bloom.

"My father told me the island has one tree," Marga said. "The fey hazel. And my mother is buried beneath it. That must be the one."

Marga and Finn climbed to reach the spot. The tree's branches were filled with ragged-edged leaves, and hung with flowering catkins and small green nuts that looked like elfin faces in green hoods. Marga and Finn sat under its branches and enjoyed the shade it provided from the sun and shelter from the wind. After so many years of searching for this place from a distant shore and distant cliffs, Marga felt a peace she had never known. She sensed her mother's presence, as surely as the company of any living person.

"I want to explain all that has come to pass to my mother," Marga said, "but I hardly know where to start."

"If your mother was before you now," Finn said. "What would you say?"

Marga remembered the night of the ball and all she had spoken of to

Nula-na-Nekon. Marga had wanted her mother to understand how much her daughter loved her. Nula had responded, *Let go of that weight. Walk into your own future.*

"I would tell her that I think of her every day," she said. "And now, because of her, because of all she endured, I am seeking my destiny. One I never could have dreamed."

"Are you ever afraid of what comes next?" Finn asked.

She looked out at the shore, which seemed a long way below them, and the sea that expanded to the horizon, just like the cliffs from home. "Every day," she said. "But I am grateful to have you with me, darling Finn. My map, my sextant..."

"My north star, my southern cross..."

She smiled.

After a moment, Finn asked, "May I address your mother?"

"Of course," she said.

"Hello, ma'am," Prince Finn said, his tone serious. "I am honored to finally meet you. I am in love with your daughter, and I intend to marry her. And when I do, I shall care for her as best as I can."

Marga reached to Finn's hand, and they looked upon the ocean and felt the salted wind kiss their faces. After some moments, they dug a hole in the earth below the tree and interred the small box containing Henry. Then Finn and Marga listened to wind and water and bird calls until the sun began to sink toward the horizon. After a time, the two traced their steps back past the empty houses to the beach where a rowboat awaited to bring them to the ship.

After the sun sank below the horizon, a single light went on in the last croft house on the lane. A woman looked out the window at the rowboats that met the great ship.

"There you go, my love, my goddaughter, my queen," said Nula-na-Nekon. "Rule with strength and always favor peace. You have made your mother proud. You have made all your mothers proud."

The events that took place in the yard at Bowmore House on that fateful day would be remembered by all who were present for the rest of their lives, for in the course of one hour on a sleepy morning when most of the kingdom was still in bed, a prince turned into a lad and a kitchen girl became a princess. Orla was overjoyed that her sister's true nature had finally been discovered. Liisi was greatly cheered when Finn told her that, as sister to the princess of Gallia, she would be considered a distinguished guest at Glengoe Castle.

Rhona allowed herself to be carried away with the many exciting events that followed. Lord Warin was forced to dissolve the debt, and now there was proof that Rhona had not ended her friend's life, so he no longer posed her any threat. According to the will of the Princess of Gallia, funds were allocated to repair Bowmore House and replace the furnishings. Doors that had long been locked were opened, boards were peeled away from windows, and the house's previous stateliness was restored.

Still, Rhona carried in her heart a very great pain. She realized that she had put her dear friend's daughter through a terrible ordeal: she had isolated her, forced her into servitude, and failed to recognize her worth. Rhona had discouraged the girl's spirit so she could nurture and display her own daughters. Yet, somehow, the girl prevailed. Marga had greatness within her, it seemed, and Prince Finn had recognized this long before he even knew her name. One thing was clear: the girl was never really a cinder, she had always been a blazing spark, a balefire, a shooting star.

But Rhona realized she had treated her stepdaughter the same disgraceful way her relations had treated her. This thought wakened her night after night, drenched with sweat, shaking from nightmares she could not recall.

On a day that was foggy and cold, Rhona decided to take a southward walk along the coast. She stepped carefully along a crumbling footpath that veered close to the edge of the high cliffs. She was grateful for the cold and solitude, and the churning ocean waters and the cries of the black ravens who flapped their wings and cawed in the mist.

Rhona did not know how long she had been walking when she came upon a small chapel, built of local gray stones. The edifice made a lovely scene, perched on a small knoll with the ocean behind it, and an expanse of slate sky overhead. How had she never come upon this chapel before? She did not know, but it matched the feeling in her heart— ancient, ashen, isolated, silent. She looked upon the chapel for what seemed like a long time before she had the thought that she might gain entry. Gingerly, she went to the heavy door and gave the iron handle a slight push. The door would probably be locked, she thought, or, if unlocked, a service was proceeding inside. But the door did open, and it revealed a small, empty chamber. Inside was dark like a cavern; the place was neat and tended. One standing candle burned near the entrance, and Rhona used it to light a few more candles in memory of those she had lost. Then, the room felt not warm in temperature, but warm in spirit. Rhona took a seat upon one of the wooden benches.

After a time, she spoke into the room's silence.

"Ailen, you went to the island where I was supposed to be sent and you found sanctuary and a future. This makes me so glad. You died too early, but not because of a queen's vengeance. You died in peace, loved by your family."

She hung her head and was quiet for a few moments, then continued. "By some strange twist of fate, your daughter was sent to me. I do not pretend to know how this happened. I only know that if I had had more compassion, I might have understood...a child alone in the world needed my protection. And I failed to provide it. I failed you."

She sniffed away tears.

"I wish you were here so I could tell you how sorry I am," she said. "Ailen, I wish you were here."

Suddenly, the door squeaked open behind her, and Rhona stopped speaking. Footsteps walked lightly down the stones in the aisle beside her. Out of the shadows, a young girl of about ten years old appeared. Rhona felt the girl's eyes upon her before she looked up to see the child standing in the aisle before her, watching. The girl was tidy enough and wore a simple dress, her light hair tied neatly. She stood and stared at Rhona; Rhona thought this behavior strange and somewhat rude.

"Hello, child," Rhona finally said, pushing the tears off her cheeks.

"Hello, ma'am," she said.

Rhona did not know what to say next. "Have you come here to say a prayer? Or are you lost?"

"Perhaps I am here to pray for the lost," she said. "Tell me about lost."

"Pardon?" Rhona said.

"Explain lost to me, if you please," the child said.

Rhona smiled, though puzzled at the nonsensical request. "Lost is what you are when you are not where you intended to go, my dear," she said. "Perhaps it is what you are when you realize...you are not the person you thought you were. Lost is the moment you understand you are the worst kind of monster: the kind that should have known better. The kind that should have *done* better."

The child smiled vaguely.

"Oh, my child, I shouldn't speak of such wicked things to you,"

Rhona said. "You are young and perfect; you need not know what awfulness is contained in the world." She hung her head in her hand.

"There, Rhona," said the little girl. She put her small hand on Rhona's shoulder. "Stand and walk with me around this place."

Rhona regarded the girl, her face lit by shadowy candle flames. "How do you know my name?"

"I have always known your name," the girl said.

Rhona forced her eyes to focus and glanced at the back of the chapel. "Little girl, where is your mother? Do you live nearby?"

"Come with me," the little girl said again. "Let us speak of the day you were born."

Rhona stared with narrow eyes at the girl. Something about her was strange, familiar and haunting at the same time. "Speak your name."

"Walk with me. I'll tell you a story and shall say my name after forty strides," she said.

Rhona stood and took a deep breath. She looked around to see if the child had a guardian nearby; the chapel was empty. She offered her hand and the girl took it.

"Forty strides, then? That will bring us around the back of the chapel and up the other side," Rhona said.

"Yes," the girl said.

They took five steps. "That's five strides right there, child," Rhona said. "If there's something you wish to say, you should do so."

"Yes," the little girl said quietly. "Rhona, you have done terrible things. And still, you could not forestall who Princess Marguerite would become. Nay, at the final moment, you revealed it."

Rhona stopped walking and looked the little girl in her eyes. "How do you know such things? How speak with such authority? Your name, please."

"That was only ten strides," she said. "I promised to tell you at forty. Patience."

Rhona sighed. "Carry on."

"You were born on a cold day in a cold season," the girl said. "Your mother gave you the warmth you needed to complete your journey into the world. Summer came, and your parents loved you with the love that lights a parent's heart. But seasons change quickly, and the following winter was bitter cold. Your father was a wood cutter and there was plenty of wood to make it through."

The child's words sounded like fairy stories until very suddenly, they didn't. "What do you know of my father?" Rhona demanded.

"He was a good man, strong and tall. I can see him now, chopping down trees," the girl said, looking up at Rhona with pretty blue eyes. "And I see him now, upon his bed, his body stricken with fever. I can see his spirit prepare to leave his body."

Rhona stopped walking and released the girl's hand. "What sorcery is this?"

"I was summoned to speak with you."

"Who made this summons?" Rhona asked.

"Rhona, humans believe they know everything about the world, but the earth holds many secrets," she said. "One is this: all trees are connected by their roots. They speak to each other in a language people cannot understand. The trees surrounding Bowmore House heard your tears. Word reached a hazel tree standing alone on a far-off island, and the bones of the woman buried beneath it asked me to visit you. To tell you, Rhona, you are forgiven."

Rhona blinked. She swallowed. "How many more strides?"

"Ten," the girl said. "But it doesn't matter, you already guessed my name. I knew you would."

"Nula-na-Nekon," Rhona whispered. "Why are you appearing to me?"

"Let's walk another moment," she said, resting her head against Rhona's arm. "There is more to my story. In the bitterest core of winter, there was a terrible storm. After your father died, your mother became ill. When she could no longer care for you, she did the only thing she could, though it broke her heart: she brought you into Dunford Town, and left you with your kin, a cold family with no love in their hearts."

Rhona knelt down to look at the girl in the face. When she looked closely, she saw that the girl's face was not solid. It was a series of faces. Yes, this was what Ailen had told her after she met the spirit in the woods. *The face wasn't one face, Rhona, it was so many, all different ages, one after another after another...*

"What do you know about my mother?" Rhona demanded.

"With no shoes upon her feet, your mother carried her daughter through the woods, through the snow, to the place where she would be safe."

"She brought me to Ara Dun," Rhona said. "The great house on the edge of the wood."

"The family had wealth of coin and stature, but they had no goodwill," she said. "Your mother knew this, but she had no other choice."

Rhona looked so deep and long into the girl's eyes, she thought she could almost see the young woman, her own mother, sick and grieving, carrying her baby through the snow.

A sob reached Rhona's throat, and she heaved with it.

"Your mother prayed that you would survive," the girl who was Nula said. "When you were safe inside the doors of the grand house, she had but moments to live. She stumbled toward the town, and into the snow. Then she found a quiet place to rest."

Rhona bent her face down. "A quiet place to die."

"When the snow melted, townspeople found her body, but nobody knew who she was," the child said. "The residents of Ara Dun told you she would someday return for you. And you waited. And you fought the voice in your heart that told you she had forgotten you. You have been fighting ever since. Stop fighting, dear Rhona. You did not keep the princess from becoming who she was, and you could not have done so had you desired such. Because of the love of your mother, you survived many terrible winters. But things are different now. Rhona, for the sake of your own daughters and the generations to come, hold on to the love. Release the cold."

Rhona's throat was choked with tears. "I shall try," she said. "Thank you, Nula."

Young Nula smiled and her eyes twinkled. "Do not forget," she said. "On the road through Dunford Town, you were a true friend to one in need, one who lies now beneath a tree on a distant island. Our family shall never forget your kindness. From this day forward, we wish you only peace, dear friend."

Epilogue

The carriage brought Princess Marga on the bumpy road past the gate and on to the grounds of Bowmore House. Marga's heart swelled when she saw the churning waters of the Morisar Sea. She put down her window and let the salty air blow her face.

"Sir?" she said to the driver. "Do you mind stopping here? I'd like to walk the rest of the way."

He pulled the reins and stopped the horses. "Here, Your Highness? I am to bring you to the door. And once there, formally announce your presence."

"I know but I'd like to get out here," she said. "This is my first time home in a long while."

"As you wish, Your Highness," he said.

The footman—a mere man this day—helped Marga out of a carriage, which, though beautiful, was made of wood and brass, only, and lacked the sweet, earthy aroma of the pumpkin carriage that had brought her to the castle on a magical night. Some days earlier, she had traveled by ship back to Dalkeith and Braemuir Kingdom, and she was grateful to alight from the carriage, stretch her legs and breathe the air of home. The salty air, tinged with the perfume of apples, settled her belly, still uneasy from the journey. As she walked toward Bowmore House, she felt like she was reuniting with a good friend. And the friend was now improving after a period of neglect: a dozen young men were perched on the roof hammering down new shingles, and in the yard, workers and servants rushed about, building things and setting up decorations.

Marga was glad to see it. When she reached the house, she considered ringing the bell. But then she decided to go around to the back, and enter through the door to the kitchen, the one she had gone through a thousand times. The kitchen was full of servants, all of them so busy and preoccupied they did not notice her. For a moment, she stood and watched. Bowmore House had been built to bring people together, to celebrate. Finally, she thought, the house was fulfilling the role it was always meant for.

Marga noticed a young man squatting in front of the kitchen fire, shoring up logs. She went to him and glanced up at the flue.

"I think there's a crack up there," she said quietly. "You should ask someone to inspect it. Otherwise, every time it rains, the fires will be quenched."

He scowled and looked up. "Yes, I have been suspecting as much." Then he realized who had addressed him and stood. "Your Highness," he said, bowing his head. "Pardon me for not recognizing you."

"Nonsense," she said. "We are all family here. What's your name, young man?"

"I am Gerald, Your Highness," he said.

"Gerald," she said. "I did this job for many years. Tending fires is a constant chore, but the heat from these fires allows people to live here. Keep the fires well, Gerald, and respect them. Do not let them get too hot, for the ashes spark and spit. If they diminish, you must start your efforts over. Fires are a living thing. Care for them as such."

By now, everyone in the kitchen had noticed her and they all bowed and curtsied in reverence.

"Thank you, my friends," she said. "Please, carry on. You have a wedding to prepare for, have you not?"

"We do, Princess," said a woman. "Back to work, everyone!"

Marga smiled and continued through the halls. She passed the door to the pantry that led to the stairs that went to the tower. She put her hand upon it and remembered the morning when Mother Rhona had locked her inside. She'd thought her stepmother had done so out of spite or rage to think that Marga might abandon them. But no, Rhona had only needed to thread a needle of possibility, and suddenly, it was confirmed: she was not Cinder, the lowly orphan, but Marga, the Princess.

Princess. It was a label she still found clumsy and incomplete. Marga had never really believed it applied to her until she met her grandfather, King Mattieu of Gallia. When he explained that someday she would be queen, she believed him. To be a princess was not so much a matter of choosing and wearing fine frocks and letting ladies constantly adjust one's hair, but of preparing to lead a country. She still had much to learn.

Marga walked slowly through the house and noticed something amazing: sunlight poured through the windows. Doors that had long been closed and locked now opened on to warm, inviting rooms. She saw no paint peeling off the walls, nor broken trim or crumbling plaster, or even a single cobweb or streak of dust. Paintings had been restored upon the walls, rugs were washed, and the air was clean.

Marga smiled. Bowmore House had come back to life.

She climbed the stairs and walked down the corridor—one she had traveled so many times, carrying wood and trays of tea. This time, she had only a small parcel tucked into her pocket. She knocked on Liisi's door.

"Come in, Celia," Liisi called. "I have been reading to pass the time, but I am entirely too nervous. I think I should try on my dress—" But when she saw Marga standing in her doorway, she squealed and ran to her.

"You came!" she said. "Mother wasn't sure if you would."

"There is no other place I'd rather be," Marga said.

"Where is Finn?"

"He is at Glengoe Castle, visiting his own family," Marga said. "And where does the 'painfully handsome' Earl of Lachlan pass the day before his nuptials?"

"Hunting with Prince Eiran, I suspect," she said. "Callum is the prince's advisor and closest friend. Did I write you about how we met?"

"You said you met him at the king's ball, but that night, you paid him no mind because he was not the son of the king," Marga said.

"That's right!" Liisi exclaimed, laughing. "I met him again when Queen Eleanor invited us to the castle for a banquet. I don't remember dancing with him at the ball, but he says I did. I danced with many young men that night."

"Including my husband," Marga said.

"Yes, but his heart was already won," Liisi said. "Callum, is, oh Marga, he's everything. Handsome, smart, accomplished at archery and swordsmanship. And he makes me laugh so much, sometimes he has to tell me to quiet down. Can you believe it?"

"I believe you are very much in love," Marga said.

Liisi stopped smiling and looked at Marga. "My wedding will not be like yours," she said.

"My wedding was a spectacle," Marga said. "Designed by my grandfather's advisors to delight the people of Gallia. Not all of them are pleased that the heir to their throne was born in a foreign land. So, when Finn and I wed, it had to be a grand affair."

"Oh, but it was so wonderful," Liisi said. "The parties, the music, the flowers...and your dresses were like works of art. And fireworks! I'd never seen such magic!"

Marga chuckled. "I am glad you enjoyed it."

"Tell me, old, married sister," she said. "What wisdom do you have for me?"

"It's only been two years," Marga said. "I suppose I'd say, make time to talk to each other. Sometimes, Finn and I get so busy, we have to steal away during some event for a quiet moment." Marga stood and wandered around the room. She went to Liisi's window and looked out at the sea.

"My new life is not always easy. Finn has kept me steady through it. I don't know what I would do without him."

"You found a good man," Liisi said.

"This is very true," Marga said. "Oh, is that Orla's headstone? You said you could see it from your room."

Liisi stood next to Marga. "My dear Orla. I cannot believe I must get married without her."

"She made the trip to my wedding, and I barely spoke to her," Marga said.

"But she was so glad you returned to say goodbye before the end," Liisi said. "We all were."

"Thank you, Liisi, for writing to tell me she was ill," Marga said. "I would not have missed the chance to see her. The stone looks lovely from here."

"The stone mason did a beautiful job. Thank you for sending him," Liisi said. "Mother was glad that Orla's resting place has a beautiful view of the sea."

"Orla deserves it," Marga said.

"She does," Liisi said. "Marga, I think of you often. I want you to know, those days were hard. I have changed much these past years."

Marga turned to Liisi and took both her hands. "My dear, we were both other people then. And we survived those days so we could reach these days, and now here we are. All right, take a seat. I have a small gift for you."

Liisi sat down again on her bed. Marga extracted the box from her pocket and handed it to her. Liisi opened it. "The broach!" she exclaimed, eyes wide. "The one I wore to the ball! But this belonged to your mother."

"She would want you to have it. You looked so lovely when you wore it to the ball," Marga said. "I hope you wear it tomorrow. And keep it for always."

Liisi stood and hugged Marga. "Thank you." Liisi set the box down on her dresser. "I am so nervous. What if my feet cannot walk? What if I forget what to say?"

"All you have to do is breathe," she said. "Everything will be perfect. Now, tell me, where is your mother?"

"She is likely outside," Liisi said. She peeked out her window. "Yes, there she is. She has taken on gardening of late."

"Has she?" Marga said. "My mother used to have the most wonderful gardens here."

"This is Mother's plan," Liisi said. "She uncovered the parcels that used to be your mother's gardens. She wants to replant them in memory of Ailen."

"Truly?" Marga asked. "How wonderful. Well, let me go and greet Mother Rhona. I shall see you later for tea."

Marga left Liisi and made her way back down the hallway. The door to Rhona's room was slightly ajar, so she glanced inside. There was the small cot her stepmother had slept in for years, but the room was different: on her desk was a vase full of wildflowers. And Marga had the strange sensation of needing to shield her eyes: sunlight poured through the windows. Mother Rhona had removed the boards. The view over the ocean had been restored, and it was as magnificent as Marga remembered it.

Her mother had loved that view so dearly.

Marga smiled and continued down the stairs, out the front door and into the yard. She found Mother Rhona kneeling in a garden plot. She wore a light-colored dress and a straw hat to shield her from the sun. Hearty gloves over her hands were stained with dirt.

Marga could not remember ever seeing her stepmother wear any color other than black.

"Well!" Rhona exclaimed when she saw Marga. "When last we

heard, the princess was not sure if she would attend her sister's wedding."

"I did not want to miss Liisi's day."

"Liisi will be so pleased," Rhona said. "I wish you had told us you were coming. I would rather not have greeted the Princess of Gallia covered in mud."

"It brings me joy to see you tending these gardens," Marga said. "And you have made a good deal of progress on the house. It looks better each time. I confess, I have already been inside. I glanced at your bedroom; what a joy to see the boards removed."

Rhona stood and peeled off her gloves. "It's time to let the sun into the house," she said. "I was thinking of you just the other day, and now I cannot remember why..."

"Show me the gardens," Marga said. "I would love to see what you have planted. And I have news."

"Oh, of course I remember!" Rhona exclaimed. She grabbed Marga's hand. "Follow me."

Rhona dashed into the house with such energy, Marga had to practically run to keep up with her. Rhona stopped at the door of the pantry. "I will not lock you inside this time," she said. "But do you have energy to walk up the stairs? You are not too tired from your journey?"

Marga smiled slightly. "I confess, I am tired," she said. "But I always loved the view from the tower."

"Good," Rhona said, smiling. "Come along."

Marga was even more tired than she initially realized, and took a deep breath to fuel her climb. By the time she reached the top, she was almost breathless.

"Come," Rhona said. She looked out the windows at the sea, picked up a brass telescope and turned to her left, lifting the scope to her eye and adjusting it. "I have been searching for the island of St. Kiana. And I believe you can see it from up here."

"What?" Marga said. "I used to search for it constantly."

"We were opening up the rooms, and when I unlocked your father's study, I found his nautical maps." She took a pile of old, brown maps from atop a wooden chair. "Did you ever look at these?"

Marga looked over her shoulder. "No," she said. "I would have liked to."

Rhona shuffled through the maps, turning them over and sideways until she found what she was looking for. "Here it is," she said. "I thought St. Kiana would be in that direction." She pointed straight ahead of them.

"That is where I always looked," Marga said. "Though I had no spyglass."

"This also belonged to your father. He kept it locked in a cabinet. I learned that the island is actually situated slightly to the north. That direction." She pointed to the side at an outcropping of rocks and looked at it through the telescope.

"That's no island," Marga said. "Those are only skerries."

Rhona put the map in front of Marga. "Look at the map," she said. "The island is not the first series of dark shapes on the horizon, but the second."

Marga took the map and studied it.

"They appear to be one group, but that is an illusion," she said. "They are miles apart. The dark shapes that are smaller are further off, you see. That's..."

"St. Kiana," Marga said. Rhona handed the telescope to her and she looked through it. "All these years, I was searching for my mother's island. But I was facing the wrong direction."

"Only slightly," Rhona said, and she put her hand on Marga's shoulder. "Sometimes we only need to change the direction of our attention a little bit for things to come into focus. I am so glad you are here, my dear. This discovery made me so happy, and there was nobody I could tell who would care as I did."

Marga put the scope down and embraced her stepmother. "It makes me feel like my mother was with us the whole time."

"Yes," Rhona said. "I wish we could flatten time. We might set the clock back some years, then we could all be here at Bowmore House together: You, me, Liisi, Orla *and* Ailen."

"That would be wonderful," Marga said. "But I would not care to undo time. The storms I went through, the storms we all went through, brought us to this place."

"You have such wisdom, my dear."

Marga smiled sheepishly. "I hope I have some wisdom. I shall need it. Mother Rhona, I am expecting a child."

Rhona smiled, wide and broad, and embraced Marga. "My girl, I am so happy for you."

"Do not tell anyone," Marga said. "Tomorrow is Liisi's day, only. But I wanted to tell you in person."

Rhona held Marga's hands. "You are so much like your mother," she said. "She would be so proud of you. And though it is not of my doing, I am also proud."

"Thank you, Mother Rhona," Marga said. "A sage once told me that every small thing has something extraordinary and grand inside. I have always believed this. And if we can each believe this about ourselves, there is no end to what we can accomplish in this world."

"I agree, my dear," Rhona said. "I heartily agree."

The End.

About the Author

Elizabeth de Veer is the author of the novel *The Ocean in Winter*. She has a Master of Theological Studies from Harvard Divinity School and has been admitted to writing residencies at the Jentel Artist Residency, the Hambidge Center for Creative Arts and Sciences, and the Virginia Center for the Creative Arts. She is a member of several writing groups, including Grub Street Writers' Collective of Boston, the Newburyport Writers' Group, Sisters in Crime New England, Boston Author's Club, and the New Hampshire Writers' Project. She lives in Georgetown with her husband, daughter, and labradoodle.

About the Press

Sea Crow Press

Sea Crow Press publishes compelling fiction, nonfiction, and poetry with strong voice, deep heart, and a connection to the natural world. From the windswept shores of Cape Cod to imagined climate futures, our books inspire, engage, and endure.

We are committed to amplifying voices and sharing stories that matter. Alongside our acclaimed eco-lit and regional titles, we publish historical fiction and immigrant stories that illuminate the resilience of individuals and communities across time and place. These narratives deepen our mission by honoring cultural memory, celebrating diverse experiences, and revealing the ways in which history and migration shape both people and landscapes.

At Sea Crow Press, every book reflects our belief that stories rooted in place can move the world.

www.ingramcontent.com/pod-product-compliance
Lightning Source LLC
LaVergne TN
LVHW032004070526
838202LV00058B/6293